Henry Christopher McCook

**Old Farm Fairies**

A Summer Campaign in Brownieland Against King Cobweaver's Pixies

Henry Christopher McCook

**Old Farm Fairies**
*A Summer Campaign in Brownieland Against King Cobweaver's Pixies*

ISBN/EAN: 9783743400689

Manufactured in Europe, USA, Canada, Australia, Japa

Cover: Foto ©Andreas Hilbeck / pixelio.de

Manufactured and distributed by brebook publishing software (www.brebook.com)

Henry Christopher McCook

**Old Farm Fairies**

# Old Farm Fairies.

## A Summer Campaign in Brownieland

## King Cobweaver's Pixies.

A Story for Young People,

BY

HENRY CHRISTOPHER McCOOK,

AUTHOR OF

" Tenants of an Old Farm," "American Spiders and Their Spinningwork," etc., etc.

———

ONE HUNDRED AND FIFTY ILLUSTRATIONS.

———

GEORGE W. JACOBS & CO.,
103 South 15th Street.
A. D. 1895.

PRESS OF
AVIL PRINTING COMPANY,
PHILADELPHIA.

In Tender Recollection of

Boyhood's Home, Loves, Joys, and Trials Among the Hills of

ever dear Ohio,

I dedicate this Book

to the

MEMORY OF MY BROTHER

# RODERICK SHELDON MCCOOK

Late Commander United States Navy.

An able, honorable and patriotic officer, he waxed valiant in fight

both on sea and land

for his Country's honor and defence.

On this page

The Author would keep green his Name

as the

Roommate, Playmate and Companion of Early Days.

# PREFACE.

This preface shall be a personal explanation. The following book was written during the winter of 1876–77, more than eighteen years ago. Its origin was in this wise: Some of my readers will know that for more than twenty years I have studied the habits of our spider fauna. During the first years of these studies, the thought came to me to write a book for youth wherein my observations should be personified in the imaginary creatures of fairy lore, and thus float into the young mind some of my natural history findings in such pleasant form that they would be received quite unconsciously, and at least an impression thereof retained with sufficient accuracy to open the way to more serious lessons in the future.

It further seemed to me that the fairies of Scotland, with whom I had been familiar from childhood, might afford vivid personalities for my plan. Accordingly, the spiders were assigned the part of Pixies or goblins, the ill-natured fairies of Scotland and Northern England. The Brownies, or friendly folk, the "gude neebours," or household fairies, were made to personify those insect forms, especially those useful to man, against which spiders wage continual war. Moreover, to express the relations of the lower creatures to human life, and their actual as well as imaginary interdependence, human characters were introduced, and conflicts between Pixies and Brownies were interwoven with their behaviour.

(v)

This purely personal statement has been intruded upon the reader to explain that the Brownies, as represented in this book, are not imitations. They antedated, by a number of years, the popular creations of Mr. Palmer Cox. The writer well understands as a naturalist that priority depends not upon originality of intention or invention, or even of preparation, but upon precedence in publication. It will be found, however, that my conception and treatment of these wee folk differ from those of Mr. Cox. As they appear to me from the recollections of childhood, they have a more serious aspect, a more human-like nature, which ought not to be wholly sacrificed to their jovial characteristics. I have therefore presented the Brownies as beings with humanized affections, passions and methods reflected in miniature.

I confess some qualms, on the scientific side of my conscience, at compelling my friends, the spiders, to play the part of Pixies. But there seemed no other course out of regard both to common belief and the necessity imposed by the facts. As I went on with the work, I wondered at the ductility with which the current habits of the aranead tribes yielded to personification. The water spiders permitted the introduction of smugglers, pirates and sailors; the burrowing and trapdoor spiders opened up tales of caves and subterranean abodes; the ballooning spiders permitted an adaptation of modern military methods of reconnoissance; and so on through a long list of aranead habits.

In order to make this more apparent, and to give adult readers, parents and teachers, and the older class of youthful readers, a scientific key to the various situations, brief notes have been added in an Appendix, to which foot-note references have been made in most of the chapters. Moreover, the natural habits personified are interpreted by figures set into the text with no explanation but the legend written thereunder.

The crudely drawn cuts which figure in the pages as "The Boy's Illustrations" are exact reproductions of sketches made by a lad in my own family, between eight and nine years old, to whom, with others, the manuscript was read as a sort of test of its quality. Encouraged by the advice of one of the keenest and most sympathetic students of child life in America, I have ventured to give a few of these drawings to the public, as a curious study in the operations of child-mind.

I had agreed with myself not to print the Brownie Book until my scientific work upon the spiders was finished, and the manuscript remained untouched until the winter of 1885-6. At that time I seemed to see the nearing end of my studies, and portions of the Brownie-Pixie story were distributed to various artists, among them Mr. Dan. C. Beard and Mr. Harry L. Poore. Some of the illustrations at that time made, appear in the following pages, bearing date 1886. "Tenants of an Old Farm" had now appeared, and was so well received that it was thought advisable to connect this book with that by an "Introductory Chapter" intended for older readers, and which gives the key to the motive of the story. Early in 1886 I recalled all contracts and arrangements for publication, as a prolonged sickness compelled me to drop scientific work and defer the issue of the "American Spiders." On the very day that the binders placed the first finished copy of the third and last volume of that work in my hands, the "copy" of "Old Farm Fairies" went to the printer.

H. C. McC.

THE MANSE, PHILADELPHIA, *May 21, A. D. 1895.*

# THE INTRODUCTION.

# AN INTRODUCTION.

☞ This Chapter is for Grownups only. Children will please skip it.

## THE SCHOOLMISTRESS AND THE FAIRIES.

In the south yard of the Old Farm at Highwood there stands a noble Elm tree. Its massive proportions, the stately pose of its furrowed trunk and the graceful outlines of its drooping branches have often drawn my pleased eyes and awakened admiration. There is nothing in Nature that better serves to stir up human enthusiasm than a fine tree; and as our vicinage for miles around abounds in worthy examples of American forest growths, there is ample opportunity for such sentiment to be kept aglow in the hearts of the Tenants at the Old Farm. Yet it must be confessed that there is also occasion at times for a kindling of quite another sort, when the stupidity, perversity, and penuriousness of men wage a vandal war against the noble monarchs of the woods.

The fall of a huge tree is a touching sight. See! the trunk trembles upon the last few fibres that stand in the gap which the axman has made. A shiver runs through the foliage to the summit and circumference of the branches. The tree-top bows with slightest trace of a

lurch to one side. Then it sinks—slowly, faster, fast!
With no undignified rush, but with a stately sweep it
descends to the earth. Crash! The ground trembles at
the fall. The nethermost branches in their breakage
explode sharply like a farewell volley of soldiers over a
comrade's grave. Boughs, twigs and leaves vibrate, as
with a passionate earnestness of grief, for a few moments,
and then are still. There, prone upon the forest mould
the glorious monarch lies, majestic even in its fallen
estate. A few bunches of human muscle, a keen steel
edge and a scant fraction of time have destroyed two
centuries of Nature's cunning work.

Well, one is inclined to so vary the version of a certain Scripture Text that it shall read "a man was in-
famous" rather than "a man was famous according as
he had lifted up axes upon the thick trees." *

Of course Mr. Gladstone, and the multitude of undis-
tinguished axmen who delight to fall a tree, have an
honorable and lawful vocation. Trees ripen, like other
animate things, and when they are full ripe they may be
felled; when their time has come they ought to fall;
when the exigencies of higher intelligences truly require, they also must fall before their time. But, this
brings no justification of that murderous idiocy which
sets so many citizen sovereigns of America to slaughter-
ing the grand sovereigns of the plant world.

However, all this perhaps has little to do with our
great Elm, except, that one must be grateful that it has
been spared to cause the eyes to rejoice in its beauty

* Psalm lxxiv. 5.

and to refresh us with its shade. We built a rustic seat against its trunk, and there in the warm summer days

FIG. 1.—The Forest Monarch's Fall. The Brownie's Grief and Anger Thereat.

and evenings which succeeded the winter of our coming to the Old Farm, I was wont to sit and meditate, and sometimes doze. It was a favorite spot with me, but others of the family often shared it with me, or enjoyed it by themselves. This will well enough introduce a matter which I have now to lay before the reader. It came to me from the Schoolmistress, who, I venture to hope, is not forgotten by the readers of "The Tenants of An Old Farm."

My dear Mr. Mayfield:

The package that I herewith send you has a strange history which I beg to recite ere you break the wrappings and examine the contents of the parcel.

It happened during one of the warm days of last June that I sat on the rustic bench under the Great Elm and read Mr. Lowell's "Vision of Sir Launfal." I closed the book and thought, with an exquisite sense of its beauty and fitness, upon the poet's opening verses which contain a description of June, and in which are these lines:

> "'Tis Heaven alone that is given away,
> 'Tis only God may be had for the asking;
> There is no price set on the lavish Summer,
> And June may be had by the poorest comer."

As I conned the words my eyes slowly wandered along the landscape, and my heart rejoiced in the royal bounty of beauty which the poet sings. Then my vision returned to the objects just around me, and gradually became fixed upon some of the living things about which you have kindly told us so much new and interesting. Indeed, they seemed already like old friends, and I watched with keen zest their various movements.

How bright everything was, and how peaceful the tone of Nature! Butterflies flitted by, beating the air in their leisurely way, then rested on leaf or flower while they opened and closed their wings with graceful, fan-like movements. The winged Hymenoptera dashed by with the sharp, quick wingstroke of their kind, or hung humming above the flowers. Honey-bees, Carpenter-bees, Digger-wasps, the blue Mud-dauber, the brown Paper-wasp, Hornets and Yellow-jackets were busy at their various occupations. One dusted pollen into its " basket ; " another dumped aromatic pellets of sawdust from a cedar rail ; another scooped up mandible hod-fulls of mortar at the edge of the brook ; others plucked chiplets of old wood from a weathered fence post ; all seemed happy, and devoted to peaceful industry.

The great green Grasshopper was in hearing, if not in sight, the veritable " hopper " whose long threadlike antennæ and wedge shaped head you have taught us to recognize as marking the true from the so called grass-hopper or locust. He sat upon the tall grass on the bank of the Run close by the spring house, and shrilled his piping love call to his mate. The annual Cicada, too ("Pruinosa" you called it), was sounding his amor-ous drum from the trees with a volume and sharpness of sound that far exceed those of his cousin german the Seventeen Year Cicada. His silent ladylove might occasionally be seen flitting from bough to bough. An Orbweaving spider's web was spun upon an adjacent bush, and three courtiers were established at different parts of the margin of the snare awaiting the complais-ance of Madam Aranea the housekeeper. Near my feet a bevy of Fuscous Ants* were tugging with great to-do at a crumb of sweet cake, while their fellow formicar-ians were equally concerned in covering and screening the gate of their nest that lay to the right under the verge of the Elm's shadow. Birds of several species

---

* Formica fusca.

were near by; Robins whistled in the meadow, a Vireo
sang in the tree tops, Sparrows twittered around the
birdcote; Hens cackled in the barnyard, and wakened the hearty, answering "Tuk-aw, tuk-aw!" of the
big red Rooster. Out in the lane Sarah's conch shell
was sending a melodious call to Hugh whom the Mistress had bidden her to summon from the wood pasture.
The whole aspect of Nature, indeed, was so charming
that I was soothed into a delicious repose of body and
mind.

I am conscious, dear Sir, that I shall lay a heavy tax
upon your credulity by what I am now to relate. Or,
perhaps, you will smile and say that your friend Abby
has fallen to dreams and visions, and like some of
her young pupils has imagination so little disciplined as
to be quite unable to distinguish between a vivid wak-
ing fancy or dream of sleep, and a real occurrence.
Very well, I must bear your unbelief as best I may, and
at all events you will listen to my story.

Will you believe that among the Tenants of our Old
Farm is a nation of Fairies? You have not suspected
their existence heretofore; but then, neither did I suspect that legions of curious beings are all around us
until the wand of your knowledge had touched my eyes,
and opened them to the wonderful life histories that are
being wrought out among our fellow tenants of the insect world.

Such, at least, was my own thought as I saw several
wee dainty bodies spring from the backs of some Honey-
bees hovering over the white clover, after the fashion
of a rider dismounting from his horse, and another
group alight from a bevy of yellow Butterflies that fluttered low down and just above the walk. They were
joined by many others of like appearance, who suddenly

emerged from the grass, from the flower border, from the drooping leaves of the Elm, and approached me.

THE BOY'S ILLUSTRATION.
FIG. 2.—Queen Fancy and the Schoolmistress.*

They clambered up the English Ivy that clings to the south side of the tree; they climbed upon the rustic

---

* In the little company referred to further on, to whom the manuscript of this book was read, was a friend's lad, eight years old, a visitor at the Old Farm. The Mistress noticed him during the intervals of the readings busy with pencil and paper, amusing himself with such drawings as children are wont to make. A number of these had been made and thrown away ere it occurred to the good woman to call my attention thereto. I was much surprised and delighted to find that the boy had been engaged in illustrating the Brownie Book (as we then familiarly called it). It was a good sign of the value of the work that it could produce such an impression upon a child of his tender years. Moreover,

bench, and a few even ventured upon the gnarled arm against which my elbow rested. This seemed a novel occurrence, certainly; but I assure you that I was rather pleased than surprised thereby, for it at once linked itself with your strange histories of insects, and seemed a natural and matter-of-course affair. Really, I have come to think that Nature has so many rare and beautiful facts hidden away in her secret places that one must never be surprised to see or hear of the most marvelous happenings. One of the brightest and most prettily robed of these tiny people, who seemed to be a sort of queen among them, drew quite near and addressed me.

"You are not alarmed at our appearance. Good! Fairies do not visit those who doubt or fear them. We are pleased to see you smile upon us. Thanks! We give you greeting! Would you like to know who we are? Yes? Well, we are called Brownies. Our folk came from Scotland. You know where that is?"

"Oh, yes," I replied, speaking, I suppose, quite mechanically, "Scotland is the northern part of the island of Great Britain; it is bounded on the south by England, on the east by the Ger——"

"Never mind the boundary," interrupted the Brownie

the rude figures were so apt and interesting to my own mind, that I fancied others might be equally interested therein. "Why not print them?" suggested the Mistress. And upon mature deliberation that is just what I resolved to do. No one but a child could make such pictures. Let the adult, however good an artist, try as much as he may, he could not reproduce such drawings. Indeed the better the artist, the further would he come from achievement. That children will take at once to these reflections of a child's mind, appears quite probable. Moreover, to the thinking adult they must have a special value as a psychological study. With all our knowledge of children, it is still marvellous how little we know of a child's mind. These little tokens of its workings perhaps may help us to a better knowledge. At all events, a few of these "Boy's Illustrations" have been selected for engraving, and the editor will be disappointed if they do not give to both his adult and youthful readers as much pleasure as they gave to himself.—THE EDITOR.

with a dainty, tinkling laugh, "we are not a School-mistress and her Committee, and you needn't say your lesson now. It's enough for us that you know where Scotland is,—the dear auld land o' cakes! We're Scotch fairies—Brownies."

" But how came you here?" I asked.

" Oh! there's nothing odd about that; we follow our wandering Sawnies wherever they go. We have all been interested with you in Mr. Mayfield's accounts of insect life, and have been present at many of your walks and talks when you little suspected such company. Ah! we could give the Tenant some hints well worth following up! Although, he does very well, very well indeed! But we wish you to know that there are other tenants on the old farm than those Mr. Mayfield knows. *We* are here, you see! And, alack-a-day! there are other folk here not so agreeable as we!"

" Many thanks," I said, "for the pleasure of your acquaintance. I am delighted and honored by your action, Madam—Madam? what shall I call you?"

" Fancy; Queen Fancy, if you please; so I am called, although, to be sure, there is not much royal state among our folk."

" I beg your pardon, Madam Fancy! And now I—fancy that I can explain the beautiful repose that lies over the face of Nature in this royal month of June. I have just been meditating upon it with delight. How peaceful, how lovely in their peacefulness are all things around us! Yes, I see how it is! The good Brownies are abroad upon the landscape, and they have thrown the light and sweetness of their own natures upon these scenes. What a happy people you are, free from all conflict and care, and how happy those who feel the spell of your influence!"

2

"Oh! O-o-oh!" A chorus of exclamations uttered in a deprecating tone broke from the whole Brownie company.

I started, and looked around surprised beyond measure at this outburst of protesting voices. Then followed a moment of silence.

Queen Fancy spoke at last. "Yes, it is just as I supposed," she said. "You are yet a novice in Nature lore. You have much to learn, all you mortals have, ere you can know the true life of the inferior creatures. There is another side to Nature, I assure you, a very sad side, too. Come, I must teach you to read between the lines!"

She touched me with a tiny staff or wand. My mind at once was wide awake and all its faculties more alert than usual. But, curiously, the Brownies had disappeared! I wondered at this, but presently a series of incidents caught my attention which for the time quite banished all thought of my new acquaintances.

A long line of Sanguine Ants,* the Red Slave-makers, filed by me in irregular columns and crossed the walk to their nest which, as you know, is placed close by the fence nearly opposite the barn. The warriors carried in their jaws the plunder of a nest of Fuscous Ants which I have already said lies to the right under the verge of the Elm's shadow. Some warriors had yellowish cocoons, some white larvæ, a few carried the bodies (living or dead I could not determine) of their victims, and several bore upon their legs the severed heads of the poor blacks who had been slain in defence of their home, and whose decapitated heads still clung to their foes fixed in the rigor of death. I rose and followed up the column of Sanguines to the

---

* Formica sanguinea.

nest which they were plundering. Some of the kidnappers were plunging into the opened gates, others issuing therefrom laden with their stolen booty, others were engaged in fierce battle with groups of the invaded Fuscas. Only a few of the latter were inclined to fight. They seemed, for the most part, dazed by their misfortune. Numbers hung to the topmost leaves and stalks of the surrounding grass and weeds, holding in their jaws baby larvæ and cocoon cradles rescued from the invaders, with which they had hurriedly fled to the nearest elevated objects. It was truly a pitiful sight, and I began to wax indignant at the Sanguine wretches who could work such domestic misery and ruin.

FIG. 3.—A Red Slavemaker Ant with its Plunder.

"Ah!" said a faint voice close by my ear, "yet this is Nature!"

I could see no one, but recognized the tone of Queen Fancy. "True, most true!" I thought, and looked further. A little way from the Fuscas' nest, just outside the circle of confusion, I saw a solitary ant of an amber hue, the Schaufuss ant,* which you have told us is also sometimes enslaved. She was moving back and forth with cautious mien, and I easily perceived was putting finishing touches to the closure of a little hole that marked the gate of her formicary hut. A tiny pebble was placed, then a few pellets of soil were added. Then the worker walked away, took a few turns as though surveying the surroundings, and cautiously came back.

* Formica Schaufussii.

The coast was clear! Now she deftly crawled into the small open space, and I could see from the movements inside, and an occasional glimpse of a tip of her antennæ, that she was completing the work of concealment from the inside. At last her task was done, and all was quiet. Just then a single Sanguine warrior, perhaps a straggler from the invaders' army, or some independent scout, it may be, approached the spot. It walked about

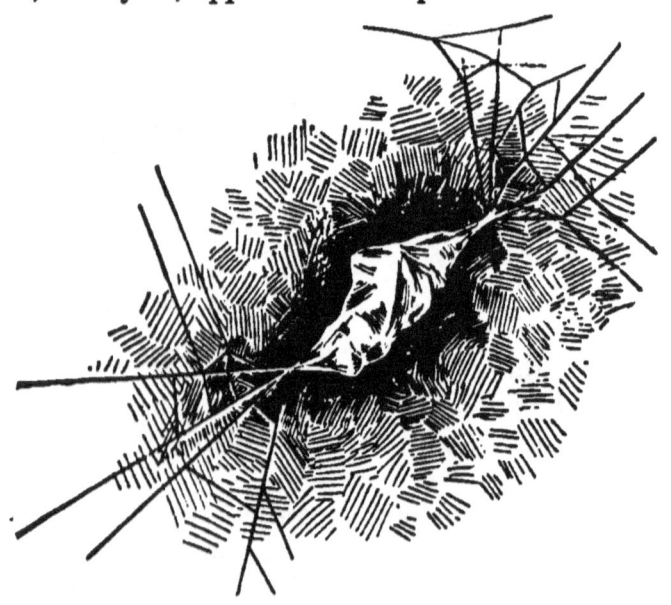

Fig. 4.—"It was Swathed Like a Mummy at Last" (p. xxiii).

the nest, which certainly looked much like the surrounding surface; sounded or felt here and there with its antennæ; passed over the very door into which the Schaufuss ant had disappeared, and although it evidently had its suspicion awakened, at last moved away.

"Good!" I exclaimed heartily. "Baffled, Sir Sanguine, baffled! I am glad that the instinct of home protection has proved too much for your wretched kidnapping cunning!"

"Aye, aye!" again spoke the voice of my unseen fairy, "baffled this time, perhaps. But can you be sure that the slaveholder scout will not be back again, with a host of its fellows, and do its work more surely?"

FIG. 5.—The Orbweaver Captured by a Wasp.

I had not thought of that, and indeed, I was pained to think it when suggested. Now I left the two nests, the plundered one and its preserved neighbor, and followed the column of Sanguines which stretched a nearly straight line of red and black for several rods, to their home. The kidnappers were bearing their prey into the open gates. Look at this! Crowds of blacks in a high state of agitation came forth to meet and greet the

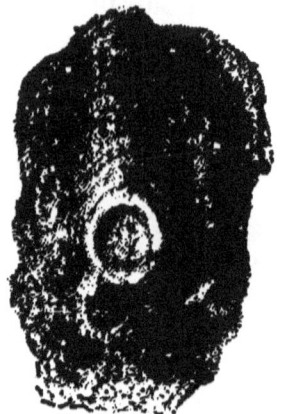

plunderers of their own fellows! Yes, these were the domesticated slaves of the Sanguines, themselves Fuscous ants, the same species and perhaps from the very nest that was now being desolated. And there they were rejoicing in the booty, welcoming home the robbers, and if naturalists tell us truly, had even urged them forth upon the Expedition.

Fig. 6.—"The Clay Sarcophagus on Yonder Barn."

"That's the worst of all!" I exclaimed aloud, unable to suppress my indignation. "One might find excuse for the Sanguines, but for this unnatural behavior—"

"Unnatural!" echoed the unseen Brownie Queen, "unnatural? No, this, too, is Nature. You are only reading between the poet's lines of peaceful beauty. You will learn your lesson by and by."

I went back to the rustic seat beneath the Elm, and thought. A butterfly flew by. I followed its flight. "Oh! that is too bad!"

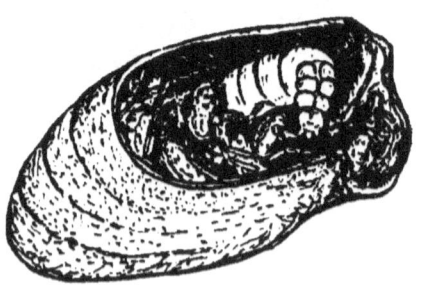

Fig. 7.—"For a Ravenous Wasp Larva to Devour."

I cried involuntarily. It had struck the snare of the Orbweaving spider. It struggled helplessly in the toils. Swiftly the aranead sped from its pretty leafy tent along its trap line, and in a moment seized and began swathing its victim. A thick ribbon of pure white silk streamed from the spinnerets, and enwrapped the butterfly round and round as it was revolved by the spider's feet. It was swathed like a mummy at last, and left lashed and hanging to the cross lines, while its captor mounted to her nest and began leisurely to haul up the captive preparatory to a sumptuous meal.

My pity had hardly time to express itself ere another insect form swept by. It was a blue wasp, a Mud-dauber. It flew to the Orbweaver's web. Another victim? It is

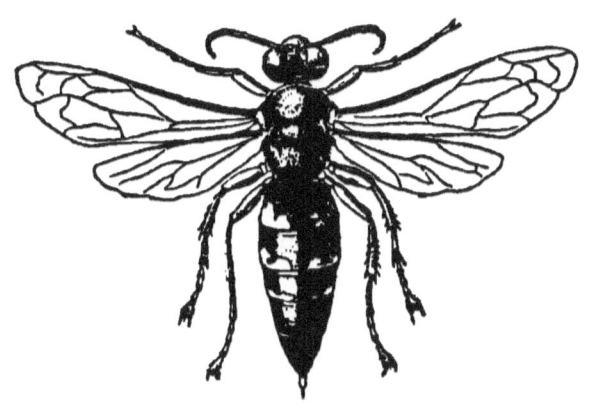

Fig. 8.—The Cicada Wasp, Sphecius speciosus.

within the toils! The spider leaves her prey and darts along the trap line. What? will she not venture? No! she recoils. But too late! The Wasp has seized her, plunged its sharp sting into her body, and shaking the bits of web from its feet flies away. I know what that means. The clay sarcophagus on yonder barn wall shall receive another morsel of preserved meat for a ravenous wasp larva to devour.

What had I to say about this incident? This; I found myself unconsciously asking, "What will destroy the Wasp, in its turn?" But I had no leisure to meditate an answer.  A beautiful creature flitted past me, whose colors of orange and black were distinct even in flight.  It was the fine, large Digger-wasp,* the largest of that family among our indigenous insects.  Just then from the branch of a small oak a Cicada sounded his rolling love call.  A note not very melodious to human ear, it is true, but it throbs with the passion of affection, and must have been sweet music to his mate on the branch near by.  Unlucky lover! your love sonnet has sounded your doom.  It shall be your death song.  See! my beautiful Wasp has pounced upon the amorous Cicada, and pierced and paralyzed like the spider before him, he is being borne to a grave in that grassy bank.  There, in the Wasp's burrow, buried alive though with a semblance of death, he shall feed the maw of a hungry worm.

" It is mother love!" exclaimed the unseen Brownie Queen, sadly I thought and tenderly.  " But mother love seems cruel sometimes; and it alone has not taught the Wasp to spare the mating love of its fellow insects."

This is not all that I saw, but this is such as I saw on that memorable occasion.  My experience started a train of meditation that was the reverse of agreeable.  But what could I say ?  I had been observing the facts of Nature, nothing more nor less.  I looked away over the landscape again and my feelings were not what they were before.  Underneath the surface of all this beauty and summer repose I seemed to feel the beating of a fevered pulse.  Yes, the Doctor of the Gentiles spake truly: "The whole creation groaneth and travaileth in pain."†  Yes, I was beginning to read between the lines!  Verily, I perceived that the insect world in the matter of anxiety, struggles and sufferings, in passions

---

*Sphecius speciosus.          † Romans viii. 22.

of love, hate and covetousness, is after all in some sort a miniature of our own world of human beings.

I do not know how long I sat pondering these things, but I was presently conscious that my Brownie friends had returned.

"You have changed your opinion about some of the inferior creatures, have you not?" began Queen Fancy. "I know that it must be so. And now it remains for you to change your opinion about us. You think we are perfectly happy, never touched by such conflicts and cares as mortals and insects have. No! it is with us as it is with you and all the rest. One idea runs through all Nature and all her creatures high and low. All alike, from gnats and fairies to mastodons and men, have friends and foes, perils and pleasures, pains and joys, loves and hates, bitter disappointments and proud attainments; watchings, cares, strifes, battles, defeats, heart desolations, sickness, oppressions, despoilment, death— all these and the reverse of all these happen to us all."

"It is true!" I answered, "I see now that it is quite true. The fact that creatures are small and unknown to us, and outside our ordinary region of feeling and thought, does not hinder them from having joys and sorrows, trials and triumphs even as we have. I will never think of Nature again, and of the insect world in particular, without remembering this double side of its life history."

"That is very good," said Queen Fancy, "and now we wish you to remember also that Brownies are a part of Nature and share the general rule. Our lives are so interwoven with all natural surroundings, and with your- selves as well, that we feel keenly everything that goes on around us. But enough for this time. I promised you something further about our history. Now I make the promise good. I am to deliver to you the records of some of our kin which have lately fallen into our hands. You will read them; write them out carefully, and give them to Mr. Mayfield to edit and print. Nobody can do that so well as he. Indeed, his name and his stories about our Old Farm Tenants have gone among our people on the far Ohio border; and that is the reason why these records of the Brownies and their wars have been sent hither to be given into his care. There, I have done."

Queen Fancy clapped her hands and a herald at her side blew upon a tiny shell, a wee miniature, for all the world, of the conch shell which Sarah the cook blows for dinner. Suddenly, a vast host of little folk issued from the grass plat along the slope toward the spring-house. They were arranged rank upon rank, whole companies in column, and they all were drawing at ropes no bigger than a lady's hair. Presently, I saw the round top of a rolled parcel emerge above the summit of the slope. It moved slowly, and I was puzzled to know by what force it was impelled, until I saw that it was mounted upon a toy cart which was being drawn by the Brownie host. On the night before I had been reading (it was a curious coincidence!) Wilkinson's account of the Ancient Egyptians, and had been especially interested in the manner in which their bulky architecture had been reared, and particularly in a picture that showed a colossal stone statue of some sovereign being drawn upon a sled by an army of laborers. The Brownie exploit reminded me of these old Egyptians. Here were the little folk of our Old Farm showing mimic reproduction of life on the Nile in the days of Abraham! Strange!

The Brownie host never stopped until the parcel

reached my feet. Then the Queen called a halt, and, turning to me, said: "Abby, Schoolmistress, we commit this precious roll to you. Receive it as a sacred trust; do our will concerning it, and be forevermore the Brownies' good friend." She clapped her hands, the herald blew his shell bugle, and in a moment the entire host had melted away into the foliage and were lost to sight.

I have not seen them since, but I have tried to fulfill my part of the trust which came to me so curiously in

THE BOY'S ILLUSTRATION.
FIG. 9.—Brownies Bringing the Roll of Records.

the drowsy hours of that June day, and now I deliver my work to you that you in turn may fulfill your portion of the apportioned duty. That you will not fail is the confident hope of

Your obedient servant,
ABBY BRADFORD.

"What do you think of that?" I asked, as I finished Abby's letter, for I had read it aloud to the Mistress.

"Perhaps," said the Mistress, looking up from her embroidery, "we had better open the parcel."

A familiar twinkle colored her smile, that raised a momentary suspicion that she perhaps knew something more of the contents than she chose to tell. The advice was good, albeit deftly dodging my question, so I cut the wrappings and exposed a roll of fair manuscript. "It is a story," I remarked, after glancing over the pages, "a sort of historical fairy tale, I fancy. But, hold! what is this?" My eye had fallen upon some sentences that arrested attention, and I read several continuous pages.

The Mistress interrupted the reading: "Well, what has interested you? And what have you to say about the whole affair?"

"I have been reading here a curious adaptation of the habits of my spider pets, and it is neatly put. And here is another of the same sort." I turned to a chapter further on, and read with great satisfaction a few pages more. "Really," I exclaimed, "the natural history is good, and is fairly inwoven with the tale. I have changed my opinion of the work; it is evidently an attempt to bring out some of the most interesting habits of our American spider fauna by personifying them with the imaginary creatures of fairy lore. You want to know my opinion of the matter? As to the manuscript I shall not, of course, venture an opinion until I have read it with some care. As to the author—well, perhaps you can tell better than I. When did Abby write it?"

The Mistress waited a moment or two and then in her quiet way replied, " Pray, how should I know ? Abby is of age, ask her ; she can speak for herself."

Thus the affair of the Brownie records rested until I had gone over the manuscript more carefully. Then the Mistress was again consulted.

" Will you print the papers ? " she asked.

" I am in doubt what to do. I think that it might find a kindly welcome, but—I fear the verdict of the public, especially the clientage upon whose favor its fate most depends—the young people. Though, to be sure, it is evidently not written wholly for them."

" I have a suggestion," the Mistress remarked. " Let us take two evenings in the week and read it to our farm people. They form a typical audience, I am sure, and their judgment will be a fair test of the possible verdict of the public at large."

" The very idea ! " I cried. " You have come to my help, my dear, with your usual practical wisdom. Let us have the readings."

Behold us, then, the entire Old Farm family, with the exception of Abby, who was absent on a visit to New England friends, seated around the great Elm during the long June evenings, trying the merits of the Fairies' history. When the early tea was over, we took our seats (or rather positions, for some of the party preferred to recline upon the grass), around the tree, and the reading began, and continued until twilight. Sometimes I read, sometimes the Mistress, and in three weeks the story was finished.

"Now for the verdict," I said. "The children first. What say you? Shall we print the Brownie book?"

"To be sure," said Joe, "why not, Sir? I think those wars and adventures with the Pixies are just the thing for boys like me."

"I would print it," said Jennie modestly. "I think the Brownies' love stories are pretty indeed; though I don't like so much fighting, and the Pixies are just horrid."

"Print it, Sir!" cried Harry enthusiastically. "I'm sure boys like me will want to hear all about the Moth, Wasp, Bee and Butterfly ponies, and the curious, wise tricks of the Spider-pixies."

"As for me," said Hugh, "I'm young enough yit to relish a fairy story uv mos' any sort. So I vote with the youngsters to prent the book."

"My 'pinion hain't much good, I reckon," said Sarah, who stood half concealed behind the Elm with her hands upon her hips in her favorite posture. "An' I hain't no sort uv notion uv witches an' sich, no way. Tho' laws-a-massy! I b'lieve in 'em; 'v course I do! But somehow, I don't feel over comfo'ble to hev sech things a-prentin' about our Ole Farm. W'at's people goin' to say about sech goins-on, any way? I don't mind about the Brownies; like es not ther be sech folk. An' w'y not here as well as other places? I don't know w'ere they'd find a nicer home than jes' aroun' here; an' I'm pos'tive my kitchen's trig enough for any kind o' fairies as ever was. Folks as hev sense enough to use a couch shell, now, as them Brownie heralds do, would be

jes' likely to settle at the Ole Farm. But es for them
Pixies—w'at's the use uv sech critters, anyhow? 'Tain't
no ways comfo'ble to think thet they mought be squattin'
on our premises. Howsomever, I'd prent the book, I
reckon. Leastways, ye kin do it, fer all me, 'f ye're a
mine ter. My notion is it's a sight more interestener
nor the Say-an-says. Though, they was worth prentin'
too, that's a fac'!'"

"Now, Dan, it's your turn," I said; "what say you?"
The old colored man sat on a low stool at the outer
margin of the family circle, with his face leaning upon
his hands. He raised his head, laid his palms upon his
knees, rolled his eyes expressively and gave his verdict
with all the solemnity of a judge passing sentence on a
capital offender.

"'Pears to me, Mars Mayfiel' an' Misses," he began,
"dat dat's a powerful good story, an' a true one, too!
W'y, I've seed dem wery Brownies myse'f. Uv coorse
I hev!" he exclaimed emphatically, turning an indignant glance upon Sarah, who had uttered a significant
guttural expression of unbelief. "W'at do you know
aboout Brownies, Sary Ann, I'd jes' like to know?
Pixies is more in your line, a heap sight! Down in ole
Marylan', now, dar's a power ob Brownies and Fairies
an' all sech folkses. 'Tain't ebry one as gits to see 'em,
dough. Dey's mighty 'tickler 'boout w'at company dey
keeps, I kin tell *you!*

"I doan say es I eber seed any on 'em roun' dis Ole
Farm,—an' I doan say es I didn't. But dat's needer
hyar nur dar. Dey's hyar, I knows. I've done seed de

signs ob 'em, many's de time. W'y, lookee hyar! How d'ye tink dem insecks an' bugs and tings w'at Mars Mayfiel' tole us aboout, done foun' out how to do dar peert tricks? Hit stans to reason dat sech critters ain't got de larnin' fer sech cunnin' doins. W'at wid dar nes's, an' burrows, an' cobwebs, an' cute little housens, an' all dat, dey show heap moah sense dan some w'ite folks es I could name. Now, whar dey gwine to fin' out all dat, I ax agin, an' how is dey gwine to do it, unless de Fairies helps 'em? Dey jes' kine ob obersee de job; dat's how it 'pears to me.

"Den dar's dat gubner Wille—shoo! He ain't no sucumstance ter w'at I knows 'boout how de insecks, an' fairies, an' goblins an' dem kine ob beins hes to do wid we uns. No, no!"—and he shook his head with serious gravity—"no, Sah! hit won't do ter go back on dat. We cullud folks knows heaps ob larnin' aboout dem critters; an' dey's jes' wove in, an' in, an' in, an' out ob dese yere mohtal libes ob ourn! Dar's de Deaf's-head moff, an' de catumpillars, an' de antemires, an' de death watch, an' de cricket, an' de money-spinners, an' de measurin' worm—sakes-alive! Dar's signs an' warn-ins fer we uns in dem critters agin all de Pixies, worl' widout en'. Amen. Yes, Sah, hit's all right; dat's a true story, an' no mistake."

"But, Dan," I said, "you haven't told us yet what you think about printing the story."

"Needer I have, Sah!" the old man replied, rolling up the whites of his eyes and shaking his shaggy, gray poll. "Needer I have! an' wat's moah, I ain't gwine

FIG. 10.—Our Farm Family in Literary Council.

ter. I doan see much good in dem kine ob books no how—specially de picters. Dar's like to be bad work aboout dem tings. Hit doan do ter be too fumwiliar wid such tings. W'at's de good? Dar's no tellin' w'at dey mought do ter we'ns, ef dey gits sot agin us. You bes' keep clar ob dat business, Mars Mayfiel'. De ole Bible's good 'nough fer me, Sah; an' hit says dat much larnin' makes a man mad, an' books is a-wearisome to de flesh. An' dat's a fac', Sah,—leastways, readin' an' a-studyin' on 'em is. You kin do w'at you's a mine ter, an' I 'low you'll prent de Brownie book, any way. Hit's mighty good hearin', I'll say dat fer it, but—" he shook his head once more, and was silent.

The next day I wrote to the Schoolmistress as follows:

The Old Farm.

My dear Miss Abby:

I have gone over the manuscript that you sent, and on the whole I approve of it, and agree to print it with such editorial notes as Queen Fancy has suggested. We have also—the Mistress and I—read it to the Farm family, having revived our last winter's "Say-an-says" for that purpose. I have even translated bits of the story into simpler form and speech for the youngest member of our household, four-year-old Dorothy. Our young people are enthusiastic in their admiration, and vote to print the book. So do the others, with the exception of Dan, who is noncommittal. But the old fellow enjoyed the reading as much as the rest. He thinks the story a true one, and declares that he has seen the Brownies! You know his boundless super-stition, and his odd habits of personifying all living things and talking aloud to them as he goes about his work. I have no doubt that he has peopled his little world with many queer imaginary creatures who may well stand to his undisciplined fancy for Fairies and Goblins, Brownies and Pixies. He has unwavering faith, also, in the occult influence of such beings and of insects generally upon the destinies of human kind.

By the way, this unexpected deliverance of Dan's has eased my mind as to one feature of the story, viz : the manner in which the life and behavior of the Willes are interwoven with, and interdependent upon, the movements of the Brownies and Pixies. Since I have thought more about it, I have greatly abated the fear that the verisimilitude of such relations might not sufficiently appear to readers.

In point of fact, the creatures of the Insect World, as personified in the story, have had and shall have much to do with determining the lot of man. The plagues of Egypt as written in the Book of Exodus, furnish an example ; as also the incursions of cankerworm, locust, caterpillar and palmerworm recorded elsewhere in Scripture. African travelers tell us that the tetze fly has so circumscribed the geographical bounds within which certain domestic animals can live, as to greatly limit or modify civilization. We all know examples of the effects of mosquito supremacy at certain points of our country in determining the fortunes of men or places. The familiar stories of Bruce and the Spider, and Mahomet and the Spider, are also in point as showing how great interests may hinge upon the behavior of an humble animal. Here are facts enough, surely, to justify us in facing the public with Governor Wille and his relations to the imaginary folk of the story.

In conclusion, I must say that I have been greatly

interested to note how admirably the habits of my spider friends admit of personification. The so-called engineering, ballooning, cavemaking, sailing, and other operations, are so accurately described by those words, that the manlike qualities, motives and passions attributed to the actors seem almost natural. At one moment I find myself accepting the representations as a matter of course, and anticipating the conduct described on the very ground of known natural habits. At another time I am startled at the strong tone of human behavior that the descriptions so easily admit. Certainly, this is something more than what the naturalists have called "anthropomorphism." What is the mysterious ligature that binds in this sympathy of movements the sovereign will of immortal man and the automatic brain cell of a spider?

Pardon me! it was not in my purpose to start so profound a question of philosophy and physiology. I only meant to say that the wishes of yourself and your Brownie acquaintances shall be cheerfully granted, and the manuscript be given to the public.

I am, very truly,

Your Friend,

FIELDING MAYFIELD.

# THE BOOK.

# Old Farm Fairies.

## A Summer Campaign in Brownieland

### against

## King Cobweaver's Pixies.

# CHAPTER I.

Not many years ago a company of Brownies lived on the lawn at Hillside, the home of Governor Wille. Since the Brownies are Scotch fairies, one must ask how they came to be dwelling so far away from their native heather upon the green hummocks of the Ohio.

The question takes us back to the early part of the Nineteenth Century, and to a Manse and glebe on the banks of Loch Achray, the beautiful little lake that lies at the entrance to Trosachs Glen, quite near the foot of Loch Katrine in Scotland. Here dwelt Governor Wille's grandfather, a godly minister of the Gospel; and here he lived until there grew up around him a large family of sturdy lads and lasses. Often had the good minister looked over his household as they sat around the table eating with keen relish their cakes and oatmeal porridge, and wondered: "How shall I provide for them all? How shall I find fitting duty and engagement for these eager hearts, restless hands, and busy brains?"

At last he answered: "I will go with them to America, and join my brother there on the banks of the Ohio River."

Now the Manse and glebe were the seat of a nation of the wee fairyfolk whom Scotchmen call Brownies. The Manse site is on the skirt of Ben An's lowest slope; and across the Trosachs road, upon a point that pushes into the Loch, stands the kirk amid its kirkyard. The Brownies were fond of this home, but they loved the

(3)

Manse folk much more dearly; and so when they heard the plan to emigrate to the New World, they resolved not to allow their friends to go to America without an escort of their fairy companions and caretakers.

A General Assembly of all the Manse Brownies was therefore called, to meet under the "hats" of a clump of broad toadstools growing on the mountain slope, close by the barn. The place was crowded from the stem of the central toadstool to the rim of the outer hat. Outside this clump the spears of grass, the drooping bluebells, and purple blossoms of heather were covered with boy Brownies, who climbed up delicate stems, smooth blades and gnarled stalks, much as city lads mount lampposts, trees and awnings to gaze upon a procession. From these points they looked upon their elders, quite as anxious and earnest, if not as well informed as they.

When the Assembly had been called to order, the King of the Brownies asked, "Who will volunteer to go to America with our dear friends, the Willes?"

There was a mighty shout; not one present failed to answer: "I!!"

The explosion fairly shook the roof of their toadstool tabernacle. Thereat the old monarch sprang to his feet, removed his plumed hat, and stood uncovered, bowing his white hairs and venerable beard before the Assembly, in honor of their noble response. The elders waved their tiny blue Scotch bonnets, wept, laughed and hallooed in turn. The youngsters danced upon the heather bells and swung from the grass blades until the tops swayed to and fro, and cheered again and again for the Willes, for the King, for the Brownies, for everybody!

By and by the King brought the Assembly to order, and proposed that a colony be drafted from the whole company to go to the New World. "I shall claim the privilege of naming the leader of the Expedition," said he, " and I name Murray Bruce. The rest may go by lot."

Whereat the Brownies cheered again, for they were always pleased to respect their good sovereign's wishes, and Bruce was one of the wisest, steadiest, and bravest of their number. He was tall, strong, comely, and in the prime of his years. Then the lot was cast. The names of all the active Brownies were placed in the tiny corol of a blue bell, which served as a voting urn. The King drew out fifty names, and these were the elect members of the colony. The interest was intense as the drawing went on. Again and again the King's hand sank into the urn, and came out holding the wee billet that decided some Brownie's destiny. As the name was announced, there was silence; but thereupon a flutter of excitement ran through the company; a whirl of noisy demonstration marked the spot where the fortunate nominee was receiving the congratulations of his friends; sometimes a cheer was given when a favorite or familiar name was announced.

"How many names have been drawn?" asked the King.

"Forty-nine," answered the Lord Keeper. Amid profound silence the last name was drawn and announced:

"Rodney Bruce!"

It was the Captain's brother, a young and promising sailor, who had won much praise for daring adventures with water pixies on "the stream that joins Loch Katrine and Achray." His name was welcomed with cheers, and then a buzz of disappointment arose from the crowd who heartily envied the "Fortunate Fifty."

However, the disappointment soon passed away, for Brownies are a cheerful and contented folk. The hum of voices ceased, and the people waited to know what might be needed to forward the comfort and success of the emigrant escort.

"How shall we get off?" said Captain Bruce. "Has your Majesty any orders or counsel? Has the Assembly any advice?"

That was a puzzling question. The Lord Keeper, Lord Herald, and all the other lords and nobles shook their heads wisely and said nothing. Some one called out the name of "Rodney, the sailor," whereat the old Lord Admiral turned up his little red nose, looked contemptuously at the speaker, and muttered something about "land lubbers." As no one had any advice to venture, all waited for their sovereign's opinion.

"Hoot!" said the King at last, "Ye shall juist gae your ain gait. Howiver, ye maun steal awa' unbeknowns, I'se warrant ye; for Parson Wille, good heart! will never allow ye to risk anything for him. But how? Well, I dinna ken; ye maun e'en settle that amang yoursels."

The difficulty was no nearer solution than before. There was another long pause. It was broken by a voice that called from the outer edge of the Assembly.

"I can tell you how!" It was Walter MacWhirlie who spoke, one of the chosen escort.

"Come to the front, then," said the King, "and say your say."

Every eye was at once fixed on the bold speaker. But MacWhirlie, nothing abashed, leaped from the heather stalk on which he stood, and making a double somersault above the whole company, landed erect upon the edge of a leaf whereon sat the King and lords.

FIG. 11.—Brownie MacWhirlie Comes to the Front by a Double Somersault.

"Ugh!" said the monarch, starting back; for Mac-Whirlie had well nigh alighted on his toes.

"Queak!" cried the Queen; and "queak, queak!" screamed the Princesses, tumbling over one another in their fright.

"You rude beast!" growled the Lord Keeper, laying his hand upon his broadsword.

But the youth and boys cheered, the young Princesses began to giggle, the old folks laughed outright, the Queen smoothed down her ruffles, the good King composed his countenance and smiled, and the Lord Keeper smothered his indignation and put up his sword.

"Speak up, laddie," said the King. MacWhirlie bowed low first to the royal party, and then to the lords. (My Lord Keeper's brow cleared up somewhat at that.)

"I was passin' thro' the barn the morn," he began, "and saw the gardener packin' the auld kist that lies on the barn floor, with tools, seeds, roots and herbs. It's a gude place for hidin', is yon kist."

"That it is," exclaimed the Queen laughing, "I've had mony a game o' bo-peep in 't mysel'."

"Aye, aye, so it is!" was the hearty assent from all parts of the hall, while the lads on the outside signified their approval by cheers for the old chest.

"A gude place for hidin' is yon auld kist," continued MacWhirlie. "I ken naethin' like it for Brownies. An' if your Majesty please, we can a' ride to America safe eneugh in that."

"It is gude counsel," cried the King, clapping his hands. "Forbye, I would na thoct it frae sic a giddy pate as yoursel', MacWhirlie. Many thanks, however, and mak' ready quarters in the auld kist for your journey to the New World. Herald, dismiss the Assembly."

Lord Herald skipped to the front and sounded a bugle, which in sooth was nothing more than a tiny shell fitted with a dainty mouth-piece.

"Hi-e-iero ! ee-roo !"

FIG. 12.—The Old Chest on its Journey Across the Allegheny Mountains.

Then he struck his staff thrice, and cried, or rather intoned in a loud voice these words :

O-eez ; O-eez ; O-eez !
Bide by the King's decrees !
Brownies-O-bonnie, and Brownies-O-braw,
Hither gae, hame gae, Brownies awa' !

At the last word the Assembly arose, and speaking all together, responded,

Brownies aye, Brownies a
Leal and true, awa', awa' !

Then they separated, the elders moving soberly, the youth scampering off hither and thither, leaping, chattering, cheering, making the grass blades twinkle with their good natured frolic. In a moment the toadstools were deserted, and a great spider-pixie crept under the vacant central hat, and began to shake his head and talk to himself while uttering a low, harsh, chuckling laugh.

Bruce, Rodney, MacWhirlie and all the elect escort, together with their families, made the voyage across the Atlantic safely though somewhat uncomfortably. But their trials were not over when they landed in Philadelphia. The chest was hoisted into a big road wagon covered with canvas, known as a "Conestoga wagon," and wheeled on for many days over the Allegheny mountains. Down by old Fort Pitt it trundled, along the banks of the beautiful river Ohio, to the frontier village of Steubenville. There the wagon stopped. Parson Wille built his cabin on Hillside. The Brownies, happy as the beasts and birds that were turned out of Noah's Ark after the flood, were released from their prison in the old chest, and took up once more old duties and pleasures in the clearings, cornfields and garden of the new home.

That was many years ago. The good parson has long since been received to a fairer Home than either Scotland or America ever gave; but his grandson, Governor Wille, lives at Hillside. It is not the same Hillside that the brave and godly minister first built his log cabin upon, you may be sure. Great changes have occurred. But the same Brownies are there; as good natured, as frolicsome, as fond of their friends and as true to them as ever, yet, we are sorry to say, not so fortunate and happy. What has troubled them?

# CHAPTER II.

When the Assembly of Brownies, which had been held at the old Scotch Manse, was quite dispersed, a spider-pixie entered the vacant tent and began to spin a web. He belonged to a race of sprites as vicious and cruel as the Brownies are kind and good. They are called spider-pixies because they do much of their mischief by means of silken webs or snares which they spin, and in which they catch their enemies. The fact, however, should work no prejudice against those remarkable creatures, the spiders, which are doubtless worthy of all the loving attention that naturalists give them.

The chief enemies of these Pixies (next to themselves, to be sure) were the Brownies. Not that the good little fairies wished to harm any creature; but then, as the Pixies wished harm to every one, and were always showing their ill will by naughty tricks, the Brownies, out of very goodness, tried to thwart their evil plans and save intended victims from harm. Thus it came that the Brownies and Pixies lived in continuous warfare. Many a battle had they fought on and around the Manse glebe and kirkyard, for the Pixies hated Parson Wille most cordially, and dearly loved to annoy him.

The Brownies were just as hearty in their love, and by close watching, hard working and brave battling they had well nigh driven their enemies from the place. Only once in a while a few, more daring and cunning than the rest, would break through the boundaries and make a foray upon the forbidden grounds.

(11)

Among the most successful of these leaders of mischief was Spite the Spy. He was a great sneak, shrewd and sly, and well deserved his name. He was a coward in the main, and loved best to do his mischief in an under-hand way. But for all that, he was so full of malice that he could be quite venturesome rather than miss a chance to work harm to those whom he hated. Thus it came that in spite of his natural cowardice he had a fair reputation for boldness. It was this miserable fellow who crawled into the tabernacle as the voices of the Brownies died away among the grasses.

How came he therein? Having chanced to hear of the proposed Assembly to consider the interest of the Manse folk, he set himself to spy out the proceedings. How should he do that without being discovered? "Let me think!" he said. He climbed up a tall weed that grew on the border of the Manse farm, swung himself by a thread of silk from a leaf, and hung there awhile, head downward, while he meditated.

"Ha! I have it!" he cried. He pulled himself up again hand over hand, scampered down the weed and plunged into the thick forest of grasses. He went swiftly, though cautiously, for a while. Then he ascended a tall spear of timothy, perched himself atop of the bearded head and reconnoitered.

"Yes, there it is," he said to himself. "I see the brown hat of the toadstool tent; and—let me see—yes, sure enough, there is the Black Pebble under which cousin Atypus used to have her nest. Any Brownies about? No, the coast's quite clear. But, caution, old fellow! you are pretty sly, but you may be caught after all. And they'd make short work of Spite if they got hold of him once, I warrant." At this he chuckled, puffed out his eyes, and swelled up his round pouch as though it were a fine thing to be quite deserving of the Brownies' anger.

Spite was not long in making his way to the Black Pebble which was at the outer edge of the Brownies' meeting place, and was imbedded in a little bank of

FIG. 13.—"Silken Snares in Which They Catch Their Enemies."

sandy earth at the base of which the toadstools grew. He began to scratch in the surrounding soil. His claws soon struck something that gave him pleasure. It was a bit of silken tissue.

"Ha! I am in luck! Here is the door of the burrow. Now we shall see, brother Brownies, and hear too; and

4

if there's any mischief agoing Spite the Spy will have his spinner in it."

Spite had come upon the door of a cave or tunnel. When a few more grains of sand had been thrown aside he lifted the tissue door and entered. It was dark at first, and there was a musty smell in the air. Spite did not care for that, and in a moment ran to the far end of the cave and back again. This strange place had once been the home of a Burrow Pixie. It was a tunnel scooped out of the sandy earth.* It ran horizontally for a short way, and then sloped downward. It was lined around the sides, top and bottom with a tight silken tube, and was about half an inch in diameter. It was, therefore, a tunnel within a tunnel, a silk within a sand one. The silk supported the sides so completely that not a particle of soil could pass through. The upper part of the tube projected from the earth, falling forward so as to form a flap which protected the mouth of the burrow or cave. At first the tube had been much longer and was bent and carried over the surface among the moss. This was the door which Spite had been looking for, and whose discovery so much pleased him.

"Well, well," said Spite, talking all the while to himself, "this is lucky indeed. It must now be several moons since cousin Atypus was cut off by the Brownies, and here·is her old place just as good as ever. It looks right into the meeting house. How fortunate! But I must fix up this door a little, or I shall have those suspicious fellows smelling around here; although I doubt whether they know anything about the place. They caught Atypus when she had ventured out of doors."

Meanwhile Spite was busy with the door. He laid a dry leaf and a few bits of dry moss around the edge of

---

* Appendix, Note A.

the pebble, then gently lifted the silken flap and crept within. He made a wee hole in the flap, and through this saw and heard the proceedings of the Brownies. Little did the good folk suspect that one of their

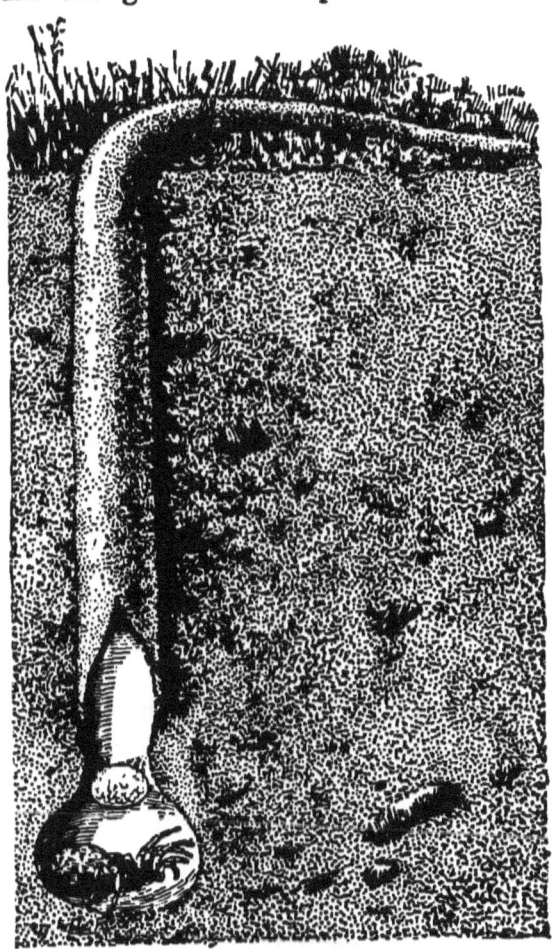

Fig. 14.—English Atypus in Her Burrow.

enemies was so near, almost in their midst. As for Spite, he was in high glee, although he was not without fears. The boy Brownies had climbed atop the Black Pebble, and crowded and capered upon it until they were like to shake it from the bank, and send it arolling into the Assembly.

"Serve 'em right, the little plagues," snarled Spite, "if the old rock did get loose, and break all their necks in the avalanche. Only, that would make a gap in my burrow, and—well, it isn't pleasant to think of the consequences."

Moreover, MacWhirlie and the restless youngsters who were mounted on the herbage that grew above and around the Pixie's cave, were continually tramping over the moss around the door, rocking to and fro on the overhanging heather sprays till the roots fairly shook, and scrambling up and down the little slope and over the flap itself. No wonder that Spite's heart seemed to jump into his throat occasionally.

However, the door of the cave was so cunningly disguised and fitted into the bank, that Spite was not discovered. He was well satisfied, for all that, when the meeting was dismissed and the last of the Brownies disappeared. He pushed open the flap, peeped out, then crawled slowly into the light, crept down the slope and entered the vacant meeting place. He was hungry; the labors and excitement through which he had passed had quite exhausted him. He therefore crouched behind a toadstool stem, and, after waiting patiently a while, sprang upon and devoured a hapless fly and beetle that chanced to straggle that way. Then he wiped his jaws with his hairy claw, rubbed his cheeks and head quite in the fashion of pussy washing her face,* stretched a few silken threads from the stem to the ground, and turned away.

"There," he said, "I leave those few lines to show that I have been here, and that Spite the Spy is sharper

---

* Appendix, Note B.

than all the Brownies. Now for home! King Cobweb
will be interested in what I have to tell. As for Parson
Wille and his Brownies, perhaps they shall not escape
us quite so readily."

Spite gained great applause by this adventure, and
when it was resolved to send out to the New World some
one to watch the motions of Parson Wille, and do all
the harm possible to his kind Brownie guardians, who
but Spite the Spy should be chosen? "You need take
but few companions," said King Cobweb; "there are
plenty of our folk in that country. I shall send a letter

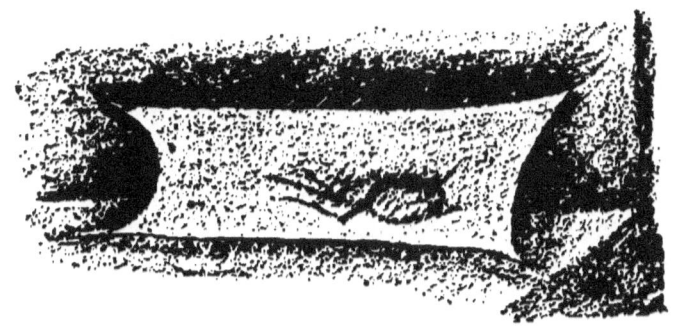

Fig. 15.—" Having Overspun Themselves."

with you to my cousin, King Cobweaver, and you can
muster a goodly company in America."

Now what should Spite do, but make his way straight
to the old chest. He discovered that in one corner the
joints of the planks had sprung open a little. "That
will do bravely, I think!" He crept into the crack to
try if it fitted his size.

"Very good indeed," he exclaimed, and then ran to
report.

King Cobweb was quite satisfied. Spite thereupon hid
himself in the open seam with two other Pixies named
Hide and Heady, and, having overspun themselves with

a silken covering, made the voyage to America in the old chest with the Brownies.*

When safely landed at Hillside, he reported to the nearest tribe of Pixies.    He was received with great favor as a distinguished foreigner; was feasted, petted, and his wonderful skill in strategy heralded everywhere. In short, he was quite a lion, and his fame was even greater in America than on the other side of the Atlantic. Spite took his honors gracefully, enjoyed them hugely, acknowledged them publicly, hobnobbed with his friends, and took occasion when talking in private with his two countrymen, to ridicule the customs and manners of American Pixies.    That was very mean, to be sure; but what better could you expect from Spite the Spy?

In the midst of all his junketings and sight-seeing Spite never once forgot the great object of his journey. He was spinning out his plots against the Brownies, counseling with his American friends how he might worry, injure and destroy them, and forming leagues for that purpose.

That was the beginning of troubles for the Brownies at Hillside.

----

* Appendix, Note C.

# CHAPTER III.

The war upon the Brownie colony thus begun by Spite the Spy had been waged from year to year until the third generation of the Willes, Governor Wille himself, occupied Hillside. Sometimes the Pixies got the advantage, sometimes the Brownies; but on the whole the Pixies gained ground. Slowly the Brownies were being driven in towards the Mansion house, followed closely by their foes. At last the malicious persecutors, led by Spite, pitched their tents and reared a strong fortification at the upper end of the Lawn. Their scouts bivouacked beneath the very windows of my Lady Governor's chamber. This would never have been had not Governor Wille lately grown heedless of his good fairy friends, and left them to struggle without his sympathy and aid. For Home Brownies lose heart and cease to prosper when their Home patrons and allies forget and neglect them. The Brownies were sore distressed. What should they do?

Early one morning the Captain and Lieutenant were in close consultation. The Brownies watched them anxiously as the two slowly walked back and forth underneath a rose bush in a border near the west window of the parlor. The point under discussion was this: " Shall we make another appeal to Governor Wille, or shall we first try an assault upon the new Pixie fort ? "

The decision was soon announced by the bugle call to " fall in." From every quarter the Brownies crowded eagerly, and the column moved toward the north-western corner of the Lawn.   There lay a pool formed by a stream that bubbled from beneath the springhouse at the foot of the hill.   The Brownies called the pool "Loch Katrine," in honor of the lovely and historic water in their old Scotch home from whose neighborhood they had come.   Just beyond the "outlet," the point at which the Spring Run issues from the pool and goes singing down the hillside, the new Pixie fort had been erected.   It was called Fort Spinder, and was

FIG. 16.—The Demilune, or Crescent Barricade.

a sign and token that Spite and his tribes had gained and meant to keep a foothold upon the Lawn, the Brownies' special domain.

In a brief space the Brownie army had surrounded three sides of the fort; the fourth side faced the Lake, and was safe from approach of land troops.   Then Captain Bruce sent out a number of scouts to view the Pixie works and report upon their strength and the best points for attack.   Let us join the Captain and his staff, and listen to these scouts as one after another they return with their reports.   We shall thus learn

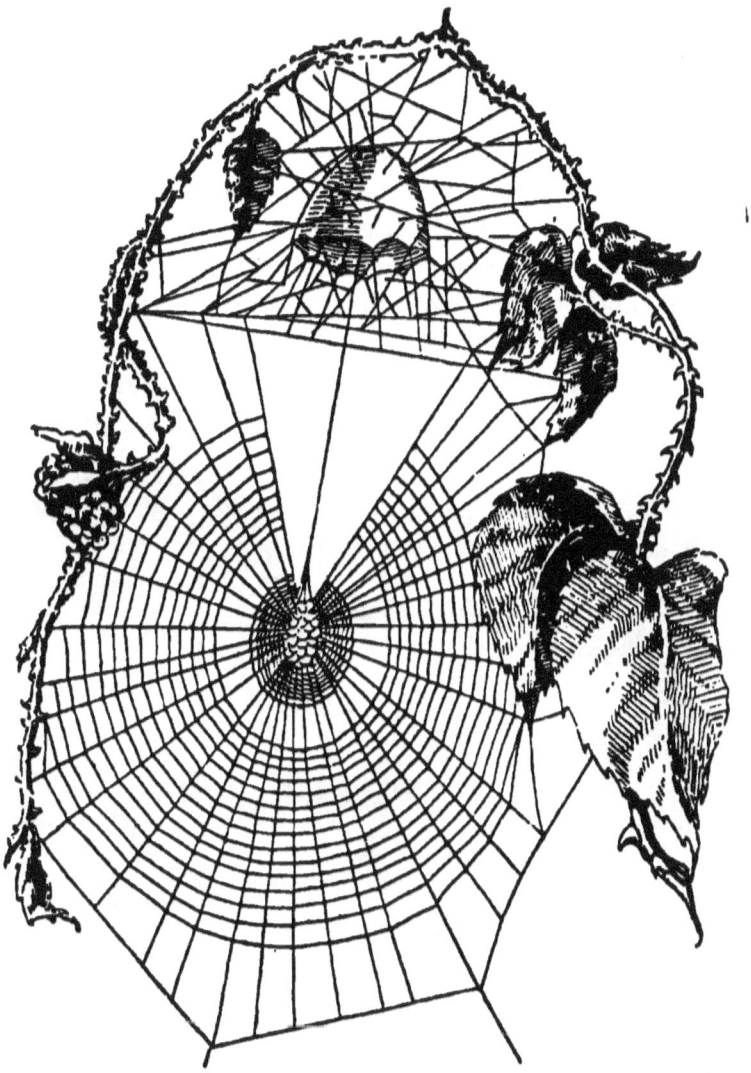

Fig. 17.—The Bell Shaped Turret of Pixie Globosa, of the Wheel Legion.

(21)

something of the Pixies' deft handicraft and cunning ways.

"The first obstacle that I met," said Sightwell, who was the first scout to report, "was a line of barricades occupied by the Wheel Legion. This is formed of round webs woven upon grass and weeds, closely joined to one another and strung in a semicircular form along the whole front of the fort. Armed pickets are stationed at the open centrals of the snares. At either end of this crescent or demilune is a large orbweb, surmounted

FIG. 18.—Fort Spinder.

by a tower. One tower is wrought out of leaves lashed together by silken threads; the other is the bell shaped turret of Pixie Globosa.*

· "The centre of the demilune is occupied by a company of the Tubeweaver Legion. They have built a broad, irregular pavilion above and around the surface foliage, whose margin is lashed by strong cords to grass stalks and other herbage. Near the middle is a long tubular entrance which opens out upon the top." †

---

* Appendix, Note A.       † Note B.

" Did you venture into it ? " asked the Captain.

" No ! I climbed a tall weed to reconnoitre, and from the summit noticed that Pixies, whom I had seen to pass underneath the canvas, appeared again through a round hole in the roof and thence passed down into the camp. Then I descended, cautiously made my way through the grass, and came near enough to see the opening into the tube, which is really the southern or front gate to the encampment. It is set close to the ground and is well

THE BOY'S ILLUSTRATION.
FIG. 19.—Fort Spinder as the Boy saw it.

concealed. It is guarded on each side by a sentinel. From my weed-top observatory I could see that beyond the demilune, and between it and the fort, the main camp of the Pixies is pitched. The space is well covered with tents, and everything inside seems to be settled into homelike and comfortable condition."

" Yes, yes ! " exclaimed Bruce with an impatient gesture. " The wretches evidently intend to stay—if they can. But what else did you observe ? "

"Nothing important. I thought best to return with this news, while Glideaway, who went with me on the scout, went around the demilune to observe the front of Fort Spinder. He ought to be back ere long."

True to his friend's prediction, Glideaway soon appeared, slipped quietly into the circle of officers, touched his Scotch bonnet and awaited leave to report.

"Well," said Bruce, "what have you to tell?"

"When I left Sightwell," the scout replied, "I hurried around the west side of the demilune, which bends in pretty close to the fort, and ends in a tall, silk-lined leaf-tower. This is used by sentinels as a sort of guard house, but I managed to slip by unobserved. I got into the Pixie camp and moved about unnoticed, passed along the whole front of the fort and came out on the east side. The walls of the fort are under charge of the Lineweaving Legion, who built them. They consist of single silken cables, crossed, knotted and interlaced into a mass several inches thick. The cables are interwoven with and lashed to the blades of grass and sprigs and foliage of meadow weeds, forming a strong wall."

"Could our troops break through or climb over it?"*

Glideaway shook his head doubtingly. "It would be a difficult task. Engineer Theridion directed the construction and his work is thorough. However, it might be done, and I for one am ready to try, Sir."

"And I, and I!" cried in chorus the officers and men who stood around.

"Thanks, my brave fellows," said Bruce, his eyes kindling with pride. "We shall doubtless have a chance to try your mettle before long. What are the defences of the front walls?"

---

* Appendix, Note C.

"In the centre of the wall is a gate built by Engineer Linyphia of the Lineweavers. It is a high dome hung amidst a maze of crossed lines and protected beneath by a curtain floor, which is swung from the dome. The dome is pierced for defence and observation, and a strong guard mans the curtain. The main entrance to the fort is here, and all who go in must pass underneath it, and through the guard.

"At each corner or angle of the fort is a gate like the central one, except that the dome is reversed and becomes a bowl. On the flanks or sides the fort is built and manned by Lineweavers and is precisely like the front."

"Very good," said Captain Bruce dismissing the scout. "Who will report as to the river front and interior?"

"We detailed our most skillful men for that service," Adjutant Blythe answered. "Sergeants Clearview and True have charge of the scout. It is a nice and dangerous service, and we can't expect an early return."

"Let us away, then, to put our command in the best condition possible; and when the report comes in I will summon you."

The morning had quite worn away when the news came that the scouts had returned. The officers speedily gathered at headquarters, where Sergeant True and three of his men were waiting. Where could the others be? Were they lost?

"We skirted the eastern face of the fort," began Sergeant True, "and reached Lake Katrine. Then we saw that the fort is built some distance from the water on the crown of the hill that forms the shore, which there slopes down to the lake. The defences on the water front are like those on the other side, but not so heavy. The tower at the angle is different, however. It has been built by the Wolf Legion, and Captain Arenicola is in command. It is a pentagon or five-sided turret of dry twigs, like a log chimney, and is silk-lined within.* The Pixies' skull-and-bones flag floats from the top.

"Here we held a consultation and agreed to divide our party. Sergeant Clearview with Corporal Dare and three men undertook to survey the river front. It fell to myself to explore the interior of the fort, aided by Corporal Swiftsure and two men, Lookclose and Tread-light. Having bidden good-bye to our companions, I explained to my men the delicate and dangerous work in which we were engaged. Then we divided our squad into two parties. I took Treadlight and pushed forward, having bidden Swiftsure and Lookclose to follow at a distance that would leave us just in view. In case of discovery or accident to either party, the first duty of the other was to escape and tell at headquarters the facts already learned.

"The fort is so newly built that the surface is not yet thickly covered with snares, traps and crosslines. This greatly favored us. We found the chief part of the fort to be an immense Tubeweaver's tent built by Engineer Agalena. The central tube runs downward toward the Lake, and opens out near a tower that guards the water front. The tent is built around tall weeds which stick out like the poles of a circus pavilion, and from their tips strong guy lines stretch to various points on the roof, thus bracing it up. †

"We skirted the vast edifice as far as the central front gate, just opposite to which we found another of Arenicola's turrets. From this point, sweeping around toward the Lake, and fronting the tower on the south-west angle, is erected a strong tent of the Tegenaria

---

* Appendix, Note D.    † Note E.

type. It is composed of a thick sheet like that of Agalena, but this is drawn up at the margin, making a sort of breastwork. Along the pouch-like depression within are many sentinels for whom openings are pierced in the breastwork. The system ends in a tall round tower, in which Captain Tegenaria has his observatory.*

"We wished to cross the path between the front Linyphia gate and the opposite tower, but it was so thronged by passing Pixies that we dare not venture. We therefore turned back, thinking we had discovered enough, and ought not to further risk losing what we had learned."

"A wise and patriotic decision," said Captain Bruce, "but how did you get out of the Pixie quarters?"

"It was not so easy to get out of their den as to get into it," said Sergeant True, "as is usual when dealing with Pixies. We had scarcely taken the back track when a terrible racket sounded from the tower behind us. Now we saw that a big drum hung from the top of the turret, upon which a gigantic Pixie was beating furiously. We knew that this must be Drummer Stridulans whose beating sounds the various signals of the Pixies. He was now sounding an alarm, which stirred the fort with great excitement. Sentinels sprang to their posts: warriors poured out of their quarters and

FIG. 20.—Arenicolas' Tower and Stridulans' Drum.

* Appendix, Note F.

ran to the ramparts. Soon companies were seen hurrying toward the lake front, and amid all the rush and clatter Stridulans' drum kept up its dolorous booming from the turret.

"A score of times we barely escaped detection by the Pixies who were running to and fro; and we lay in our ambush almost breathless, nearly hopeless of keeping concealed, and ready to sell our lives at the greatest cost to our foes. Then we saw an officer run up and signal the tower. The drum ceased, and squads of Pixies began to return from the lake front in a quieter mood.

"We were anxious to know the cause of the alarm, and of its conclusion too, for we feared it might concern Clearview and his party. Words dropped by passing warriors confirmed our suspicions; but of the result, whether good or ill to our companions, we could gather nothing. When the fort had settled into quiet we continued our retreat; and here we are, Sir. But, it was trying work and a close shave. We crawled through the grass like snakes the whole way, until we had gone around the outer wall and were fairly out of sight of pickets and lookouts."

Sergeant True's report caused great uneasiness in the Brownie camp as to the fate of the river scouting party. At last an unusual stir around headquarters showed that something important was afoot. An anxious crowd gathered before the tent door, peering inside, where Sergeant Clearview could be seen in the midst of a circle of officers. He looked sadly draggled and worn; his face was bruised, his clothes limp and stained, and alas, he was alone! Let us hear his story.

"When we parted from Sergeant True we slowly moved along the edge of the Lake keeping under shelter of the sloping bank, and screening ourselves behind the tall grass at the water's brink. We passed nearly one-half the lake front of the fort, which we found pro-tected in the same manner as the other sides, except that the works are not so heavy. The Pixies clearly intend the navy to defend that quarter from assault. However, no ships are anchored in the stream. Indeed we did not even meet a boat of any sort until we came to the remains of the Old Bridge that stood, as you remember, nearly opposite the centre of the fort, where

THE BOY'S ILLUSTRATION.
FIG. 21.—The Pixie Waterman's Skiff.

the water gate is placed. There we came upon a skiff moored among the rushes.

" 'Here now is our chance,' whispered Corporal Dare. 'Let us seize this boat, and we can safely pull along the whole lake front.'

" I agreed to this, as there were no Pixies in sight on shore. 'However, we must take no risks,' I said ; 'there may be a waterman hidden or asleep in the bottom of the boat. We must approach quietly, and from all points so as to cut off escape to the shore.'

5

" We crept through the reeds, and at a signal rushed together upon the skiff. Three Pixies, huge fierce fellows, sprang from the bottom of the boat and began a vigorous defence. One of our men was cut down instantly, but the rest of us clambered over the gunwale and made a hand to hand fight with our foes. The conflict was severe; we were nearly evenly divided as to numbers, although the Pixies had much the advantage as to size. However, we killed two of our enemies, but could not prevent the third from escaping. He leaped into the lake and ran fleetly over the water. We lost sight of him behind a clump of weeds, but knew that he would at once give the alarm.

" ' Come, my men, be quick!' I cried. 'Take the oars; there is only one chance for us; we must push into the stream and pull for life."

" The order was obeyed; we were soon beyond the rushes in clear water, and having pushed the boat into the current, put her bow down stream, and bent to the oars with all our might. For a few moments we thought we should pass the fort unobserved. Then we saw several Pixies running out of the gates toward the shore; others joined them; the boom of an alarm drum somewhere within the fort floated over the water, and in a brief space the shore was lined with angry troops. We could see Spite the Spy directing affairs; and soon a large boat shot out from the banks full of armed Pixies.

" ' Out to sea,' I cried, ' Out!—and pull as you never did before. Our lives depend on it.' It was vain. The boat gained rapidly upon us, and soon nearly touched our gunwale.

" ' Cease rowing, lads,' I cried. 'There's nothing left but to sell our lives as dearly as possible.' Corporal Dare seized a boat hook and plunged it into a Pixie

officer who was about to board us.    But another took
his place, and another, when he too had fallen.

"Taught caution by these losses, our assailants drew
back from us, and while Dare stood on guard, Dart and
Dodge, the two other surviving Brownies, and myself
again took the oars.    We reached the swiftest part of
the stream where the current sets in heavily toward the
shore, and I saw that we must drift in upon the beach.
This also the Pixies saw, and seemed content to keep
near us, without taking further risk.    The crowd on
shore followed along our course waiting for the final act.
We were very near, but tugged away, hoping against
hope that we might be carried past the jutting point and
escape.    Perhaps some such thought struck the Pixie
boat commander, or it may be his crew could not restrain their fury.    Several of them leaped out of the
boat and ran toward us upon the water.    Some water-
pixies joined them from the shore.    Our boat was seized.
We dropped oars, and a death struggle began.    Dart,
after a gallant fight, fell dead in the boat.    Dodge was
overpowered, captured and bound.    Corporal Dare was
at last dragged into the water by two sailors with whom
he was in a hand to hand conflict and the three sank
together.

"I was alone.    Wounded, nearly exhausted, overpowered by numbers, what could I do?    It was folly to
fight the whole Pixie force.    Plunging my sword into
the face of the boat captain, I threw myself backward
into the Lake as though wounded unto death.    Amid the
horrible clangor and applause of the Pixies' victory cry
I sank.    I struck out beneath the water, swam as far as
I could, and cautiously came up to the surface.    As
good fortune would have it, I arose almost within reach
of a floating leaf.    This I grasped, edged myself around

to the open water side, and drifted. I saw that the two boats were being pulled ashore by the excited captors, who were holding aloft on the points of their spears the body of poor Dart. There was great rejoicing, of course, and then the crowd slowly dispersed, bearing with them their prisoner, Dodge, and doubtless thinking that the rest of the Brownie party had been slain.

"Meanwhile, I drifted on, and in spite of every effort to the contrary, drew nearer the bank. The Pixie guard had now been doubled, and I feared that I had escaped death only to fall upon it in another form. The leaf lodged, and unluckily upon a bare, sandy point. There was not a blade of grass behind which to find shelter. I therefore clung to my rude raft, which swayed up and down, and turned round and round so that I had hard work to keep my hold. Still, treading water, I followed with the leaf until it reached a spot where some driftwood had lodged.

"'This is my chance!' I thought.

"I crawled up on the sand and lay down behind and beneath the flotsam. The warmth of the sun was pleasant, for I was chilled by the water, and was so exhausted that, would you believe it? I fell asleep! But my nap was a brief one. It was broken by the sound of voices, and starting up in a daze, I attracted the attention of the Pixie guard boat crew engaged in patrolling the Lake. They turned the boat to the shore, with a hurrah, and several leaped overboard and dashed toward me upon the water.

"There was nothing for it but to run, and that I did; over the level, sandy bank, on, on—toward the tall grass beyond. The boat's crew were soon on my track; the shore sentinels joined them, and away we all sped pell-mell. Affairs seemed blue enough, it is true; but I had

FIG. 22.—Sergeant Clearview Takes Refuge in Argiope's Nest.

(33)

already escaped so wonderfully that I had high hope
that I should yet reach camp and tell my story. At last
—it seemed an age!—the grass was reached. I plunged
into the thicket, but the Pixies were close at my heels,
too close to admit of escape, for they were all fresh and
I quite worn out. As I passed a tall clump of grasses,
I caught sight of a great pear shaped egg-nest of the
huge Argiope Pixie. I knew it well, for it was an
abandoned nest of the past autumn, built there during
one of the successful raids of our enemy. A happy
thought came to me. I rushed into the grasses beyond
the nest, then turned, and doubled sharply upon my
track, ran back, sprang into the clump of grass and
weeds upon which the nest hangs, and swung myself
toward it. There is an opening in the side, a sort of door
or window for the escape of the young. Into this I
dropped, and lodged safely upon the flossy paddock
inside. I had barely got in when my pursuers dashed
by at full speed into the jungle which they had seen me
enter. The whir and clatter of their rush I could hear,
as many of the crew passed just beneath me. On they
sped; the noise grew faint, fainter, and died away. Then
I knew that once more I was saved. The bed upon
which I lay was a soft one; it was made, in fact, of
purple and yellow silk; but I was not much inclined to
sleep, you may be sure. I lay close, however, until I
heard the sound of returning footsteps. Back the Pixies came in singles, pairs, triplets, squads; and by their
manner and utterance I learned their disappointment
and rage.

"At last the place was quiet, and I ventured to look
out of my little window. No enemy was in sight. I
crept forth, descended, and crawling on hands and knees,
after many adventures which I need not mention, passed

the front of the fort, entered the space beyond, and easily found our camp. This is my report, Sir. It is a sad enough one, but such are the risks of scouts; and I can truly say for my brave comrades and myself that we did all that we could." *

"No one will doubt that," said Captain Bruce. "We deeply mourn the loss of so many brave and good comrades. May their memory be green forever!" He withdrew his hat, and bowed his head. All present did the same, and stood in silence for a moment.

"We all must bear the chances of life and war," resumed the Captain, "and now let us take up the next duty. What shall be our policy? We have heard the reports of the scouts; shall we make an attack?"

The council of war thus invoked, long and earnestly considered the question. Had not their hearts and hands been burdened and stayed by Governor Wille's neglect, the Brownies would have joyfully ventured an assault even upon such a stronghold. As matters stood, however, they judged that an attempt would only lead to useless loss and further discouragement. They recommended that the siege of the fort be continued as closely as possible, and that meanwhile Captain Bruce and Lieutenant MacWhirlie make another appeal to Governor Wille. Thus the council closed.

---

* Appendix, Note G.

# CHAPTER IV.

## THE BROWNIES VISIT GOVERNOR WILLE.

All that their unaided powers could do the Brownies had now done. But the higher Decrees of Nature had linked their destiny with the will and conduct of the Household whose welfare they guarded. Mysterious relation! you exclaim. True; and the creatures of the Universe are bound to one another and to the Great Whole in relations whose mystery none has fathomed, and which perplex the wisest. So what could the Brownies do, or what could men do in like estate, but continue steadfast in watching and duty, and do their best to change the wills upon whose action turned weal or woe, success or failure?

The truth is, Governor Wille had fallen into bad ways. It was a proud day to the Brownies, and joyously had they celebrated it, when their friend had been elected Governor of the Great State of Ohio. But joy had been turned into mourning. New faces began to be seen around Hillside, and they carried little spiritual force and beauty upon them. Rude voices, coarse laughter, profane words, angry tones were no longer strange sounds in the Wille Mansion.

The lads who read this will soon be voters. Let them mark this: the man who goes into political life must take heed or he will be swept away from safe moorings by a class of so-called "party friends," who are poor companions and worse counsellors, and who elbow and crowd away the best elements of community. Now, Governor Wille did not take heed. He gave himself up to those who surrounded him for low, selfish ends, and drifted under their convoy into perilous channels. As the Governor fell off from the good old ways, the Pixies triumphed at Hillside, and the Brownies lost control. That was the state of things when these Records began. Indeed, it had well nigh come to such a pass with the Brownies that they ceased to ask : How shall we beat back the Pixies? and were beginning to wonder, How shall we escape with our lives?

There could not have been a better leader than Bruce. He was bold but prudent, having courage without rashness. He was cool, hopeful and persevering. All the fairies loved and trusted him. He had risked his life a hundred times for them and theirs. He was covered with scars. Amidst all troubles and losses he had not lost heart. But now he was cast down and doubtful.

Never did captain have a better helper than Lieutenant MacWhirlie. Active, tireless, with spirits that never drooped, and zeal that never flagged; prompt, obedient, brave and intelligent, MacWhirlie was a model officer. His one fault was that he sometimes failed in caution; careless of his own life, he was apt to risk unduly the lives of his men. But in the wild, guerilla warfare that the Brownies waged, such a fault seemed very like a virtue. Therefore the Lieutenant was loved by his troopers and honored by all. Affairs were truly serious when MacWhirlie became discouraged; and he was discouraged now, beyond a doubt.

The fact that the Pixies were fortified upon the lawn, and encamped therein, bag and baggage, was bad enough. Yet this difficulty, courage, patience and skill might overcome. But the destiny which linked their success with the behavior of Governor Wille, bore heavily upon the good Brownies since the Governor had taken to evil ways. Therefore the Captain and Lieutenant set out with heavy hearts for the Mansion. A crowd of Brownies followed a little way behind their officers. They saw them cross the Lawn, spring into the great Sugar maple tree, run along the lowest limbs and swing themselves upon the sill of the chamber window. The window was open. Governor Wille sat beside it in an easy chair, reading a newspaper, and enjoying the fresh morning air.

The Brownies saluted him. He dropped his paper and answered the greeting heartily.

"Welcome, good brothers, a thousand welcomes!" His tone grew less cheery as he spoke the last words, for his eye caught the grave bearing and sad faces of his visitors. He knew at once that they must have come on serious business. Indeed, he might have guessed that at first, for except at Christmas times, and on birthday and wedding anniversaries, the Brownies rarely entered the Mansion unless some urgent need required. They were always near at hand, the Governor well knew, and hovered about house and grounds doing kindly deeds in secret. But the family did not often hear or see them. In fact, Governor Wille had been so busy, and was away from home so often, that he had lost much of the old family interest in the gentle little people who loved and guarded him and his so tenderly. Yet, he had not wholly forgotten them. They had visited him several times of late with complaints about their own dangers, and warnings about his. He had thought lightly of the matter, and of that, indeed, he was a little ashamed. But, then, he was so busy!

He rose from his chair. "Brothers," he said, "Your sober faces bode a gloomy message. I know you are never pleased to waste words. Speak your errand freely. What troubles you?"

"Brother Wille," answered Bruce, "we bring nothing

FIG. 23.—The Pixies Spinning Gossamer over the Eyes of Governor Wille and Dido.

new. It is the old trouble about the Pixies; the same complaint and warning that we have urged upon you of late more than once. Our enemies—and well you know they are yours too!—are pressing closely upon us. They have driven us to the lawn at last, and even upon that they have built their fort and camp. A little space further and we must flee into the house. And what most troubles us is that they will follow us. Ah, brother Wille, our hearts are sad at the thought of Pixies filling your home! We have done our best and we come to you for aid. You must help us drive back these wicked spirits. That is our petition, and our request."

The two Brownies stood quietly with their bonnets or Scotch caps under their arms. Governor Wille impatiently crumpled the paper in his hand, came to the window and replied. "Tut, tut, Bruce, it certainly can't be as bad as that. You are a little blue this morning, I fear. Why, when did Brownies ever give up to Pixies? It was never heard of!"

"Softly, brother Wille," said the Captain. "That has often happened, right here at Hillside, too! And it will happen again you may depend on't, if Wille and Dido do not soon bestir themselves to help their old home fairies."

Governor Wille hesitated, ahemmed, and at last said: "I am loath to meddle in this affair, and really, I don't see that there is such pressing danger. I have little fear for my good, brave Brownie friends. But,—I shall talk to Madam Dido about it, and if she is agreed, look out for aid, and get your troopers ready for a good chase after the Pixies."

The two Brownies withdrew, leaving the house by the way they had entered. They looked sad, although they tried to hide their feelings from the friends who awaited their coming.

"What is the news?" cried the Brownies.

"Nothing as yet," answered Bruce. "But we hope for good news soon."

"What will come of all this, Captain?" asked Mac-Whirlie privately.

"Very little, I fear," was the answer. "I can't think what has come over the Governor of late. The Pixies seem to have spun their webs over his heart."

"Over his eyes rather!" said MacWhirlie, "or his hands and feet. His heart is still true to the Brownies, I am sure. But he can't or don't understand our troubles and his own perils."

"Well, well, we shall soon know." With that poor consolation they sat down on the edge of the lawn by the gravel walk and waited.

Presently Governor Wille and his wife Dido came out of the house, and walked slowly up the path. Wille was relating his interview with the Brownies.

"What do you think, wife? I fancy their stories about the Pixies are a good deal exaggerated—by fear of course I mean, for Brownies are clear truth always. Bruce said that the lawn was full of their tents and nets. Do you see them? I cannot see one, and I've been looking all along the walk." *

"I quite agree with you, my dear," said the affectionate Dido. "As for the Pixie snares, I can see no more of them than you. Perhaps we had better wait a few days before we interfere."

"A few days!" sighed Bruce, who heard all the conversation. "It will be too late by that time, I fear!"

---

* On a dewy summer morning one sees the fields and shrubbery covered with innumerable spider webs of various sorts. By midday these webs are invisible. What has become of them? In truth, the sun has simply dried the dew which clung to the delicate filaments of the webs and thus made them visible ; and from careless eyes the webs are hidden as was the case with Governor Wille. — THE EDITOR.

# CHAPTER V.

## MADAM BREEZE COMES TO THE RESCUE.

"Come!" cried the Captain at last. "Moping is no part of duty. If Governor Wille won't help us, we must seek allies in other quarters; and for the rest trust to our good swords."

He raised his bugle to his lips, and sounded a note or two, whereat his Adjutant appeared.

"Blythe," said the Captain, "order out my pony, and get ready to attend me to Hilltop. And you, Mac-Whirlie, see that every Brownie is armed and ready for work of any kind at a moment's warning. No fuss, please; keep everything quiet as possible. I don't want Spite the Spy to suspect any unusual movement. He'll give you credit for a little lack of caution when he finds you in command;" and the Captain laughed pleasantly as he said this. "But mind! it mustn't be the genuine article, now. Try for once to beat Spite at his own favorite tactics. Draw off the cavalry pickets, but see that your troopers are ready for the saddle. Look to the pioneer corps, and see that the axes are in good order. Saunter around carelessly as you like, but keep your eyes open. Come, Blythe!"

The last words were spoken to his Adjutant who already stood holding the Captain's butterfly pony Swallowtail, as well as his own. The Brownies sprang upon the creatures' backs and rode away.

MacWhirlie watched the forms of the horsemen until they were lost to view behind the gable of the house.

" Heigh-ho!" he sighed, "the time was when the journey to Hilltop was a safe and pleasant ride. But it's
a bold feat nowadays, with Pixies waiting at every
corner, and their webs flapping on every bush. But
I must e'en leave the Captain with Providence and go
about my own business."

The afternoon was well advanced when Bruce and
Blythe halted their jaded ponies under the shade of

FIG. 24.—Bruce and Blythe on Their Way to Hilltop.  Pixie Attus Tries
to Lasso Them.

a laurel bush, a little way from the Lone Aspen on
Hilltop.  "Poor fellow!" said the Captain as he stroked
Swallowtail's drooping wings.  "It was too bad to bring
you on such a service, with plenty of stouter nags in
the stable!  But we had to run the gauntlet of the
Pixies, you know, and those big fellows would never

have got through unnoticed. Think they can carry us back?" he asked anxiously.

"I doubt it, Cap'n," was the answer. "But rest and a hearty meal may bring 'em around all right."

"Very well; then do you care for them while I go to the Lone Aspen."

The Lone Aspen stood on the summit of

the hill. It was an old tree, with wide spreading branches, and great girth of trunk. The trunk was hollow, and covered with warts. One of these was quite near the roots, and was pierced in the centre with a hole which exposed the hollow within. Bruce stopped at the foot of the tree

THE BOY'S ILLUSTRATION.
FIG. 25.—Bruce Whistling for Madam Breeze.

beneath this opening, and blew a peculiar note upon a whistle which hung by a chain about his neck. There was no answer. He whistled again. Still no response. Along the rough scales and ridges of bark running up and down the trunk, a stairway had been made like the rounds of a ladder. Upon this the Captain climbed towards the opening. He stepped out upon a bulging wart and peeped within the tree. It was empty. Again he blew his whistle. The echoes rolled up and down the hollow trunk and died away far above toward the branches, where a faint streak of light shone through an opening like the one in which the Brownie stood.

"This is strange!" exclaimed the Captain. He turned, and looked up at the Sun through branches of the tree. "Surely, Madam Breeze should be at the Lone Aspen at this time of day! However, I must climb to the window and wait. He sat down on the window ledge, and as he was tired out by long journeys, hard labors and sleepless nights, in spite of himself he fell into a doze.

"Ooo—oo—oo!"

A sound like the tones of a distant bell awoke him.

"Ha, she has come!" he cried, and jumped to his feet. Madam Breeze was passing with her attendants through the door. Her voice sounded through the hollow trunk as she swept into it. In a moment the Captain felt her breath upon his cheek, and presently stood face to face with her at the window.

She kissed him heartily, brushed the hair back caressingly from his forehead, and addressed him in a sprightly, kindly way. Madam Breeze was an Elf of pleasing appearance; plump to the verge of stoutness, but singularly graceful and airy in all her movements. She was troubled with an asthma which interrupted her speech with frequent attacks of coughing and wheezing, much to her discomfort and the disturbance of her temper. She had an odd fashion of expanding and contracting in size either suddenly or gradually. This occurred oftenest during her attacks of asthma, and to those who first saw this, the sight was a startling one.

"So my brave little Captain," said the Elf, "you've been whistling for the Breeze at last, have you? Ah! I thought you would come to it some day. But you always were such an independent little body—hoogh!

6

And you have come to the little fat lady at last, hey? Well, I'm heartily glad to see you—hoogh!—and you'd have been welcome long ago—wheeze! Sit down and tell me your errand." She bustled about all the while and kept everything and everybody around her in a whirl of excitement.

"There, now, I've composed myself to listen—wheeze! But I suspect that I know without being told—hoogh! However, say on, while I sit here and rock myself." The merry lady twisted together a couple of boughs into the shape of a rude swing, and seating herself among the leaves, swayed back and forth, wheezing, coughing, oh–ing and ah–ing, while Bruce told the story of his troubles.

"And now," he concluded, "I appeal to you for help." He took the whistle from his neck and laid it in the Elf's hand. "This talisman has always opened a way for Brownies to the heart and help of you and yours."

"Tut, tut!" said Madam, throwing the chain around the Captain's neck again, "Put up your whistle—hoogh! No need to remind Madam Breeze by that of the claim of the fairies upon her and hers. And so these horrid Pixies have worried the life out of you? And you tarried all this time before coming to me?—Wheeze, wheeze! Confound this cough! And you didn't go to my gentle Lady Zephyr this time, hey? Her balmy breath wouldn't quite suit your present purpose? Ho, ho, ho! Good stout Madam Breeze for you, hey?—Hoogh! Aha, I see that Brownies, like other folk, when they get into trouble prefer the useful to the ornamental. Well, well, you're right enough."

Whereupon the jolly, kind hearted Elf swung and rolled herself about and made the leaves of the Lone Aspen fairly dance with the voice of her laughter.

FIG. 26.—Captain Bruce Appeals to Madame Breeze.

"Now to business!" Madam Breeze sobered down just one moment as she spoke. "How did you come here? On the ponies, hey? Call Blythe."

Bruce blew his bugle. Presently Blythe clambered up the ladder and saluted the Elf.

"How are the ponies, Blythe? Pretty well done out, hey? Not fit for the journey back? In a pinch are you? So I thought. Well, you Brownies do miss it sometimes, you must confess." Madam ran on asking and answering her own questions without giving Blythe a chance to speak a word. However, she seemed, through some mysterious news agency of her own, to know everything without information from the Brownies.

"Need fresh horses? Just as I supposed. Here, here —Whirlit,—wheeze,—hoogh! (Confound that cough!) Blythe, call Whirlit for me. The rascal!—he's always out of the way when I want him."

Notwithstanding the bad character given him by his mistress, Whirlit was at the window in a moment.

"There, keep still now, and listen!" Madam herself was quite as restless as the frisky Whirlit while she gave her orders, bouncing back and forth all the time among the leaves. "Still, I say! Put Swallowtail and Blythe's pony in the stable, and get out my Goldtailed matches. Order all hands to be ready to leave immediately. Quick! Off with you!"

Whirlit sprang from the window, turning a score of somersaults or more on his way to the ground. He returned presently, leading a pair of Goldtailed moths. They were beautiful insects with soft downy plumage, snowy white color, and a tuft of yellow hair at the end of the tail.

"Aren't they beauties," cried Madam, casting an admiring glance at her splendid matches. "And fast, too.

And thoroughly trained. And what's the strangest thing about them, they're not worth an old straw in the day time. They hang around on the bark here as spiritless as a toadstool. But the moment evening comes they spruce up, and hie—away! they're brisk enough then. Queer, isn't it? But I keep 'em just for night work. Now we're all ready for a bout with the Pixies. Pooh! the nasty beasts! I hate to soil my breath with them and their clammy snares. But Brownies can't be left to suffer. Ready, Captain? Yes? very well, then, mount and away!"

The afternoon was nearly gone. Below Hilltop the woods, orchard, house, lawn and garden all lay in shadow. The Goldtailed matches were in fine spirits. Their energetic mistress kept close behind them buoying them up, and urging them on, and in a short time they reached the spring at the foot of the orchard back of the mansion.

"Halt!" cried Madam Breeze. "I shall wait here in the tops of the trees, while you move forward and get your Brownies ready. Be quick, now, and when you want me, remember the whistle."

# CHAPTER VI.

### ATTACK ON THE OLD LODGE.

Bruce put spurs to Goldtail and flew across the garden followed closely by Blythe. They reached the Lawn and crossed the Brownie camp. They stopped at the Captain's headquarters under the Rose Bush. Everything was in confusion. MacWhirlie was pacing back and forth in high excitement; a group of Brownies surrounded him, talking and gesticulating violently.

"Silence!" cried MacWhirlie, stopping suddenly, facing the excited group. "I tell you that I will not stir a hand in this thing until Captain Bruce returns, or until it is settled that he will not return this night. I love Rodney as fondly as you; he is my dearest friend, the Captain's own brother, my comrade in a thousand fights and forays. But it would bring on a battle were I to consent to follow my own heart and your wishes. That would ruin us all. I cannot; dare not, will not! I must obey my orders. Silence, I say!"

Bruce leaped from Goldtail's back and walked hastily into the midst of the group. The Brownies did not notice him until he stood by MacWhirlie's side.

A clamor of surprise, satisfaction, and grief greeted him. The Lieutenant's face brightened; then clouded again, as with sympathy and pain.

"Speak, MacWhirlie," said the Captain. "What has happened? What is wrong with Rodney? Quick, and tell the worst at once."

"He is shut up by the Pixies along with his boy Johnny."

(50)

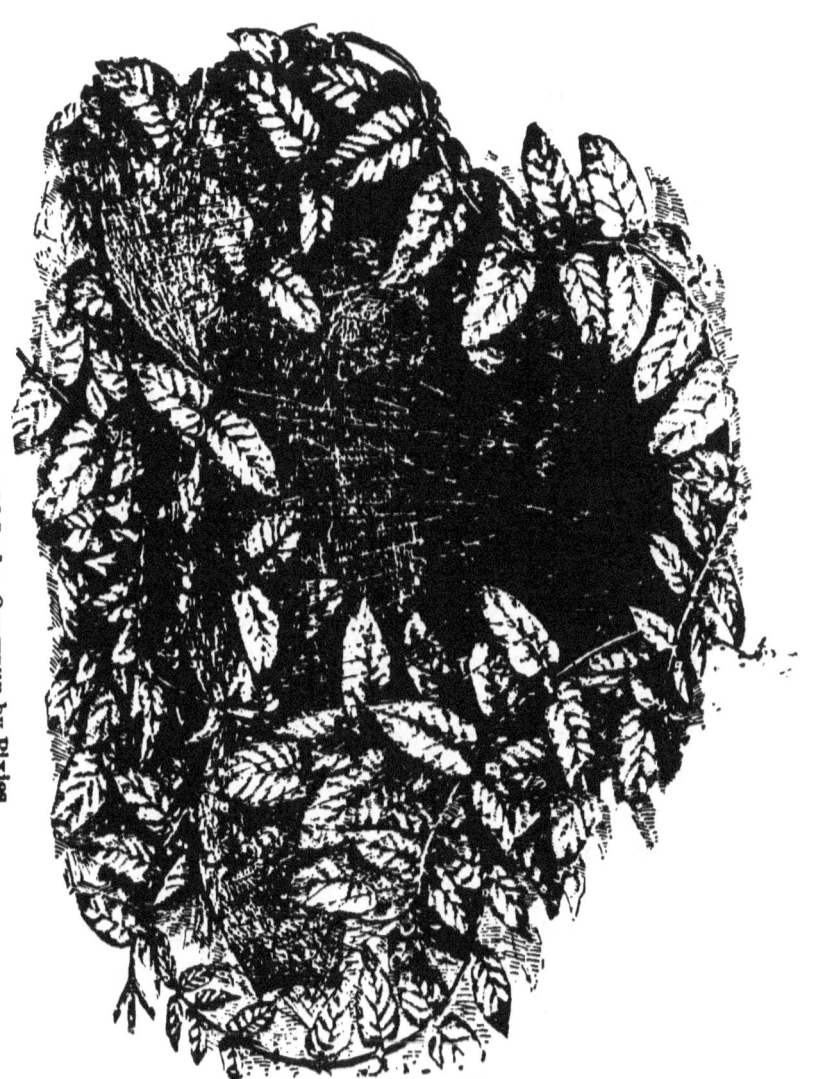

FIG. 27.—The Old Lodge Overspun by Pixies.

(51)

"What, Rodney captured! I never would have thought it. How did it come about?"

"It was not exactly his own fault, Sir. He had been busy about the boats all day—you know we were to have everything in order,—and I had asked him to look after his sailors. He took Johnny with him—not an hour ago, Sir,—to have a last look at matters. He did not want to take the little fellow, but the lad was bent on going; and besides he is a brisk young Brownie, and quite able to look after himself. Rodney was busy at the rivulet about some naval affairs and left the boy for a few moments on shore. Just then one of the butterfly ponies flew by and strolled off toward the Pixie picket line. Johnny saw its danger and ran to bring it back. He had gone but a little way when he was seized by one of the Pixie scouts, who are always hovering around now, and clapped into one of our old lodges which they have covered with spinningwork and are using as a guard house." *

"But Rodney? How came he into their hands?" the Captain cried.

"I am coming to that. The Commodore heard Johnny's cries, sprang on shore, and rushed upon the old wretch who had captured the lad, and who was spinning a rope across the door. He cut him down with one blow of his cutlass and ran into the lodge to get Johnny."

"Ha! that was well done!" exclaimed Bruce.

"Yes, Sir, but he wasn't quick enough. A squad of pickets heard the fuss, and before Rodney could repass the door they had blocked it up with their snares, double lashed and sealed it, and,—there they are!"

"How did you find out all this?"

"Why, of course, some of the sailors also heard the

* Appendix, Note A.

boy's cries and followed the Commodore; but only in
time to see how things had gone. They ran back to the
camp, and here they are, clamoring, threatening, plead-
ing to get me to order all hands to the rescue of Rodney
and his boy."

"Have you done anything?"

"I have set guards to watch the lodge and report continually how things go. For the rest I have tried to
keep the camp in perfect quiet."

"How goes it with the prisoners; are they well?"

"Yes," answered Pipe the Boatswain, "the Commodore
has his boy in the very furthest end of the lodge, and he
stays there walking back and forth before the lad, cutlass
in hand. They haven't dared to molest him yet. He
sounded his bugle once or twice, and I know he wonders
why his friends, especially his old tars, have deserted
him. It's well nigh broke our hearts, Cap'n."

"It was hard to resist the pressure, Captain," said
MacWhirlie, "and harder still to control my own heart.
But I did what I thought my duty. I stand ready to
suffer for it if I erred. And now that you are back all
I ask is to lead the rescue. I will save Rodney and his
boy, or leave my carcass with the Pixies."

"My dear fellow," said Bruce, "you did quite right.
God bless you for your love of me and mine but especially bless you for your firmness on this occasion. It
would have been a sad day for us all if the life of our
nation had been risked for the sake of one however dear
to me and to us all. Now, get ready for action! Is all
in order for the assault?"

"Everything."

"Then rally the men. We will advance with all our
force. We must first save Rodney and his boy. Then
we shall clean out the whole Pixie nest. The battle

word is 'Rescue.' Madam Breeze waits yonder in the orchard to join us."

How the order flew through the Brownie camp! Love for Rodney, and the news of the near presence of their powerful ally put hope and courage into all hearts. Every man was in his place. Even the older boys had taken arms, hoping for permission to join in the battle or at least the chase.

The Captain led his men swiftly and cautiously by a roundabout route to the site of the old lodge, which was

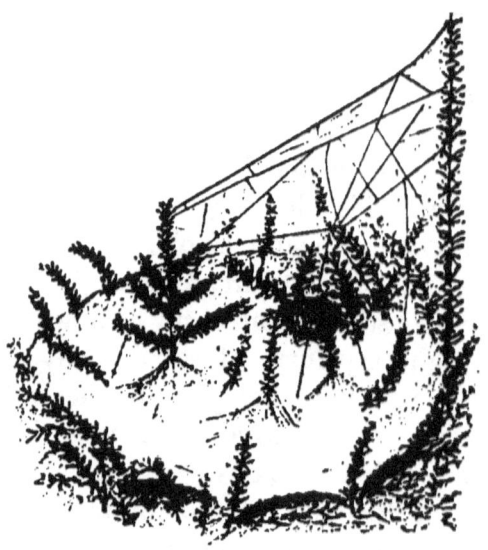

at the extreme eastern flank of the Pixie camp. He skirted the Lawn, passed the spring, and struck the bank of the rivulet at the foot of the orchard. There he waited until the full moon had risen above the hills, and slanted her rays along the river and into the bosom of little Lake Katrine.

FIG. 28. —A Tubeweaver's Den.

"Hark!" said the Captain at last.

"Hark," the word passed in a whisper along the line.

Up in the tree tops Madam Breeze and her train were waiting for the signal. Not waiting patiently, indeed, for they rocked and rolled among the round topped apple trees, and swung to and fro among the tall pears, rustling the leaves, shaking down the fruit, and whistling among the branches. But there they were, all ready, eager to rush upon their foes.

The Brownies had now reached a point well to the east of the Pixie camp and fort. Just beyond them was the lodge, now changed into a tubeweaver's den, in which the Commodore and his boy were confined. Captain Bruce halted the column and distributed the men throughout the tall grass. He formed a half circle looking toward the old lodge, the pioneers or axmen being in the centre.

"Steady, now, a moment," he exclaimed in a low tone to MacWhirlie. He fell upon hands and knees and glided through the grass. He was back in a few moments.

"It is all right. Not more than a dozen Pixies are on guard, the rest are beyond the demilune in the camp at supper, carousing, singing and making merry over Rodney's capture. Poor fellow! He is seated in the far end of the lodge holding Johnny on his lap. The boy has cried himself asleep. The Commodore has one hand on his sword and rests his face upon the other. Neither friend nor foe seems to be expecting us."

"Attention!" The order ran in low whispers around the line.

"Ready!"

"Ready." This word passed from officer to officer in the same way.

Then the Captain stepped to the head of the axmen, put his whistle to his lips and blew a long blast. The shrill notes cut through the air. Rodney heard it, lifted up his boy, leaped to his feet and cried:

"Come, Johnny, up! Wake! It is a rescue!"

The Pixie guards heard it. They grasped their weapons, and crowded together before the door of the lodge. Spite the Spy and his horde heard it as they feasted and made merry. They hastily seized their arms.

FIG. 29.—Spite and His Pixie Friends make Merry Over
Rodney's Capture.

(56)

"What's in the wind, now?" muttered Spite. "That beast of a Bruce is at the bottom of it, I warrant." But none of them seemed seriously to expect an attack. The Brownie camp had been quiet all day. Their Captain was known to be absent; their Commodore was a prisoner; there had been no sign of any unusual stir.

Up in the orchard where she swung impatiently among the tree tops, good Madam Breeze heard the same call.

"Ah! there it goes at last. Thank our star for that. What! Whirlit, Whisk, Keener and all the rest of you, do you hear? Up and away—away! Oo—oo—Ooh!"

The Brownies were crouched in the grass, every nerve strained to the utmost, every eye fixed eagerly upon their leader, awaiting the word of command. It came at last. Bruce dropped his whistle, drew his broadsword, and shouted the welcome word, "Charge!"

With a wild hurrah the column closed in upon the lodge, MacWhirlie leading one wing, Pipe the other, and Bruce at the head of the axmen leading the centre.

It was a complete surprise. The guard of Pixies broke, parting to right and left. One squad fell into the hands of the sailors and were all slain. The others fared little better with MacWhirlie and his troopers. The door gave way before the strokes that the Captain and his pioneers rained upon it, and Rodney with his boy in his arms sprang out. Three times three hearty cheers rang in the evening air as the brave hearted sailor came forth a free man.

"Brother Rodney," said Captain Bruce, "there is not even time for greeting. Send your boy to the rear. Take command of your men. We are to charge the whole Pixie camp and fort. Madam Breeze is behind us. You know the rest. Forward!"

# CHAPTER VII.

## HOW THE FORT WAS SAVED.

By this time the Pixies in the main camp had recovered from their surprise. The Brownies' battle-cry
"Rescue" showed plainly the object of the assault. The
Pixies were used to war's alarms; and, as for their
leader, Spite, lack of promptness and skill was not
among his faults. Therefore Rodney had scarcely been
set free ere Spite had his followers in line. However,
he did not expect an attack upon himself, for he fancied
that the Brownies had been too much cowed lately to
venture upon the offensive. He thought they would be
satisfied with rescuing Rodney, and would then retreat,
and that he determined to prevent.

"Come, my lads," he shouted, "we must not let these
creatures escape us this time. Teach them what it is to
break into a Pixie camp. Fall on them! Give no
quarter; spare no one, let your battle-cry be 'Death!'"
He ran to the front as he spoke, shaking in one hand a
poisoned dart and holding in the other his war club.

The Pixies followed keenly enough, shouting their
terrible watchword. But their confidence was dashed as
they saw the Brownies, so far from retreating, actually
forming their line of battle in front of the demilune.
The Pixies paused at this sight. Even Spite hesitated
a moment. In that moment a shower of arrows rained
upon them from the Brownie bows. Then with a ringing cheer the brave fairies charged. The two columns
closed. Above the clash of weapons and clamor of
battle were heard ever and anon the voices of the Pixies

(58)

FIG. 30.—Elf Whirlet Comes to the Rescue of Captain Bruce.—(Illustration by Dan. C. Beard.)

(59)

sounding the war cry "Death," and the cheery tenor of the Brownies answering with the sweet word "Rescue."

The leaders of the two parties were in the thickest of the fight. Spite was well seconded by his two lieutenants, Heady and Hide, and the rank and file of the Pixies behaved valiantly. The Brownies had gained much by their first onset upon the picket line and outposts, but, on the other hand were far the weaker party. It were hard to say which army might have won the fight had they been left to themselves; but this was not to be. Madam Breeze swept down upon the struggling lines. For a moment she hovered over the battle confused and angry at the prospect.

"Why, what can I do?" she cried. "Here, Whirlit, Keener, Bluster—you rogues, stop I say! Don't you see?—hoogh! You can do nothing against the Pixies without injuring the Brownies. They're so mixed together that I can scarce tell one from the other."

Whirlit had already thrown himself into the midst of the fight. He espied Captain Bruce and bounded to his side. Two great Pixies were rushing upon the Captain with uplifted spears, and wide open mouths from which terrible fangs were thrust. With one puff of his keen breath Whirlit sent both these warriors spinning and tumbling in the dust.

"Thanks!" cried the Captain, "That was a kindly service right bravely done." Whirlit threw himself over and over again as a token of his satisfaction, and then said:

· "Madam awaits your orders. She fears to mix in the fight lest she may do more harm than good. What shall we do? Make haste, please, the old lady is very much excited and won't wait long. She'll be in mischief if—"

" Silence, Sir ! " said the Captain sternly. " Don't
speak in such terms of your mistress. Tell Madam
Breeze with my compliments, to knock over the Pixie
camp, houses and fort, and leave the enemy themselves
to us."

" Whew ! " whistled Whirlit as he leaped into the
air. " A peppery Brownie, that ! Served me right, however."

He found Madam Breeze almost bursting with anger,
confusion, anxiety, excitement and the exertion of self-
restraint.

" You imp of ingratitude ! " she began, " how could
you dare—"

" Madam," cried Whirlit, interrupting her, " the Captain says, with his compliments, you will please knock
over the Pixie camp, tents, houses, fort and all ! "

Madam's brow cleared in a moment. " That I will,"
she answered in her usual jovial tones. " Hie—away, my
hearties ! come, come now ! ' Blow, ye winds, and
crack your cheeks ! ' "

Thereupon Madam Breeze and her company fell upon
the Pixie camp. The breastwork or demilune that had
been woven around the outer bounds was leveled in an
instant. Then the clamorous crew fell upon the circle
of huts and tents that stood next within. It was not so
easy work here.

" Whoop ! " shouted Whirlit, as he threw himself,
with full force, back foremost, against one of the broad
canvas sides. " Ugh ! " was the next exclamation heard
from him as he bounded back like an india-rubber ball
and fell sprawling among tent pins and ropes.

" Ho, ho, ho ! " The merry laugh of Madam Breeze
rolled out through the hurly-burly at this discomfiture
of her page. " Try it again, Whirlie, it's easily done,

7

you know! You'd make a fine base ball, now, wouldn't you? Ha, ha!"

Whirlit did try again; then Whisk and Bluster and Keener; and last of all Madam Breeze threw her round body against the tent. The ropes snapped, the walls tumbled together, and in a trice the noisy Breezes had sent ropes, canvas, and poles streaming away into the air, broken into a hundred pieces.*

One after another the Pixies' dens, nests, tents, huts, barns and storehouses shared the same fate at the hands of the busy wreckers. In a few moments the ruins of the camp were scattered in confused heaps upon the earth, or were floating off upon the wings of the storm. The females, or Pixinees, who with their broods of young had been left in possession of the camp, at first showed fight. But they soon saw that resistance was vain, and fled into the fort, where they hid themselves in the sheltered corners and angles, or cowered against the lee side of pebbles, leaves, clumps of grass, and the various rubbish that littered the ground.†

All this time, the conflict was raging between the Brownies and Pixies outside the barricade. Great as was the clamor raised at the overthrow of the camp, the noise of battle was so loud and the feelings of the combatants so intense, that none knew what havoc Madam Breeze was making. A lad ran into the rear line of the Pixie troops calling for the chief.

"Back to your mother, boy," was the gruff response, "and leave the battle to warriors."

"But mother has fled into the fort. The house is broken down. The camp is attacked. The barricades are leveled. Everything is ruined. I must see the Captain."

---

* Appendix Note A.     † Note B.

The evil tidings rapidly spread, and even before it reached the chief the line began to waver, and fall back toward the camp. Spite fell into a towering rage when the message was brought to him. He cursed Madam Breeze. He cursed the Pixie who stopped the messenger, and thus caused the bad news to spread. He cursed Bruce and the Brownies. He cursed his own eyes, also, although he might have saved himself that trouble, for they had never been a blessing to anybody.

"But cursing won't mend matters, Chief," said Lieutenant Hide. "The fort still stands; we can fall back to that, and save what we may."

"Drummer, sound the retreat," cried Spite; "and Hide, do you fall back with the right wing to the fort. Orderly, bid Lieutenant Heady take command and cover the retreat. Tell him to fight every inch of ground."

Then Spite turned upon his heels and hurried to the rear. In truth, he was not sorry for an excuse to withdraw from the fight. He stumbled over the ruins of the camp at every step. It was a complete wreck. Not a tent, not a building of any kind remained, except the fort, to which he bent his course. It was a huge structure, as we have seen, braced and strengthened by every art and effort at the Pixies' command. But Spite's heart failed him as he looked around, and saw how everything else in camp had vanished away before the mighty breath of his adversaries.

"See!" he exclaimed, "Madam Breeze and her train have just attacked the fort. Will it hold out, I wonder?" With this thought in mind he hurried forward.

Keener saw him coming, and recognized him at once. "There comes Spite the Spy!" he shouted. "At him, boys! let us toss him in one of his own sticky blankets!"

"Aye, aye," answered Whisk, "suppose we fling him over the horns of the moon, and let him—"

"Let him stick there," cried Whirlit, finishing the sentence. Whereat the trio pounced pell-mell upon the Pixie chief.

"Very well, my lads," exclaimed Madam Breeze, "you're quite welcome to a monoply of the old beast. Phooh! How he smells of poison! He well nigh takes my breath. Fort smashing suits me better." With these words she threw herself against the Agalena wing of Fort Spinder. Every cord and canvas in it shook with the violence of the onset. But it was unbroken. Again and again the stout Elf cast herself against the walls; the cords creaked and seemed about to part, but so elastic were they that they swayed inward with a heavy surge and then back again. The weeds, blades of grass and twigs to which the ropes and beams were fastened bent under the weight of the blast, but were unbroken.

All this time Spite was struggling with the three Elves. They pinched his skin, they plucked at his cheek, mouth and nostrils. They almost blinded him with blasts which they cast full into his eyes. They pulled his clothes, and held him by the limbs. But he kept on his path. Stoutly, stubbornly he fought his way step by step until he stood at last before the gate of the fort. He was seen at once, and a dozen of the inmates ran forward to admit him.

"Not for your lives!" he shouted. "Don't leave a crack open, if you can help it, for these blusterers to enter. It would be ruin to open the gate."

He looked around him. Hide and his party were still a goodly distance away. He could hear above the voices of the storm the rousing cheers of the Brownies as they pressed more and more closely upon Heady, who was doggedly giving way, disputing every inch of ground. Whirlit, Whisk and Keener had left him, at the beck of Madam Breeze, and now joined that lusty Elf in their assaults upon Fort Spinder.

"What is done, must be done quickly," thought Spite. "May all the furies seize the old monster! She has broken a breach in the roof. See! the garrison, aided by the women and children, are doing bravely. There; that villain Keener has cut his way to the inside of Fort Agalena. And there go Whisk and Whirlit after him. How the walls sway back and forth! The roof bulges upward. The reprobates! They are trying to break through the roof. If they do that and Madam Breeze gets in, all is lost; away will go the whole building with a crash. What shall I do? If we could only anchor the roof! But there's no ballast about. Hide and his men are far away yet. Confusion seize them! Why aren't they here now?"

It was a trying moment for the interests of the Pixies. All seemed to turn upon the fate of the fort; and that to depend upon one person. But that person was Spite the Spy, and he had never yet been wholly without resources. Hopeless as the case appeared, he was equal to the emergency. He would save the fort if it could be saved! He jumped from the weed-top which he had mounted for better observation, and plunged into the midst of the ruins of the camp. He stopped before a pebble almost the size of his own body.

"That will do, I think," he muttered. He seized the stone, twisted a cable around it, and dragged it away toward the fort. It was but a moment's work to climb upon an overhanging weed, fasten the cable to a branch and swing the stone over upon the roof. The canvas sheet sank downward under the pebble's weight. Spite watched it with keen interest. The elastic stuff swayed upward and downward several times, and seemed about to settle firmly, when Whirlit leaped upward against it with his strong shoulders. The pebble flew off the roof, spinning through the air close to the head of the Pixie chief, who looked on from his perch among the leaves.

" Failure ! " muttered Spite.

" Try again, old fellow ! " shouted Whirlit from the inside, where he was capering in high good humor above the heads of the enraged inmates.

FIG. 31.—" He Jumped from the Weed Top."

" Good advice," Spite responded with feigned cheerfulness ; " I will try again. And succeed next time, too ! "

A mocking laugh followed him as he swung himself down the weed by his rope ladder, and hurried off again into the ruined camp. On— on—on ! He stopped at last.

" This is it—the very thing. But, can I manage it ? " He stood before a broken twig as thick as his own body and five or six times as long as himself. Think of a man carrying a log as thick as himself and twenty-five or thirty feet long ! That was something like the feat that Spite undertook.

" But I can do it," he said ; " I *must* do it ! " The

energy and strength of despair were upon him. He seized the beam with his long arms, bowed himself to the burden and lifted it. Tottering with the weight, and stumbling over the debris of the desolate village, he laid down the beam at last at the foot of the tall weed.

The task was not ended. He twisted a cable around the log and mounted into the foliage. He stood a hundred times his own height above the weight he wished to lift. Would he ever get it up? We shall see! He hauled upon his rope until it was stretched to its utmost. Then one end of the stick slowly rose above the earth; up—up —until the other end was in the air. See! it swings quite free. It is rising

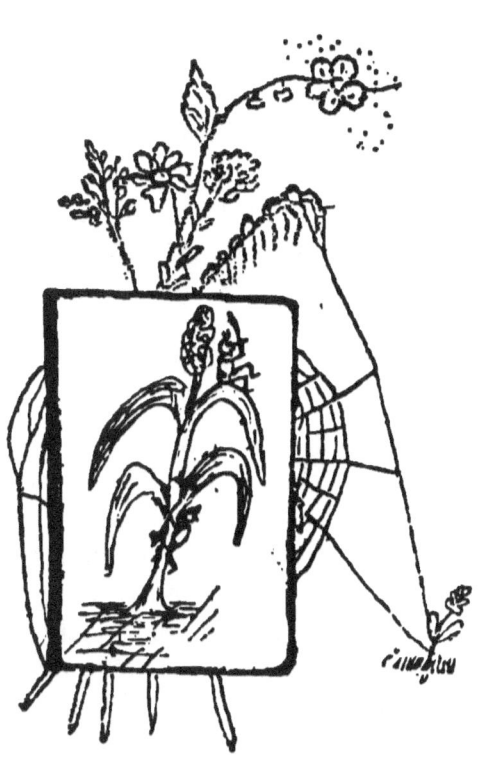

THE BOY'S ILLUSTRATION.

FIG. 32.—Spite the Spy Climbs a Weed to Reconnoitre.

higher and higher. Hand over hand, the strong and patient workman is drawing the beam slowly and surely toward the top of the plant.*

Madam Breeze began to be concerned about this new effort of Spite's. A few more stout assaults and the roof must give way dragging with it walls and all.

* Appendix, Note C.

But what if Spite should manage to get his great log anchor on it? It would hold the roof so steady that no power at her command could move it. Moreover, it would bear the roof down toward the ground, and so prevent Whirlit, Keener, and Whisk from breaking through by stretching the elastic cords upward until they snapped. They could make no headway by pressing downward since the earth stayed the cords in that direction. And how could they heave the roof upward with a great log lying on it?

"I don't want to begin this affair all over again," quoth Madam Breeze, "for in sooth, I'm pretty well out of breath now—wheeze! A few more turns will use me up. Therefore, my good Mr. Spite, I fear that I must interfere with this logging business of yours."

So saying, she flung herself upon the beam, as it hung far up in the air, slowly mounting to its place. It swayed up and down a moment, as an object fastened to an elastic thread will do, and then—crash! the rope snapped, and the log fell to the ground.

Not a whit discouraged by this disaster, Spite looped the end of the cable over the weed, and before Madam had fairly got her breath again, he had made fast the log, reascended the bush, and was pulling might and main upon the rope.

He had his reward. There was no second breaking of the cable, although Madam Breeze threw her weight upon the log. It reached its position. It hung nearly over the roof. Spite tied the rope, crept out upon the branch, reached down to the log, and with one push of his long arm swung it inward and over the roof. At the same time he cut the cable. The log dropped to its place. The roof that had been bulging out, just ready to burst, sank into its true position. The walls were anchored now. The fort was saved !*

Madam Breeze gathered all her strength for a last onset. Whirlit, Whisk, and Keener on the inside vigorously seconded her attempt. But it failed.

" Well, well," said Madam, " I give it up! I'm out of breath—clear blowed—hoogh! I've scarce wind enough to get home with—wheeze ! Come out of that, lads. Our work is done for to-day."

The three Elves crept, rather crestfallen, out of the opening in the roof made by the pebble, and the whole party without more ado, or another word, puffed back to Lone Aspen. Spite sat upon the branch and watched their departure. He rubbed his hands, and said, "Aha!" He knew that he had

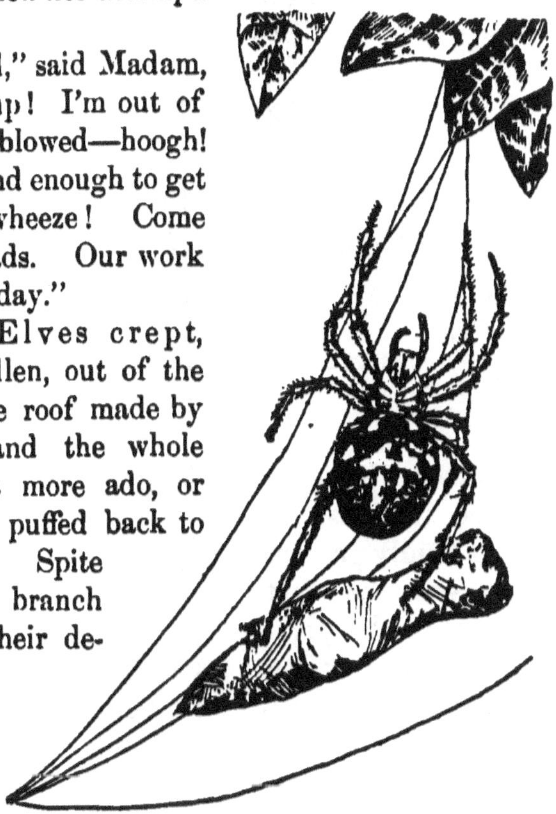

FIG. 33.—A Spider Drawing up a Swathed Grasshopper to its Leafy Den, " Hand Over Hand."

done a deed that would gain him glory among the Pixies. That was pleasant; but after all, that which pleased him best was the thought that he had saved a Pixie fort from which to plot and war against the good Brownies.

---

* Appendix, Note D.

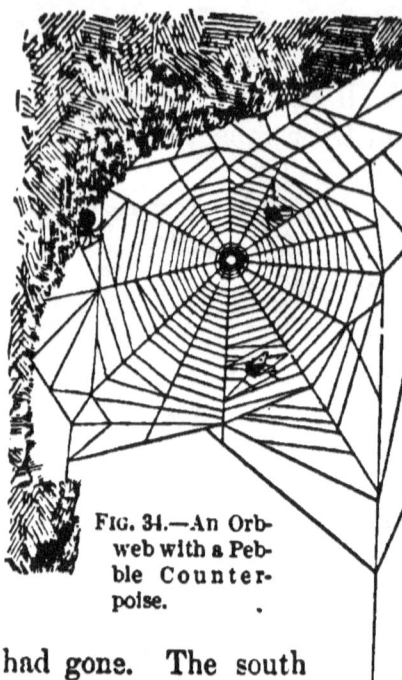

FIG. 34.—An Orb-web with a Pebble Counterpoise.

Yes, my dears, one may be clever, wise and accomplished, but very, very bad withal. As poet Burns truly sang:

"The heart aye's the part aye
That maks us right or wrang."

Hide and his company of Pixies came up to the fort soon after Madam Breeze and her retainers gate was thrown open, out and mingled with their the deed by which Spite The hero of all this praise resting, surveying the He had need of his wisest torious Brownies were outer line of the demi-Heady and his division

had gone. The south and the inmates ran friends, loudly praising had saved the fort. sat quietly on his perch field, and thinking. thoughts; for the vic-already beyond the lune, steadily driving before them.

Spite dropped to the still swung upon the fort," he said to the homes are gone, and place for you now. the soldiers, "we must and keep it. The sun

ground by the cable that bush. "Go back into the fugitives. "Your own that will be the safest As for us," addressing make a last stand here is nearly down. If we

can hold the position for a little longer, night will bring
relief, and give time for some plan that shall change the
fortune of battle. Advance!"

The line moved forward to support Heady. The site
of the fort was well chosen for defence. It stood upon
a swelling height of the lake shore, with a space of
smooth grass in front. On this little plain, a short distance beyond the height, at Spite's command the Pixies
began putting up a breastwork. They wrought rapidly,
weaving together grass blades, leaves
and twigs, and spinning between them
ropes and webs. Spite, himself, with
a few of the ablest warriors went to
assist Heady in holding back the
Brownies. The plan succeeded; by
the time the fighting force was ready
to fall back, the workers
had thrown up a rampart
behind which the entire
army retreated in good order. A series of skirmishes
began along the line of
breastworks, but the even-

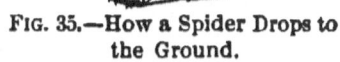

FIG. 35.—How a Spider Drops to
the Ground.

ing shadows soon fell and separated the combatants.

The Brownies were in fine spirits. They were confident of complete victory on the morrow. A line of
cavalry pickets, under Lieutenant MacWhirlie, was
posted throughout the plain, which skirted nearly three-
fourths of the knoll on which the fort stood. These
pickets were ordered to keep moving the whole night,
thus keeping strict guard upon the Pixies at the points
whence they were most likely to make a sally or seek to
escape. Sentinels were also placed on the lake side or
rear of the fort. In that quarter the bank sloped toward

FIG. 36.—"Weaving Together Grass, Leaves and Twigs."

the lake, and was dotted with bushes that straggled singly and in clumps to the water's edge. Soon the camp fires and lanterns of the Brownie army were glimmering along the outer border of the plain and through the copse by the lake side. They looked like fire-flies dancing among the boughs, and indeed they were encaged fire-flies, or bits of fox-fire from decayed stumps. As the whole country was now open to Captain Bruce, he had no trouble in securing supplies for his troops, so that the Brownies went to the night's rest or duty with refreshed bodies as well as hopeful spirits.

Matters were not so pleasant with the Pixies. The provisions laid up within Fort Spinder were not abundant, and Spite had to order all to be put upon short rations. Moreover, their hunting ground was quite limited, of course, and the game on which they were used to prey had been frightened off by the late commotions. However, the lights from the watch fires of their enemies drew some unwary and over curious night wanderers within the confines of the fort, and the hungry Pixies were able to catch a few of them. As for Spite, their chief, he was silent and moody. After mounting the guards, and giving necessary orders, he threw himself upon the ground, wrapped his blanket around him and began to think. We shall learn the fruits of his plotting, by and by.*

---

* Appendix, Note E.

# CHAPTER VIII.

## THE SANITARY CORPS.

In the centre of the Brownie camp were three large
tents, the officers' headquarters, the hospital tent, and the
marquée of the Sanitary Corps. These were wrought
out of large leaves, deftly stretched upon frames, with
edges overlapping like a tiled roof, and anchored to the
ground by small pebbles, heaps of sand, and by tent
pins of thorns or splinters.

The Headquarters' tent was occupied by the chief
officers, Bruce, Rodney, MacWhirlie and Pipe. The

Fig. 37.—The Hospital Tent and Marquée of the Sanitary Corps.

Hospital tent was devoted to the sick and wounded.
But one would not easily imagine who were the occupants of the Sanitary tent; we shall therefore lift the
door of the marquée, and peep within.

It is a snug place. In the centre, well up toward the
roof, a large fox-fire lantern hangs from the ridge pole

which sheds a soft light throughout the interior. A
strong odor of herbs and ointments fills the place, the
reason for which soon appears. Four wee Brownie
women are busy with retorts, jars, boxes, lint, bandages,
and various other articles of the healing art.

The oldest of the party, judged by our human standard, has reached that uncertain boundary of womanhood
which divides maiden from matron. One might venture
to call her an "old maid" Brownie, and perhaps she
would not deny it, for that is a class—God bless them!
—whom the Brownies dearly love. But no one could
aver that the fairy woman had suffered loss of charms
by advance in life. One glance into her face shows how
pure, gentle and good must be the disposition that has
wrought the tracery of such sweet expression around
her features. Her name is Agatha; she is the only
child of Captain Bruce, and one does not wonder,
having once seen her, that even the Brownies call her
Agatha the Good. She is spreading upon tiny bandages
out of a tiny jar some kind of ointment, the recipe for
which you may be sure is in none of our dispensaries,
but which the Brownies call Lily Balm.

The young Brownie who attends her, not as handmaid
but companion, is called Grace. Her face is such a
goodly one, her manners are so gentle, easy and winning,
her every movement so graceful, delicate and yet so full
of life, that we shall not be surprised to hear you say:
"Surely, she must be the Fairy Queen herself!"

At the other end of the tent, kneeling over a brazier
filled with coals, is the third member of the Sanitary
Corps. She holds above the coals a retort, in which she
is distilling Lily Balm. Her back is toward us and her
face is hidden. There! you have caught a glimpse of it
as she turned her head to speak to her companion. The

cheeks are flushed, the eyes are bright with the glow of
the coals, there is an earnest, pitiful look in their deep
blue that speaks of thought intent upon present duty.
But there is also a strange light therein, a light as from
some far away world, that throws an air of mystery
around this person and bids your thoughts pause rever-
ently as they run on in judgment concerning her.　This

FIG. 38.—A Peep Inside the Sanitary Tent.　Faith Distilling Lily-Balm.

is Faith, the daughter of Rodney the Commodore.　She
is young as the Brownies count years, and was born "at
sea," that is, upon the Lake Katrine of Brownieland,
through which flows the Rivulet at the foot of the
Orchard.

At Faith's side is her companion and friend, Sophia, the daughter of Pipe, the Boatswain. There is a mixture of boldness and shyness in her manner that strikes one at once. Her movements have the snap and positiveness of a practical woman. Her eyes sparkle with intelligence; there is in them a keen, questioning look which tells that she loves not only to know, but to know the reason why. If she were not a Brownie you would probably say she was a pushing sort of person; that you scarcely could decide whether she was more curious or sincere, more dreamy or practical, more skeptical or credulous. But that she is beautiful you would not hesitate to say. She is busy among the herbs, sorting them, making ready material for Faith's retort.

Now that you have seen this Sanitary Corps, and learned their names, you may drop the door of the tent and we shall go on with the story.

"Come, Grace, we have done quite enough for the present," said Agatha. "Bring the bandages and let us go to the Hospital. Have you lint and balm in your satchel? Very well. That is all we need now. Faith, hadn't you better leave off distilling, and help us for a while with the dressing?"

"Yes; if you wish it," answered Faith, "and we can stop now as well as not."

The pots and herbs were set aside, and Faith and Sophia followed Agatha and Grace through the rear door of the marquée. They crossed into the Hospital under a covered way that united the two tents. The Hospital was a spacious tent, or rather several large tents or marquées, joined in one. Along each side on the rude cots hastily made from dried grass and leaves, lay a number of wounded Brownies. The sufferers turned their eyes upon the Nurses as they entered, and

8

at once their faces lit up with pleasure. Agatha and her friends went from couch to couch carrying the blessings of their healing art. Some of the men had hurts that had not yet been dressed. These were first carefully washed. The lint, which the Nurses carried in their satchels, was laid upon the wound to absorb the poison, and the balm applied.

A Pixie uses his fangs, when fighting at close quarters, with terrible effect. His mouth is a tremendous piece of machinery. The jaws are each armed with a sharp,

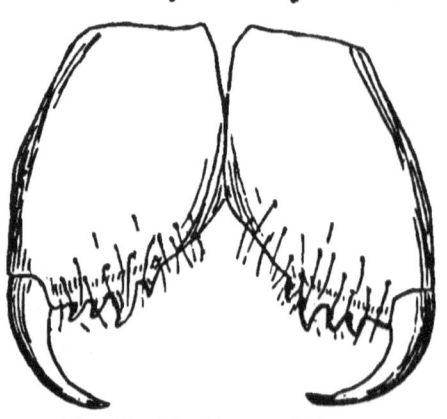

FIG. 39.—The Jaws and Fangs.

movable fang, pierced near its end. When the Pixie bites, a poisonous fluid flows through this hole into the wound.* In battle with Brownies the Pixies try to come to close quarters. Being much larger and more powerful, they seize them in their hairy arms, strike their fangs into them, and spring back quickly out of reach of the Brownie's sharp sword or axe. All this is done so rapidly, that often ere the victim has time to strike a blow he has been wounded and cast down, and his assailant is out of reach. The poison leaves a painful wound in the Brownie's flesh, frequently disabling, but never killing him unless the heart be reached. Indeed, no Brownie ever perished by any form of violence except drowning, suffocation or a heart stroke.

For the hurt made by Pixie fangs the Lily Balm made by the Sanitary Corps is a sure remedy. If

* Appendix, Note A.

applied at once upon soft lint, which absorbs the poison, the relief is immediate. But in any case it will ease the pain, and in the end cure the wound.

The uses of this balm, and all the services which the sick require, were well known by Agatha and her aids. They always followed the army; no risk or toil was shunned by them upon their noble mission. They were the wards of the nation, and the favorites of the army. Moreover, for why should we keep it a secret? every one of them was dearly beloved by a worthy youth, who had the joy of being loved in return.

The four Nurses made the round of the Hospital, visited every couch, and applied or ordered needed remedies. At the end of the tent was a group of Brownies, with wounds which required treatment, but were not serious enough to hinder from duty. Their hurts were quickly cared for, and one after another the party dropped out until only one was left. He was a tall, shapely youth, who stood within the shadow of the gangway with his face muffled in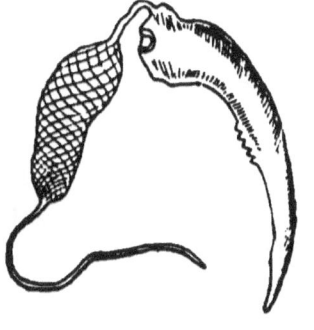

FIG. 40.—The Poison Bag and Fang.

a cloak. As the last of the group was dismissed from the Nurses' hands he stepped forward into the light, dropped his cloak, saluted the Nurses, and advancing to Sophia's side held out toward her his left arm. The sleeve had been ripped up, and a blood-stained bandage surrounded the forearm. Sophia's cheeks grew pale, and she uttered a low cry of alarm.

"Why, Sophie," exclaimed the youth, "what has possessed you? One would think you had never seen blood before. Come, my good lass, it is only a scratch, and a few drops of your Lily Balm will make it all right."

Sophia now found voice. "What a fright you gave me! Are you sure that you are not badly hurt, True? Quick! let me undo the bandage." The blood came back to her cheeks which now were hot and flushed. Her fingers trembled as she clipped the bandages with

Fig. 41.—Sophia Dressing Sergeant True's Wounded Arm.

the scissors that hung at her belt, bathed the wound, and tenderly laid on lint and balm. Sophia was one of the best and most impartial of nurses; but it must be confessed that her fingers passed more gently over that swollen arm; that her eyes had a more pitiful look upon that hurt; that she lingered longer about the details of bathing, anointing and bandaging that wound than she had done in any other case. Do you blame her?

And Sergeant True was a model patient. Indeed he seemed quite to enjoy his wound, or at least the treatment of it. Agatha, after a few kind inquiries, had busied herself in giving instructions to the ward nurses and watchers. Faith and Grace had withdrawn to their own tent.

"I am glad you came to me, True," said Sophia as the last stitch was taken in the bands, and the sleeve was being gently fastened to its place.

"Didn't I wait, just to make sure of that?" answered the Sergeant. "Why, it is almost worth while to get a scratch like this for the pleasure of having you doctor it with those canny fingers of yours. Many thanks!"

"But I don't care to practice my art on you, remember! Good bye!"

The words were spoken in the gangway as the handsome Sergeant passed out, and—though it is by no means certain,—something very like the sound of a kiss followed close upon them.

"Good bye!"

Ah, how many times the words are uttered on the border of shadows that shall pall loving hearts. It is well that good-byes can be said in happy ignorance of the morrow.

# CHAPTER IX.

The four Brownie maidens were once more together in their own quarters. There was little said for a long time. The meeting between Sophia and her lover had awakened tender and anxious thoughts in the hearts of all. Agatha was following in imagination the agile form of Lieutenant MacWhirlie, as he went the grand rounds of his pickets. The thoughts of Faith were with Adjutant Blythe who, somewhere in camp or field, served at the Captain's side, his faithful squire and counsellor. Grace's musings were of the gallant and stalwart Ensign of the Corps, Sergeant Lawe.

It would be too much to say that the Nurses had no anxiety about the safety of their lovers. But then, they had been bred in the midst of war's alarms. They knew that their fathers, kindred, and friends were brave, experienced, skillful, and devoted to one another. They had learned to regard war risks as matters of ordinary life and business, and were rarely troubled about them. There was special reason why they should be even more light hearted than usual that night. Yet, so strangely run the currents of one's thoughts, that these maidens were all sad.

There was some reason, indeed, why Agatha and Faith should feel thus, for the old saying fell true in their case about the course of true love not running smooth. Captain Bruce refused consent to the marriage of Agatha and MacWhirlie. The two had waited long, patiently, devotedly ; yes, and hopefully, although

(82)

they had often known that "hope deferred" which "maketh the heart sick." Every one thought the Captain's conduct strange. But he never gave any reason, except that Agatha was too grave, and MacWhirlie too gay for a well balanced marriage. As obedience to parents is one of the unchanging laws of Brownieland, no one could oppose.

Now, it so happened that Commodore Rodney had taken up a like notion concerning his daughter and Adjutant Blythe. "Blythe is too jovial, and Faith is too serious," said the Commodore. "They could never sail smoothly in the same ship on a whole life's course." An odd feature of this trouble was that each of the fathers pooh-hooed the objection of the other, and each uncle was highly pleased with his niece's choice! The best of Brownies, like other people, have their whimsies. Grace and Sophia had no such sorrows to vex them, and were looking forward to their wedding on the next Thanksgiving Day.

Enough for the present of these disappointments and hopes. The night watch in the Hospital has just been changed, as have also the outer sentinels. Blythe, for it is he who attends to this latter duty, has sounded a soft note on the whistle that hangs against the rear door of the Sanitary Tent. It is the signal that the Nurses are wanted in the Hospital. Night duty is divided between them, two of them always watching in the Hospital, while the others sleep in the marquée. Agatha and Grace have the first watch to-night, and pass into the Hospital. But Faith knows whose lips had sounded the call, and comes in to exchange a few words with her lover.

"Good-bye!"

Why should she, too, have come back with a tear upon her cheek?

The light is turned down low in the fox-fire lantern.
The yellow hospital flag flaps lazily against the staff.
The full moon hangs over Hillside.  The tramp, tramp
of the sentinel grows dim and clear by turns as he
recedes from or nears the door.  The noises of the camp
have died away and silence reigns at last over plain, fort
and field.  Both Brownies and Pixies are weary with
the day's battling and sleep well.  Faith and Sophia,
too, after a long talk about their trials and their loves,
their hopes, fears and joys, have fallen asleep in each
other's arms.

The stars that mark the midnight hour are fast has-
tening into the zenith.  The sentinels walk their beats
with weary pace.  The relief guards will soon be on the
rounds.  Faith and Sophia stir in their sleep uneasily
as though dimly conscious that the whistle will soon call
them to duty.  There is a soft touch, as the touch of an
angel's finger, upon their cheeks.  It seems to rest upon
their eyes, their lips.  It is pressed against their nostrils.
It stays their breathing.  They turn restlessly on their
couch.  They toss their arms, but the soft touch is on
them, too.  Cannot they awake?

Yes, their eyes are open now.  Is it a dream?  Is it the
vision of a nightmare?  Two forms, the terrible forms
of their foes, the Pixies, are bending over them, wrap-
ping them around in the silken folds of their snares!

Alas! it is no dream.  The most dreaded of all their
enemies, Spite the Spy, chief of the Pixies, and Hide
the son of Shame, are crouching at their bedside.  The
maidens start from their pillows, but fall back again
hopeless.  They are bound hand and foot as with grave-
clothes.  They are wrapped in a winding sheet of gossamer; enshrouded alive.*

---

* Appendix, Note A.

Spite reckoned truly that the next impulse of the Nurses would be to scream. He thrust his hairy face close against their cheeks, and hissed from between his lips, "Utter one sound and you die! Keep still and you shall not be harmed."

Sophia swooned quite away. Faith closed her eyes and waited in an agony of fear. She felt Spite's strong arms placed around her. She was lifted from her couch; was borne through the tent. She was in the open air, and the breeze blowing upon her cheeks

THE BOY'S ILLUSTRATION.
FIG. 42.—Spite and Hide Carry off the Nurses.

revived her. She opened her eyes. In the clear moonlight she could see Hide pushing through the side of the covered gangway, close by the rear door of the marquée, carrying Sophia in his arms. With an instinct of hope that no terror could check she lifted her voice and screamed with the energy of despair. She felt the Pixie's hot breath upon her cheek; an awful oath sounded in her ear, and a rude hand smote upon her mouth. She fell back unconscious.

Let us follow backward the thread of our story into the Pixie's camp where we left Spite keeping his solitary watch, that we may account for this sudden appearance in the heart of the Brownie encampment. Spite could not sleep. Anger, mortification, hate, disappointed ambition, all the evil passions were ablaze within him, as he thought of what the Brownies had already gained, and of their assured victory on the morrow. His troops discouraged, provisions cut off, Madam Breeze (for aught he knew) ready to side again with the Brownies,—his utter defeat, the loss of the fort, and the massacre of his people seemed certain.

"If we could abandon the fort," he muttered; "if we could quietly steal out and leave the enemy watching an empty camp? That would be our salvation! But we can't; those troopers of MacWhirlie's are patrolling the plain, and the woods in the rear are swarming with pickets. But—I don't know?—"

He sprang to his feet, crossed over to Hide's quarters in Fort Tegenaria, bade him join him, and walked hastily to the line of breastworks on the lake front. He stopped under a bush that stood within the entrenchment. The night was cloudless, and by the moonlight streaming through the leaves, the two Pixies saw stretched among the upper branches a round, vertical web. It was the inner abutment of a bridge that once extended from Fort Spinder to Lakeside, but had been long in disuse.

"Do you know the condition of the Old Bridge?" asked Spite. "It has been a long time since I crossed it."

"I know little, except that I have heard some of my boys say that the piers on this end are in pretty good condition, and that some of the cables are still up."

Fig. 43 —" A Round, Vertical Web"—p. 86.

"Very well," said Spite, after musing a few moments, "let us explore a little. You always used to be ready for a scout, Hide, and I suppose have not forgotten your old cunning. The Brownie sentinels are just beyond us, there. Yon big fellow's beat runs under the middle of the second span."

Hide was quite as ready for the adventure as Spite. Without more words the two swung themselves into the bushes, climbed up the sides of the abutment wall, and were presently at the top.

"Here are the cables, at any rate," said Hide. "Only two of them, however. The rest are broken off. They hang down the sides of the abutment, and over the ends of the branches."

"Pull on the one next you," cried Spite, who had himself laid hold of one of the sound cables, and was pushing down upon it with all his might. "Mine holds. It is fast to the second pier in yonder bush, I am sure. How with yours?"

"It is all right," answered Hide, "I am willing to venture on it."

Nearly fifteen hundred millimetres distant was another and taller bush in which pier No. 1 of the bridge was built. The Pixies could not see this since the darkness of the night and the shadow of the leaves hid the white outlines of the web-wall. But they knew that it must be there, and therefore crept upon the silken ropes each upon one, and began their journey.*

Three thousand millimetres above the ground, for the whole distance from bush to bush over that single coil of rope those two creatures crawled. The cables shook, swayed and bent down, but neither parted, and the adventurous Pixies landed safely on top of the pier.

* Appendix, Note B.

The next pier was in a clump of bushes thirty-five hundred millimetres away, not in a direct course, but angling slightly across the field. The architects of the Old Bridge had taken advantage of the brushwood between the hill and lake. But as the shrubs grew at irregular distances from each other, and in various lines of direction, the course of the bridge was somewhat broken from the right line. Only one cable remained of those that had united pier No. 1 and pier No. 2. The scouts must therefore cross singly. To add to the danger a Brownie sentinel was stationed underneath the cable, about midway between the piers.

FIG. 44.—A Cobweb Bridge Across a Path.

"What say you, Hide?" asked the chief, "shall we go on?"

"What have you to gain by it, Cap'n? That's the question with me. Tell me what you intend by exploring this old suspension bridge, and I'll say whether it seems worth the risk."

"Certainly," said Spite. "My plan is to repair these cables by bracing the old ones, and putting up new ones, so that we can abandon the fort secretly, if we are pressed too hard. We could pass the whole force across the bridge by night, embark in our vessels, and cross the lake to the other shore, or to the island. The point I want to settle is, whether the cables are so far good that we can make a good roadway in the time at our command. We must do night work, repairing as well as crossing; and if we are hard pushed by the Brownies, we shall have to do some rapid engineering. That's the plan; what say you?"

"Good," cried Hide, "very good! It will be a fine stroke to slip away and leave the enemy to watch bare walls. Ha, ha! I fancy I see their solemn faces, on the discovery of our flight." Hide grew quite merry over his conceit.

"Very well then, that settles it. Here goes!" So saying, Spite stepped upon the single cable and began the passage. He moved slowly at first, until he found that the line was strong enough to bear him; then he increased his gait, and soon landed upon the top of pier No. 2.

Hide perceived that Spite had reached the pier, for the cable had ceased to vibrate under his movement, and accordingly began his voyage. Midway between piers he saw the Brownie sentinel approach. He passed underneath the cable humming some pretty ditty as he paced his beat.

Overhead just above him hung the black form of the Pixie. Hide paused and peered downward upon the unconscious Brownie. His eyes swelled with hate; his

breath escaped with a hissing sound, he bowed his back
in readiness to spring down upon the sentinel.

"Fool!" he muttered at last, "would you risk the
discovery of all for the sake of one miserable Brownie
more or less in the world? Ha! it was a great temptation; and I was mighty near yielding to it. Might have
broken my neck, too! I don't know, though;" and he followed the sentinel's retreating form with gloating eyes;

FIG. 45.

Unseen Dangers. Pixie Hide
Threatens the Brownie
Sentinel.

"I believe I could have dropped right down upon the
rascal, and throttled him ere he could have piped a
note. I'm sorry now that I didn't do it! But, no
matter; I'll get him some other time."

The sentinel, meanwhile, with steady gait passed onward under the cable and out of sight behind the bushes.
He never knew how nearly he had escaped death that
night, nor even suspected that peril threatened him.

Hide hurried over the remainder of the cable, and joined his comrade on the pier.

"Well," whispered Spite, "my heart was beating a tattoo of terror lest you might be rash enough to pounce upon that fellow. Really, I expected to see you take the leap. It was lucky that you controlled yourself. It would uncover all were we to start the Brownies' suspicions in this direction. We must keep all quiet on this side the fort. Now for the next pier! How does it look on your side?"

"There are a half dozen perfect lines here."

"Good. There are three here in prime order. Where is the next pier?"

"Over in that oak sapling to the right. The span is the longest in the bridge, about five thousand millimetres.

"Jolly, jolly!" exclaimed Spite in great glee. "We are now sure of most of the way. This long span needs little repairing. The first two we can fix up, I am quite sure. Now for the last."

They were not long in running across the third span; but when they reached pier No. 3, they found no traces of the cables which once united it to the lakeside abutment.

"Bad!" said the Pixie chief. "It will have to be built anew, that's all. It's lucky, too, that the worst break is on the last span, for we can repair here with less risk than elsewhere."

"Moreover," said Hide, "we have a double chance for escape, the river as well as the bridge."

"True; and now let us finish our observation by finding out the condition of yonder abutment." The pair descended to the ground, crossed to the willow in which the last pier had been fixed, and found it in quite as good repair as the others.

"All right!" exclaimed Hide.

Spite said "Jolly!" one of his favorite slang expletives, which he thought particularly good since he had lately borrowed it from one of his English cousins.

Highly pleased with what they had learned, the Pixies turned their faces homeward. As they crossed the space between the shore and pier No. 4, they had full view of the Brownie encampment from a vine covered old stump.

There the line of cavalry guards stretched along the plain, encircling the fort. Beyond, the camp fires of the main army glimmered amid the grass, weeds and bushes. A profound silence hung over the whole

Fig. 46.—Spite and Hide View the Brownie Camp.

scene. Both camp and fort were locked in the deep repose of midnight.

"Captain!" said Hide. He stopped and looked steadfastly toward the camp.

"Say on, comrade."

"I followed your venture," continued Hide, "will you risk mine?"

9

"That depends," answered the chief. "What is it?"

"Just to make a private visit to the headquarters yonder and pay our respects to the Brownie Captain. We are now inside the picket line. We can make a circuit around here by the lake and come up in the rear of the tents. The sentinels will not be numerous there, nor very watchful. It's a chance if there are any at all. There is little risk in the matter, just enough to give it spice. And—who knows? there might be a chance to end the campaign by putting my dagger into Murray Bruce's heart; or, failing that, you might bag that little fairy flame of yours, and carry her off to the fort. That would be 'jolly' indeed! Come, what say you?"

Spite hesitated. The plan seemed plausible. Hide was a prudent fellow, and not apt to take unusual risks. But then, there *was* the risk that he and his second in command might be taken, or cut off. And what would become of the Pixie cause in that case? It was not a prudent act. But then, again, it was a strong temptation. Assassinate Bruce? or, seize Faith?

"Lead on," he cried, "I'm with you."

The yellow flags of the hospital and sanitary tent were their guide. Hide's theory about the sentinels they found correct. They stole through the camp, passed the rear of the hospital, and paused before the marquée of the Sanitary Corps, which they took to be the officers' headquarters. A peep through the flap of the tent showed them their mistake, and revealed the sleeping forms of Faith and Sophia.

"We stop here!" said Spite, pushing aside the door. What followed has been told.

# CHAPTER X.

## THE GOLDEN MOTTOES.

Faith's cry breaking upon the midnight stillness was heard throughout the camp. The wounded in the hospital started up in their beds. The attendants ran toward Agatha and Grace supposing that the cry came from one of them. The two Nurses stood holding each other fast, trembling violently, their eyes fixed upon the door. Bruce ran from the headquarters tent, sword in hand, followed by Blythe, Rodney and Pipe. There was no need to sound the alarm, for the Brownies were running from all parts of the camp to headquarters.

"What is it? A night attack?" Nobody knew. "What was it—that terrible cry?" Nobody knew that. The sentinels had seen nothing. Then came MacWhirlie riding into the camp at full speed on one of the Goldentailed matches, which Madam Breeze had presented him.

Some one exclaimed: "Hah! this explains it! The picket line has been attacked by the Pixies. The Lieutenant has come for help."

No! He too had heard the cry, and had come to learn the cause. All was quiet along the plain.

Leaving the perplexed throng outside, let us re-enter the hospital. Agatha and Grace had recovered from their fright. The excitement caused by the alarm, the sudden and violent action of the soldiers in starting up upon their couches, even leaping from them, had re-opened many wounds so that they were bleeding freely.

(95)

Some of the worst cases had fallen back fainting. All was confusion within the place. The helpers were hurrying hither and thither. From the outside the Brownies were running in and out with the pointless questions usual in times of panic. Agatha's heart was touched at the sight. The voice of pity within her at once mustered her disordered faculties.

"Grace, Grace," she cried, "this will never do! Hasten to the marquée and bid Faith and Sophia come to the aid of these poor fellows. Quick! and bring all the lint that you can find. Guards!" she continued, calling to the sentinels at the doors, "keep out the people. We must have quiet here. Howard," addressing the head helper, "look to your aids! Brothers," she spoke to all attendants now, "remember your Golden Mottoes!"

FIG. 47.—"Silk Ravelled from Cocoons of Spiders."

She pointed as she spoke to the eastern side of the tent, sweeping her hand along the line of wall. Silk banners hung thereon, upon every one of which a Golden Motto was embroidered, together with various emblems, designs and tracery. Rich effects were produced by using the many hued scales on the wings of butterflies, the brilliant shells and elytra of beetles, and minute feathers of humming birds, which were embossed upon the cloth with silk raveled from cocoons of moths and spiders.* The ban-

ners were the gift of the Sanitary Corps whose cunning fingers had made them. Let us follow the rapid motion of Agatha's hand and read these Golden Mottoes.

The design of Banner One is, on a blue shield, a carrier pigeon in full flight, with a message tied by a ribbon about its neck. In the surrounding border are grouped and interwoven arrows and other emblems of speed and promptness. The motto is:

QUICKLY DONE IS
TWICE DONE.

The design of Banner Two is, on a blue shield, a silver

Fig. 48.—A Spider's Cocoon Nest.

pyramid, the North Star shining above it. In the border are wrought figures of a frontiersman with his rifle in

* Appendix, Note A.

hand standing among rocks and great oaks; a pilot at his wheel; an Indian shooting rapids in his bark canoe; a whaleman at the bow of his boat with harpoon poised. The legend is:

COOL HEAD GIVES HELPFUL
HANDS.

The design of Banner Three is, on a red shield, a full orbed golden sun with the old fashioned cheerful human face wrought upon it, and bright rays shooting out in all directions. In the border are anchors, flowers, song birds, sporting Brownies, winsome figures and emblems. The motto is:

CHEERFULNESS IS BOTH
BALM AND BROTH.

Banner Four, although not the most beautiful in point of imagery, is the most costly, the most carefully wrought and the most striking of all. On a purple shield two points, one above the other, one in chief and one in base are repre-

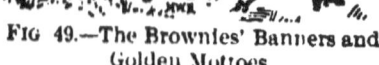

FIG 49.—The Brownies' Banners and
Golden Mottoes.

sented by golden stars, and these are united by a straight line. The motto is:

OUR LIFE LINE A RIGHT LINE.

The border consists of various mathematical instruments, a rule, square, dividers, sailor's compass, etc., and running all around the banner through these are the sentences "Straightway From Knowledge to Duty," "Duty First, Duty Last."

It has taken some time to note these decorations, but only a moment was consumed by the glance that Agatha and her aids cast upon them. That glance and the voice of their fair leader acted like a charm. The words had scarcely been uttered before the helpers were scattered through the tents and at the couches of the suffering. Agatha herself kneeled beside a wounded soldier, rearranged the bandages, and poured in fresh balm. She had cast more than one impatient look toward the side door that led into the Sanitary tent, wondering why Grace had not already come back with Faith and Sophia.

The rear door of the hospital, near which Agatha was kneeling, was pushed violently forward and Grace entered. She was capless, her hair streamed over her shoulders, her whole appearance showed anguish and agitation.

"They are gone!" she cried. Agatha rose hastily and threw herself into her arms.

"Gone? who? Faith? Sophia? Gone!—where? Speak, girl, what do you mean?"

"Oh, I cannot tell. Something dreadful has happened. They were not in the room when I went in. I supposed they had gone out to learn what was the trouble, and ran into the crowd to seek them. Nobody knew. Your father and uncle, and Pipe, and all the rest were there,

but no Faith—no Sophia.  They knew nothing of them.
They are searching for them now.  They fear that the
Pixies have carried them off.  Oh, Agatha! what shall
we do?"

Ah, Agatha, do you remember the Golden Mottoes
now!  Will she remember, think you?  Her frame
shook with emotion; her hands were cold; beads of
moisture gathered on her pale forehead.  She spoke in a
dreamy way, as though talking to herself: "Carried off
by the Pixies?  Gone?  Cousin Faith gone?  Sophia
gone?"

Then she started as from a trance.  There was a
tremor in her voice, but she spoke quietly, as one who
had struggled with her own heart and got the victory.

"Grace, God help them!  But our duty lies here.
There is no time now for grief.  There is no call on us
to take part in the work and peril of delivering our
sister Nurses.  Others will do it better than we.  Our
duty is plain.  And is just before us.  Mine is here.
Grace, dear, yours is there!"

She pointed first to the couch at which she had been
kneeling, then to one across the aisle, and quietly turning from her companion, knelt down again by the
wounded Brownie, and took up the dropped thread of
her labor of love.  When she lifted her eyes Grace was
at her post.  Noble conquerors!  These are the victories
of those who be better than they who take a city.

# CHAPTER XI.

Meanwhile, the light of fox-fire and fire-fly lanterns was glancing everywhere through camp and field, showing where eager searchers were scattered looking for the lost Nurses. Rodney was well nigh frantic with grief, and ran here and there among the tents calling the name of his daughter. Only the echo of his voice came back to him out of the night. Pipe was as one paralyzed. He leaned against the wall of the tent with folded arms, and eyes fixed upon the spot where his child had lain. His mute sorrow was pitiful to see.

Blythe and Sergeant True entered the tent. The Adjutant's bright face was clouded; the tall form of the Sergeant was bowed.

"If one only knew!" said Blythe. "It is this terrible uncertainty that is so hard to bear. If I knew where they were, I could cut my way through legions of fiends to save them, or die trying."

"Is there no trace at all?" asked True.

"Not the slightest. It is only a suspicion"—he lowered his voice—"that they have been carried off by the Pixies. No one dares even name it to the Commodore and—" nodding toward the Boatswain

"But that is not reason," answered True. "It is important that we should know the worst, at once. For one, I mean to find out the truth, if I can, and face it manfully."

He stepped to the couch, which lay just as it had been left by the Nurses. His hand caught upon a thread of gossamer that lay upon a pillow. He looked more closely. There was another, then another, then a thick strand of the silken material. He rose with the delicate filaments floating from his fingers, walked to the lantern, and held his hand within the light. Blythe followed every motion.

FIG. 50 —A Brownie Link Boy with a Fire-fly Lantern.

"Do you see?" cried True. "There can be no doubt of it. Some of the enemy have passed the lines, entered this tent, woven their snares around the sleeping maids, and escaped. One of the two Nurses uttered that cry as they were being carried off. We must look for them in the Pixies' fort or on the way to it."

"That is truth," said Blythe, "and the sooner we begin the search the better."

True walked up to Pipe and touched him tenderly upon the shoulder. The Boatswain looked up vacantly.

"Ah, my lad, it is you!" he said at last. "Where is our Sophia?"

"Boatswain," said True, holding up the hand to which the gossamer threads were still clinging, "Sophia is in the Pixies' fort or on the way to it. And you and I must bring her back. Come, rouse up! Be yourself again!"

Pipe started from his lethargy. He looked at the floating strand of web-work; listened to True's statement; passed his palm against his brow, then seized the Sergeant's hand.

"My boy, you are right! And I have been acting the fool! Poor girl! poor girl! Come—let us not delay. To the Pixies' fort! Ho, my brave tars!" Even while he spoke Pipe stepped to the door of the tent and put his whistle to his lips.

"Stop, stop!" cried True, laying a hand upon his arm. "Remember the proverb: Make haste slowly! Are we sure that our lost ones are at the fort yet? May we not find some other traces of them that will enable us to go to work more intelligently? Don't call your men. They are scattered abroad in busy search. They are doing no harm, and may do much good. Let them alone for the present. You and I can follow this trail a litttle further."

There was a cool head at last on the track of the fugitives. The fact gave at least a glimmer of hope. True first inquired carefully of Agatha, Grace and others in the hospital, as to the exact point from which the shriek had come. They all agreed that it had been made close by the rear of the tent, so near that it seemed to be inside.

"That determines our first step," said True. "Now for lanterns and the sharpest eyes among you. We shall search here," he continued, and led the party just outside the tent, and set them to scanning every bush, grass blade and weed in the vicinity. The Nurses had been asked to join the search for a little while, and fortune gave to Agatha the first important discovery.

"Here!" she cried, "I have a trace!" She had plucked from a thistle stalk a bit of gossamer.

"I too!" cried Pipe, holding up a similar object.

"And I!" said Grace, who was in advance of the party.

"Stop!" exclaimed True. "Stand where you are until I get the line of the trail."

Agatha stood nearest the tent. Pipe was beyond her and a little to the right. Grace stood some distance from both in a

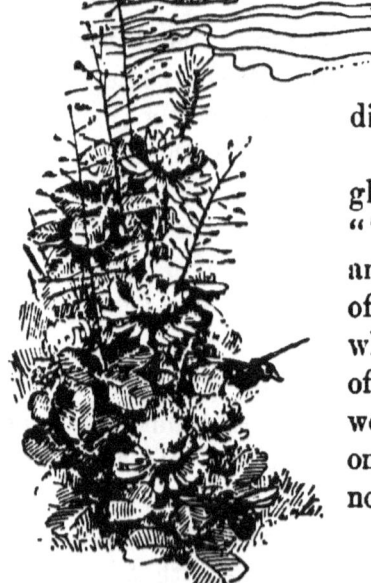

direct line with Agatha.

"That will do," said True, glancing up at the North Star. "The line runs due north, and straight from the rear of the camp. Start again while I make some inquiries of the Adjutant. Blythe, a word with you. Who was on guard over there, to the north?"

"No one."

"Impossible! Blythe, you couldn't—"

FIG. 51.—"From a Thistle Stalk a Bit of Gossamer."

"Stop!" exclaimed Blythe, his voice choking with emotion. "The Captain bade it. And Rodney, and Pipe,—and myself, alas, alas! we all councilled it. The men were weary. A strong picket line entirely surrounded the fort. They were picked men with MacWhirlie at their head. We knew that no force of the enemy lay in our rear. No one dreamed of danger from that quarter."

"Say no more," said True. "Regrets are useless now.

I see how it is. A party of stragglers or spies has stolen in here while we slept. Faith and Sophia have been surprised while alone in the tent."

" But what motive?—" began Blythe. A shout from the searchers interrupted him. It was Pipe's voice.

" We have struck the trail again ! "

" Who has it ? "

" Howard there, and myself."

" Steady ! let me see. Here are our first traces, where those three lanterns hang. Hold up your lights to the points where you found the last signs. That will do. There, do you see? Two of the first lanterns are.

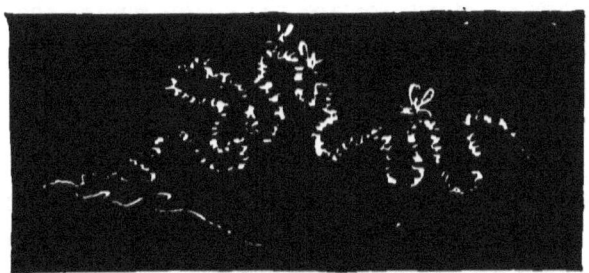

Fig. 52.—"A Bit of Gossamer."

in line with Howard's light, the other in line with Pipe's. And the two lines are nearly parallel, showing the paths. by which the two maids were borne away. We are on the trail. Due north still ! Forward, once more ! "

Step by step the trail was followed by threads caught here and there upon leaves and branches. It continued to bear northward for a goodly distance, then turned westward as though the fugitives were making gradually toward the fort. There it was lost for a while, and when discovered again was once more bearing north. Again it turned westward, and was lost completely in the plain that encircled the fort, just where it bordered on a strip of sand that ran down to the little lake.

# CHAPTER XII.

Sergeant True stood on the edge of the plain considering what should next be done. All signs of the trail had ceased as soon as the searchers had come out of the grass and brushwood. There could be no trail upon the flat plain, the Sergeant knew. A large party had just returned from searching the wood between the lake and the fort. There was a bare possibility that the fugitives had ventured to cross the plain, and run the gauntlet of the picket line into the fort; a little stronger possibility that they had skirted the wood by the shore and pushed on down toward the outlet where the Pixie navy lay. True therefore questioned the returning searchers:

"Have you seen anything?"

"Nothing. Lieutenant MacWhirlie has had the entire strip between lake and fort thoroughly guarded ever since the alarm. Nothing could have passed, he says. Nothing has passed that has left any trail. The Lieutenant has sent scouts down the shore to make sure."

Rodney and Pipe heard the report with heavy hearts, Hope was fast dying within them. "Must we give it up?" cried the Commodore. "Is there no deliverance?"

"There is but one way by which they could have escaped us," said True, pointing toward the lake. "Is it possible that we have been mistaken, and that pirates

(106)

have done this outrage after all? Commodore, have there been any boats or ships off shore lately?"

"Not one," answered Rodney. "Both fleets are lying by for repairs, for the last fight used them up pretty well. We've been doing shore service ever since."

"It is most strange! But we must search the shore thoroughly in this neighborhood, at any rate."

The bank of the lake was presently covered with Brownies eagerly scanning by the light of their torches and lanterns every foot of ground.

"We have it, we have it!" shouted Rodney. "Come here, Pipe! and you, Waterborn. Look at this!" Immediately a crowd surrounded the excited Commodore.

"Stand back!" he cried; "don't push down so close upon the shore until some of the sailors have seen these marks. A boat has landed here within the last half hour. See the wash of the waves upon the sand! And just there the bow has scraped. What say you, lads?"

"There is no doubt of it," responded Pipe, after a careful examination. Waterborn, the mate, held his lantern to the water line and after a moment's inspection gave the same opinion.

"Here," exclaimed Blythe, "is the crowning proof!" He plucked from the shore a handful of silken threads that had caught upon the sand and gravel which covered the spot where Faith and Sophia must have lain. Yes, they had found the trail again; but only to lose it in the waters of Lake Katrine.

"What shall be done?" asked Rodney.

"We must follow you now," answered True. "The path lies upon an element of which I know little. You and the Boatswain are at home there. To you who are most wronged Providence gives the opportunity to undo the injury. We yield to the navy, now. Lead on ; we'll follow you, you may be sure."

Rodney and Pipe had scarcely been themselves since the first tidings of their bereavement. Their wills seemed benumbed by the blow. They followed Sergeant True like little children. But now that responsibility was laid in their hands, they roused themselves to duty. They were the keen, shrewd, sailor chiefs once more. Subdued still by their grief, but alert and intelligent, they took up the work before them.

"'Tis an element that leaves no trail," said Rodney, "yet it will go hard, but my gallant tars shall find the lost ones. We'll scour every nook and beat every bush along shore, if need be. We'll pluck the dear captives from under the black flag or we'll sink every timber in the fleet! What say you, lads?"

A hearty cheer was the sailors' answer. The whole company on shore joined in it. And it did them all good.

"You can not tell which direction the boat has taken, of course," said True. "But have you any opinion at all about it? You must start out from some view point. What shall it be?"

"That is exactly what I have been asking myself," said Rodney. "I have a notion that the boat, wherever it came from, has crossed to the island or gone down to the outlet to join the fleet. I incline to the latter view. The island is lightly garrisoned ; the Orchard Camp is nearly deserted ; the mass of Pixie troops are shut up in Fort Spinder. Naturally, the robbers would take to the fleet as the safest place."

"That is good reasoning, Commodore," said Water-born, "and there is only one thing that weakens it. The wind would be dead against them going downward.

For the last half hour it has been blowing due north—straight upon the island."

"True; but we shall see presently. The first thing is to rally our men. Boatswain, pipe to quarters."

"Aye, aye, Sir!" answered Pipe, and the shrill whistle sounded through the air and along the water. A few stragglers who had joined the various searching parties gathered in at the call. But most of the sailors and marines were already present.

"Now lads, we must away to our ships. Fall in! Forward, march!" The column started up the shore at quick step, and was soon lost to view.

10

# CHAPTER XIII.

## RAFT THE SMUGGLER.

Spite and Hide saw that Faith's cry had aroused the Brownies, and pushed at their utmost speed directly from the camp. It did not occur to them that they might be tracked by the threads of web-work torn off by leaves and twigs from the cords with which they had bound their captives. But they did fear that one of the Nurses might again cry out; and they stopped long enough to fasten gags upon their mouths.

Several times the Pixie chiefs turned toward Fort Spinder, hoping to reach the Old Bridge by the way they had come. But their progress was checked by bands of Brownies scattered everywhere in the direction of the fort. The lights of the searchers were seen dancing throughout the entire plain, and running hither and thither in confused lines among grass and shrubbery.

More than once the Pixies were on the point of being discovered. Several times they had to crouch under the leaves, lest they should be seen by parties of excited searchers. Indeed, their safety lay in the fact that the Brownies were so much excited; and had all been as self-possessed as the cool headed True, Spite and Hide would have been captured.

At last they reached a point where the plain sweeps down to the sandy bank of the lake, which is a natural basin widened into an artificial pond. The brook that flows from the Hillside spring runs through it. There is an island in the middle of the lake, covered with grass, moss and ferns. In honor of the old home the Brownies called the lake Loch Katrine, and the island Ellen's Isle, names which the Pixies refused to acknowledge, and called the pond Lake Arachne and the island Aranea Isle. On this little sheet of water, and its inlet and outlet, the navies of the Brownies and Pixies floated; and here was the scene of many a battle between Rodney and his sailors and the Pixies and pirates.

Spite and Hide paused on the border of the plain to consider. It was not far to the pier of the Old Bridge along which lay the path to the fort. But the space between them and that point was swarming with Brownies. MacWhirlie had mustered his entire troop, and set them to patrolling the plain. Throughout the woods, from the foot of the hill to the very lakeside, sentinels were posted at short intervals, and burdened as they were the Pixies could not pass that line.

"Well, Hide, what shall we do?"

"Do? Humph! there is little choice left us now. I will follow my chief. Lead on!"

"Lead on? Whither?" Spite snapped his fangs angrily as he spoke. "You got me into this scrape. It was a foolhardy adventure. Now get me out! I know you have something to advise."

"Very good! Let us kill these pretty captives of ours," said Hide with a sneer, "and cut our way through to the pier. Or, if you lead the way with them, I'll follow."

Spite looked down upon the unconscious form of Faith.

"I see no way out of this," he said. "To break through the line would be certain death. It looks as though it had come to that at any rate. May the foul fiend take you for tempting me to this madcap raid! Hide, Hide, bethink you, I pray!" Spite's voice was trembling with—fear, shall we say? Without awaiting reply from his companion, he took Faith in his arms and ran down to the edge of the water.

Hide followed him. He had long suspected what no one else had dreamed of, that Spite at heart was a coward. He had little love for his chief. Indeed, the thought was not new to the ambitious Lieutenant that Spite alone blocked the way of his own promotion to the headship of the Pixies. That he would be a worthy leader he, at least, did not doubt. He enjoyed his Captain's agitation, and was pleased to keep him upon nettles. He had already settled a plan of escape.

Spite eagerly scanned the surface of the lake.

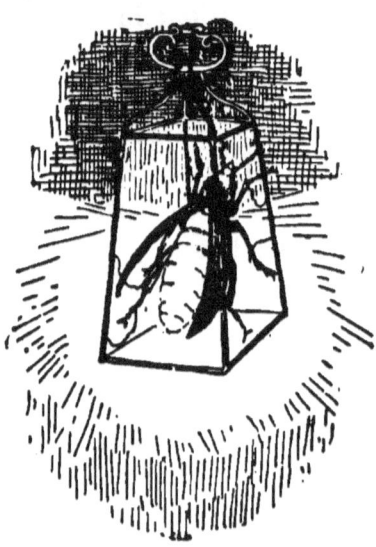

Fig. 53.—Brownie Fire-fly Lantern.

"It's no use looking for the navy, Captain," said Hide. "There it rides, away down by the outlet. We must pass the Brownie pickets to get at the boats. Might as well cut through to the pier!"

"Is there no escape then? This is terrible! We shall be slaughtered outright." He pointed to the semi-circle of lanterns and torches drawing closer and closer upon them, marking where True and his party were following hard upon their trail. Spite dropped his burden, sat down, and fairly wrung his hands in despair. Yes, Spite the Spy, the chief of all the Pixies, did that!

Hide highly enjoyed the distress of his Captain. He had proved what he had long suspected, and, best of all, he had gained a hold upon Spite that would give great advantage over him in the future. He saw that it was high time to drop this malicious by play and address himself in earnest to escape.

"Cheer up, my brave Captain!" he cried, "I think I see a way out of this."

"Hah! Is it so?" Spite was too much elated with hope to notice the sneering tone of his Lieutenant.

"You shall see; wait here a moment." He ran along the sand to a clump of ferns that bent over from the bank until they kissed the water. He

FIG. 54.—The Nurses Carried Away on Raft Dolomede's Yacht, the Fringe.

mounted one of these and disappeared. Soon the drooping tips of the ferns lifted up, parted, and a curious craft glided out from the cove formed by the bended foliage. What a snug and secret harbor it was! The vessel touched the bank close by the spot where Spite stood, and Hide jumped ashore.

"Now then," he cried, "all aboard! We have no time to lose." He lifted Sophia from the ground as he spoke, carried her to the boat and laid her down in a leafy canopy or cabin. Spite followed with Faith.

"Push off now!" said Hide to a tall Pixie who had charge of the vessel. He put his paws against the shore and shoved vigorously. The waterman did the same, and the boat shot out into the lake. A brisk wind was blowing along the surface of the water, and the craft was soon off shore and out of danger.

The lanterns of the Brownies were seen bobbing along the bank just above the spot at which but a moment before the boat had been moored. A group of lights marked the point at which the trail had been lost, and where True and his party were now standing perplexed.

"Ugh!" said Spite as he watched the scene. It was hard to tell whether the sound betokened pleasure or displeasure. He was greatly relieved at the prospect of escape, but was not in the most amiable humor, for all that. With the easing of his fears came the thought of how he had exposed his weakness. His pride was hurt. He felt humiliated. He knew that Hide had been trifling with him, and his wrath grew hot thereat. He vowed revenge in his heart, but was too wise to show his feeling then. "I can wait!" he said. He glowered upon the Lieutenant, but soon cleared up his face and spoke cheerfully.

"Truly, friend Hide, you seem to be a person of varied resources. Pray, how chanced you to come across this waterman and his boat?"

"The fact is, Cap'n?" answered Hide laughing, "I have to keep a little private yacht for my own use. There are certain things, you know, for which one cannot well use the government ships. This is my friend, Raft Dolomede. Raft, allow me to present you to my chief, Spite the Spy. You see, Captain, my American friend has great respect for our community, although he does not belong to us. He has been brought up on this

lake ; is a skillful sailor, willing to obey orders, take his
pay and ask no questions. He runs on his own hook—
is a privateersman, in fact, on a small scale. We understand each other pretty well, and, of course, I knew
where he kept his boat moored. He's not on very good
terms with our cruisers; for, in sooth, he doesn't quite
understand our revenue laws. I fear, now, that it
wouldn't do to look closely under these leaves! There
might be something contraband.aboard besides these fair
Brownies. Hey, Raft?"

Raft's boat was a home-made affair, but was ingeni-
ously built. Dry leaves had been gathered into a mass,
and fastened together with silken threads. To this had
been added a mast, a sail, a jib and other fixtures so
that the structure was a cross between a raft and a
schooner. The leaves served admirably the varied uses
of hull, sails, storerooms, beds and barricade. They
caught the wind and drove the boat along as well as a
ship's canvas. They were soft dry couches for sailors
or passengers. The hollows and crevices between them
were the "hold" of the vessel and gave ample storage.

Raft, the owner of this craft, was a handsome specimen
of the family of water-pixies. He wore a coat of
chocolate brown, trimmed with a broad orange band,
and covered with double rows of white buttons. His
trousers were pale red. He was quite at home on the
lake with his yacht, and was such a skillful swimmer
that he might really be said to walk on the water instead
of swimming through it.*

"How shall I put her head now?" asked Raft. "We're
bearing nor' east by east, and with this wind will soon
strike the cave yonder on the orchard shore. Shall I
keep her so?"

---

* Appendix, Note A.

"What say you, Captain?" asked Spite. "What are we to do with these, now?" pointing to Faith and Sophia.

"The first thing to be done, it seems to me," said Raft, casting a pitying look upon the nurses, "is to give 'em a little breathing privilege. If you don't take those rags off their figure-heads, and give 'em a breath of fresh wind, they'll soon be dead Brownies." With that he opened the sharp claws on one of his hands, like a pair of scissors, and without more ado cut the bands that had been placed as gags around the captives' mouths.

FIG. 55.—"Murderous Assaults Upon One Another."

"All right!" he said, resuming his rudder, "go on with your palaver. But heave ahead lively, or we'll be across the lake before you decide."

Spite had been in a deep study. At last he said, "We must go to the island."

Raft glanced inquiringly at Hide, who nodded assent. "Aye, aye, Sir. Port-a-helm it is." He turned the bow toward Ellen's Isle.

"We can easily find lodgings for our fair prizes there," continued Spite. "But what about Fort Spinder? That is what troubles me. How are we to get back? It is now too soon after the alarm to think of running the pickets. Even if it were possible to do that by night as things are now, it would be madness to try it by daylight. And yet, we must get some word to our people soon, and have them out of that fort by to-morrow night, or—" Spite paused and looked serious.

" Well ? " said Raft.

" Well ? " said Hide, " or —what ? "

" You know quite as well as I! " answered Spite.
" There will not be a corporal's guard of Pixies left in
Fort Spinder, that's all ! "

Hide shrugged his shoulders and looked grave. He
had known very well what Spite meant, and he had a wife
and children in the fort. There was a long pause.
Spite and Hide were in deep and anxious thought.
They could imagine the wild natures shut up within
Fort Spinder venting their native savagery in murderous assaults upon one another.* What could control them
when the absence of their two chief officers should be
discovered ? Was there any chance for them to return
to the fort ? or any other way to prevent the catastrophe
which they dreaded ? The wind freshened, and in the
meantime the " Fringe " (as Raft called his yacht) was
rapidly approaching the island.

---

* Appendix, Note B.

# CHAPTER XIV.

Faith and Sophia were much relieved by Raft's considerate act. They had never thought to be grateful to a Pixie, but they felt gratitude toward the smuggler as he cut the bands upon their mouths. Their limbs were still bound, but they could turn upon their sides or backs, and look into the quiet, starlit sky. Their minds were in a whirl of wonder, uncertainty, terror. They had scarcely taken in the full horror of their condition. Captives in Pixies' hands!

Their hearts had beaten fast with fear when Raft drew near, but the kind words and act of the bluff sailor revived their hopes a little. Perhaps even the Pixies might take pity upon them and restore them to their home! At all events, it lessened their suffering to be free to breathe naturally, and it was a comfort to be able to talk together, instead of looking into each other's faces in mute wretchedness. They were near the bow and their captors were in the stern of the boat with Raft; they could therefore speak freely in whispers without fear of being heard. On the contrary, the three Pixies spoke aloud, as though not caring to conceal their thoughts from the prisoners, or not thinking they were overheard. Thus, much of their conversation reached the nurses' ears.

Spite and Hide sat thinking. Raft stood at the tiller and kept the boat steady on its course. Not a sound was heard except the ripple of water against the sides

of the vessel as it moved rapidly onward through the
darkness.

"Faith, dear Faith," whispered Sophia, "I cannot
make it all out. Where are we? What is to be done
with us? How came we here?"

"We are on Lake Katrine, Sophia, and we are sailing
toward Ellen's Isle in a Pixie yacht. That much I
am sure of. I know nothing more. But alas! I dread
the worst. What can we expect from our terrible foes?
And then the hatred they bear father and uncle—oh,
my poor, poor father!" The thought of their friends'
grief and anxiety for them awakened a fresh train of
anguish in the captives' hearts. They laid their heads
down upon the leaves and wept together.

Forsaken! Lost! The waves laughed and danced
merrily by them as the bow cut the water. The stars
looked down coldly from the great solemn heights of the
sky, and twinkled and winked upon them as though
careless or ignorant, or even in mockery of their fate!
Why had such a sorrow come upon them?

"Captain Spite," said Hide, at last.

"Well, Hide, what is it?"

\*    \*    \*    \*    \*    \*

"Oh Faith, do you hear that?" whispered Sophia.
"We are in the hands of Spite the Spy and his Lieutenant! Heaven defend us now!"

Faith answered with a groan.

\*    \*    \*    \*    \*    \*

"I have thought," said Hide, "that we might sell our
prisoners. If we keep them, they will be a world of
trouble and risk. Dispose of them, we get out of our
scrape handsomely, save the garrison and people in the
fort, get vast credit for valor and strategy, and start a
fresh campaign full handed, with good chance to regain

our lost ground.  I don't see any way out of this, but
to put up our fair prizes at ransom."

"Well," said Spite sharply, "go on!"

"Not much more to say, Cap'n.  Let's go in, or send
Raft in with a flag of truce.  Offer to give up the Nurses
if Bruce and the Commodore will raise the siege of Fort
Spinder.  I believe they'll do it."

"Aye, aye, that they will!" said Raft heartily.  "It's
a sensible plan, and as manly as sensible; for, the fact
is, I don't relish this making war on women."

"Faugh! no cant, please!" sneered Spite.  "Anything with Brownie blood is our game.  But you're
mistaken.  Bruce and all the rest, that Sergeant True
particularly, would take the high moral grounds about
the business, and send back word: 'Better all die than
compromise Truth and Duty, or give up the pursuit of
wrong.'  They wouldn't do what you expect.  I doubt
if they would even receive our flag of truce."

    \*     \*     \*     \*     \*     \*

The hearts of the prisoners fluttered between hope
and fear as they heard these words.  Home again!  The
very thought gave them joy.

"Faith, we shall be ransomed, I know!" exclaimed
Sophia.

Faith was silent.

"Oh, Faith, you don't believe they would do that?"
again whispered Sophia when Spite had ended.  "Surely
your father would consent! and dear True also—"  She
stopped and caught her breath quickly as though a cruel
doubt had suddenly seized her new fledged hope.

Faith was still silent.

    \*     \*  .  \*     \*     \*     \*

Raft next spoke.  "Well, that's amazing to me!
Now, I think if my gal was in the hands of two such—"

he paused as though at loss for a word. "Two such—accomplished villains;" he continued, "I reckon you'll think that complimentary, gentlemen ;—I wouldn't stop to split hairs very long, I can tell you. I like grit, too; but I can't say that I admire it at the expense of those pretty things over there."

"Captain," said Hide, "wouldn't Bruce compromise by simply letting our folks retire from the fort unmolested? March out with arms, banners, and all the honors, and leave the Brownies to occupy the old shell, and destroy it at their leisure? I say try it anyhow."

"So do I," said Raft. "That proposition ought to double the cape of the sharpest scruple. Say you'll land your cargo; hoist a flag of truce; and I'll run in shore within hailing distance. Or, if you like it better, I'll undertake the matter myself."

The Pixie chief made no answer. Faith and Sophia listened to hear their fate pronounced, with feelings wrought up to the highest pitch. Spite rose and walked excitedly up and down the deck. He stopped and looked at Faith. He seemed about to yield. He raised his eyes to the water, then cast them upon the island which was now just ahead of them. Then he stood like a statue gazing at some object which hung in the air beyond the bow of the yacht. A fiendish smile passed over his face. For a long time he was silent and motionless.

"Gentlemen," he said, "I'm much obliged for your council. But I have a better way. Fort Spinder shall be empty before to-morrow's sunrise, and its garrison and contents safe on the orchard side of the lake in Big Cave Camp. Patience! You shall know my plans as soon as we have put our prisoners in a secure place."

He spoke like a new person. There was an air of

confidence in his manner, and a jubilant ring in his voice that gave assurance to his companions. They were quite content to wait and trust the chief. Besides, the boat was now touching shore. The bow grated upon the sand. Raft jumped off and made the Fringe fast.

"Come now, my dears," said Spite, approaching the Nurses, "we will go ashore and take things a little easier."

Faith and Sophia were once more stricken with despair. The hope of being ransomed had been dashed by this mysterious plan which Spite had hinted to his comrades. What it was they could not even conjecture ; but it meant imprisonment, death, it may be worse than death to them in a Pixies' den. Resistance they knew was vain. They could only plead for mercy. They lifted up their voices together and with crying and tears sought to move the pity of their captors.

"Tut, tut !" said Spite, "if you will behave yourselves there shall not a hair of your head come to harm. Bless your pretty faces, we don't mean to eat you. Come, cheer up! We intend to take you to a snug and comfortable house, a palace in fact. You never spied a prettier place, I warrant. You shall be with friends who will know how to take care of you. 'Pon honor, you shall not be harmed. There now !"

With an effort at consolation which sat awkwardly upon him, he cut loose the web-work shroud that enveloped Faith, and without more ado picked her up and jumped on shore. Hide followed with Sophia.

The two Pixies ran along shore a short distance, and then began to ascend the bank. They stopped near a tuft of grass on a mossy slope, where Spite laid down his burden and began to examine carefully the surface. A bunch of moss somewhat dried, and heaped up in a careless way, attracted his attention. "Here is our place!" he exclaimed, and tapped against one side of the heap. There was no response. He seized the moss and shook it vigorously. Thereupon, one side of the moundlet suddenly opened, pushing outward like a door.

An old Pixie, large and gaunt, thrust out her head, and cried, "What do you want? Begone, or I'll—"

"Oh, no you won't, Mother Tigrina! Don't you see? It's Spite, my good old lady. Open quickly! There, that will do. Come on, Hide."

The officers entered, carrying Faith and Sophia. The place in which the party now stood was a domed chamber or vestibule, lined in all parts with white silk. The tapestry was spread over the interior of the moss heap, which was in fact a hollow ball built up by skillful workmanship, although the rude exterior had the appearance of a chance accumulation. At the outer end of this mossy dome an oval portion had been left unattached to sides and bottom, and was fastened at the top alone by the silken lining. Thus was formed a rude sort of door, hinged at the top, which the occupant could raise at will or fasten by overspinning from the inside. This dome was in fact a vestibule or outer approach of a deep cave or tunnel, which slanted into the ground for a short distance and then turned downward.* This cavern was held by Spite as a sort of country seat or castle, which he had dignified with the name of Aranea Hall. It was in charge of Dame Tigrina whom we have just seen in possession of the place. She was a monstrous character, even among her own nation, but what she lacked in grace she made up in her rude devotion to the Pixie cause and leader.

* Appendix, Note A.

"You see, Dame Tigrina," said Spite, "I've brought you two nice companions. You can't complain of being solitary now."

"Humph!" said the old hag, looking fiercely upon the Brownies.

The Nurses were carried into an inner room of the cavern. Its walls and ceiling were hung with beautiful white silk tapestry. The floor was covered with a purple silk carpet; cushions formed of yellow floss and fibres of plants were spread for couches and chairs.*

"There, my lassies," said Spite, "you never slept in such a room as this. I am sorry that I must leave you immediately, but you shall be well cared for. Be happy! and expect me soon." He dropped the curtain partition or portiére and Faith and Sophia were alone in their prison palace.

---

* Appendix, Note B.

# CHAPTER XV.

Fort Spinder was in a ferment. The unusual stir in the Brownie camp was seen by the pickets on the outer barricades, and they at once gave the alarm, thinking that a night attack was to be made. The garrison sprang to arms. The Pixies swarmed to the breastworks; the Pixinees (as the females were called) mounted the ramparts of the fort.

Now arose the trouble that Spite had anticipated.

"Where is the Captain?" The word ran from mouth to mouth along barricades and breastwork. The Captain was not to be found.

"Where is the Lieutenant, then?" The inquiry ran through the Tegenaria quarter with the same puzzling result. Presently a sentinel who had mounted guard near the abutment of the old suspension bridge reported that he had seen the two officers climb the pier and go out upon the cables.

"Have they returned?"

No he had seen nothing of them since.

A rumor was started, and ran through the lines, that Spite had been captured by the Brownies, and that had caused the unusual excitement in their camp.

Then came another rumor that made headway amid whispers, hints, and mutterings of "Treachery!" "Cowardice!" "Desertion!" "Sold out to the Brownies!"

So the leaven of riot and panic began to work. Some bewailed the missing officers as martyrs; some cursed

11                    (125)

them as traitors; all mourned their absence as a fatal blow to their own safety. Irritated by the uncertainty, worn out by watching, fasting and fighting, the two parties readily passed from words to blows.

"They are true as steel!"

"They are false traitors!"

"You lie!"

"Hah! take that!"

Words like these, followed by the clatter of claws, and the sharp rasping of fangs were heard in every quarter. Luckily the third in command, Lieutenant Heady, was no milksop. He had seen riots and rebellions before and had quelled them. In stubborness, cunning and ferocity he was a genuine Pixie. Fortune, it seemed, had made him chief, for the time, at least. And chief he would be, or cease to be at all.

He summoned a squad of the most courageous guards, and with them passed along the line of barricades. Quarrels were broken up with a strong hand, both parties being impartially beaten. The seditious were warned, the orderly praised, the doubters cheered, the timorous encouraged.

That answered for a little while.

Once more the riot began.

Heady and his patrol renewed their round. But as soon as a tumult was silenced in one quarter it arose in another. No sooner had the police squad reduced matters to quiet and moved to another point, than the riot broke out afresh behind them. Finally it gathered such headway that the Lieutenant was compelled to retire. The ill feelings which the rioters had vented upon one another were turned against him. The combatants united to wreak a common vengeance upon Heady.

"He is a usurper!"

" He wants to be chief himself ! "

" He has made way with the other officers so that he may seize the command ! "

" Down with him ! Death to the tyrant ! "

" Death ! Death ! Death ! "

The whole seditious element of the garrison gathered together, and moved in a solid mass upon Heady and his little band of aids, who had fallen back toward the tower that united the two main quarters of the fort.

"Aha ! " said he, " is it that you are after ? Very good, my brave boys ! There are two who can play the game of death, as you shall learn ! "

The Pixinees had assembled upon the rampart and were looking down grimly upon the tumult in the parade ground or open space beneath. Heady called to them to open the tower gates. Now, strange to say, Heady was a universal favorite among the Pixinees. Which one of his particular qualities won their admiration it would be hard to say, but

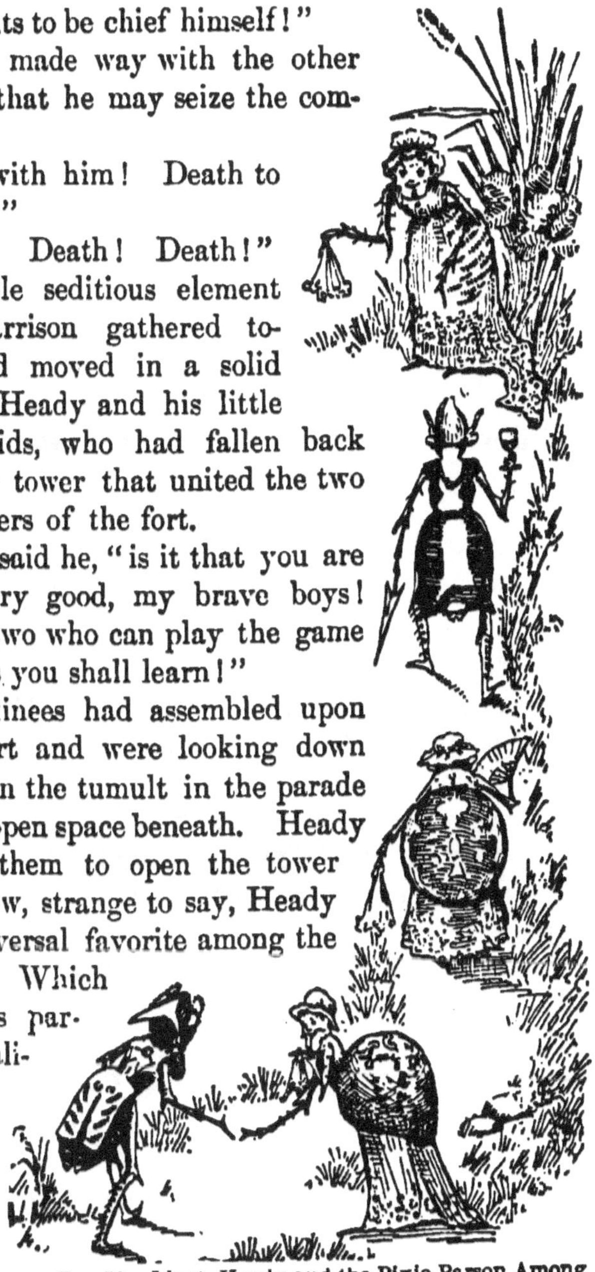

FIG. 56.—Lieut. Heady and the Pixie Parson Among Admiring Pixinees.

the cross-grained and savage old crumdudgeon had a host of enthusiastic friends among the Pixinees of Fort Spinder. They always stood up for him, and the cunning fellow knew well that he could count upon them now; especially as the Pixie Parson,* who had great influence among the Pixinees, was also his warm friend.

The gates of the tower flew open immediately, and an excited crowd of Pixinees gathered about their favorite. They leaped from the ramparts. They climbed down the walls. They thronged the gate. Their forms fairly swelled with indignation. They were ready at a word to fall upon the insurgents.

The mob paused at this demonstration. They did not like the look of things. They began to consult among themselves. A few in the rear ranks of the main body dropped out one by one and sneaked off toward the barricade. Heady spoke a few words to his Amazon squad, and then approached the rioters. He advanced several paces from the gate and addressed them.

"Gentlemen, you have chosen to submit this little difference of opinion to a very grim sort of a judge called—Death. I am ready to argue the case, and—there is the court!" He pointed to the group of angry Pixinees.

The leaders of the riot held a brief whispered consultation. They were quite taken aback at this turn of affairs.

"Come, gentlemen," continued Heady, in the same cool, sneering tone. "The court is waiting. Are you ready for trial?"

There is no telling what the issue might have been had not the current of feeling been suddenly arrested.

---

* Appendix, Note A.

During these moments of tumult a thin white speck had been floating in from the lake. It sailed above the tops of the trees, hovered over the fort, and gradually settled down toward the parade ground. A voice was heard to issue from it :

"Pixies, ahoy—oy!"

All eyes turned upward. A balloon hung overhead and just beyond, toward the lake, another and another could be seen.

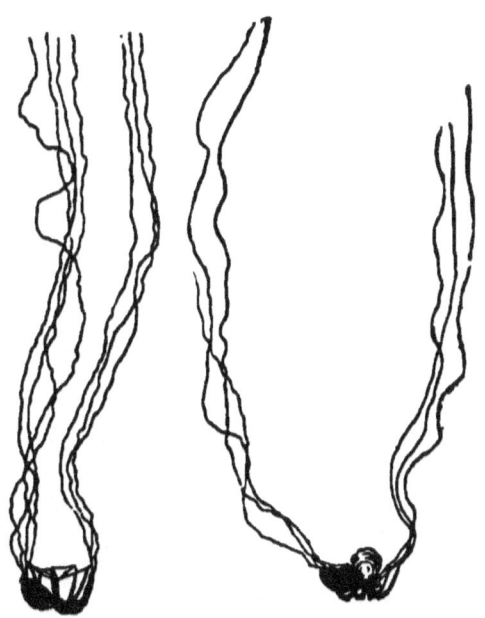

"Lay hold of the ropes!" called a voice from the nearest of these ships of the sky. "We want to descend here. We bear a message from your chief."

A score of willing hands were reached out, and the cords, which

FIG. 57.—"A Balloon Hung Overhead."

by this time dragged upon the ground, were seized. The little vessel, thus steadied, began to descend. It touched the ground in a vacant space between the rioters and the Pixinees. A small Pixie stepped from the basket, and looked inquiringly around. He was dressed in a dark gray coat, with broad white stripes; breeches pale colored and spotted, and a black vest over which a white-haired beard was streaming. He seemed much puzzled at the strange grouping of the

parties around him, who for the most part had kept their
positions, but were looking quietly on, their interest in
the new arrival having nearly soothed their wrath.

"I should like to see Lieutenant
Heady," said the stranger. "I have a
message for him from Captain Spite
and Lieutenant Hide."

FIG. 58.—Gossamer's Balloons.

"I am the person you seek," said Heady, stepping
forward.

"If you will pardon me a moment, Sir," said the
stranger, "and give me some help in getting my comrades anchored, I will deliver my message."

The second of these little voyagers of the air reached a position above the fort, and cast out cords and grapnels. He soon anchored. Then another and another followed until five had safely landed.

The interest of the fort Pixies in these æronauts had now quieted the passions that had been so near fatal explosion. Here was news from their missing officers. All would now be well! By common consent both parties put up their weapons and gathered around the messenger.

"There is nothing secret in my orders, Sir, I think," said the balloonist who had first landed, "My name is Lycosa. Here are my credentials. My orders I will give when you are ready for them."

"Say on, then!" said Heady, "You couldn't have come with them at a luckier time. What news from our chiefs."

"Good news," answered Lycosa; "they crossed the bridge, raided the Brownie camp, seized two of the Nurses—the Commodore's daughter and the Boatswain's —and have them safe on the island to hold as ransom for your safe and quiet departure."

This news was received with unbounded favor and applause, not hearty, ringing cheers such as Brownies give, but a noisy clatter of fangs. The applause ceased and Lycosa resumed.

"The capture of these prisoners was a masterly stroke. The chiefs stole into the Brownie camp, seized their captives from the very headquarters, and made off with them. A scream from one of them aroused the camp. The hue and cry was raised, and by the barest chance Spite and Hide got off to sea on board a smuggler's yacht."

"With their prisoners?"

"Yes, all safe. They are in limbo now, ready to be exchanged if need be. But the Captain hopes to keep them for another and worse difficulty than the present."

Fig. 59—Spite Sends off Lycosa and his Balloon Corps.

"Humph!" grunted Heady, "that would be hard to find, I fancy. Go on!"

"He sends word by me that the old suspension bridge is passable; that a few cables stretched across spans Nos. 1, 2 and 4, will make it a quite good route. I am here with my companions, not only to bring the message, but to do this work of repair."

"But when is it to be done," asked Heady, "and how are we to make a landing in face of the enemy's camp? The Brownies would climb the piers and cut the strands under us; or would send their cavalry up to do it, and attack parties crossing.

"They would swarm on the shore and prevent our landing. They would have us at great disadvantage, for they could destroy us one by one. A pretty plan that! Perhaps our chiefs had better come and try their own chances in it. No! let them send out their she Brownies and try the ransom." Heady spoke with much warmth and the Pixies applauded.

"Not so fast, General," said Lycosa, like a good diplomat conciliating Heady with a high sounding title. "All that has been attended to. The Fringe, a fast yacht, has gone down to the outlet with your officers, to order up the navy. The ships will be anchored off the Old Bridge within two hours. It will then be the hour just before dawn, which you know is the darkest of the night. We can have the bridge ready for travel by that time. Both your chiefs agree that the Brownies will then be quieted down and will sleep more soundly because of this disturbance. One of us, however, is to make a balloon reconnoisance before the start from the fort shall be made, to see whether all is quiet. The navy will land your party as fast as they arrive, and we can get over, it is thought, before daylight. Should the movement be discovered, the ships can resist any onset until all the garrison are off. That is the plan which I bring. The chief orders the trial. If it fails, the ransom plan will not."

Heady looked sullen, shook his head, and meditated

for a few moments. No one spoke. All waited for his decision.

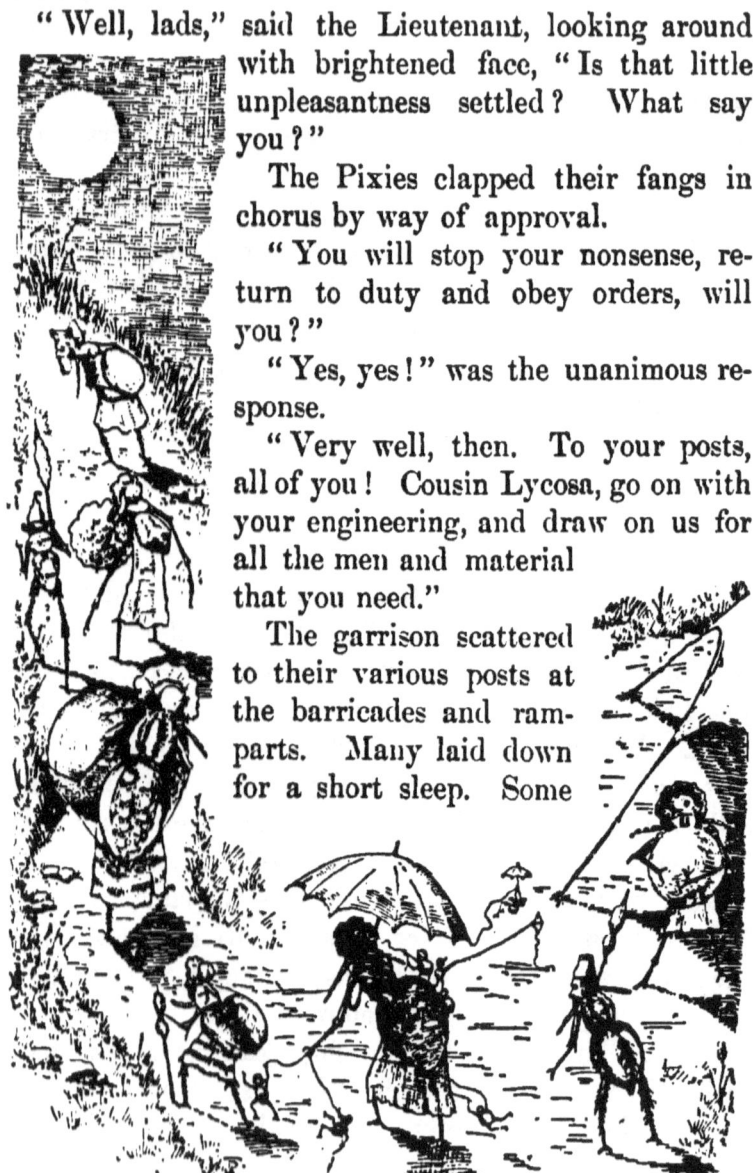

"Well, lads," said the Lieutenant, looking around with brightened face, "Is that little unpleasantness settled? What say you?"

The Pixies clapped their fangs in chorus by way of approval.

"You will stop your nonsense, return to duty and obey orders, will you?"

"Yes, yes!" was the unanimous response.

"Very well, then. To your posts, all of you! Cousin Lycosa, go on with your engineering, and draw on us for all the men and material that you need."

The garrison scattered to their various posts at the barricades and ramparts. Many laid down for a short sleep. Some

FIG. 60.—The Pixinees Leave Fort Spinder, Carrying their Cradles and Babies.

went out with Heady to look after repairs upon the
bridge. The mutiny was over. Once more Spite had
saved Fort Spinder. It was Lycosa and his companions, just alighting upon Aranea's Isle in their balloons, that had fixed the attention of the chief while
the Fringe approached the shore carrying the captive
Nurses. The whole plan of rescue flashed upon his
mind: he would send a balloon message to the fort,
and with it engineers to direct the repair of the Old
Bridge and the proposed escape thereby! Meantime
Hide and himself would bring up the fleet to convey
the garrison across the lake.

Lycosa and his chief assistant Gossamer lost no time
in beginning work. Their balloons were anchored by
strong cords to grass stalks, and hung in the air swaying
backward and forward ready for the embarkation.
They were hammock shaped silken structures, quite
wide at the middle, and gathered into a point at each
end. From the bow and stern floated filaments of silk,
which served the purpose of gas in human inventions
for air locomotion, that is to say, they buoyed up the
balloon so that it floated aloft.

The Pixie aeronaut was seated in or beneath his hammock. Gossamer's hammock or "car," was a rather
broad, close ribbon of silk; but Lycosa's was a light
meshwork affair, just enough for his body to rest upon,
and which he aptly called his basket.* When the time
came to ascend, the stay lines would be cut, the balloons
rise up and be carried along by the breeze. If he wished
to go higher, the balloonist opened his spinnerets, set
his tiny silk factory agoing, and thus by adding to the
number and length of the filaments increased the buoy-
ancy of the machine. If he wished to descend he gathered up the floating lines into a little ball underneath

* Appendix, Note B.

his jaws, something like a seaman reefing sails, and as the surface exposed to the air was diminished, the balloon descended.

"Let go the ropes!" shouted Lycosa, as he climbed by a thread into his car, which swung beneath the netted hammock. The ropes were cut, and away the voyager

FIGS. 61 and 62.—Madame Lycosa and American Dolomede Carrying Their Cocoons.

went to the Old Bridge, followed by his brother balloonists. Assisted by the fort engineers, they stretched new cables across the broken spans, and strengthened the old ones. An hour's steady service finished all needful repairs. Then Lycosa ascended from one of the piers, made a survey of the Brownie camp, returned and reported that the camp had settled into its usual quiet. Rodney and his sailors were off to the inlet. Being certain that the lost Nurses were not in the fort, the Brownies had recalled the extra pickets. There was little more risk in crossing the bridge than had attended the venture of Spite and Hide, especially as a fog now hung over the shore. Lookouts were placed upon the shore pier to watch for the fleet. All baggage and portable material were packed. Some of the Pixinees took their children upon their backs, like Madam Lycosa; others carried their round, silken cradles in their jaws, like Madam Pholcus, or lashed beneath their bodies, like Madam Dolomede. *

Fort Spinder was stripped and ready to be abandoned to its fate.

Soon Lycosa's signal flag was seen flying from above the pier. The fleet was in sight! The

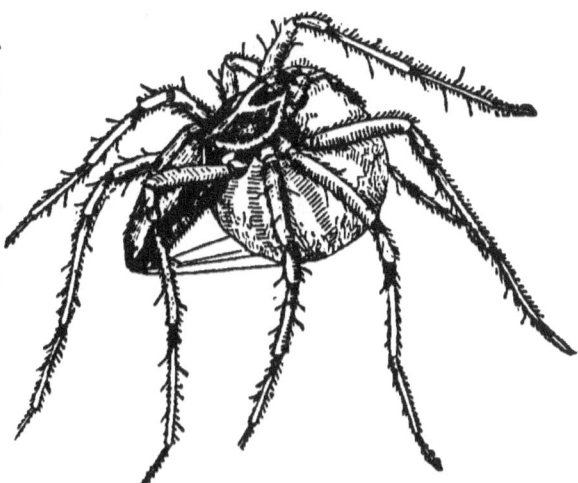

Fig. 63.—Madam English Ocyale Carries Her Cradle Lashed to Her Body.

news was passed rapidly from mouth to mouth along a line of sentinels stationed on the bridge. The garrison was set in motion. In a short space of time the whole force had gone over without accident, and without a sound loud enough to alarm the Brownie pickets, a result much assisted by a contrivance of Lycosa's. To prevent the noise made by vessels mooring to the shore, he caused all the ships to anchor some distance from land. He then attached cords to the masts and bowsprits,

* Appendix, Note C.

and by means of his balloons carried them directly
from the bridge to the ships. Thus there was no
tramping from abutment to lake across the bank. There
were no splash of oars and wash of waves by the plying
of boats from shore to ship.

The last soldiers had embarked. The cables were cut,
the anchors weighed, and with a favoring breeze the fleet
crossed the lake and anchored in Big Cave harbor on
the opposite or orchard shore. One of their camps or
villages was located here, and the wearied Pixies were
disembarked and comfortably housed.

# CHAPTER XVI.

## BROWNIES ON A LARK.

After the evening meal there usually comes a lull in the duties of Brownie camp life. Pickets have been told off and stationed at their posts; camp fires are kindled, and the soldiers gather around the glowing light, stretched upon the grass underneath the shadow of leaves and flowers, or seated on rude stools of pebbles and twigs. In chat and story they forget the fatigues and dangers of a soldier's life. They spin yarns of past adventure, tales of "moving accident by flood and field" and "perils in the imminent deadly breach;" they discuss the chances of the campaign, the strategy and behavior of the enemy, and the merits of their commanders. Jokes, quips, merry anecdotes and witty sayings run around the circle, and ever and anon hearty peals of laughter break out upon the still evening air.

"Ho, lads! Tone down your mirth a bit!" cried the officer of the day to one of these groups, in the camp before Fort Spinder.

"Aye! aye, Sir!" was the response, and for a moment silence fell upon the circle.

"Say, boys," at last exclaimed one of the company, "let's get out of this and go for a lark. I have a capital idea in my head."

"Ho, ho!" cried Brownie Highjinks; "Twadeils really has an idea in his head! I'll warrant it's a lively one. Out with it! I'm for any fun that's not against general orders."

"Well then, lads, come close together and listen."

Twadeils was one of two brothers who had got their somewhat peculiar name from their daring and mischievous spirit which kept them and most people around them in a whirl of excitement and adventure. Their chums nicknamed them the "Twa deils," and the two words at length became one, and the lads were called Twadeils Senior and Twadeils Junior. But among their fellows they were simply known as "Twadeils" and "Junior."

The Brownies grouped themselves around Twadeils, heard his plan, and with little question gave hearty assent. An hour and place of meeting were fixed; and after discussing details of the proposed lark in whispers as they bent over the camp fire, the merry plotters retired to their tents.

In due time they were up and assembled at the rendezvous. The group that now started out upon their secret adventure was made up of Brownies from all arms of the service. The navy was represented by Brownies Barck, Ferrie, Wetman and Obersee; the cavalry by Brownies Gear, Saddler, Martingale, Hosson, Howrode and Barnit; the infantry by Halfrick, Highjinks, Esslade and the two Twadeils. A merry crowd they were and as bold as merry. The story of their night adventure we are now about to tell.

They silently stole from camp; passed the sentries without much trouble, and reached the bank of the lake close by the point where the Brownie picket line touched the water. They were in a shallow depression formed in earlier time by an overflow of the lake. The water rose almost at this point to the surface of the shore, and only a narrow ridge of sand hindered it from flowing down the dry channel over which, indeed, it often ran during freshets.

Twadeils set Obersee and his sailor companions to form a raft. They were handy at such work, and soon had a number of beams lashed together into a rude raft that was secure enough, at least for such adventurers as those who expected to use it. The rest of the company were set to digging at the sandy ridge which banked the lake. All sorts of implements were used, drinking cups, table pans, shovels extemporized from splinters, stalks and chips picked from driftwood on the shore. Indeed, the Brownies had been trained to turn a hand to such duty without use of spades, shovels, picks or other trenching tools.

By the time the raft was ready, a cut had been made through the sand almost to the verge of the lake, and the water had already begun to trickle over the top. Then the final order was given, and all the Brownies fell to with zeal, and removed the remaining sandy barrier. Soon a breach was made in the shore through which the lake water began to pour. The spirits of the Brownies rose with the rising flood, and when at last enough water had entered the channel to float the raft, they let it swing out into the stream, and were afloat upon the swift running current.

Their purpose was now made plain. They intended to drown out the Pixie pickets, overflood and override the barricade, and get into the heart of the Pixie camp. But there were some difficulties in the way that these reckless spirits had not considered. The water was as frisky as themselves, and would not confine itself to the course in which they had expected it to run, but turned hither and thither, crawling among clumps and tufts of weeds, grass and bushes, whose tops presently appeared above the surface of the current, and lay in the way of the raft as it floated down stream.

12

"Look out there in front!" cried the leader; but before the raft could be pushed away it bumped against a bush. Several Brownies were tossed into the stream, and were pulled up with diffi-culty. Now the raft was off again, and its crew, a little more careful, managed to avoid the snags that threatened them in front.

Soon the cry arose: "Look out on the right!" Too late again, for the raft was caught in an eddy and driven among the bushes on the margin of the little torrent. Some of the crew clambered upon the bushes; others plunged into the stream, and by dint of pushing and pulling, and many hearty but subdued calls, and with much laughter, the vessel was released from the bushes and pushed again into the cur-rent. At this moment Ess-lade saw the form of a Pixie upon an overhanging bush. He lay along the stem with arms and legs stretched out before and behind and held close to-gether, thus so tightly em-bracing the plant that it was difficult at first to distinguish him therefrom.

Fig. 64.—Tetragnatha's Mimicry of a Green Twig.

"Aha!" said Esslade, "I know that trick of yours, Master Tetragnatha. I have seen you and your kin try to cheat us before this by snugging yourself along stems of plants, and keeping your great green coat and legs down tight to 'em. You fooled me that way once, but you can't do it again. Here boys, we must get the old rascal out of that!"

So saying he sprang into the bush, laid hold of a limb, and swung himself up to where the Pixie lay. Several of his comrades quickly followed, but Tetragnatha had no mind to meet them in fair combat. He jumped up, and leaped from the stem into the midst of the current. This sudden movement surprised the Brownies. They paused, and gazed wonderingly at their foe, whom they knew to be no water-pixie, and therefore expected to be engulfed in the stream.

"Well," exclaimed Wetman, "that was a foolish trick. Might as well have stayed to be killed as to jump into that current and be drowned; for drowned you surely will be, old fellow."

But Wetman was mistaken. To the surprise of all the Brownies, Tetragnatha instead of sinking, spread his legs upon the water, floated for a moment or two with the current, and then in the face of the stream began slowly to approach the shore.

"What can this mean?" asked Gear. "How does the creature manage it? What sort of hidden machinery has that Pixie within himself to enable him to go contrary to the current into the bushes on yonder shore?"

"Don't know, but we'll try to find out. So after him boys, after him!" cried Twadeils.

The order was quickly obeyed, the raft was swung into the stream, and partly urged by the current, and partly impelled by poles and oars, the Brownies followed the fleeing Pixie and almost overtook him. They were just a little too late, for a moment before the raft touched the shore, Tetragnatha reached a low-hanging twig and climbed to the top of a bush.

The Brownies, however, were determined not to be foiled, so once more a party sprang into the limbs and leaves, and followed the retreating Pixie. Tetragnatha paused a moment, as though considering whether it would be better to meet his enemies in open fight, or a second time try the stream. But his foes were too many, so he leaped upon the water. This time he varied his method, for he made one end of a long cord fast to a branch, meanwhile holding on to the other end, so that when he alighted on the water the cord stretched out behind him. This stayed and buoyed him up as he ran off at full pace upon the surface of the stream.* As he went, the thread stretched out, and seemingly would have made no end of lengthening had not one of the Brownies cut it. Tetragnatha was discomfited only for a moment; then, to the surprise of his pursuers, instead of sinking beneath the flood rode upon it, and turned his course towards the shore. This time, however, the Pixie's way led along a belt of bright moonlight that glimmered through the branches.

"Aha, lads!" exclaimed Rownie, who was standing at the bow watching an opportunity to annoy his enemy, "I see what's the mystery! The Pixie has spread a sail! Look there! you can see it if you stoop low and catch a side view of the silk as it shines in the moonlight! Do you see now? Tetragnatha has lifted his body from the surface of the water and has set his spinning machinery a-going; and now you may see the outspun threads glinting in the moonlight. A long pencil of silken lines is spread out from the spinnerets above him, while at the same time he has fastened his feet together by a little silken raft. The raft buoys him

---

* Appendix, Note A.

FIG. 65.—Pixie Tetragnatha's Escape.—(Illustration by Dan. C. Beard.)

upon the water; the floating filaments act as sails; the wind is blowing right toward the bank yonder, so that in spite of the current which heads off this way, the creature is able to sail over the surface of the water. There he goes!   He is bound to make land."

Rownie had seen truly.   This was another of the tricks of that strange and cunning craft which was continually being unfolded before the Brownies' eyes.   Tetragnatha was now safe on dry land, and scampered off among the bushes.

Once more the adventurers pushed into the current. The stream bore to the opposite side, making a long curve which brought them close up to the picket line of their own troops.

"Hush!" cried Twa-deils, "Yonder is one of our sentinels, close up to the edge of the stream!   Down flat on the raft, every one of you; quick, and lay low till we are quite past." The Brown-ies tumbled at the word

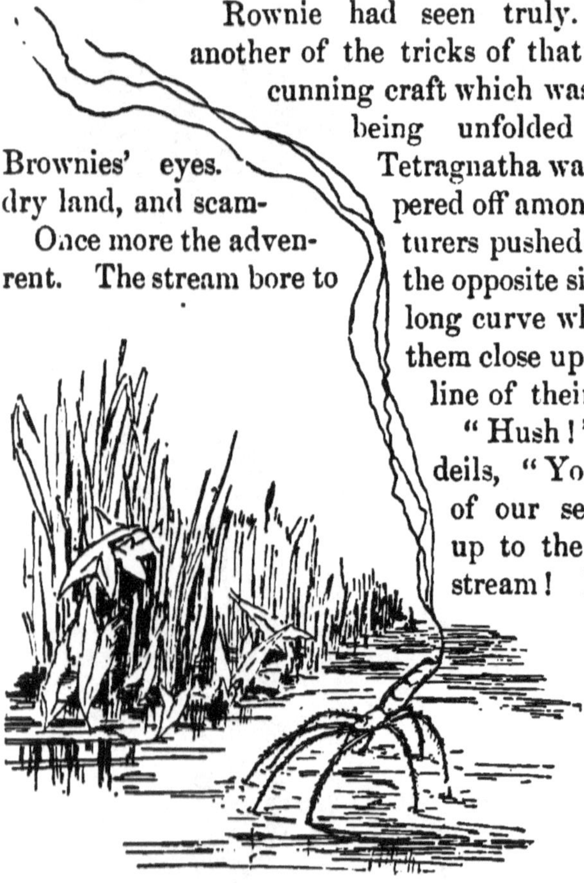

Fig. 66.—Tetragnatha: "The Floating Filaments Act as Sails."

and spread themselves along the logs in as small space as they could assume, although their position was any-thing but comfortable, for the water continually washed over them, or spurted up upon them through the chinks of the raft.

"Ahoy, there!" cried the Brownie sentinel, "What boat is that?"

No answer, and the raft sped silently by.

"Halt, there!" shouted the sentinel, running after the vessel. "Halt, I say, or I will fire on you."

He paused, raised his bow and let fly an arrow. It was well aimed and sank into a log close by the head of Highjinks. Indeed it pierced his Scotch bonnet and tore it from his head. This fidgety Brownie could no longer be restrained, and although the raft had now been carried quite out of reach, he leaped to his feet, pulled out the arrow, waved it and his bonnet above his head, and called to the sentinel, whom he knew well:

"Say, old chappie, save your shots for Pixies. Don't you see, you rascal, you've spoiled my hat, and—"

"Lie down, you ninnie," cried Twadeils in a whisper, "you'll give us away! We'll be stopped, taken back to camp, and put in the guard house, every one of us!"

Thereupon several Brownies quietly pulled Highjinks down upon the logs. By this time the raft had swung round a clump of brushwood, leaving the sentinel gazing in a dazed way after the mysterious vessel. Scarcely had they rounded the point when a huge Pixie darted from the grasses near them, and, after making a few rapid strides upon the current, dived into the stream.

"Hello! here's game," cried Twadeils. "Stop the raft a moment." Ferrie swung the bow around. Saddler and Barnit seized the ropes and jumped into the nearest bushes; then holding back lustily, the clumsy vessel was soon stopped.

"Now get her up to the place where the Pixie went down," said Twadeils. "I know him well. He is one of the Dolomede band of water-pixies. Sixpoint Dolomede they call him. Steady, here he is!"

Looking down into the water the Brownies saw Six-point clinging to the stem of an overflowed plant.

"What a curious looking creature he is!" exclaimed Hosson. "He has put on a coat of armor that shines like silver even through the water. How did he get it?"

"Don't know," exclaimed Halfrick, "but I will see whether it is proof against my spear."

He steadied himself upon the raft and drew back to strike. The sharp implement cut through the water, and as Halfrick leaned over the edge of the raft to watch the result of his stroke, he was suddenly made conscious of an effect very different from that he had counted upon. He could not have been more surprised if an earthquake had struck him.

Sixpoint, at the touch of the spear, unclasped his hold upon the stem, darted upward, and struck with full force against the under part of the bow, which shot upward into the air until the raft stood on one end in the water. It was much as though a huge whale were to come up underneath a fishing boat. Halfrick was heaved into the air like a rocket, and after several somersaults alighted in some near-by boughs. The rest of the company slid along the logs and dropped together into the stream. A more surprised set of Brownies perhaps never was seen. They arose to the surface, sputtering and struggling, and one after another laid hold of the raft, which had now righted itself. But as they climbed up at one end, Sixpoint clambered upon the other. His weight dragged the bow under the water, and the stern tossed into the air throwing the Brownies forward. They were flung directly upon the great Pixie, who was as much surprised by the sudden movement, which he took for an assault, as were the Brownies themselves, and

FIG. 67.—Pixie Sixpoint Upsets the Raft.—(Illustration by Dan. C. Beard.)

backed off into the stream dragging down the bow with him.

Meantime the Brownies had returned toward the stern of the raft, and as Sixpoint let go his hold the bow rose in the water. This see-sawing of the vessel and the oddity of the proceeding touched the Brownies' risibilities, and they began to laugh. Soon the whole party were in a tumult of mirth, in the midst of which Dolomede gravely thrust out his forepaws, deliberately climbed upon the raft and began to look around. Thereupon several of the Brownies dropped into the water beside the logs. Among these was Gear, who, while he floundered about and ducked his head, said, " Wh—wh—what's become of the brute's armor? don't you see he has stripped it off? Wh—what do you think he has d—d—done with it ? "

" Such a fellow ! " said Junior, who was treading water beside Gear, " I believe you would ask questions and study problems in Natural History if you were dying. Here lads, " he added, " it's a burning shame that this Pixie has possession of our raft. Let's up and at him ! "

The party climbed out of the water, drew their weapons and cautiously advanced, but Sixpoint thought discretion the better part of valor, for, without waiting for his enemies to attack, he dropped into the stream and sank beneath the surface. The Brownies rushed to the edge of the raft just in time to see the Pixie moving out of reach from stem to stem of the submerged plants.

" Look, boys ! " cried Gear, " He has his silver armor on again. How is the thing done? It looks like magic ! "

" Suppose you dive down and ask the old fellow, dear boy, " said Highjinks. " No doubt he will lend you a brand new suit for yourself, if you like."

Dolomede was by this time quite hidden from view, and any attempt to follow would have been vain. So

Twadeils ordered all hands aboard, and once more set sail.

Perhaps we may stop to explain the point that puzzled Gear. The silver armor was nothing, in fact, but bubbles

Fig. 68.—"The Triple-Decked Tower of Linyphia."

of air that clung to Sixpoint's hairy coat. It is the fashion of water-pixies to spread out the numerous hairs upon their furry skins just as they plunge beneath the surface of the water. Portions of air within the spaces between the hairs cling around the body, held thereto by the pressure of the surrounding water. This air gathers in round bubbles which shine like silver, and have somewhat the appearance of a coat of mail. They probably furnish the air for the creature to breathe while in the water, and they of course disappear into the atmosphere the moment the surface is reached.

Once more the Brownies were afloat, and now they drew near the barricades, and saw the damage wrought by the flood upon the Pixie defences. The water had overflowed the demilune, so that only the end towers showed above the surface ; and these swayed to and fro before the force of the rushing current and under the weight of the Pixie sentinels who, as it seemed to the Brownies, must have been driven to refuge within them, so suddenly had the flood broken out. The triple-decked tower of Linyphia was crowded with these fugitives.

"Now, lads," said Twadeils, "here's our chance for fine sport. What say you? Shall we push our raft right over the barricade to the gate of the fort? Or stop and pick up some of the fellows imprisoned here in the towers?"

"It is bad policy to leave an enemy in one's rear," said Rownie.

"You mean that a Pixie in a bush is worth two in a fort, don't you?" exclaimed Ferrie.

"It will soon be time for us to be in our quarters," said Howrode, pointing to the faint blush of coming dawn in the eastern horizon. "If we are not in by reveille it will be rather hard on us. We will not be able to get through more work than we can find here among these towers."

These opinions were heartily endorsed by the majority of the party, and the raft was directed toward one of the central towers.

# CHAPTER XVII.

## HOW THE LARK ENDED.

The water had risen around the demilune, covering the entire line of works except the tall towers above the two ends and on either side of the central gate. The raft was steered toward the tower at the western end. This was a dome-shaped structure wrought by bending together and lashing several leaves, which then looked like the crown of a peaked hat. The inside was neatly tapestried with silk, and on all sides of the opening, which looked downward, were strung guy ropes and cross lines. Above the whole, was curved, like the plume of a helmet, a leaf with a long stem, whose point was bent downward and fastened to the roof.* This formed a watch tower or lookout for a sentinel who could thence scan the surrounding space and give warning of approaching danger.

"Yonder is the lookout, lads!" said Twadeils as the raft swung toward the tower; "but he seems to be taking it very coolly, for although he must see us, he makes no sign of giving warning. But, we had better not trust to that; push on as fast as possible, and put him beyond the power of raising an alarm. Give way, lads, give way heartily!"

"Aye, aye, Sir!" was the answer, and the raft soon lay alongside the tower.

"Fasten the painter to one of those lines," was the next order. "Gear, you may lead the cavalrymen to the lookout, and I'll head the attack on the main tower."

* Appendix, Note A.

(153)

"All right," said Gear ; " I know the company which the fellow up there belongs to.   A keen lot they are, too, as bright as the scarlet uniform that gives them the name of the ' Cardinal Company.' *   Come on, Brownies ! "

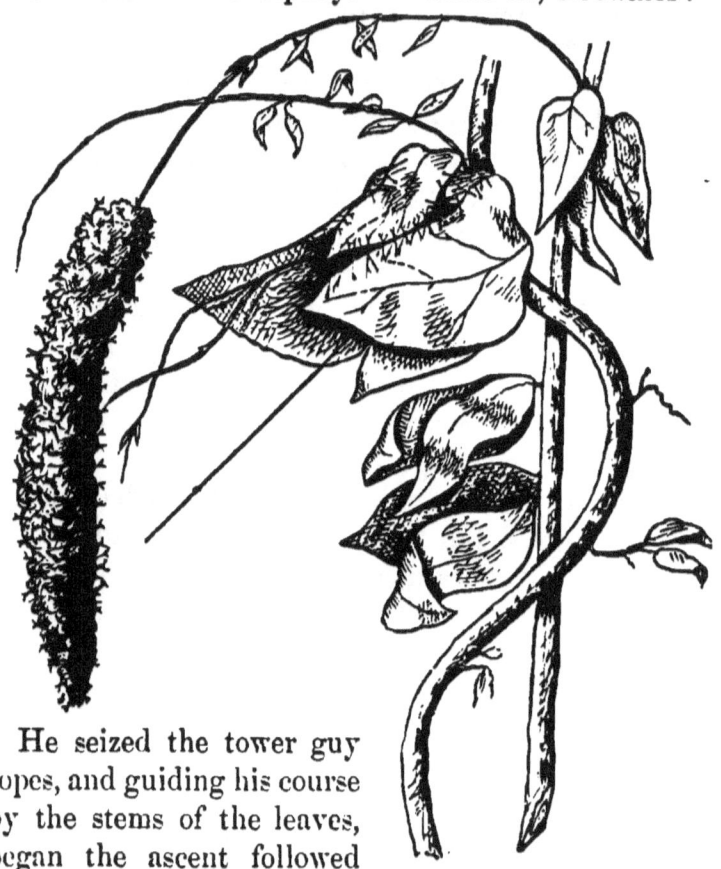

He seized the tower guy ropes, and guiding his course by the stems of the leaves, began the ascent followed closely by his comrades, Sad-dler, Halfrick and Barnit.

FIG. 69.—Leaves Lashed or Sewed Into a Turret Den.

Up they went, hand over hand, everyone trying to beat his leader to the top, which they were not long in reach-ing.   As they hung at the edge a moment and looked over it, they saw the Pixie watchman standing rampant

<hr />

* Appendix, Note B.

at the opposite side of the lookout. His scarlet tunic shone bright in the moonlight, and the metallic green of his fangs glistened as he gnashed them together in defiance.

"Surrender!" shouted Gear.

Cardinalis shook one arm threatingly by way of answer. The Brownies now made a rush toward the Pixie, but before they could reach him he vaulted into the air, and pass-ing over his as-sailants' heads, lit on the oppo-site side of the lookout. The Brownies could not check their speed and tum-bled against and over one another, as they reached the spot where the Pixie had stood.

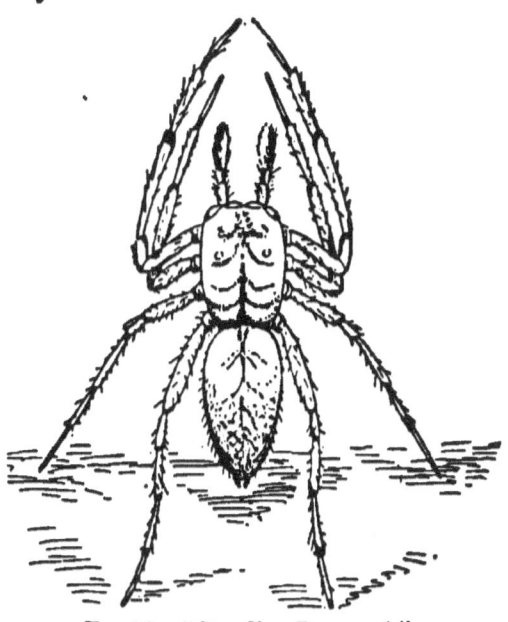

FIG. 70.—"Standing Rampant."

"Well jump-ed," cried Gear, recovering himself, "but you shall not miss us next time." He seized the dragline, which the vaulting legionaries always stretch behind them when they jump, and gave it a stout tug as he faced about. Cardinalis cut the line with his claw, and turning sharply faced his foes, and as they approached backed quietly down the stem of the leaf to the roof of the tower.*

"Foiled again," cried Gear, as the squad of Brownies

* Appendix, Note C.

scurried after the retreating Pixie, "but you can't escape us a third time." His boast was too soon made, however, for before his party could reach the tower, Cardinalis had scampered down the guy ropes to the Brownie raft. Thither he was followed by Gear and his men who were now well warmed to their work and boiling with vexation at their two failures. Halfrick was the first to reach the raft, and as he charged with poised spear, Cardinalis sprang upon him. Halfrick sank upon

FIG. 71.—"Well jumped!"

one knee, dropped the end of his spear to the deck, and received upon the point the force of the assault. The spear point penetrated the Pixie's breast, but the staff was shattered, and Halfrick borne to the deck. His comrades were at his side in an instant, but before he was relieved, the dying Pixie buried his fangs in his shoulder.

"Has any one a cruse of Lily Balm?" asked Gear. No one answered. The thoughtless fellows had not counted upon accidents and wounds when they planned their lark.

"Too bad, too bad!" Gear exclaimed. "But we must do the next best thing." He tore the skirts of his coat into strips and tied a bandage tightly around the shoulder between the hurt part and the body. He then put his lips to the wound and sucked the poison into his mouth. Halfrick had already fallen into a stupor, and was laid in an easy position upon the raft, where his comrades watched him with sad countenances.

In the meanwhile how fared it with Twadeils and his

party? They had little difficulty in mounting to the tower, but as they entered the leafy dome, they found themselves faced by the huge proportions of Shamrock, the tower-keeper. Near him were two Pixies belonging to the Vaulting Legion who had taken refuge from the flood within the tower, and whose bright eyes shone out of the deep shadows wherein they lay.

The Brownies had a hard task before them, for they must hang to the tapestried sides of the tower with one hand, while they kept the sword arm free. Moreover, they were to attack from beneath, and face an assault which coming from above would be much more serious. But they knew nothing of fear and little of prudence, and pushed on holding their swords above them, which thus formed a bristling circle of points against which their enemies must cast themselves if they chose to attack. The moonlight shone brightly upon objects beneath, but little got within the dome, and all above them was in shadow; only the outlines of the Pixies dimly showed against the white tapestry of the walls.

Silently and slowly, but steadily the circle of Brownie sword points moved upward into the shadow, narrowing as they rose. The affray promised to be a bloody one, and even the most reckless of the party had begun to feel the sobriety of the moment, when the advance was suddenly arrested by a voice calling from above them.

"Halt! We surrender!" It was Pixie Shamrock that spoke.

"Halt!" echoed Twadeils, although the command was scarcely needed, for his company had stopped at the first word. Yet, they suspected a Pixie trick, and every arm held the sword blade more firmly, and all eyes were more keenly on the alert.

Shamrock perceived that the Brownies distrusted him,

and again spoke: "We are in earnest. No trick is intended. Descend, and we will follow you and give ourselves up. We have good reasons for our strange action. We have been deserted and deceived by Spite the Spy and our own friends, and shall not now throw our lives away to please or profit them. You may trust my word."

After a brief whispered consultation, Twadeils concluded it wise policy to accept the offered surrender, and gave orders to descend. It must be confessed that he was glad to do this, for he began to fear that serious results would follow, and even that if they should be victorious, precious lives would be lost. There was no relaxing vigilance as the Brownies descended, and when they reached the raft and saw the senseless form of Halfrick stretched upon the deck, they were still better satisfied that they had found so easy an issue from their adventure.

FIG. 72.—Shamrock's Fernleaf Tower.

The Pixies, true to their word for once at least, came down quietly, and let themselves be bound, after which Shamrock told the following story, which seemed strange indeed to his captors : " Our sentries were stationed last evening as usual, although it was expected that Fort Spinder would be abandoned some time during the night. 'Keep up an active patrol,' said the Captain of the Guard. 'Show yourselves freely to the enemy's pickets, until you get orders from me to retire. Then quietly and hastily withdraw from your posts, and we will go off in the last ship load.'

" That seemed all right, and the sentinels on duty, of whom we are a part, suspected nothing when, during the night, the relief guard were ordered to headquarters under pretence of receiving some secret instructions from the Chief. But they never returned. We kept watch long after the time for changing guard ; no corporal appeared. Then we sent a messenger to the fort to see what was the matter. He soon returned saying that the fort was abandoned. Not a Pixie was left except the sentinels at the posts ! We had been fooled, betrayed, deserted and given over to death by our selfish Chief, who left us as decoys to keep up the appearance that the fort was occupied, in order to deceive you Brownies. A madder lot of Pixies never was seen. If we could have gotten hold of our chiefs we would have made mincemeat of them in short order.

" But storming and swearing didn't help matters. What should we do? That was the question. We even thought of going straight to your camp and blowing on the whole mean pack, and would have done it, I think, only we feared you folks would think it a bit of Spite's strategy and cut our throats for our pains. In the midst of our deliberations a flood burst upon us from some unseen quarter. The very witches seemed to be abroad and conspiring against us. We could not imagine the source, as there was no rain. The water-pixies readily escaped to the land and are now in hiding somewhere, but the rest of us fled from point to point until at last we were cooped up in the towers. Now you can understand why, being thus betrayed, confused and mystified, we had little stomach for fighting, and preferred to surrender, if for nothing else than to get even with our miserable dog of a chief, Spite the Spy. If you'll take the trouble to go to the other towers you'll probably find all our comrades in the same mood."

Here was startling news indeed for the Brownies! What should they do? At all events, they wouldn't tell their prisoners that they were only a chance squad of runaways out on a lark! Some serious duty seemed to be before them. The suggestion to visit the other towers and bag all the Pixies therein was a strong temptation; but ought they not now to push straight to camp? An unlooked for circumstance brought the question to a swift conclusion.

The water began to subside almost as rapidly as it had risen, but the Brownies were so intent upon Shamrock's story that they failed to note the fact. The raft's bow had been tied by a short rope to the tower, and as the water ran out, the stern of the vessel gradually settled, and by the time the Pixie tale was fairly told, was quite out of water and loosely lodged upon a clump of grasses. Suddenly these gave way and the raft began to tilt into an inclined plane.

"Look out, lads!" cried Hosson, "Hold fast all! The raft's upsetting!" The warning came just in time to allow Halfrick's attendants to seize and save him from being shot into the stream. Highjinks, finding himself slipping down, flung himself into the water by a double somersault, and several others joined him, while those who clung to the raft were flung together in a huddle, Brownies and Pixies sprawling over and clinging to one another. Wetman, who chanced to be near the bow, clambered up and cut the painter, whereupon the raft fell into the stream with a splash, and the water washing over the deck gave the crew a ducking. The incident excited the mirthfulness of the Brownies, who broke into merry laughter, and those on board began to chaff those in the stream. Some one hailed Highjinks, who was cutting lively antics in the water, and struck up a familiar doggerel, something after the fashion of modern college ditties.

I.

" Here, dear
Little son,
Go slow,
Do not run!"
Go slow—oh—*er!*

II.

"Down town
Do not stray,
There dare
Not to play!"
Not to play—ay—*er!*

III.

"Near here
Is a well.
Poor More
In it fell."
In it fell—el—*er!*

No sooner was the song started than all the crew joined in it. The strain was a dolorous one, and the refrain ended in a peculiar note on the syllable "er," combining something of a sigh, a shriek and a grunt, upon which all the singers laid the full stress of their voices, and stopped with a sudden jerk. The whole effect was comical; and the third verse seemed so pat to the case in hand that it was followed by a roar of laughter that fairly raised the night echoes.

Ferrie, who was something of a wag, saw Gear splashing and spluttering in vain efforts to ascend the raft, for he was but an indifferent swimmer, and broke into an extemporized verse:

> Here, dear
> Little Gear,
> Come quick
> And I'll pick
> You out of the creek—eek—*er!*

The effort was hailed with applause, and the refrain was repeated with rousing effect by the chorus:

> Out of the creek—eck—*er!*

Gear took the sally good naturedly, and as he was quite as quick at repartée as Ferrie, sang back from the waves, sputtering and stuttering as he sang:

> M—m—Merrie Ferrie,
> Sh—sh—shallow fellow,
> Shut quick,
> Or I'll stick
> You into the creek—eek—*er!*

"Good!" shouted the Brownies, with another hearty peal of laughter, as they repeated the refrain. What a trifling matter will pass for genuine wit among friends who are all in a good humor, and ready to be pleased with every honest attempt at innocent fun!

But Twadeils thought that matters had gone quite far enough, indeed, too far. "Come, come, lads," he said, "this must end. Matters have taken too serious a turn for further mirth. Our lark must end just here. Pull the raft to shore."

"All right, Captain," said Highjinks, who had drawn himself out of the water, and stood on the end of the raft shaking himself with many grimaces. "I'll reduce myself to order, and help reduce your order to execution." Whereupon he plunged again into the flood, and aided by one or two others soon had the raft free from the entangling remains of the demilune. In a few moments it touched the bank where, with some merry words of mock farewell, it was abandoned.

Twadeils now called his comrades around him. "Brownies," he said, "our adventure has taken a more serious and important turn than I had expected. We have a wounded comrade whom we must get into the hospital as soon as possible; we have these prisoners to deliver to Captain Bruce, and above all we have news of the utmost value, which ought not to be held back a moment longer than necessary."

"But is the news true, comrade?" interrupted Gear. "Aren't we being gulled by these Pixies? Lying is their native speech."

"I have thought of that," replied Twadeils, "and am not willing to go into camp with such a story on the naked word of our prisoners; although I believe, from several circumstantial proofs, that they have told the truth this time, if never before. I propose to send out a scout to find out the facts. We shall wait here for his report. What say you?"

All agreed with their leader, and the whole party clamored to be sent as scouts; but Twadeils appointed his brother Junior, with Barck and Howroad. Junior pushed toward the fort, gradually bearing in the direction of the central gate. Soon the party passed a clump of ox-eyed daisies whose tall blooms towered above the fort walls.

"Here is a good place to make an observation," said Junior. "Barck, mount that tallest stem and tell us what you see."

Barck as a sailor was well used to climbing, and in a few moments reached the blossom; but just as he was

clambering over the edge of the white leaves, he seemed to miss his footing and fell to the ground. His fall was broken by a clump of grass, but he lay stunned and motionless.

His comrades ran to him and tried to restore him. "I never knew Barck to make a slip of that sort before," said Howroad; "he's one of the surest footed topmen in the fleet, and can climb like a monkey."

"True enough," said Junior, "and I don't understand it, but we must not allow this accident to thwart our purpose. Do you watch our comrade, and I'll try my luck at climbing for an observation."

FIGS. 73 and 74.—"Standing Rampant, with Claws Uplifted as Though to Strike."

So saying, he began the ascent, and as he was a skillful athlete readily reached the top. He took the precaution to peep over the edge before he got upon the flower, but saw nothing. The coast was clear! He stood up and turned to survey the fort, but was startled by a rustling noise at the further margin of the daisy. He turned, and drew his sword.

" Who is here?" he demanded.

There was no answer. But now gazing steadily in the direction from which the sound came, he saw the dim outlines of a Pixie standing rampant with claws uplifted as though to strike. The mystery of Barck's fall was solved ! Junior recognized in the creature before him one of the Laterigrade Legion, a well known character. His uniform was generally yellow, and he was in the habit of ambushing in yellow flowers. The daisy was a favorite resort wherein he would lay alone for many days, hugging the yellow heart of the large flower, and quite concealed from a careless observer. Sometimes he resorted to other plants, and then his uni-

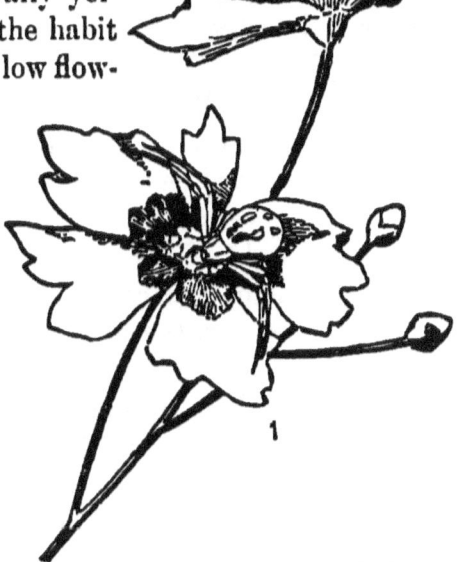

FIG. 75.—Turncoat Tom on a Daisy.
(Misumena vatia).

form took the tint of their flowers, a fact which gave him the popular name of Turncoat Tom.* As Barck had clambered upon the daisy unthinking of danger, Turncoat Tom had struck him on the head, and the mariner, quite off his guard, was knocked to the ground.

---

* The author seems to have in view a well-known Thomisoid spider, known both in Europe and America as Misumena vatia.—ED.

"You miserable, sneaking Turncoat," cried the Brownie, wrathful at his friend's mishap. "You shall pay for this dearly!" and thereupon he assaulted the Pixie furiously.

A duel on a daisy! It was a strange occurrence even in Brownie world. The duel was of short duration, for a skillful stroke of Junior's sword severed one of Turncoat Tom's claws, whereupon he sidled, crabwise, over the edge of the daisy, after the fashion of his tribe, and leaped sheer of the flower into the grass beneath, fortunately on the side opposite to where Barck lay. Junior peered over the edge and saw the form of his wounded adversary glide into the shadows and disappear.

"Well," said the Brownie, as he put up his sword, "I dare say that is another of the abandoned sentinels, and he has been punished enough. Let him go!"

He turned once more to survey the fort, which lay under the full light of the moon, quite exposed in every part. It was silent as a cemetery. Not a sentinel was seen at the gates, on the walls, on the towers, or on the parade ground. Not a boat lay at the landing. Not a sign of life anywhere except on the Arenicola tower, where the grim flag of the Pixies floated from its staff, having evidently been left, like the sentinels of the demilune, to keep up the impression that the fort was still occupied.

Well satisfied, Junior descended and was pleased to find that Barck had now recovered consciousness. He had no idea what had happened to him, only knowing that as he crawled upon the daisy a sudden stroke, like a shock of electricity, had fallen upon his head and smitten him to the ground. With a sailor's superstition, he was disposed to think the fall the result of some miserable witch work. Junior having relieved his mind

FIG. 76.—"A Duel on a Daisy." Junior and Turncoat Tom.

(167)

on this subject, dispatched Howroad to report to his brother and recommend that all the Brownies join him with their prisoners. Twadeils approved, and by the time the party had come up Barck was well enough to join in the march with a little aid, and was soon as lively as the rest.

All were now in the best of spirits. Twadeils resolved to pass through the fort by the central gate, go out by the water gate, and re-enter camp by the lake front.

"Lads," he said, when he had told his plans, "we had expected to slip through the lines before reveille, be safe in our quarters for morning duty, and keep our lark to ourselves as a theme for campfire yarns. But all that is now done for. Public duty requires us to go in openly and make a full breast of all our doings. We deserve punishment, of course, and shall get it; but we may hope to get off easily, for we bring great news. Then, we have three Pixie prisoners; and as we go through the fort we will haul down yonder black flag and carry it home as a trophy, and a rare one it will be. The one drawback to all this is poor Halfrick there. But let us hope that the Nurses can yet pull him through safely. And now, attention! Forward, march!"

Off they set, then, in high spirits, which, however, they faithfully kept within the bounds of quiet mirthfulness. They moved cautiously until they had passed the central gate; but once within the fort, they found that the place was beyond doubt deserted. Hosson and Wetman were sent aloft to pull down the Pixie flag from Arenicola's Tower, and having secured this valued trophy, they hurried homeward. Notwithstanding their leader's warning, the highly excited Brownies could not wholly restrain their joy as this emblem of their wicked enemy's power descended from the proud place where it had floated in triumph and defiance. Highjinks started in a jubilant voice a popular camp song, which seemed quite pat to the occasion. His comrades at once united with him in the rollicking strain, whose chorus at least we may venture to quote.

> " Del-en-*do* est Car-tha-*go !*"
> Car-tha-*go* has got to go ;
> For the Romans, don't you know,
> They have sworn it shall be so.
> Car-tha-*go* has got to go !
> " Del-en-*do* est Car-tha-*go !* "

Think of it! A Brownie scouting party singing a Brownie camp song in the centre of a Pixie fort! It was an inspiring thought, and with a ringing stress upon the refrain that woke loud echoes through the silent streets, halls, and towers of Fort Spinder, the Brownies sang.

Then with three cheers and a tiger, the jolly crew once more yielded to Twadeils' remonstrance, composed themselves to quietude and marched briskly away. Nevertheless, frequently as they moved along they kept time to the hummed notes of the chorus :

> " Del-en-*do* est Car-tha-*go !* "
> Car-tha-*go* has got to *go !*

# CHAPTER XVIII.

## WOOED BUT NOT WON.

Notwithstanding the fatigues of the day and night Spite did not seek rest. Leaving the command of Orchard Camp with Hide, he went aboard the "Fringe" and sailed over to the island. The boat was run in under the willows, and at his own request Raft went with Spite to the lodge of Dame Tigrina.

"You would be more welcome if you'd come at a respectable season," was the greeting which the old creature gave her master.

"Well, well, mother, you must bear with me this time. It isn't often I trouble you. And, you know, you never lose anything by serving me. How are your new boarders? Asleep, I hope?"

"Asleep? not they! They have done nothing the whole night but weep, and pray, and bemoan their condition."

"Poor things!" said Spite, "I suppose they are pining to see me, again! Hey, mother?"

Dame Tigrina showed her fangs in what was intended for a grin, and led the way into the "Brownie Bower," as Spite merrily called the place where Faith and Sophia were confined.

"Good morning, my pretty birds," said the chief, as he entered the chamber. "It is rather early for a call of ceremony on young ladies. But, really, you must excuse me for once, as time is precious just now. Besides, I come on business,—business of great importance. And that is always a good excuse for untimely visits."

The Nurses rose as the Pixies entered the room. They stood with arms clasped about each other, casting beseeching glances at their dread enemy, but saying nothing.

"Come, Mistress Faith," continued Spite, "I have some private words to speak to you. Now no scenes, please! If you want to be well treated act sensibly. There, Sophie, you can go to the other side of the room. What I have to say concerns Faith alone."

He loosened the clasped arms of the captives and led Faith aside. The Brownie maiden shrank back from the Pixie's approach, drew herself up and stood facing her persecutor. Her face was sad almost to despair, but a quiet firmness in her eyes showed that although she thought best to be silent, she had braced herself to resist or suffer to the utmost.

"I am a plain, rough-spoken person, Faith," began Spite, "and I shall waste no words in telling you my wish and purpose. I love you. I want you for a wife. I mean to marry you."

Faith started, shrank back yet further, drew herself up yet more, but remained silent.

"I don't wish to marry in my own race, for reasons which I do not care to explain. But I have long felt the need of some one to preside over my household. I have chosen you to that honor. Are you ready to accept it without more ado?"

Faith's cheeks blushed crimson at these words. Her eyes flashed as she answered: "Spite, chief, Pixie, fiend! —whatever you call yourself, what evil spirit could have devised such an unholy scheme? Faith ally herself with you? Never! Do the worst you can do at once. I can die. I am not afraid to die. Strike! But say no more of a matter the very thought of which is revolting." She spoke quietly, but there were firmness and fire in her tones before which even Spite quailed for a moment.

He was not long abashed. "That sounds very fine," he replied, "and I suppose is the proper thing to say, and all that, in such cases. Let us take all such high and virtuous stuff for granted, however, and come straight to business. Now first, you have such an offer as no Brownie ever yet dreamed of. You may be queen of the Pixies. You shall have a palace—yes, a score of palaces if you like. Servants, honors, garments of the richest silk, table luxuries from air and earth and water—everything that heart could possibly wish of honor, riches and comfort shall be yours. What have you to say to that?"

"That not all the kingdoms of this earth, could you bestow them on me, would buy me to be a Pixie's bride."

"Then, second," continued Spite, not noticing the reply, "you will be in a position to act as a mediator between your people and ours. You could have many opportunities for doing good to your friends and kin. The alliance which I propose would also give you a power for good over our people. Even if you were asked to make a sacrifice, it would be your duty to do so since thereby you would widen the sphere of your influence. What do you say to that?"

"I say, as I have ever been taught, that it is not lawful to do evil that good may come. It is a delusion and a snare to say that such a wicked union as you ask could have any other than a disastrous end."

"Then, third," continued Spite with the same cool indifference to Faith's indignant words, "third and last, you might as well submit gracefully to your destiny. You can't help yourself. You are in my hands. I shall marry you whether you like or no. You will only bring sorrow and pain upon yourself and friends by your stubbornness, and will do no good in the end. I have finished my business. I don't mean to press it just now. Think over it carefully. If your good sense is equal to your reputation, you will conclude to live queen of the Pixies, with a good heart. The next time I come I shall expect to have your betrothal kiss. I leave you now to refresh yourself with sleep. Good night!"

While Spite was thus addressing Faith, Sophia in the other end of the room was approached by the smuggler.

"Oh, Sir," she cried, "you showed us kindness on the boat. I know you must have a good heart, even if you are a Pixie. Have pity on us, and save us from this horrible dungeon."

"Softly, softly, my pretty lass," responded Raft. "You are right enough in thinking that I pity you. But it is not so easy always to indulge one's self in that luxury. It would be a mighty costly one if I were to carry it to the length you ask. But I have a proposal that may make it all right. There, listen coolly. Don't cry, please! That quite unmans me. You can get out of this trouble in an easy and pleasant way.

"Get out of this trouble?" repeated Sophia with hope and joy. "Quick, tell me how!"

"So! I am ordered by Lieutenant Hide, who is second in command over the Pixies, you know, to propose marriage to you in the name of his oldest son Halfway."

"Oh! you are mocking me!" cried Sophia, clasping her hands, and her countenance changing from hope to horror. "You cannot mean that?"

"No, certainly I am not mocking," said Raft mistaking her meaning; "he's in dead earnest, I am sure, and will stand by his proposal. He means just what he says. He wants a Brownie wife for his boy."

14

"O Sir," exclaimed Sophia quickly, "you misunderstand me. Nothing could induce me to listen a moment to such a proposal. I would never, never marry him!"

"Ah! that's the way the wind blows, hey? Well, there's no accounting for tastes. Young Halfway is counted a likely chap, and the best match in the country. There are scores of young Pixinees who would jump at such an offer."

"Don't speak of it! It is an insult. I would die a thousand deaths first. Never, never!"

"Well, well, you needn't go on so about it. I'm sure I meant you no harm, and I've done my duty to my captain. Hide can't gainsay that."

Sophia sank upon a cushion and wept violently. Raft looked upon her tenderly. At last he spoke:

"Look here, Miss Sophia, it may be that you'd take more kindly to a sea life, now, than to one on shore. If you can't marry Halfway, what do you say to Raft? You will be free as air to come and go, and be queen of the "Fringe," the fastest yacht upon the waters. You shall have no captains or lieutenants over you, nor anything else, but your own sweet will and choice. You can visit your kin when you please, spend half the time with them if you like. And, maybe, they would be willing to have me spend a good deal of time with you in the Brownie camp. P'raps I might take to Brownie ways, by and by, and turn out a sort of fairy myself. Who knows? What say you, my pretty? Speak up and don't fear! If you'll give me the right to call you my own, I can find the way out of this cave for you and your friend Faith too, I'll be bound! Well, what is it?"

Sophia's amazement during this address was unbounded. She dropped her hands upon her lap, lifted

her face and with round wondering eyes gazed in a be-
wildered way upon the smuggler. Her heart had been
somewhat drawn toward Raft on account of his kindness. The one glint of sunshine in all the deep darkness
and horror of their position, had been the rough courtesy
of this Pixie sailor. But to marry him? Oh! how
could she listen to such a proposal?

Yet she dared not stop Raft lest she should anger the
only one who had shown himself friendly. If she
should speak out her whole heart, would he not turn
against her and Faith with bitterness? Then, for just
one brief moment—the thought of her helplessness
flashed upon Sophia's mind. All was lost to them.
They were already as those who had gone down among
the tombs. Would it not be right for her to save Faith,
at least, by complying? Faith would be free!—Raft
had promised it. She herself might be delivered from
the power of Spite and Hide, who would compel her to
marry Halfway. True, she would be a Pixie's wife.
But how much better Raft than Halfway! How much
better to be free upon the Fringe, than imprisoned in
Dame Tigrina's halls? To be permitted to see home
and friends as often as she wished! Ought she not to
make the sacrifice, and save dear Faith?

The temptation flashed before her imagination for a
moment—only for a moment. With a shudder, and a
blush of self-reproach that she had even allowed the
thought to rise, she put the temptation aside.

"O Sir," she exclaimed, bursting into tears, "I pray
you say no more! You have showed me some kindness; have pity on me now. I cannot do what you ask.
I am betrothed to Sergeant True. The laws of my race
would not allow a marriage with you or any other of
your people. Such concord, fellowship, and communion

we may never hold with Pixies. We dare not be thus
unequally yoked together. Indeed, I would not offend
you, but—"

"Tut, tut," exclaimed the smuggler interrupting her,
"there's no offence in particular. If you don't accept,
it's your own look out. However, I can do nothing for
you in that case. If you were my wife now, I should
have a right to protect you and yours against all my
kith and kin. I would do it, too! But as you don't
choose that, I must e'en stand by my employer, and do
the best I can for him. So, say no more about it.
There! the chief is ready to leave, I see, and so good-
night!"

The two Pixies left the room, and Faith and Sophia
were once more alone. Their grief was pitiful to see.
There was not a ray of hope for them. O that they
were dead! or, that they had never been born! So they
moaned, and wept in each other's arms for long, long
hours, until Nature hushed their anguish into the for-
getfulness of sleep.

While the Pixie chief was off upon his mission of un-
righteousness, the Brownie captain had also gone upon
a journey. Leaving the command to MacWhirlie he
started for the mansion with Blythe and True. The
old Dutch clock in the hall rang out the hour of four
as they entered the chamber window by the Virginia
creeper that covered the side of the house. Night was
beginning to yield before the advance of coming day,

> "And now Aurora, daughter of the Dawn,
> With rosy lustre purpled o'er the lawn."

How sweet, fresh and still the old place looked after
the trials, fatigues and perils of the past day and night!
But there was no time to indulge pleasant sentiment.
Many dear interests hung upon their haste. They crept

through the window blinds, and mounted the bed posts
to the coverlid close by the sleeping Governor.

Bruce spoke. Wille turned uneasily in his sleep, but
made no answer. Blythe touched his face with a sword
handle. The Governor threw up his hand, opened his
eyes, plucked at the netting of the canopy and muttered,

"I say, wife, the mosquitoes have got under the bar.
It's very annoying!" Then he lay down again to sleep.

Once more Bruce spoke, but more loudly, "Governor
Wille, Wille, Wille!"

"Oh dear!" sighed the sleeping man, "I do think
the everlasting singing of those mosquitoes is worse than
their bite. Couldn't you keep them out, wife?"

"Come, come," cried Bruce impatiently, "It is we—
the Brownies. Wake up! Wake, and listen to us, if
you have any love or pity for your old friends."

Governor Wille was now aroused and sat up in his
bed and looked down sleepily upon his fairy friends.
He yawned and rubbed his eyes. "Well," he began,
"this is a strange visit, truly. What is wanted now,
pray?" Bruce briefly related the late events, and be-
sought his aid to recover the lost Nurses.

"But I don't see what I'm to do!" exclaimed Wille.
"How can I bring back the poor lasses? I don't know
where they are, I am sure. What shall I do about it?
I say, wife—wife! Dido, wake up! Here are the
Brownies. Spite has captured Faith and Sophia. Dear
me! can't you wake? You're a precious sleepy head!"

Dido awoke in half the time that Wille had taken; but
then gentlemen look at those things so differently when
it concerns their wives! Wille and Dido held a short
conference, which was interrupted by many yawns from
the Governor, and finally Dido announced the conclusion.

"Governor Willie has been up all night," she said;

" He returned at a late hour from Columbus, and is worn out with business, travel and loss of sleep. He must rest now. After breakfast we will go out to the lake and join you in the search after Faith and Sophia."

" When do you breakfast?" asked Blythe.

" It will be quite late to-morrow—ten o'clock at least, I suppose."

" And you will not be ready to help us before eleven or twelve, then?"

" I think that is quite likely."

" Cannot you come without the Governor?" suggested Blythe.

" No, I couldn't think of that. We never undertake such things separately. Good morning, now."

Dido pulled up her night-cap, retied the strings, and laid her pretty head upon the pillow. Her husband was already breathing heavily, off asleep while Dido was talking.

" But, madam," said True earnestly, " twelve o'clock may be too late. You are trifling with this thing! We ask you to pity us and help us. You know the Golden Motto, 'Quickly done is twice done.' If you want to help us at all you must make haste."

" Hush-sh!" said Bruce, taking the Sergeant by the arm and leading him away. " Don't you see? They are both asleep already. We can do nothing more now, I fear. Come, we must once more fall back upon our own resources."

True left the bed unwillingly. He muttered and sent back reproachful looks as he moved away. He may have been too much interested to judge calmly, but he had decided opinions about the conduct of Wille and Dido—sleeping while Faith and Sophia were in Pixie bonds! He spoke out, too. But his words were unheard. The trio left the chamber and hastened back to camp.

# CHAPTER XIX

## A BATTLE ON LAKE KATRINE.

Commodore Rodney and his brave tars were not long in reaching the inlet, where the Brownie fleet lay moored. The damages received in the last sea fight were so far repaired that the ships were ready for service. Sails were shaken out, cordage stretched, anchors weighed, and before dawn the whole navy was crossing the lake under full sail.

Rodney's flag-ship was called the Emma, and was built after designs of the Brownie Naval Constructor. Its hull was cunningly framed from leaves cut, bent and stretched into proper shape. Its sails were delicate leaves fastened upon miniature masts, whose cordage was twisted from fibres of plants.

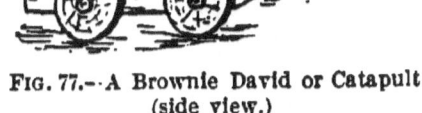

FIG. 77.--A Brownie David or Catapult (side view.)

Its armament was thus fashioned: bits of elderberry stalk were cut into short lengths and the pith removed, leaving "barrels" which were thrust out of port-holes or laid along deck. A rod or "plunger" fitted into each barrel, the outer end of which was lashed to a string tied to the ends of a bowed strip of elastic wood, hickory for the most part, whose ends were braced by stiff pieces to either side of the barrel. To the end of the "plunger" several ropes were fastened. Then tiny pebbles were dropped into the tubes against the head of the rod through holes in the breech. To fire the gun, the Brownies drew the plunger back as far as the elastic strip would allow; then suddenly let go the cords, which the gun crew usually did with a great hurrah. The bended strips sprung into position, forcing the plunger forward, thus driving out the pebbles to a goodly distance. For these cannons or catapults the Brownies had the odd name of "davids."

The other vessels of the fleet were smaller than the

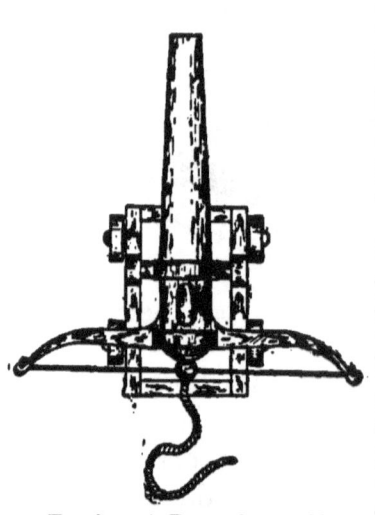

FIG. 78.—A Brownie David (top view.)

Emma, but were rigged and fitted out after the same manner. Their names are: the Ken, commanded by Pipe; the Trusty, commanded by Waterborn; the Old Honest, commanded by Tradewind; the Perseverance, commanded by Coral; the Hope, commander Fluke; the Steady, commander Temperance; the Kind, commander Takeheed. These were the principal vessels and their captains were good and tried men.

The Brownie national flag was white, with a blue canton or field; upon the latter was a white cross saltier, known as St. Andrew's Cross, within the centre of which was a red flaming heart surrounded by a wreath of thistle blooms and leaves. The Brownie "Jack," after the fashion of American and British fleets, was simply the blue field as above described, without the white fly. Commodore Rodney's pennant was a white streamer, bearing thereupon a white water lily, the long stem of

which was bent into the form of the letter "E," as used
in script, and the whole displayed upon a green leaf.

It was a pretty sight to see the tiny fleet, with sails
all set and colors.flying, swiftly riding the water.
The current of the brook carried the boats well on
towards E l l e n 's Isle. Off the western point
of the island they left the stream and proceeded
slowly along t h e northern shore.

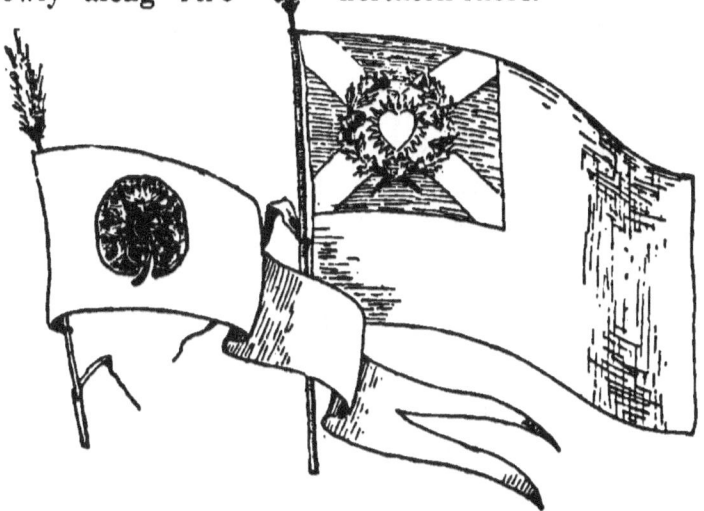

FIG. 79.—Brownie Flag and Pennant.

"Sail, ho!" cried the lookout on the foretopmast cross-
trees of the flag-ship.

"Where away?" asked Rodney.

"Dead ahead!"

"Hah! that's strange. What do you make her out
to be?"

"I can't say exactly, owing to the mist upon the
lake. But I take it to be the Styx, the flag-ship of the
Pixie squadron."

"Keep a sharp eye ahead," said Rodney. "The Styx
was anchored at the outlet last night and can hardly be
off there."

"I see her plainly now!" said the lookout, "and she is not alone, sir. Three other sails have just hove in sight."

"It's the Pixie navy, then?"     .

"Aye, aye, Sir. And they're standing up the channel with every sail set."

"Strange!" muttered Rodney. "How did they know of our movements? Is there a traitor among us? Is it all chance? Or has this something to do with the loss of my poor child? No matter! There the enemy is, and we must make ready to receive him. Ho, there! Make signal, prepare for action!"

The flag that telegraphed this order to the fleet was run up, and soon the merry whistle piping the men to quarters was heard upon deck. Little preparation was needed. All were longing for the fray. Every heart yearned to do somewhat to rescue the captured Nurses and avenge the injury put upon their beloved commanders. The sun had now fairly risen, and the mists slowly rolled up from the surface of the lake. The whole Pixie fleet was seen standing up the channel, as the strip of water between the island and the orchard was called. The wind was from the northwest and therefore favorable to the Pixies, who were bearing down rapidly upon the Brownies.

The vessels of the water-pixies are built in the same style as Raft's yacht, the Fringe, but much larger in size. Admiral Quench commanded the fleet, and the names of his most important vessels, with their masters, are as follows: the "By and By," Master Slipknot; the "Despair," Master Strangle; the "Goodtime," Master Drown; the "Littleone," Master Sineasy; the "Fast," Master Wildoats; the "Doubt," Master Shallow; the "Smoke," Master Stunt; the "Cigarette," Master

Sapforce, whose mate was Mr. Nicotine. More efficient captains and crews never spread sail or drew cutlass. They were devoted to their Admiral and thoroughly united in hatred of the Brownies. They had the advantage over their enemies in strength and number, and with a favoring wind, were confident of victory.

The Pixie sailors were popularly known (after the

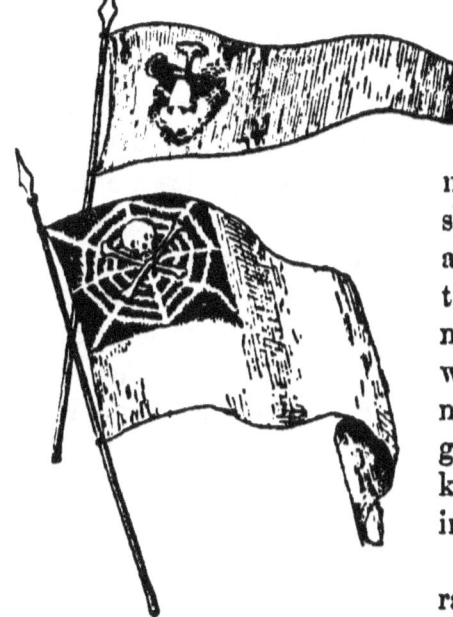

name of their flagship) as the "Stygians." The Brownie tars had also a popular name,—"Natties," which, unless it be a nickname for "navigators," the author knows not the meaning thereof.

As the two fleets rapidly neared each other a red silken flag was run up to the peak

FIGS. 80, 81.—The Pixies' Flag and Pennant.

of the Styx. It showed on a black canton, embroidered in white silk, a round spider web within which hung a skull and cross-bones. Admiral Quench also had his pennant, a red streamer upon which was blazoned a golden chalice held inverted in a sable hand over burning coals.

Fortunately for the Brownies the wind chopped around into the north just as the two fleets came within gun shot. The advantage in manœuvring, which before had been wholly with the Stygians, was now equally divided. As the black and red flag floated from the peak of the Styx, the Natties opened fire with their davids. The pebbles tore through the sails of the Pixie ships and wrought much damage among the crews.

"Close up!" telegraphed Quench from the flag-ship.

Stygians prefer to fight at close quarters. They have no weapons like the Brownie davids, fit for doing battle at long range, and therefore bear straight down upon the enemy; fling out from their spinnerets grapnels of silk cable; leap upon the enemy's deck and with fangs, swords, spears, and lassoes fairly weigh down and over-power their foes. A company of trained boarders known as the Vaulters, commanded by one Saltus, were especially formidable. Their duty was to station them-selves upon a yard-arm, cross-trees, top or shroud, and attach their bodies thereto by elastic ropes; thence they would leap down upon their foe, seize him, and by the backward rebound of the cord, draw him with them-selves up to the point of departure. When thus seized and carried aloft a Brownie rarely escaped.

The sudden change of wind enabled the Natties to keep clear of their powerful adversaries. They tacked back and forth across the channel, avoided the Pixie ships and poured in at long range their david shot. Rodney, however, had no thought of shunning a hand to hand fight. He had determined upon a decisive struggle. He believed that his Natties in their present humor would be invincible. Having therefore pounded the Stygians thoroughly with his davids, and thus dis-abled one or two ships and weakened several crews, he hoisted the signal "Bring the enemy to close action!"

The order was received with cheers and briskly obeyed. The Natties bore down upon the enemy and poured in volley after volley of shot. The Stygian sails were riddled, masts were knocked over, decks were covered with wounded Pixies; splinters flew in the air like snow flakes.

The fleets were now within grappling distance. The two parties stood with weapons drawn, eager for the meeting that should test their courage, skill and strength. The ships closed. Hull grated upon hull; yards interlocked; the grapnels were hove; ship to ship, all along the line, Stygians and Natties were coupled in conflict. The Kind and Tattle, the Trusty and Fast, the Hope and Despair, the Old Honest and the Littleone, the Perseverance and the By and By, the Ken and the Doubt, were locked together. The Tipple and the Treat were both alongside the Steady, the Smoke and Cigarette were doubled against the Wholesome, and the Styx and Goodtime had grappled the Emma.

In some cases the Natties were the boarder, in others the Stygians. The better policy of the Brownies was to stand upon the defensive in these hand to hand fights; for the network of cords and ropes with which the rigging and decks of the Pixie craft were filled, made it perilous for Brownies to land upon them. There were some, however, bold enough or rash enough to venture, and not always without success.

The Emma was somewhat larger than the flag-ship of the Pixie squadron; but as the Styx was aided by the Goodtime in the assault upon her, Rodney had heavy odds against him. Yet he and his brave tars were so thoroughly wrought up and eager for battle that he cared nought for that. He bade his crew stand by to repel boarders. They were ranged on either side of the deck. Admiral Quench brought up the Styx on the port side. The Stygians swarmed in the rigging. They hung upon the yards, which projected over the Emma's deck, ready to drop down thereupon. They flung out their lariats to entangle the Natties stationed on yards and ratlines.

Arrows flew in clouds from the Emma's deck and rigging. Then casting aside their bows (all except the sharpshooters stationed in the top), the Brownie sailors closed to their work. The battle had begun in earnest. For a few moments there was a confused mingling of Stygians and Natties. Brownie cheers

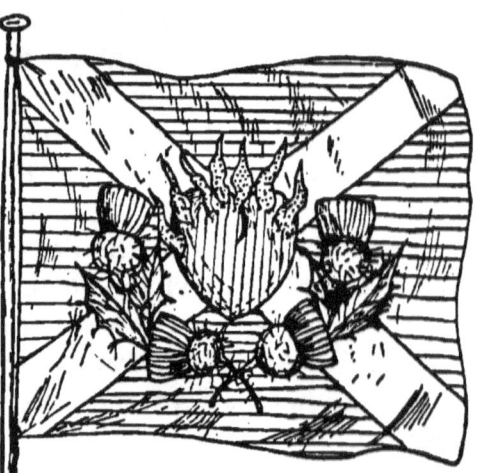

FIG. 82.—The Brownie "Jack," Blue Field, White Saltier, Red Flaming Heart, the Flames of Gold.

blended with the rasping clatter of the Pixies' drum beaten by Stridulans and his drum corps. A constant splash—splashing was heard, as pairs of combatants dropped from the shrouds into the lake, where the battle was often renewed, both parties sometimes sinking together in death.

As yet no Stygian had kept foot upon the Emma. Every onset had been repulsed and the Pixies hurled back. But the Brownies were not always to be so fortunate. A strong party headed by Quench broke through the line of defenders, and fairly got foothold upon the Emma. In the confusion Master Drown led a

vigorous attack from the Goodtime, and gained a footing
in the starboard waist. For a moment the Natties gave
way. Victory seemed to woo the Stygians, who were
pressing upon their enemies, exultingly shouting their
watchword, " Death ! "

In this crisis, Commodore Rodney raised the Brownie
war cry. " Rescue, rescue ! " he shouted ; " Remember
Faith ! Remember Sophia ! To the Rescue ! Follow
me ! "

He ran upon the advancing line of Stygians swinging
his cutlass above his head. It was a Damascus
blade, a famous weapon in the Brownie history
and traditions,
which went by the
name of "Straight."
The commander of
the Emma, Captain
Ask, advanced
side by side with
the Commodore.
His voice was
heard above the

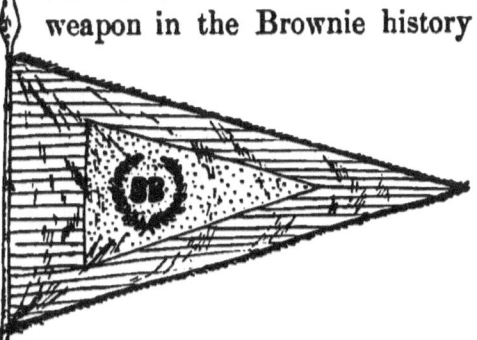

FIG. 83.—Flag of Brownie Brigade of
Cavalry, Blue and Gold.

clamor of battle and discord of Pixie drums
echoing the call " Rescue ! " as he poised aloft his battle-
axe, the " Bigbelief " as his sailors used to call it.
Rodney's sword and the battle-axe of Ask cut great
gaps in the Stygian ranks. The Natties followed close
upon their leaders, and soon the Pixies were driven back
again to the sides of the ship.

There they made a stand. In the drift and swirl of
the conflict it happened that the leaders of the contending crews were brought face to face. Admiral Quench
had steadily fought his way toward Captain Ask ; Ask
had as eagerly pressed toward the spot where Quench

was fighting. They met at last. Quench flung upon
the Captain's face and arms a cloud of network. The
delicate threads, striking like a lasso against Ask's up-
raised arm, enveloped it, and the enswathed member
sank helpless at his side.* His eyes were filled with the
silken filaments, so that he was well-nigh blinded. A
mocking laugh broke from Quench's lips as he leaped
forward upon his foe with out-reached fangs.

It would have gone hard with Captain Ask had not
the mate of his ship, whose name was Angel, been close
behind him. He had followed and guarded his beloved
commander throughout the entire battle. Quickly the
mate cut the network that bound Ask's arm, tore the
filaments from his eyes and dashed his own cutlass into
Quench's face. The Pixie paused a moment, staggered
by the blow. In that moment Ask recovered himself,
raised his axe and struck the Admiral. His aim was
somewhat turned aside by the web filaments, still clinging to his arm. The blade of Bigbelief missed the
Pixie's head and sank into his shoulder. The force of
the blow carried both combatants to the deck. Ask
rose to his feet, seized Quench in his arms, lifted him up,
put forth all his strength and threw him into the lake.

Meanwhile Rodney had come upon Drown, the master
of the Goodtime. The fight between the two was short
and decided. Drown was pinned to the mast head by
the Commodore's sword; Rodney's left arm was severely
wounded, and his face badly torn. Before he could
withdraw his sword a score of Stygians led by Deceit,
the master of the Styx, set upon him. Natties hastened
to the rescue, and waged battle gallantly around their
chief. Rodney seized a marlinspike, for he had no time
to withdraw his cutlass, and with his unwounded arm

---

* Appendix, Note A.

laid about him vigorously. Deceit fought his way through the line of Natties until he reached the mast whereto his comrade, Master Drown, was pinned like an insect in an entomologist's box. He drew forth the cutlass, and was about taking Drown in his arms when Rodney fell upon him. Deceit turned the cutlass against its owner. But it was an awkward weapon in the new hands and did little hurt. A blow from the marlinspike broke the Stygian captain's arm and sent the cutlass ringing upon deck. Deceit closed immediately upon Rodney, seized him with his uninjured claws, and ere the Commodore could again raise his arm, bore him to the bulwark of the ship, mounted the rail, and was about to leap into the water with his captive. Fortunately, Rodney with his right hand laid hold upon the shrouds and thus delayed for an instant the Pixie's fell purpose. A volunteer sailor in the Emma's crew, our old friend Sergeant Clearview, had picked up the Commodore's cutlass as it dropped from Deceit's hand. He was at Rodney's side in a moment. He clasped one arm around the chief as he hung over the rail, and with the other buried the blade of Straight in the bosom of Deceit.

The Stygian captain loosed his hold, fell back into the lake and sank out of sight. A dozen willing hands had by this time seized the Commodore, and he was borne fainting to his cabin. Thus it happened that two of the chief officers of the Brownie navy owed their safety, that day, to the prompt and loving aid of their followers.

We left Quench struggling in the lake whither Ask had tossed him. This was a small matter to the Stygian admiral, for he was a famous swimmer, and disabled as he was, had no trouble in reaching his own ship's side.

He clambered up the man ropes and was helped aboard by his sailors.

"Cut adrift," were his first words, "and signal the same to the fleet!"

So cut adrift it was, on board the Styx and Goodtime not only, but throughout the squadron. Had Rodney not been disabled, it is doubtful whether the Stygian ships would have got off from the Emma so easily. As it was, they were suffered to swing loose, but were not permitted to leave without some parting compliments.

"Man the guns!" cried Ask. The Natties stood to their davids, and shot rattled upon the retreating ships so freely that the crews were driven below, leaving on deck only enough to navigate the vessels.

Throughout the two squadrons various fortunes befell the ships. The Steady had fared somewhat worse than the Emma. Commander Temperance was badly wounded, and had not the signal to cut adrift been given in the very niche of time, the good ship might have been captured. The Wholesome was badly damaged by the Cigarette and Smoke, and her captain, Lustyhealth, was carried below sorely hurt. One of the Stygian vessels, the Despair, was sunk by the Hope. Its captain, Master Strangle, got off on one of the boats, however, much to the sorrow of Commander Fluke who tried hard to lay hold of the rogue. The Tattle was captured along with its master, Backbite, by Commander Takeheed of the Kind. This miserable, sneaking Pixie was lashed to a mast of his own ship, and as the Kind towed the Tattle through the Brownie fleet he was greeted everywhere with groans and jeers by the true-hearted sailors. They were not used to treat prisoners after this fashion, but had small compunction in the case of this fellow Backbite.

As for the rest of the ships, it must be enoug h to say that all the officers and crews did their duty well. Special mention may be made of Boatswain Pipe. Even before the signal to cut adrift had been hoisted upon the Pixie flag-ship, Pipe had so closely pressed the Doubt, that its master, Captain Shallow, had already cut off his grapnels, and was in full flight toward Big Cave Harbor.

The Ken followed peppering her adversary with david. shot. But Pipe soon saw that the Doubt would slip away from him, and gave up the pursuit, returned to the fight, ran his ship alongside the Despair, leaped upon her deck at the head of his boarders, and fell upon the crew who were engaged with the Hope. It was through this timely reinforcement and the bravery of Pipe the Boatswain that Commander Fluke was able to sink the Despair with all her crew, excepting the boat's crew that escaped with Captain Strangle to the Tipple. Having finished this valiant service, he pulled away in an open boat to the aid of the Wholesome, and by his timely reinforcement saved that craft from the clutch of Captains Stunt and Nicotine.

# CHAPTER XX.

## A NAVAL MONSTER.

While these exciting events were occurring, Twaaells and his chums having finished their "lark" were slowly picking their way towards the Brownie camp with their prisoners and wounded comrade. It was past sun-up before they sighted the pickets, for a heavy fog having arisen from the lake, they must needs stop and wait for the day. At the guard line they were halted only a few moments, but taken at once to headquarters, where they told their news in full, and turned over their prisoners. Thence they were marched away to the guard house where, after a hearty breakfast, they turned in for a sound sleep. They were quite content to take their punishment, and happy that their adventure had turned out so much better than they had dared to hope. Half-rick, who had been sent to the hospital, rapidly improved, and it may here be said, fully recovered under the Nurses' skillful care. When the party learned the unhappy fate of Faith and Sophia they were deeply grieved.

"I saw the lights of the searchers at one time," said Gear, " bobbing here and there through the bushes ; but I was fool enough to think that it was a guard detail out looking for us, and so said nothing. Alas, alas! Well, I don't believe I'll ever go on another lark!" But he forgot his good resolve before long, and the time came when he was as keen for a night adventure as ever he had been.

Late in the morning the whole party, amid the mingled cheers and chaff of the camp were brought before Captain Bruce who had returned from his visit to Governor Wille.

"Brownies," he said, "you have been guilty of a serious breach of discipline by leaving the camp without orders, and that in the face of the enemy. It is true, you have done great public service; but that has been more by good luck than good management or good intent. The result might have been different, and not only damaging to the Nation, but fatal to yourselves. You deserve a greater punishment than you have received; but this is a time of sore grief and peril to our Nation, in which the best service of all her sons is required for every moment. I therefore dismiss you with this public reprimand and the imprisonment already inflicted. Remember that no deeds, however brave, can entitle one to praise when they are done in defiance of discipline, and in disobedience of superiors. Go; report to your several commands, and henceforth confine your energies to the discharge of regular duty and obedience of lawful orders."

"Don't you think you were a little too severe with the boys, father?" asked Agatha, who was present during the reprimand.

"Perhaps I was, daughter; but I hardly think so. Some kinds of craft will bear a good deal of ballast. But all our young Brownies are alike; they will have their freaks and larks no matter how serious affairs may be. However, these lads are among the most skillful soldiers in camp, and they will be none the worse either for their fun or their punishment. The rogues! What a lark it was!" And in spite of the heavy burden on his heart, he smiled at the remembrance of the

Fig. 84.—"They Entered the Leafy Towers."

adventures which had been told him. "It seems the climax of absurdity that a mere squad of youngsters should plan an assault upon a strong fort, and actually gain possession of it too, by a freak of fortune!"

Now orders were given to raze the empty fort. The Brownies had been keen to enter and destroy the place as soon as Twadeils had reported its abandonment; but MacWhirlie forbade action until Captain Bruce's return. The eager soldiers swarmed over the barricades, through the gates, and along the vacant streets. They entered the leafy towers in search of lurking foemen, and finding none cut the binding threads and let the leaves unroll. They severed the stay ropes of the conning tower of Pixie Thaddeus, and the whole structure collapsed. As the repaired suspension bridge stood intact, and the shore was strewn with the litter of a hasty flight, the manner of the Pixies' escape was easily explained. But the whereabouts of the garrison was not made out on account of the fog that overhung the lake. That however was

lifting, and the Pixie fleet would soon be in sight.
The soldiers went to work heartily. Breastworks, barricades, gates, towers, walls, ramparts, bridge and piers
were assailed with such zeal and vigor, that in a short
time the remnants of Fort Spinder were laid in pieces
upon the ground, flying in fragments through the air,
or floating in broken bits
upon the water.

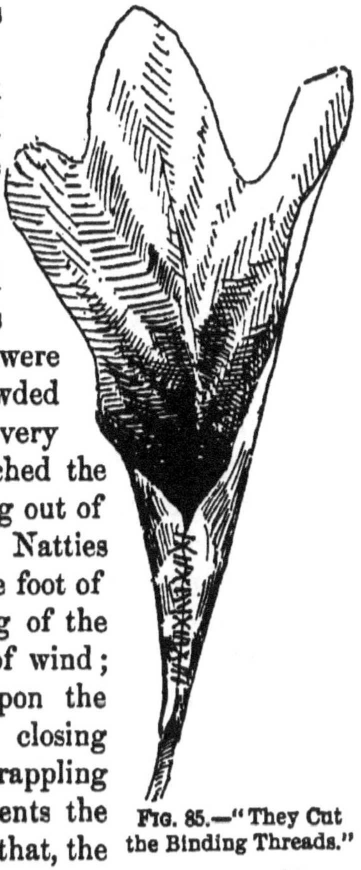

By the time this good work
was finished the sun had
scattered the fog, and left the
face of the lake quite clear.
Little columns and clouds of
mist still hung here and
there, leaving distant objects
indistinct, but both fleets were
in sight. The Brownies crowded
down to the bank, and from every
elevation and tree top watched the
battle. The Stygians pushing out of
Big Cave Harbor, and the Natties
coming into sight around the foot of
the island; the manœuvring of the
vessels under the change of wind;
the effect of the davids upon the
Pixie craft; the onset, the closing
together of the ships, the grappling
of hull to hull, all these events the
excited soldiers saw. After that, the

FIG. 85.—" They Cut
the Binding Threads."

two fleets were so huddled together that none could say
which side was victorious.

Some of the cavalry mounted and pushed off over the
lake to see for themselves. But the Bee and Butterfly
ponies dared not come very near the ships, lest their

wings should be caught in the rigging and they and
their riders destroyed. They came close enough, however, to notice the turn of battle. Couriers passed
back and forth bringing to Bruce news, now good now
bad. At last they reported the Stygians in full retreat,
and that the Natties had gained a great victory. Cheer
upon cheer greeted this tidings. The shouts from the
shore rolled across the water, and were heard by the
Brownie sailors who answered their comrades heartily.

A yacht was dispatched for Captain Bruce, who, accompanied by Blythe and True, crossed to the Emma to
consult with Rodney as to future movements. The
Stygians had retired to Big Cave Harbor, and there for
some time they were likely to stay. They could be seen
from the fore-top busy upon deck and rigging repairing
the damages of battle, as the Natties, also, were doing.
Dinner was now over; a pleasant hum of voices sounded
through the fleet. The decks were cleaned from the
litter of conflict. The sad rites over their fallen comrades were decently but speedily paid. The sailors
awaited eagerly the issue of the officers' consultation.

Captain Bruce returned to the shore. Blythe and
True remained with the fleet, and were assigned to the
Ken under care of Pipe the Boatswain. Now a rumor
ran through the squadron that an immediate attack was
to be made upon the Stygians by the whole Brownie
brigade; that MacWhirlie had gone around with the
cavalry by the inlet to fall upon the Pixie camp, and
that Bruce with the infantry was to pass around to the
other end of the lake, cross the outlet and cut off retreat
from that quarter. However set agoing, the rumor well
set forth the main features of the plan agreed upon
between army and navy.

Rodney's wound was painful, but was not so serious as

to hinder active service. He went about his duties with his arm slung in bandages; a little weak in body, but as stout of heart as ever, and with brighter hopes than he had for some time dared to cherish. The afternoon was well advanced when the lookout on the Emma reported an unusual movement in the Pixie fleet.

"What do you make it out?" said Rodney.

"They seem to be getting ready to weigh anchor!" answered the lookout. "And several of their boats have in tow a queer sort of craft that looks more like a snail shell than any sort of vessel I know."

"Hah! some Pixie trick, I warrant!" returned Rodney. "But we mustn't let them escape us this time. Ho there! Set the signal to weigh anchor."

"Aye, aye, Sir," was the hearty response from Mate Angel. "It is done, Sir."

"Now signal the fleet to prepare for action."

"Aye, aye, Sir. That is done too."

"Good. Now set the order to come to close quarters."

"Close quarters it is, Sir," soon responded the prompt mate.

The Nattie ships were bearing down upon the mouth of Big Cave Harbor, arranged in the form of a half moon, the Emma in the centre of the line. Pipe led one wing in the Ken, Commander Coral led the other in the Perseverance. Already the cavalry battalion had made the crossing, and was well up to the Pixie camp, close along shore, and almost within hailing distance of the fleet. A squad under command of Ensign Lawe was left to guard the shore road and make telegraphic signals to the fleet with the wigwag flags. Lieutenant MacWhirlie with the bulk of the troops pushed on and to the rear, with the purpose of falling upon the

Pixie camp while the fleet attacked in front. The odd looking craft which had puzzled the lookout, had been towed off shore, and was now slowly gliding out of the harbor. The Stygians were seen from the Brownie ships

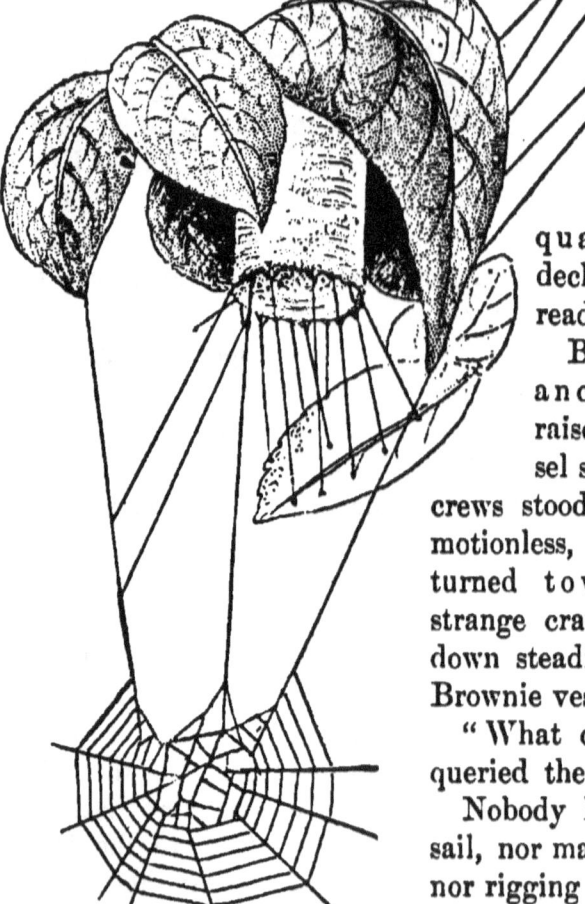

hanging in the rigging, manning the tops, swarming at their quarters upon deck, evidently ready for action.

But not an anchor was raised, not a vessel stirred. The crews stood dumb and motionless, with eyes turned toward that strange craft bearing down steadily upon the Brownie vessels.

"What can it be?" queried the Brownies.

Nobody knew. No sail, nor mast, nor spar, nor rigging of any kind was to be seen upon it. Not a sailor showed himself anywhere. It

FIG. 86.—"The Conning Tower of Pixie Thaddeus."

had no visible motive power, and went through the water as though driven by an unseen spirit hand.

"What can it be?" exclaimed Pipe, whose command lay nearest the strange vessel.

"I believe it is the new ram the Pixies have been talking so much about lately," answered Sergeant True. "They have been trying to keep it a secret, but the thing has leaked out. It looks like an ugly affair."

"Ugly? I should say so!" said the old salt warmly. "It is nothing but the cast off shell of a water snail. Call that seamanship? Nobody but a lubber or a Pixie would be willing to sail or fight in such a tub as that."

"Well, I'm only a lubber, you know," answered True, "and have but a landsman's notion of things. But to my mind that ram, or shell, or tub or whatever it may be, will turn the tide of battle against us if we don't look out. See! the davids are playing on it from all parts of our fleet. The shot bounds off its sides like thistle-down. It keeps straight on its way, like grim Fate, turning neither to the right hand nor the left. Do you see, Boatswain? the creature is making straight for us!"

"Aye, aye! let it come on. I say pooh! to all your croaking. Stand by, now, and see how a genuine sailor can knock the bottom out of all the floating brass, iron, or snail-shell pots that ever went to sea. Launch the boats, lads! We'll

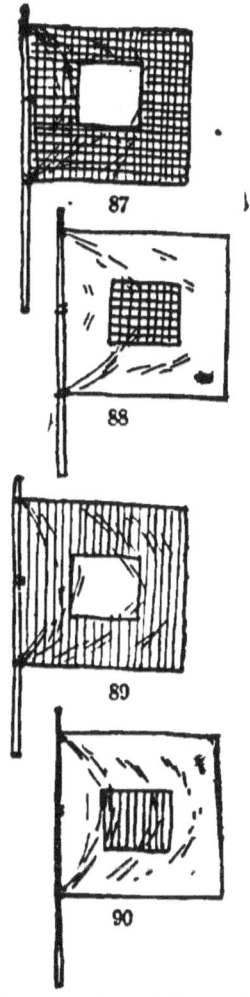

Telegraphic Signal Flags: 87, Black with White Centre; 88, White and Black; 89, Red and White; 90, White and Red.

pull up to this Stygian kettle and see if we can't ḳ ᵈd some hole in it through which our cutlasses will make way."

Next to the Ken was the captured Pixie ship Tattle, which had been turned into the Brownie navy with the new name Praise, and Clearview, as a reward for his service in saving Rodney's life, had been promoted to command her. Next to the Praise was the Hope, Commander Fluke. As the Pixie ram neared the left wing, composed of the three vessels just named, it suddenly shifted its course and bore straight down upon the Praise,

"Fire!" cried Clearview. A harmless broadside was poured upon the Ram.

"Again," shouted Clearview. "Aim below the water line; I see an opening there."

Another broadside was delivered with no better effect. On, on the weird monster moved, straight toward the ship. Every eye in both fleets was fixed upon the Praise. Every heart throbbed with anxiety.

Crash!

A groan of dismay ran along the line of the Brownie squadron. A wild yell of joy rose from the Pixie ships. The solid prow of the ram had crushed through the leafy side of the Praise, as an iron steamship would run through a fishing schooner. She sank in a moment leaving her crew struggling in the waves.

More quickly than one would have thought so clumsy a craft could move, the Ram turned and bore down upon the Hope. The Natties aboard this ship were dismayed at the fate of their comrades, but not a man swerved from his post.

"Boarders, ahoy!" shouted Fluke.

"Aye, aye, Sir!"

"Prepare to board the enemy. Drop from the cross-trees. Spring from the deck. Heave the grapnels if you can."

Brave but hopeless struggle! The Ram crushed into the Hope as into the Praise. A few of the Natties succeeded in leaping upon the smooth round turret of the enemy, only to roll off again into the lake, and be engulfed in the vortex of their sinking ship.

Two ships gone in a score of minutes! No wonder the Brownies began to get ready to bout ship and flee from this leviathan of the deep who devoured ships as behemoth the rivers. No wonder that Pipe, when he saw two-thirds of his command swept out of existence, should have felt a cold shudder run through him as this invincible and invulnerable mystery of the sea now turned its prow upon him. His order to launch boats had been executed. The three ship boats were already in the water. Pipe himself commanded one, True another, Coxswain Help the third. Lieutenant Swift had charge of the ship. Pipe hesitated only a moment as to what he should do.

"Lieutenant," he said, "look out for the ship. Tack, and if you can, get to the stern of the old kettle." He held to his prejudice even after such sad experiences. "You may find some joint in her harness there through which to send a shot. But look out for the ship, and save her whatever comes of us. Ready, my hearties?"

"Aye, aye, sir!" was the firm response.

"Give way, then—lively!"

The three boats fairly cut the water. Pipe was in advance. He tried to run his boat under the starboard side, hoping to find some port-hole or opening there. But his purpose was foiled. The Ram struck him amidships. The boat was cut in two, and the crew submerged in the waters. True's boat was just in the rear of Pipe's, and shared the same fate. Help, more fortunate than the others, avoided the blow, and passed to the stern of the Ram, which plowed on remorselessly and mutely as before, directing its course against the Ken. Help threw a quick glance upwards toward the strange vessel as it surged by his boat. A curtain of varnished silk canvas hung across the stern. It was drawn tight and fastened above, below and at the side so that the water was shut out. But Help saw one side of the curtain pushed back for a moment, and the mocking visage of a well-known Pixie officer peered out upon him. It closed, and the Ram sped on to its work of destruction.

Help dropped into its wake, checked his boat, and began looking about for any of the crews of the lost boats and ships who might yet be above water. True and Blythe were picked up. Clearview was saved. Fluke was lost. Several others, common sailors, were also picked up. But Pipe, good, gallant, dear old Pipe, was gone! He had sunk and had not risen. For a long time Help rowed around the scene of the disaster, and then with a sad heart turned the bow of his boat toward Ellen's Isle. The sturdy Natties brushed from their eyes the tears shed over the lost boatswain, and then bent to their oars, leaving their beloved Captain beneath the waves of Lake Katrine. Of all the gallant sailors who went down that day none was so mourned as Pipe the Boatswain. The tragedy of his taking off seemed all the more terrible because of the untimely fate of his child Sophia.

# CHAPTER XXI. ·

Lieutenant Swift felt bound by the orders of his late commander, all the more because of his sad fate. Accordingly he tacked ship, and avoided the stroke of the Ram, which in turn tacked, though somewhat more clumsily, and followed the Ken toward the Brownie fleet. Again Swift tacked and put the head of his ship toward Ellen's Isle. Then the Ram gave up the Ken and bore down upon the Emma, as though resolved to seal the fortunes of the fight with the destruction of the Brownie flag-ship.

Rodney was in sore straits. His officers and crew were greatly demoralized. His sailors were superstitious; and there was something so contrary to all that Natties had ever known or heard of in the character and exploits of this audacious stranger, that superstition was aroused. They could fight Pixies, but this was a sea-ghost. There was no use contending against it. There was nothing to do but bout ship and sail away. But what humiliation! And after so noble a victory! To add to the perils of the position, the Stygian ships had weighed anchor, and were closing upon the Brownie fleet hard in the wake of their Ram. At last duty overcame pride in Rodney's heart, and he gave the order to retire up the channel.

Ensign Lawe, with his squad of cavalry, had watched from a knoll on the lake shore the progress of events. His heart sunk within him as he saw the loss of the Brownie ships and crews. "I can't stand this any longer," he cried, as the boats of Pipe and True sank before the Ram's stroke. "To the rescue, my lads! Charge!"

Without waiting to see whether or no he was followed

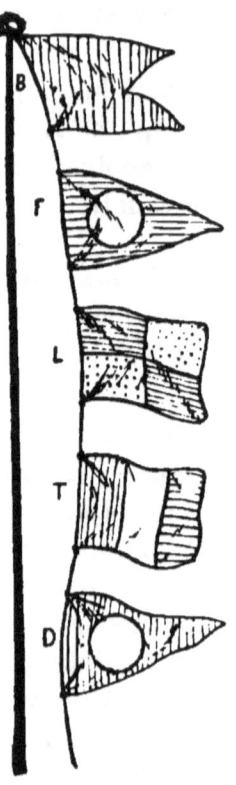

by his battalion, he mounted his bee pony and rode at full speed toward the Ram. His troopers followed, muttering loudly against their leader's folly, but unwilling to disobey. The Pixies saw him plunging through the air, and greeted him with loud yells of mockery.

"What is Lawe about?" asked Rodney.

"It looks as though he were minded to charge upon the sea monster," answered the mate.

"What folly! Why, look there! the madcap is charging almost alone upon the very front of the Ram! He is gone daft! Are you sure that is Ensign Lawe? I never knew him to do such an insane act. He is one of the coolest heads we have. It's too bad—too bad! The fellow is throwing away his life; and we've lost too many valuable officers already."

FIG. 91.—Signal Flags: B, Red; F, Blue, White Circle; L, Blue and Gold (Yellow); T, Red, White, Blue; D, Red, White Circle. Can you read the Order?

Rodney sighed, and thought of his lost boatswain, the very right arm of his fleet.

The Ram was steadily pursuing the Nattie ships now in full retreat. The wind blew up the channel. It would be a stern chase, which is always a long chase. Half the Pixie navy followed with the Ram; the other half had tacked across the lake toward the foot of the island, with the intention of sailing up the opposite channel, and thus heading off the Natties ere they reached the inlet. They had bold plans afoot, and thought to destroy the whole Brownie fleet.

This manœuvre had turned attention from the daring ride of Ensign Lawe. Yet the Ensign was not such a madcap as his countrymen declared him, nor such a fool as his foes supposed. He had seen at once that the masts and rigging usual to sailing vessels were wanting from this new craft; he could therefore approach a-horseback with comparative safety. That there must be some assailable point, some port-hole, some door, something penetrable he felt sure.

"I will find my way to it," he said in his heart; "or at least find out where it is. I will uncover the secret power that works this destruction, or find out the monster's weak points and give knowledge of it to the Commodore."

He had now reached the Ram. He swept above the prow. No opening there! He hovered over the deck. All hard and smooth there! He skimmed along the sides. No port-holes, no seams, no sign of break or opening there. He flew past the side, and hung in the air above the vessel's stern. A dart whistled by his face. He felt the vibrations of the air on his cheek.

"Hah! There is an opening then in your solid shell? That dart came from some vent. Let us see!"

He pressed his gallant nag closer to the Ram. His keen eye caught the varnished curtain that hung across the stern. He saw one side of it tremble and lift a little as he circled about it. The weak point in the sea monster was exposed! Hurrah! He would try the metal

16

of a Brownie cutlass against that varnished curtain!
If he could cut that open, the waves would rush into
the hull, and the Ram would sink into the lake with
the noble barks that it had destroyed.

Lawe tightened his bridle reins as he thus meditated,
and drew his cutlass. He dropped a little astern of the
Ram, but well to the port side, so that he might sweep
straight across the stern. He poised himself firmly, bent
over in the saddle, and cried, "Go, my good nag!"

Golden Rule, as his pony was named, sprang to the
voice of his master as though conscious of what depended
upon him. He passed across the stern of the Ram so
closely that his wings almost touched it.

Whi—rr—rr!

The Ensign's sword ripped through the curtain, and
Golden Rule shot by like an arrow.

Quickly Lawe turned and swept back again on the
same track. Again the blade cut through the curtain,
with a downward stroke this time that laid open a
vertical seam.

"Once more, my brave Golden!" said the Ensign,
patting his pony, and he swept the third time across
the face of the curtained door. The top and both edges
were now severed from the sides of the shell. The
curtain dropped over so that one corner dragged in the
water. The hollow hull of the shell ship was exposed,
and within it the angry faces of a group of Pixies.

The work wanted yet the finishing stroke. One side
of the curtain was slit down to the water line. The
waves were already washing in thereat; but the other
side was only partly severed. It needed one stroke
more—just one! That would lay the curtain level
with the lake; then the billows would roll in, and
claim the Pixies and their infernal machine for their own.

A fourth time Lawe swept across the stern of the Ram. A fourth time his good sword did its work without fail. The true eye and steady hand of the Ensign sent it home to the mark. The curtain trembled a moment in the breeze, fell backward with flap and splash upon the surface of the lake, and dragged behind, checking the Ram's motion as though it were a heavy anchor, and then weighed the stern downward to the surface. The waves broke in with a roar that echoed through the hollow hull. The groans and yells of the Pixie crew answered back the voice of the waters.

Lawe cast one exulting glance within as he rode by. But he was doomed to a more terrible trial than he had yet endured. As he sped across the opening on his fourth trip, a dark form leaped upon him from the hold. He was in a Pixie's clutch! One claw grasped the Ensign's foot, the other was buried deep in Golden Rule's breast. The pony, frantic with terror and pain, plunged and shook his wings. But the Pixie kept his hold. Lawe looked downward into his face. He saw the black visage, and sneaking eyes of Lieutenant Hide!

"Ha, ha," laughed the Pixie. "You know me, do you? Well, you've done a fine thing to-day, no doubt! Your name shall go down to posterity, of course. But I think I shall stop *you* from going down any further in that line. We shall try another sort of going down. There's nothing like pleasant company, even when one's making a voyage to the bottom of the lake! Ha, ha!"

The malignant creature spoke truly. They were sinking slowly together, horse, rider and Pixie into the lake. The weight of Hide's body might have been overcome, but the motion of the pony's wings was much hindered.

Golden Rule struggled nobly, but fell steadily toward the water. Ensign Lawe had by this time recovered from the shock of the unexpected assault.

"Grammercy, for thy courteous invitation," he said, coolly. "I choose to decline thy bidding and thy presence. In sooth, we shall part company now."

Once, twice, and again the faithful cutlass glanced in

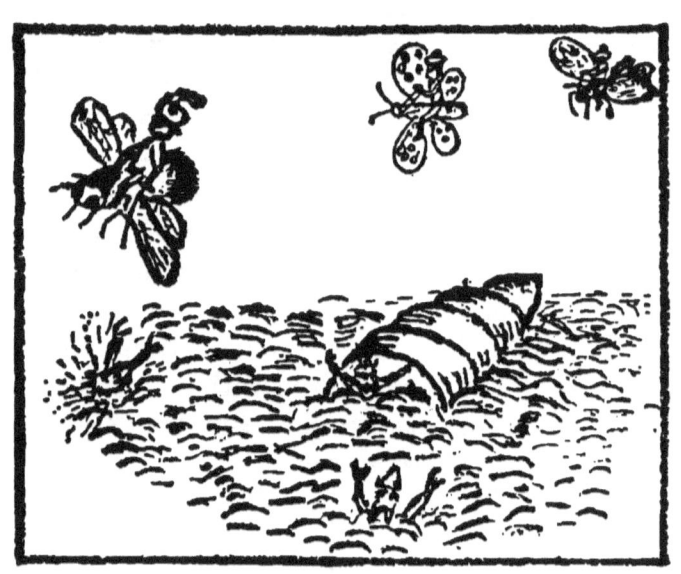

Hide. falls into the water.

FIG. 92.—The Sinking of the Pixie Ram.

the sunlight. The first stroke cut loose the Pixie's claw from the pony's breast; the second divided the arm by which his own foot was held; the third, following quickly, smote upon the head of the wretched creature as he tumbled, like Lucifer of old, into the bosom of the lake.

There was a ripple upon the water; a faint pool of blood tinged the face of Lake Katrine, and the waves closed forever above the dead body of Hide, the son of Shame. Golden Rule, released from his burden, shook his wings gladly and mounted aloft. Lawe cast his eyes downward just as the Pixie Ram settled, surged, and plunged stern foremost into the lake.

Thus perished at the hands of Ensign Lawe, the famous sea ghost, the Pixie shell-clad Ram. The machine was a brilliant thought, the conception of Hide himself. It was just what it seemed to be, the shell of a water snail. Entering this empty shell, Hide and his engineers had closed the opening with a web or curtain of varnished silk, which kept the water out.* Then paddles were fitted up in the stern, revolved by hand cranks within, and thus the vessel was directed by those inside. To ordinary assault it was invulnerable at every part except the curtain which covered the opening, and thereat had the keen blade of Ensign Lawe found entrance, and so the way to victory.

---

* It is not uncommon for certain tubeweaving spiders to avail themselves of the friendly openings of land shells and spin their web therein. The Editor must confess that he has never seen any of his spider friends whose habits resemble that here attributed to Pixie Hide. But the Author is not without authority for the use made thereof; for Jones, in his "Animal Life," a well-known and excellent book on Natural History, relates an incident upon which the story of the Pixie Ram may have been founded.—F. M.

# CHAPTER XXII.

### "HAIR-BREADTH 'SCAPES BY FLOOD AND FIELD."

The gallant exploit of Ensign Lawe had been wrought while the two fleets were under full headway up the channel. After the first outbreak of anxiety, amazement and mockery, but little attention had been paid the Quixotic affair, as all voted it. Both fleets were intent upon the management of their ships. Pursuers and pursued crowded on all sail, and as a strong wind blew from the west they were a long way from the Ram at the moment of its destruction. A shout from Lawe's soldiers, who had hovered near during the strange duel, drew attention to the Brownie troopers.

"What is that?" asked Rodney of the lookout.

"I don't see yet. Yes, I make it out now; Lawe is struggling in the air with a Pixie who must have leaped from the Ram upon his pony. The Ensign is falling into the water. No! he has cut himself loose! The troopers wave their swords and shout like mad men."

"What of the Ram? How do the lads manage to escape the darts from the—?"

"See! See!" cried the lookout excitedly. "The Ram is settling into the water. The stern has been laid open from deck to keel. The waves rush in. She is sinking! Hurrah, hurrah!" The national standard was run up upon the flag-ship, and as the Natties uncovered and saluted the colors, cheer after cheer made the welkin ring. The Brownie bugles struck up one of their favorite national airs, "The Bonnie White Flag," which begins,

The Natties over the blue waves sail,
 The Troopers cleave the air,
The Footmen tramp o'er hill and vale,
 But one is the Flag we bear!

CHORUS:
Huzza for the Flag we bear!
Huzza for the Name we wear!
We are one, we three,
Over shore and sea,
In the honors and toils we share
For the Flag and the Name we bear.
Ho—e—yo!  Tu—loo—ra—lay
The bonny white Flag for aye!

FIG. 93.—Saluting the Colors.

(211)

The noble character of the Brownies was well shown
by the absence of jealousy on this occasion.  Although
the navy had run from the Ram, the sailors cheered the
good trooper who had conquered.  However, the Ensign
took no time to indulge in hurrahs and congratulations.
He pushed to the shore, exchanged his injured pony for
a fresh nag, and rode off to join MacWhirlie.

The Stygians at first could not credit the destruction
of their naval machine, least of all that it had been
wrought by a dragoon !  Few of them had seen the combat.  They had left the Ram, as they supposed, to
follow and destroy the Ken, and had themselves pursued the fleeing Nattics at full speed.  Many of them
had just seen the vessel as she went down.  For the rest
the vacant water was the proof.  The Ram was gone !
Their hopes had now also gone.  With one half of the
fleet on the other side of the channel, they deemed discretion the better part of valor, and slowly fell back
toward their harbor again.

Rodney longed to follow them, but for several good
reasons kept on his course up the channel.  He had lost
two of his best ships, with Pipe, Fluke, True, Blythe,
Help, and many other brave men.  In the hurly-burly
no one had observed the escape of Help and his boat
crew ; they, as well as the crews of the Praise and the
Hope, were thought to be lost.  Moreover, he knew not
but another Ram might be sent against him.  Finally
he feared that if he did stop to attack the Stygians in
the harbor, the other squadron would sail around the
island, and he would thus be caught between the two
divisions.  Much to his regret, therefore, he gave up the
plan to join with the army in attacking Big Cave camp,
and sailed up the channel to meet and engage the second
Pixie squadron.

In the meantime MacWhirlie had fallen with his usual vigor upon the enemy's camp. The pickets had been driven in, and the outer line of works captured. The portable davids of the cavalry carried upon the backs of their bee ponies, a sort of flying artillery, were turned upon the tents and inner works, and the shot played merrily.

But as fortune would have it, Bruce failed to get up at the appointed time, and could not support his lieutenant by attacking on the other side of the camp. During the delay thus caused the incidents above related occurred; the Pixies rallied, and reinforced by Stygians from the returned ships, drove MacWhirlie back to the outer line of entrenchment. Here he put up breastworks, placed sentinels and picket lines, sent out scouts, and waited for his captain.

Bruce soon appeared and the line was completed around the Pixie camp, stretching in a half circle from shore to shore. The great drawback was the absence of the fleet. The Brownie commanders were concerned about the safety of their position. Could they hold it until Governor Wille came to their help? Or, would anything interfere to hinder him from keeping his promise? If he failed again, what should they do?

"However," said Bruce, "it is well not to cross a river until we come to it. Ensign Lawe, take a troop and ride over to the mansion. Get news of the Governor's purpose. Remind him of his promise. If there is any danger of another delay, come back post haste with the news. And now, my men, let us to breakfast, take a little rest and get ready for hard service. There's plenty of it before us."

Soon after the bugle had sounded the sick call, one of the sentinels on the picket line saw some one rapidly approaching from the direction of the Pixie camp.

"Halt! Who goes there?" he cried.

"A friend without the countersign."

"Advance, friend without the countersign."

As the stranger drew near he showed the form and features of a Brownie soldier. They were indeed marred and wasted, and the uniform was tattered and soiled; but a Brownie soldier the fugitive certainly was. When he had come near enough the sentinel halted him and called:

"Corporal of the guard! Post four!" When the Corporal arrived the stranger was ordered to advance to the post.

"Who are you and whence do you come?" asked the Corporal.

"What! friend Steadypace," was the reply, "don't you know me? Well, well! A Pixie prison must have made sad changes in me if you can't recognize your old comrade Dodge."

"Dodge? Dodge! Can it be? Yes; so it is! Dear old fellow!" Corporal Steadypace embraced his friend, hurried him to the guard tent, had him fed and tidied up, meanwhile relating the particulars

Fig. 94.—"The Bugle had Sounded the Sick Call."

of Sergeant Clearview's story, and what the Brownies knew of his own capture. Thence Dodge was taken to headquarters, where he was heartily greeted by the Captain, and bidden tell the story of his adventures and escape.

"Well, Sir," said Dodge, "when our boat was captured, as Sergeant Clearview has told you, I was thought

to be the only survivor of the scouting party. The
Pixies made a great hurrah over me as they led me
through their fort, and I was pelted, hooted and cursed

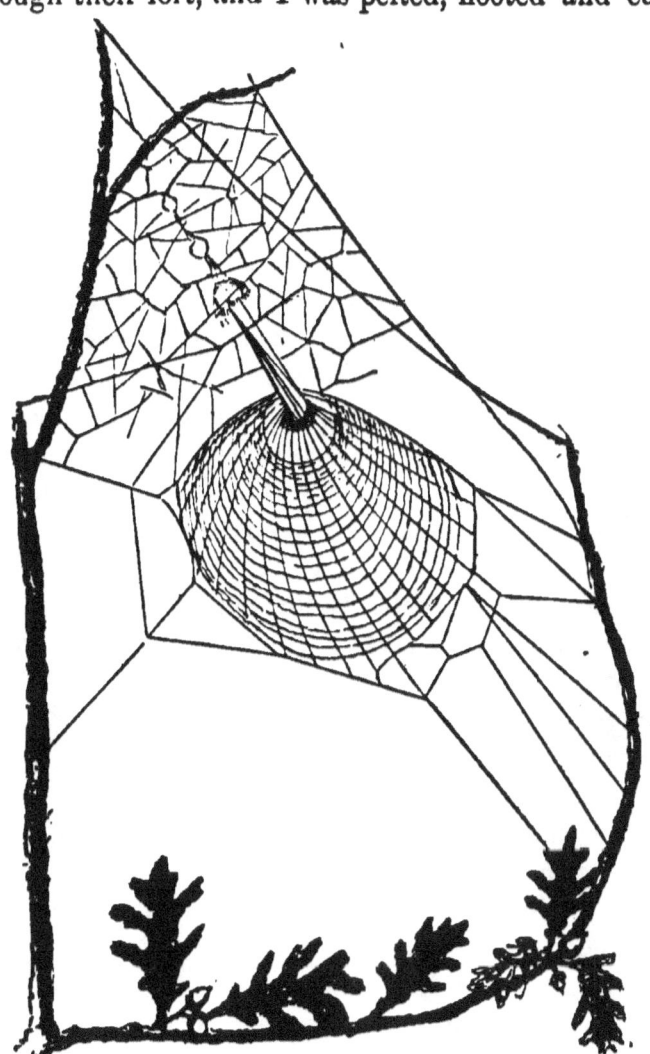

FIG. 95.—The Labyrinth.

by all the youngsters along the way. Spite the Spy
tried hard to pump out of me some information about
our plans, but failed."

"Well, my daisy," he said at last, "we'll try you
another time. Guards, take the Brownie off to the
Labyrinth."

"At this order I was led away to the shore, ferried
across the lake to Orchard Camp, and put in a prison
located on the lake side within the Pixie picket lines.
It is a curious structure, and looks as though several
architects had wrought upon the design. One of the
sides, built by Engineer Epeïra, is a delicately woven
orbweb. The other side, together with the gables, battle-
ments and roof have been built by Engineer Theridion.
The upper part of the prison is a maze of crossed lines,
in the midst of which is a dome after the style of Engineer Linyphia. Above the dome is a dry leaf rolled up
into a hollow cylinder.* I was placed within this leaf,
which served as a dungeon or cell, and just beneath me
in the little silken dome the keeper of the prison had
her station. Her name, as I soon learned, is Labryn-
thea, a suitable one certainly for the keeper of such an
establishment. Occasionally, two or three Pixies would
hang around the premises, joining in the watch or
exchanging gossip and flirtations with Madam Keeper.
A few survivors of a brood of younglings sported in the
maze, and when a small insect struck and was entangled
upon the threads, they would creep through the crosslines, seize the unfortunate prey and feed upon it."

"But Dodge, pray tell us how you saw all this from
your inner prison?" asked the Captain.

"Certainly. I didn't see anything for some time, my
leaf cell was so dark; but looking carefully around, I
found one spot where the roof was nearly worn through.
By some strange good fortune, when the Pixies searched
me before bringing me to the prison, they overlooked

---

* Appendix, Note A.

my clasp knife which I had thrust into the band of my
Scotch bonnet. I was thus able to work out a space
large enough to let my head through. I cut out three
sides neatly, and made a sort of trap door that hinged
upon the uncut end. I was engaged on this for some
time, as I had to work secretly, catch all the chippings

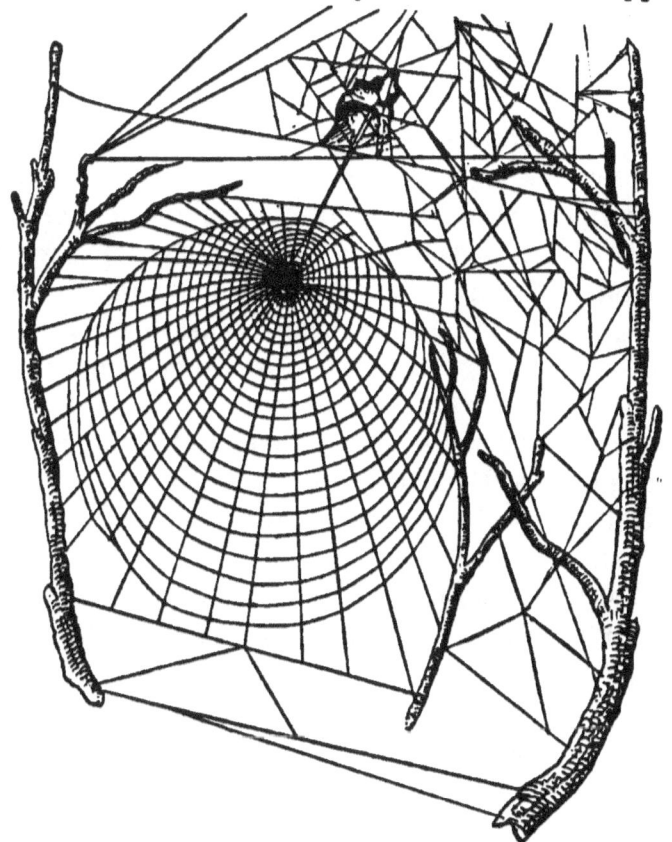

FIG. 96.—"Above the Dome is a Dry Leaf Rolled Up."

in my hat, and then conceal them in my pockets. Had
they dropped upon the domed roof below they would
have awakened suspicion. By following the lines of the
leaf veins I made a cut so clean and close that my door
was quite concealed from ordinary notice. I now had

many opportunities to peep out of my trap and see what was going on around me. I thought I knew something of Pixie tricks and ways before, but dear me! I learned more from that hole in the roof than I ever dreamed of.

"There were several Pixies domiciled on the branches of a tree that overhung the Labyrinth, whose manners especially interested me. They are practicing a new mode of harassing Brownies, a sort of patent spring net."

The Brownie officers quickened attention at this statement, for they are not only blessed with healthy curiosity, but naturally are always vigilant to meet their enemies' plots. Amidst a running fire of questions Corporal Dodge told the following story: One day while looking out of my door, I heard beneath me the voice of Spite the Spy. From the prison talk I had already picked up the news that Fort Spinder was abandoned, and the Pixies transferred to Orchard camp, and was not surprised at the chief's presence.

"Hello!" said Spite in his rough way, "Where's old Hyp this morning?"

Labyrinthea ran down her trap line, pushed her head between the bars of a window and called out, "Who's there?"

"Only myself, sweetheart!" answered one of her lovers; and thereupon he sprang out of an adjoining window and clambered up the ladder-like lines toward the keeper.* But madam was in no humor for such trifling, so she lashed the gallant heartily with a whip of silken cords that she carried at her girdle along with the prison key. The amorous Pixie retreated, more rapidly than he had advanced, amidst the jeers and laughter of the crowd beneath. The keeper again

---

* Appendix, Note B.

looked out and seeing who was there, asked what was wanted.

"The Captain wants to see old Hyp," one of his aides replied.

"You'd better put a bridle on your tongue, young

FIG. 97.—Madam Labyrinthea Lashes an Impudent Lover.

sir," was the response. "Isn't it just as easy to call folks by their proper names? 'Hyptiotes' isn't much more to say than 'old Hyp;' and besides shows decent respect to a better man than yourself."

Another burst of laughter greeted the discomfiture of

the Pixie aide; after which Spite said: "We have called to see this patent spring net that Hyptiotes has invented. Where shall we find the fellow's laboratory? It is close by here we are told."

The party was directed to the adjoining tree, a low growth of pine, where they found the inventor awaiting them. He was already stationed upon his net, which he called from its shape the "Triangle," a name, by the way, that has been transferred to himself. It is in fact a triangular snare composed of four threads gradually widening at one end and at the other converging upon a single thread. The four threads are regularly crossed in the manner of the common orbweb, and indeed the whole snare resembles a section of four radii cut out of a round snare. The line upon which the threads converge is fastened to some fixed object and on this, back downward, Hyptiotes was placed.*

When Spite's party arrived he left his position to greet them, and at once began to explain the spring net. His son was stationed on the trap line, and as he got into position I could see the whole snare rapidly tightening up until every cord was taut. "Now," said Hyptiotes, "observe that the operator holds that part of the trap line next the net within his hands. The part next the branch he holds with one foot. These two parts are drawn tight. Now see! between the lad's two feet there is a third portion of the line which is slack, and coiled up in a loose ball."

"Yes, yes," said Spite gruffly, "we all see that; but how does the machine work? That's what we want to know."

"Patience, Captain! I'm coming to that. Watch please! I will let this bit of leaf represent the insect,

---

Appendix, Note C.

or a Brownie if you prefer. I shall throw it quickly
against the net and do you note what follows."

As the scrap struck the cross lines, instantly the whole
structure flew forward with a slight snap, then as suddenly was drawn taut, and again snapped loose. This
was repeated several times. The leaf was caught by
the sudden relaxing and shooting forward of the cross
lines which by this motion were thrown around the leaf;

FIG. 98.—The Snare of Hyptiotes.

the latter, after several springs of the net, was completely entangled and hung vibrating within the snare.

"There," cried Hyptiotes, "you see how well it works!
Let me show you the principle. You have seen the coil
of slack line between the two feet. Fix your eye now
upon the foremost one. I will touch the net. See!
instantly this claw releases its hold upon the line, and

17

the whole net shoots forward as far as the coil will allow it. Follow closely, still, and you will see that the claws rapidly pull in and tighten up the trap line while the coil of slack line meanwhile again rolls up. That's the whole secret of my spring net." So saying, Hyptiotes put his front paws over his head, and stroked it forward with a self-satisfied air as though he, at least, had no doubt of the high merit of his trap.

Spite examined the structure carefully, made several more trials of its working, and then expressed his hearty approval. "Very good, indeed. I think it will be a valuable addition to our armory. Now, if we only had a few Brownies at hand for you to try it on, your demonstration would be quite perfect. By the way——" He clapped his hands together and laughed. "A capital idea that!"

He turned to his staff of Pixie officers, and made some remark which I could not hear. But they cast glances upward toward my prison, and the thought flashed upon me that Spite's sudden idea referred to me. Could it be possible? Did they mean to test their new machine on me? Two officers left the group and ran toward the main gate of the Labyrinth. I closed my trap door and with as composed frame as I could command, awaited the issue. Soon Madam Labyrinthea and the two Pixies were heard climbing up the ladder. They entered the dome; they ascended to my cell. "Come," they said without further ceremony, "follow us. Our Captain has sent for you."

I was led to Hyptiotes' grounds; the Pixies formed a wide circle around me and the inventor was ordered to go ahead. Of course my captors supposed me to be ignorant of their plans, and doubtless thought to take me by surprise. But I was on my guard, although I hid my knowledge under an indifferent mien. I secretly slipped my knife into my hand and waited.

"Go over to the opposite side of the circle!" ordered Spite. I started in a quiet walk.

"Run!" shouted Spite fiercely.

"Run, run!" echoed the whole crowd in chorus, no doubt thinking to startle and confuse me by their sudden clamor.

I quickened my gait to a brisk trot, but kept my eyes aslant toward the point where I saw young Hyptiotes waiting to cast the net. In a moment the snare left his hands and flew toward me. I dodged low to the ground and made a quick leap toward the narrow end of the snare, hoping thus to escape the worse entanglement of the wide end. I was only partly successful. In spite of my efforts I was caught in the narrow point of the net and thrown by a sudden jerk to the earth.

The Pixies set up a roar of joy, which was lucky for me, because under cover of their excitement I could use my knife unobserved. In a trice I had freed my limbs and risen upon my knees; and under pretence of struggling and swinging my arms, severed the trap line beyond the point of the snare with a swift stroke. I was free, and getting to my feet began quietly to brush the shreds of cobwebs from face and clothes.

The Pixie glee suddenly ceased. I heard the harsh voice of old Hyptiotes roundly berating his son whom he blamed, or chose to appear to blame, for the failure of his invention. I knew better, but kept my secret. However, I glanced toward young Hyptiotes who never moved a muscle during all the cursing and clamor that assailed him.* Meanwhile I slipped my knife beneath my belt and quietly awaited the will of my captors.

---

* Appendix, Note D.

"Take him back to prison," growled Spite; "We'll try him again to-morrow."

"Aye, aye," said old Hyptiotes, "and I'll then spring the net myself, and answer with my head that the miserable Brownie don't dodge out a second time."

I was led back to my cell, and my thoughts were not very agreeable, you may be sure. But I resolved to at least try to escape before the morrow. I knew my doom was sealed if I remained, and could be no worse were I caught trying to flee. I had already planned a way of escape, and made some preparations for it. I waited until nightfall, quietly opened my trap door, crept over the roof, and softly stepped upon the ladder-like lines of the maze which surrounds the prison. Just at that moment I heard a loud sound within the cell. As ill fate would have it, my keeper had taken a notion to visit me! Perhaps she was anxious about the morrow; maybe she only wished to enjoy a sight of my misery in view of my gloomy prospects. At all events, she had

Fig. 99.—"Young Hyptiotes Never Moved a Muscle."

never before visited me at that hour, and now had happened upon me at the worst possible time. I cast an anxious glance backward, and, O wretched blunder! saw that I had forgotten to close the trap door behind me. My way of exit would of course be seen at once and the cry be raised.

What should I do? Think quickly, Dodge! and think well, for your life hangs upon this moment's decision. I heard the sharp cry of Madam Labyrinthea. I could feel the swing of her body as she threw herself upon the ladder that led up to the trap door.

In another moment she would be upon the roof and I should be discovered. My first thought was to slide down to the ground and run for it. But a second thought was better. Just before me swung within the maze a triple cradle or

Fig. 100.—Labyrinthea's Snare and Cocoons. Where is Dodge's Jail?

cocoon string provided for the young Labyrintheans. I had already, in one of my former night adventures, cut open one of these, and made a burrow within. I hardly knew at the time why I did this, but it was one of my old dodges (which I had taught Sergeant Clearview, by the way), when out on a scout to take refuge in one of these vacant Pixie baby houses. They are snug and comfortable places, too. Now I saw what to do! I swung myself by a line across the intervening space, pushed open the little slit in the side of the cocoon, crawled within, curled myself up, drew down the flap closely, and waited.* My heart beat a tattoo. I could see nothing, but heard the feet of Labyrinthea rattling over the roof; felt the tremor of the lines as she sprang from them, after a pause, during which I guessed that she was looking around for me. I heard her loud alarm to the guards; felt the shaking of the Labyrinth foundations as the Pixies ran to and fro; more than once felt the pressure of feet clambering over the cocoons in the hurried rush across the maze.

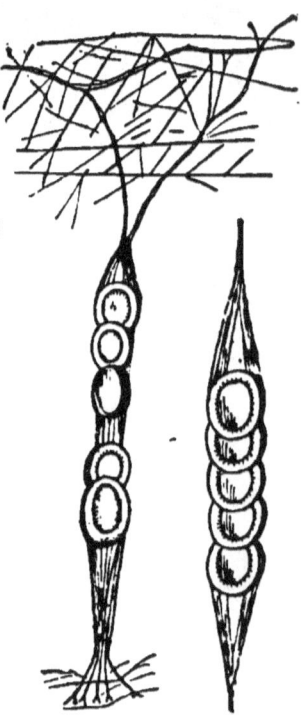

FIG. 101.—Labyrinthea's Cocoon String.

There was great commotion at the gate of the jail; then the din lessened, grew faint, rolled away and died out in the distance. No one had thought of my retreat as a possible hiding place. For the present at least, I was safe, though much cramped in my close quarters.

* Appendix, Note E.

I opened the slit for a breath of fresh air, and ventured
to look out. All was still. Shall I slip out now or not?
I queried. No! The whole Pixie host is afoot, beating
the bushes in every quarter. I cannot run such a gauntlet of eager searchers without detection. I will wait
until the pursuers are tired out and have returned.
They will give me up, will relax guard around the
prison, and beyond it the coast will be clear.

So I did. I heard the returning guards; heard Labyrinthea puffing and storming up the stairway to her
dome, and as I kept the slit in the cocoon a little ajar
could even make out her angry oaths. Her disappointment at my escape evidently softened her toward her
gallants, for I heard her exchanging views with the one
whom she had lashed away from her in the morning,
over the mysterious disappearance of her prisoner. How
could he have got off unnoticed? It was plain from the
talk that Spite suspected the keeper herself of some
connivance at my escape; but I wasn't much concerned about that.

As the day dawned everything was quiet. The keeper
and guards were asleep. Now is my time, I thought.
So I left my cramped but cosy silken retreat, slid down
the ropes to the ground, and glided away into the grass.
I got safely through the Pixie lines, made myself known
to our own pickets, and here I am, thankful and happy
as ever Brownie was or will be!"

Dodge's story was eagerly listened to, and he was
heartily congratulated upon his rare good fortune. Bruce
and his officers questioned him about all that he had
seen within the enemy's lines, and drew from him much
valuable information. Then as a reward for his skill and
pluck, and as a salve for his sufferings, he was promoted
to be a sergeant and went away jubilant to his quarters.

# CHAPTER XXIII.

The Ken, it will be remembered, made for Ellen's Isle, when pursued by the Pixie Ram. Lieutenant Swift never checked her speed until he had run his ship under the shelter of the northern shore. Thence he rejoined the fleet, after the Ram had gone down, and sailed on with Rodney up the channel.

Coxswain Help steered for the island. The Stygians lay between him and his own fleet, and should he make for Orchard shore he would risk capture. Ellen's Isle was nearest; his boat was overloaded; the Ken seemed to be already there awaiting them under the northern bank.

"Give way heartily, lads," he said, "we shall soon be on board the Ken."

The sailors pulled with a will, and although loaded down almost to the gunwale, the boat made fair speed. The sinking of the Ram, which they saw quite plainly, put fresh vigor into their arms. They could hardly hold in their cheers; but Help ordered silence, as he had no wish to call the Pixies' attention to them. The island was reached, but a sore disappointment awaited them, for the Ken had gone on, and the Nattie ships were far up the channel. Clearview climbed atop of a bush and looked across the island to the south channel.

"There is the Pixie squadron crowding on all sail toward the inlet," he said. "The Stygians are not yet in sight of our fleet, but it cannot be long before they

(228)

meet. Look yonder to the north! The other half of the Pixie fleet has sailed out of the harbor, and is running up the channel." Now the officers consulted as to what should be done.

"My duty is on the water," said Help, "I yield the chief command to our superior officer, Adjutant Blythe. Captain Clearview will take command of the boat. I shall lend a hand wherever I can."

"Very good," said Blythe; "but let us settle what is to be done first. We can fix the matter of rank afterward."

"Well said, Adjutant," remarked True. "In our condition the readiest helper has the highest rank. Let him lead us, who knows how to get us out of trouble. Can't we cross the south channel? That's our own side, you know."

"Not in one trip of our boat," said Clearview. "It was shipping water freely before we landed. The distance to the south shore is much greater than that which we have come. We might divide and make two trips, but that doubles the risk, and gives less chance to the party left behind should the Pixies land here. Suppose we wait until the fleets meet, and act as may then seem best. See! even while we speak, one of the Pixie ships is landing at the head of the island."

"Can you make her out, Captain?" asked Help.

"Yes, it's the Doubt, Master Shallow's craft. I would know the cut of her jib among a thousand."

"What are they doing?" asked Blythe. "Are they sending boats ashore?"

"Yes, they have anchored off the Big Rocks; and one, two, three boats are pulling into the cove above."

"Three, did you say?" returned Blythe. "Then let us attack them, and we shall have enough boats wherewith to leave the island. I feel that I could almost clean out a boat load myself."

"No, no, Adjutant!" answered True; "nobody doubts either your ability or appetite for fighting Pixies.

Fig. 102.—"Abandoned Snares."

But we can't afford to take such a risk. My advice is that we run our boat under these clumps of iris, and bivouac for a while beneath the thick foliage that crowns yonder bank. We shall be out of sight, shall have

time to rest the men, and can then get off safely. We
have everything to gain by waiting."

True's advice was taken. The boat was hidden,
a snug bivouac was made near a clump of hazel bushes
upon the high land beyond the shore, and the crew threw
themselves upon the grass to rest. Scouts were sent out
to beat around the neighboring foliage in search of lurking Pixies. There were many signs that they had lately
been upon the spot, such as abandoned snares and vacant
lodges, and deserted nurseries woven into balls from
the seeded and feath-
ery tops of grasses.
Apparently, all who
could march or sail
or move through the
air had gone off to
join the Pixie forces
on land or water.
Only a colony of
youngling Orbweav-
ers remained snugly
tented around a
Jack-in-the-Pulpit.
Most of them were

FIG. 103.—" Vacant Lodges."

balled in a round mass under one of the leaves, packed together, with legs and arms intertwined, and sound asleep.

One of the Scouts was keen to mount the plants,
cut the tent cords and disperse the brood of younglings.
But Blythe forbade, " for," said he, " they'll keep
under cover while we are on the island, and it's always
wise to let well enough alone. They can do us no
harm, so we'll not harm them."

Now, Captain Clearview and Sergeant True climbed
into a tree to note how the two fleets came on. With

a heavy heart they saw their squadron, after a brief struggle, sail away toward the inlet. The Doubt rejoined her companions, but one of her boats remained upon the island. What could that portend?

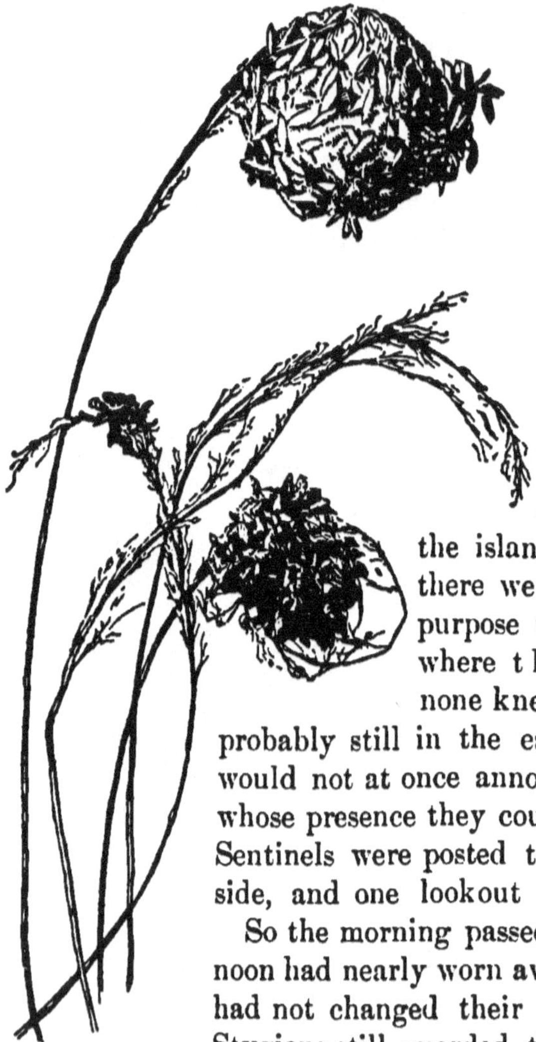

Clearview and True told what they had seen, and urged all to guard against surprise. Their enemies were on the island. How many there were, or for what purpose they stayed, or where they might be, none knew. They were probably still in the eastern end, and would not at once annoy the Brownies, whose presence they could not suspect. Sentinels were posted toward the land side, and one lookout upon the shore.

So the morning passed, and the afternoon had nearly worn away. The fleets had not changed their positions. The Stygians still guarded the inlet, but the heavy davids mounted at the mouth thereof held them in check. Two or three Pixie vessels were slowly sailing down the north channel coasting along the island. There had been no

FIG. 104.—"Deserted Nurseries Woven into Balls."

sign of the Doubt's mysterious boat's crew. All was quiet. No chance yet to escape.

A squad under Help's command was sent out to forage. They had not been gone long when the little camp was aroused by an alarm from one of the sentinels. The Brownies sprang to arms, thinking that the Doubt's boat crew had attacked them. There was a sound as of feet trampling among ferns and grasses. Some one was approaching rapidly,—several persons evidently; and they were charging at full run upon the picket line.

"Stand!" cried the guard. "Who goes there?"

There was no reply. Then one of the sailors of Help's squad, and a second, and a third leaped from the underbrush, sprang by the sentinel regardless of his challenge, and ran into the midst of the camp. They were breathless, pale, trembling, terrified.

"Well," cried Blythe, "this is something new, truly! Full sized Brownies, and Natties at that, running like a frightened rabbit from a Pixie! Why, comrades, what has possessed you? Speak, can't you?" They could not speak. The poor fellows were so overcome that they had to sit down. Water was given them, and they revived.

"Come, now," said True firmly, "this has gone far enough. What is the cause of this?"

One of the three could just utter the single word— "Pipe!" The very name set the sailors shivering again with terror.

"This is most unaccountable!" exclaimed Blythe. "What do you mean, fellow? What about Pipe? Do you mean our poor boatswain who was lost this morning?"

"Yes—yes!" gasped the sailor. "We—have—seen —him! Oh, oh!" He uttered a cry as he spoke, jumped to his feet, threw up his arms, pointed toward the picket line and fell flat upon the grass.

All eyes turned in the direction of the poor fellow's hand. There stood Pipe the Boatswain! A chorus of mingled groans, shrieks and cries arose from the company. The sailors scattered into the ferns and bushes. The officers stood their ground, but there was not one among them who would not have run had he dared.

The figure slowly advanced. The eyes were sunken, the face pale, the hair hung damp and matted around the face and brow. The clothes were ragged and clung closely to the body. The eyes had, or seemed to have, an unnatural brightness. They were fixed steadily upon the officers. Step by step, nearer and nearer the figure came. But it spoke no word. There could be no mistake about it. It was Pipe the drowned boatswain!

Now Sergeant True, like most sensible persons, knew that if there were such things as ghosts they must be harmless creatures. He had often said that; and declared that he would like to meet a ghost. But if the truth were known, he would rather have been excused just then. However, he spoke at last.

"Speak! whatever you be! Spirit, ghost, or living flesh,—tell us what you are, and why you are come here!"

The figure stopped. A strange, familiar light played upon the pale face, and glimmered around the corner of the eyes. Then into the death-like silence the image spoke with a husky voice:

"Well, shipmates, this is a rather tough greeting on one's return from a long voyage! What's i' the wind, that you all run from your old comrade, and stand staring at me as though I were a ghost? Hey, my boy, don't you know Sophie's daddy?"

FIG. 105.—"A Colony of Youngling Orbweavers as Snugly Tented Under a Jack-in-the Pulpit."

"Pipe, Pipe! it is Pipe himself!" exclaimed True, and he rushed forward and took the dear old sailor in his arms.

"There, there," said the boatswain, "that'll do for the present. Cast off grapnels, please, and save your hugging for some one who likes it better. Hello, you lubbers!"—addressing the sailors,—"get up, here! I'm ashamed of the cloth, I am. Yes, it's Pipe—who else? Want proof of it, do you?" The sailors were sitting upon the ground staring, dumb and incredulous, upon their old officer. "Well, here goes then. You know the sound of pipe to quarters, I'll be bound." So saying he put his whistle to his lips, and sounded the old familiar note.

It was enough. The frightened foragers rose and shook hands with Pipe. The scattered runaways came back. An eager crowd surrounded the boatswain to hear him explain this marvelous resurrection from the deep.

"Well, it's easily enough explained. Come to think of it now, I don't wonder that you took me for a ghost. In sooth, it is not often that a Brownie stays under water for a whole day, and comes up again, unless, may be, as a ghost."

"What! Under water a whole day?" cried Help. "You don't mean that seriously, do you?"

"Aye, aye, shipmate, that I do. It has not been half an hour since I left the depths of the lake there. I went down with the rest under the keel of that infernal old pot that the Pixies set afloat. I supposed my time had come at last. But no one seems to be willing to die even when his time has come; so you see, I struck out pretty lively, so as to get clear of the wreck and the drowning crews as I came up, and then allowed myself to rise. First thing I knew I was diving straight through the door of a water pixie's nest! You know there are some of those creatures who make a kind of hollow globe or diving bell under the water."

"Yes," said True eagerly, "the Argyroneta pixies."

"Aye, those are the fellows. Well, they stay and balance their nest with cables, which they fasten to stems of water plants; then they mount to the surface, catch a bubble of air in the little hairs of their legs and hands, sink with it and shoot it up into the nest. When it is filled they have a water-tight house filled with air, down in the very midst of the lake. It is a cunning thing even if it is made by a Pixie.

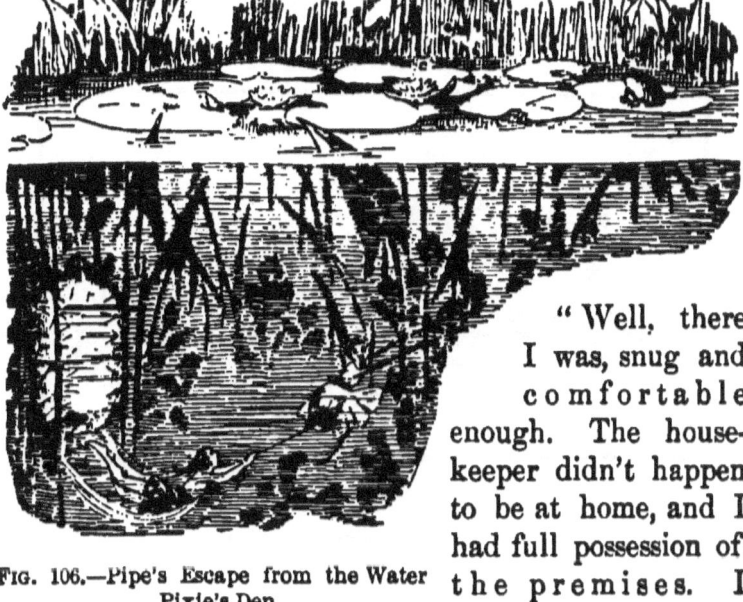

"Well, there I was, snug and comfortable enough. The housekeeper didn't happen to be at home, and I had full possession of the premises. I couldn't make up my

FIG. 106.—Pipe's Escape from the Water Pixie's Den.

mind what to do. Of course, I knew that I couldn't stay there always; but I feared to crawl out and mount to the surface. Either way my chance seemed pretty slim for life. I concluded to wait a while anyhow, and stretched myself upon a sort of web hammock that hung from the sides. I looked every moment for the landlady to report, and loosened my knife to welcome her home. However, she didn't come, and after a long waiting I fell asleep. How long I slept I don't know. I was aroused by a slight swaying of the diving bell nest. The proprietor was coming in, sure as the world! She was already half way through the port-hole. I clutched my knife and got ready to cut away. But a thought struck me. Think's I, can't I lay hold of the old lady, and get her to tow me out of this, and may be ashore? I put my knife between my teeth and waited quietly until Mrs. Argyroneta had got fairly into her cabin. Then I leaped from my hammock,

THE BOY'S ILLUSTRATION.

FIG. 107.—Pipe and the Pixie.

grabbed her by a hind leg, and yelled at the top of my lungs. Whew! you ought to have seen that Pixie get. She turned and made through the port, mounted to the surface, and flew across it like the flying Dutchman. I found it a little hard to hold on to her leg. But the creature had cast out of her spinnerets a good stout cable as she turned to leave her nest, which I seized with both hands. *

* Appendix, Note A.

" I should hate to say how many knots, an hour we rated. The Pixie went so fast that my head was kept above water by the swiftness of the motion. She made straight for the island, and upon my word, I believe she would have towed me clear ashore if it hadn't been for an accident. In doubling the edge of a cluster of water lilies my tug struck a snag and capsized. The rope slackened and I had to swim for it. Mrs. Argyroneta dived. Not relishing a second journey to the bottom of the lake, I cut the cable with my knife and clambered on top of a lily leaf. After some trouble I managed to cut the leaf loose, and as the wind and current set in toward the island, I drifted ashore just below here. I had scarcely landed when I met these hearties here, who broke off into the woods at a livelier rate than even my Pixie tug had made. That is the whole of my yarn. And now if you please, give me something to eat for I'm mortal hungry."

" What became of your Pixie ?" asked Blythe.

" Never saw her after she dived," returned Pipe. " I reckon she's going yet, for a worse scared creature, barring these three Jacks of ours, of course, I never saw. But, come comrades, here I have been spinning my yarn about my own miserable carcass, and all the time have heard nothing of the fleet. To tell the truth, I've been afraid to ask. But let me know the worst, all of it, while the cooks are getting supper ready."

The story was soon told. The good sailor was glad to find affairs had gone no worse. His joy over the ignoble end of the Pixie monitor was particularly keen.

" Humph !" he said, "just what I thought. A lubberly old pot ! And any seaman that would sail in such an affair deserves no better fate than to be sent to the bottom by a dragoon's cutlass."

# CHAPTER XXIV.

## THE WISDOM OF THE PIXIES.

In the meantime how fared it with Faith and Sophia?
The hours of captivity dragged wearily along. The
nagging and petty annoyance of their keeper were hard
to bear, but their chief dread was the coming of Spite
and Hide. They knew nothing of passing events, for
not a creature had been seen or heard since Spite and
Raft left, except Tigrina. In the depths of that Pixie
cave they were shut off from the upper world, and their
grim and vigilant guardian kept them strictly to their
rooms.

They had no heart at first to note the furnishings of
their prison. But as time passed their spirits somewhat
rallied. They began to observe the things around them,
which were wrought with exquisite taste and skill.
Tapestry, carpets, sofas, cushions, stools, couches all were
woven of silk. There were pictures and statuary, books
and portfolios bound elegantly in yellow, purple and
white silk, and illuminated with gold, bronze and divers
colors* The Nurses wandered from one to another of
these objects, which compelled their admiration and interest. The works of art were exquisitely done.

Many of the books, the maidens noticed, treated of
natural objects, laws, forces, and phenomena. The
wonders of air, earth, and sea were told and illustrated
in many volumes. Faith and Sophia were much interested in these. Their fondness for Nature was great, and

---

* Appendix, Note A.

(240)

the books and prints which lay around them in such wealth well nigh beguiled their thoughts from their griefs.

"Look at this, Sophie," cried Faith, who had just happened upon a rare volume rich in the arts of type, graver and brush. It lay by itself on a circular stand, as one sometimes sees a costly family Bible in American homes. It was plainly one of the treasures of Arachne Hall. Sophia came to her friend's side and bent over the title page which read thus:

"THE WISDOM OF THE PIXIES.

TRANSLATED FROM THE ORIGINAL OF THE LAWS OF PLUTO, AND THE WISE SAYINGS OF THE SAGES OF PIXIELAND.

ANNO MUNDI; . . . . M̄ M̄ . . . . , . . . . MDCCC."

"The Wisdom of the Pixies!" exclaimed Sophia. "That must be a curious book indeed. I never knew before that our wicked enemies professed to have a sacred book, or held to any religious notions at all. I am anxious to know what these laws of Pluto may be. Turn over the page, Faith."

"I am trying to make out this date," answered Faith. "The numerals have been erased; they appear to have been written several times, amended again and again, and finally left in this uncertain condition."

"That is just it, Faith. Observe that for the common date, 'Anno Domini — year of our Lord,' has been placed 'Anno Mundi—year of the World.' It is hard for a Pixie to acknowledge in any way the Blessed Author of Salvation to Men. Let me see!—M stands for one thousand; M, M for two thousand; the bar over the top means a thousand also. M̄ is one thousand thousand, M̄, M̄ two thousand thousand, and just there

is a gap. The other legible figures count up eighteen
hundred. That is all I can make out ; but I suppose
the Pixies mean to say that the world is a good many
thousand times two hundred thousand years old! Do
you believe it?"

"That's a ripe old age, Sophie," said Faith, "and I
neither believe nor disbelieve. How can one tell? Our
fathers only say that 'in the beginning,' whenever that
was, the world was made. But the further back one
can trace the being of the earth by established facts,
just so much further can we 'walk by sight' into the
Eternity whose sovereign Lord we receive by faith."

"True enough," replied Sophia, "the question interests me as a matter of fact simply. As a matter of
religion, I suppose it has little value. At least, I have
so heard the good minister Dr. Comingo say in conversation with Governor Wille. But turn the page, please!"

Faith turned the leaves of the book, reading aloud
the titles of the chapters. Now and then she stopped,
read a sentence or two, commented upon the sentiment,
and contrasted it with the good, pure, unselfish laws of
Brownieland. Our story need not be burdened with
much of what Faith and Sophia saw in the "Wisdom of
the Pixies," but some of our older readers will be curious
to have a few extracts. Here they are, with the head-
ings or titles of the chapters given, for the most part:

Chapter I. On the First and Great Law—Take Care
of Number One. . . . Chapter II. On the Chief End
of Life—Eat, Drink and be Merry, for To-morrow You
Die. . . . Chapter IX. The End Justifies the Means.
. . . Chapter X. On Attaining One's End: By Fair
Means if You Can, by Foul Means if You Must. . . .
Chapter XV. Showing That an Individual Cannot
Wrong a Corporation—On the Right of Corporations to

Plunder the People. . . . Chapter XVI. Showing That it Cannot be Wrong to Rob a Government. . . . Chapter XVII. Showing That Since the World Loves to be "Humbugged," it is Quite Lawful to Gratify it, for One's Own Advantage. . . . Chapter XXXV. Is Man an Automaton?

"Why, what a strange notion!" cried Sophie. "What sage starts that question?"

"It appears to be some Chinese sage whose sentiments are quoted, if I may judge by the name—Hoox Lee."

"And what has he to say about it?"

"Well, there is a good deal. Here's a section on the 'Evidence of Transmitted Peculiarities' that starts out thus: Every one has noted the interest that the young of the human species take in dolls, marionettes, and exhibitions of such figures as the famous Punch and Judy, and Mrs. Jarley's wax works. This is a universal characteristic. Whence does it arise? Why should this instinctive sympathy of children with Automata and their clumsy tricks, be so deep-seated and wide-spread? Evidently here is a fact which the wise and candid philosopher should ponder. Here, it may be, is a thread by which we may traverse the labyrinth of man's mysterious nature. The deduction cannot well be resisted, that this natural and inwrought sympathy with the Automaton, in all its varying forms, is owing to the kinship of man himself with the Simian."

"Oh, that will do!" exclaimed Sophia breaking short the sentence. "That certainly is quite as funny as the Punch and Judy which Governor Wille had shown at his children's party, last Thanksgiving Day. But is Mr. Hoox Lee in earnest do you think?"

"He seems to be," answered Faith, joining in with

Sophia's quiet laughter. "But here is the next chapter." Chapter XL. To be Found Out is the Essence of Wrong.

"Turn on!'"

Chapter XLIII. The Pleasure and Security of Drinking Liquors in Moderation. . . . Chapter XLIX. Wine and Beer Drinking the Sovereign Remedy for Drunkenness. . . . Chapter L. On the Origin of the Universe.

"Ah! What has the sage to say on that point?" asked Sophia.

"Far too much to read now. This seems to be a favorite theme with the sages; there are a great many pages. Here is the opening section : ' According to the sacred writings of the Pundits of India, a certain immense spider was the origin, the first cause of all things. This spider drawing the matter from its own bowels, wove the web of this universe, and disposed it with wonderful art. She, in the meantime sitting in the centre of her work, feels and directs the motions of every part, till at length, when she has pleased herself sufficiently in ordering and contemplating this web, she draws again into herself all the threads she had spun out and, having absorbed them, the universal nature of all creatures vanishes into nothing.' "

"Dear me," said Sophia, "how very like that is to the ' nebular theory ' that we heard the Professor discussing one evening with Governor Wille on the great porch. But pray, whence came the spider? Who made her? I wonder the sages didn't think of that question?"

Faith resumed the reading: "The natives of Guinea believe that the first man was created by a large black spider which is so common in their country, and is called in their jargon ' Ananse.' "

"Now, that is too bad!" said Sophia once more interrupting the reading. "I could believe that the Pixies came that way, but to say that men were so made! But that is the way with the sages of unbelief. They had rather think the universe to have been spun out of the spinnerets of a big black spider, than admit that in the beginning the Holy God made all things."

Faith made no answer, but stood silently turning over the leaves. The silence was broken by a sound that startled the Nurses, and struck terror into their hearts. We must go back to the Brownie's island camp in order to explain this sudden interruption.

# CHAPTER XXV.

## BLYTHE'S FLUTE.

Despite their position the wrecked Brownies were in good spirits. The restoration of Pipe had taken a load off their hearts. The reaction was so great, after their grief and the certainty of his loss, that low spirits vanished from the camp. The boatswain's resurrection seemed an omen of good fortune. The cheer that filled all hearts bubbled over in song, laughter, merry tale and joke. But as the Brownies feared to attract the attention of the Doubt's crew who were yet on the island, they kept the sound of their merrymaking within bounds of their picket lines.

Blythe added much to the enjoyment of the occasion. By some rare chance, as he was setting out for the fleet in the morning, he had flung over his shoulder his flute box, which he often carried in a little case something after the manner of a field glass. It had clung to him when the Ken's boat went down, and there was the flute, ready to swell the joy of the bivouac. Blythe was quite in the spirit to play, and all hearts were in tune to listen.

Again and again the notes of the sweet instrument murmured among the overhanging branches. Camp tunes, battle tunes, love tunes, home tunes—the hearts of the Brownies were stirred by turns with tender, pathetic, sad or fond emotions as the well known strains fell upon their ears.

"Come, lads," cried Pipe, "cannot we have a song?"

"Aye, aye, a song, a song!" was called from all sides.

"What shall it be?" asked Blythe. "I will gladly accompany Captain Clearview here, who is an excellent singer. Captain, what say you? Shall we have 'Woodmen, Boatmen, Sailors and Horsemen?' The lads like that and can join in the chorus."

"Play away!" said Clearview, and at the proper note he struck in and sang the following song, in the refrain of which all the company joined:

### THE BROWNIES' NATIONAL SONG.

#### O MERRY AND FREE!
##### OR
##### WOODMEN, BOATMEN, SAILORS AND HORSEMEN.

#### I.

O merry and free,
'Neath the wildwood tree,
Are the Woodmen of Brownieland, bonnie and dee;
 Too—ra—lah, too—ra—loo, too—ra—lay!
In the breeze there is balm,
In the sky there is calm,
Each sound in the wood is the voice of a psalm;
 Too—ra—lah, too—ra—loo, too—ra—lay!

#### II.

O merry and free,
On the lake and lea,
Are the Boatmen of Brownieland, bonnie and dee;
 Too—ra—lah, too—ra—loo, too—ra—lay!
For the trout's rushing leap,
And the water-fowl's sweep,
With the paddle's soft dip sweet harmony keep;
 Too—ra—lah, too—ra—loo, too—ra—lay!

#### III.

O merry and free,
On the wrinkled sea,
Are the sailors of Brownieland, bonnie and dee;
 Too—ra—lah, too—ra—loo, too—ra—lay!
For the creaking of sail,
And the sough of the gale,
And splashing of waves, are the songs that ne'er fail;
 Too—ra—lah, too—ra—loo, too—ra—lay!

IV.

O merry and free,
Over hill and lea,
Are the troopers of Brownieland, bonnie and dee;
　　Too—ra—lah, too—ra—loo, too—ra—lay!
It is pleasure indeed,
To be one with the steed
In his strength, and thrill with the rhythm of speed;
　　Too—ra—lah, too—ra—loo, too—ra—lay!

"Hist—st!"

The sharp prolonged sibilant that broke in upon their applause and caused instant silence, was uttered by Sergeant True. He advanced into the circle with his hand raised warningly.

"Hist! Quiet all!—except you, Blythe. Keep on with your music. Play some of your softest airs, and play until I bid you stop. As for the rest of you, I charge you, for your lives, not to speak or move until you hear from me. No matter what you see—perfect silence, remember!"

He stepped back again into the bushes and was hidden from sight. What could the strange interruption mean? The Brownies were all alive with keen curiosity. Was the Sergeant in a merry humor, and planning some trick upon the party? They suspected that. But it was not much after True's habit to do such a thing. Besides, his manner betokened unusual earnestness. Therefore, all sat still, looking into the bushes whither True had disappeared. The Adjutant promptly fell into his friend's plan. He obeyed orders, played away and waited.

"Hist! look up! But don't stop the music, and don't stir!" said True in a low voice.

All eyes turned upward. A faint rustling among the branches directed the party's gaze to the point of interest. A quaint old hag of a Pixie was slowly crawling along the twig above Blythe's head. It was our acquaintance, Dame Tigrina!

Blythe's heart fluttered a little, it must be confessed. It really seemed that the grim creature was preparing to pounce upon him. See! she is just above the musician's head. She has fastened a cable to the branch and is slowly lowering herself toward the ground.

THE BOY'S ILLUSTRATION.

FIG. 108.—Blythe's Flute Charms Tigrina.

There was a slight quaver in the notes of the flute that could not be credited wholly to the performer's intention. Yet, he behaved with wonderful coolness and courage. The music went on; not a false note, not a pause, while the Pixie was gradually lowering herself toward the ground.

When about one-third of the descent had been made, Tigrina paused and sat quite still. She was listening to the music, not foraging for victims! Blythe's flute had charmed her forth from her cell. There she hung in mid air indulging her fondness for sweet sounds. Who would have thought it of the old hag? However, it would perhaps be well to mention that it has frequently been reported that some Pixies are strangely sensitive to music.*

True's conduct was now explained. He had caught a glimpse of the Pixinee when she first left her hall, but had not been able to mark the spot from which she came. When the singing stopped and the applause began, Tigrina retreated so rapidly and stealthily that the Sergeant again failed to note the door of her cave, but saw the general direction and neighborhood thereof. He thought that if Blythe would repeat the music it would charm the old creature forth once more, and so it proved.

From his blind in the bushes he saw the cave door slowly open, and marked the spot. He saw the Pixinee peep here and there, then, satisfied that the coast was clear, return to her place above the musician, where she hung and listened as before.

True had gained his point. He did not indeed understand how near he was to his heart's great desire. But he had thought it probable that Faith and Sophia might be hidden on the island in some of the Pixie dens, and at once resolved to follow up this fortunate incident in hope that it might give a clew to a more important discovery. He quietly left his hiding place, planted himself before the spot whence Tigrina had come, and drew his battle axe.

---

* Appendix, Note A.

"Hist!" The sound directed the Brownies' attention toward him. "Close in around me when I call.
Don't move before that. Now, Blythe,—stop!"

The music ceased. No one stirred for a moment or
two; then Tigrina, as though persuaded that the per-
formance had ended, scampered up the cable from which
she hung, and hurried off toward her cave.

"Close up!" ordered True.

The company rushed forward and surrounded the
Sergeant, who now stood with axe poised, face to face
with the Pixinee. Tigrina was in the act of springing
upon True. Her claws were outstretched, her eyes were
ablaze with excitement, and in the greatness of her
wrath her fangs clattered against each other.

As the Brownies closed the circle about her, she
started, and cast a quick, terrified glance around her.
Then her whole visage changed; the arms fell to her
side; her face dropped upon her chest; her limbs relaxed;
the eyes became glassy and fixed; she suddenly sank to
the ground and lay rigid and motionless.

True lowered his axe. An exclamation of surprise
broke from the group.

"Is she dead?" asked several at once.

Pipe stepped to Tigrina's side and cautiously turned
her body with his foot.

"'Pon my honor," he said, "I do believe the old witch
has burst a blood-vessel, or had an attack of apoplexy.
She's dead as a mackerel."

"It does seem so, indeed," remarked True, who had
also examined the body. "There is every sign of death,
beyond doubt. For my part I don't wonder, for I never
saw such a swift and terrible change in any living creature as came over this one."

"Come," said Clearview, "let me try an experiment.

I know something more of the tricks of these Pixies than you. They can beat the 'possums at feigning death. Now, I venture that Madame here is as alive and awake as any of you. Stand back a little. We shall see. Bring me a cord."

A stout cord was brought by one of the sailors. Clearview approached cautiously, and looped the rope around all the Pixinee's limbs except one arm. During all this there was no sign of life.

"Hand me your axe, Sergeant." The weapon was passed to him. "Observe now," continued Clearview, "that I intend to strike just where that claw lies. If the creature is dead it will not hurt her to have it chopped off."

FIG. 109.—Attitudes of Spiders When Feigning Death.

He lifted the axe deliberately, and struck directly at the unbound arm which was stretched out motionless upon the grass. The blade sank into the ground ! The claw had been removed by a quick motion as the axe fell.

"Phew——ew !" said Pipe, drawing a long breath. "Talk about wonders of the stage ! That acting beats Charlotte Cushman all hollow."*

A burst of merriment broke from the circle of astonished and amused Brownies, in the midst of which Tigrina slowly raised her body from the ground, and sat up looking around upon her captors, quite crestfallen.

"Well," she said at last, "now you have me, what'll you do with me ?"

* Appendix, Note B.

The Brownie officers held a brief, whispered consultation. Then the boatswain addressed Tigrina.

"Old woman, we shall exchange few words with you.
You know well that your life in ordinary circumstances
wouldn't be worth a salt herring. But you've just one
chance for it. I have lost a daughter. She was carried
off with one of her companions by some of your people.
We have found no trace of the maidens yet. If you
can tell anything that shall lead to their discovery, your
life shall be spared. If not, you die instantly."

Tigrina sat with eyes fixed upon the ground. Her
face had a stubborn cast that showed indifference to life,
or determination to yield nothing for the sake of saving
it. She remained silent.

"Well," continued the boatswain, "have you nothing
to say? Do you know anything? Speak out. You
shall find us true to our word, as Brownies always are."

"For Heaven's sake," cried Blythe impatiently, "if
you can put us on the track of our lost friends, do so!
You shall not only have your life, but whatever
besides—"

"Hah! What interest have you in the silly things?"
asked Tigrina looking up quickly. Her whole manner
had changed at the first sound of his voice. Her eyes
dropped slowly from the Adjutant's face to the flute
which he still held in his hands, and there remained
fixed.

"I have a deep and tender interest in one of them,"
exclaimed Blythe. "And I pledge you my word, with
the boatswain, to stand between you and death if you
will tell us where we can find Faith and Sophia."

There was a moment's silence, so profound that one
might almost have heard his neighbor's heart beat as the
Brownies awaited the Pixinee's answer. The fate of

19

their beloved Nurses seemed to hang upon her lips. Tigrina at last broke the silence :

"You will give me my life?" she said.

"Yes!" cried a score of eager voices.

"And set me free?"

"Aye, aye!" was the hearty chorus.

"And give me—that?" continued Tigrina, pointing her hairy claw toward the flute in Blythe's hand.

"It is yours!" cried the Adjutant, flinging the instrument into the Pixinee's lap.

Tigrina clutched it eagerly, turned it over and over, as a child would a new toy, looked into it, touched the keys, put it to her ears and listened, then laid it down upon her lap and gazed at it with childish fondness. All this time the Brownies looked on impatiently, but not inclined to interfere.

"Hah!" exclaimed Tigrina, "and will it sing for me, too? Pretty bird! Sing, sing!" she said as she fondled the flute tenderly.

"Come, come, old lady," cried Pipeat last. "Be done with this nonsense! Remember that neither life, freedom, nor the flute are yours until you keep your part of the bargain. So hurry up."

Tigrina looked up again with the old fierce, sullen face. "Ugh! To be sure. Well, gentlemen, I have sworn not to tell any one where the fairies are. But that big officer yonder—," she cast a savage glance at True, "knows where I live, I reckon. There's nothing to hinder you from following up what you have already found out yourselves, is there?"

A cry of joy arose from the party at these words. The hint was taken at once. What news! Faith and Sophia were found at last ! Hurrah!

Pipe turned eagerly upon Sergeant True.

"The door, the door!" he cried, "where is the door of the old hag's cave?"

Blythe sprang forward, grasped Tigrina by the arm until she fairly winced under the pressure, and exclaimed, "are they alive?—are they safe? Speak!"

"Both!" was the answer.

The cool, clear voice of Captain Clearview broke in upon the excitement. "Come, my friends, this is not wise. You are giving way to hopes that may be dashed from you. What have you to rely upon for them all? The word of an old Pixinee condemned to death. I think she has spoken truly. But let us make sure before we show our joy. First of all, take that flute from her and bind her arms securely. We will take her with us into the cave. If she has not deceived us we will be true to her. If this is all mockery and deceit—" There was no need to finish the sentence.

By this time Pipe, True and Blythe had the mossy door of the cave pushed open. They entered the silk lined vestibule, and saw the tunnel sloping away into the hill until lost in the darkness.

"A ladder and lanterns!" cried Pipe. "Haste—away!"

"Aye, aye, Sir!" answered a half dozen hearty voices. The sailors flew to the boat, and soon returned with a rope ladder and several fox-fire lanterns.

"Are we all ready?" asked True.

"Ready!"

"Come on then! and God speed the search!"

He stepped into the mouth of the cave bearing aloft one of the lights. Pipe and Blythe followed. Then came Clearview and Help leading Dame Tigrina. Several sailors brought up the rear of the party. The remainder of the crew kept guard at the entrance.

"Hark!" The word fell from the lips of both the imprisoned Nurses at once. There was a sound as of the wind blowing through the long tunneled hall that led into their room. It came nearer. It grew louder. The maidens stood still straining every nerve to resolve the meaning of the strange noises. There could be no doubt, at last, that it was the sound of approaching footsteps, mingled with voices.

"O Sophie, it is Spite the Spy!"

"O Faith, the Pixie chiefs have returned!"

With a cry of anguish they threw themselves into each other's arms. In this movement the stand bearing the "Book of the Wisdom of the Pixies" was overturned, and with a great racket fell to the floor. The large volume opened its folios as it fell, and lay spread out upon its face under the stand.

The scream of the Nurses and the crash of the stand were answered by a cry from without. The curtain door of the chamber was rent aside, and Sergeant True bearing aloft his fox-fire torch entered. Ere he could utter a word the boatswain darted past him. Sophia had sprung forward at the first vision of her lover, and found herself clasped in her father's arms! Faith had fallen upon her knees. The drapery of her gown streamed backward partially covering the gilt and silken bindings of the Pixies' Book of Unbelief. The hands of the kneeling Nurse, just as they were outstretched toward Heaven, were clasped in the fervent grasp of Adjutant Blythe, who in a moment was kneeling at Faith's side.

It was a striking and tender scene—the kneeling figures of Blythe and Faith; Sophia fast locked in her father's embrace; True standing nearby, the central figure of the group, holding his torch aloft, gazing upon

his betrothed with joy and fondness shining through the
tears upon his check. Crowded in the door and just
within the room, were the other members of the searching party, in the midst of whom stood Tigrina casting
alternate looks of anger upon the Brownies, and desire
upon the flute which had fallen from Blythe's hand and
rolled quite near her.

Why should we dwell upon what followed? The
mutual greetings, the quick exchange of experiences, the
outbreak of emotion, joy, gratitude, love—these are
better left to the reader's imagination. One may be
certain, however, that the party did not long stay inside
the Pixie's cave. To be sure, it was a snug place, and
would have been quite safe, and no doubt more comfortable to the Nurses than the rude accommodations of the
Brownie bivouac outside. But the very sight of Aranea
Hall, even with all its beautiful furnishings, was hateful
to them. They insisted upon going away from the place
with all haste.

"It is a prison, a miserable prison, however much it
may be decked like a palace," exclaimed Faith. "Let
us out of it, immediately!"

"Aye," said Sophia, "with all its silken tapestry,
carpets, and couches it is a den of Pixies, a loathsome,
dismal dungeon. Take us out of it, take us quickly!"

The happy company returned along the tunnel, and
mounted to upper air. A second greeting awaited the
rescued fairies from the party that guarded the entrance.
The boisterous joy of the Brownie sailors could hardly
be restrained. But an urgent warning of the danger
that might be called down upon their newly found loved
ones, by discovering their presence to the Doubters on
the island, kept the outbreaking happiness within bounds.

The Brownies were true to Tigrina and left her safe

within the cave in possession of the coveted flute. But they fastened the cavern door and mounted a guard over it. Then a shelter was provided for the Nurses. As willing hands and happy hearts make light work, the night was not far gone ere a tent of leaves was built. Tired out with excitement Faith and Sophia were quite ready to retire when all was prepared for them. How happy, happy, happy they were as they lay down to sleep in each other's arms! Their joy rippled over their lips in whispered congratulations and thanks, and bubbled forth in grateful tears. Then soft deep sleep, the sleep of the good and happy stole gently upon them.

It was long before the Brownie sailors settled to sleep. Weary as they were, the wish to hear the story of the capture and imprisonment of the Nurses, was stronger than the need of rest. Thus, Pipe, True, and Blythe, to whom the particulars had been told, had to tell them over and over again. At length all were satisfied; the sentinels were stationed, the reliefs appointed, and sleep fell upon the little camp.

# CHAPTER XXVI.

## THE HAUNTED GROUND.

Our story must now go back to Big Cave Camp on the Orchard shore of Lake Katrine. Lieutenant MacWhirlie had made a vigorous attack upon the Pixie camp, using his portable davids with good success. He completely demolished a bowl-shaped battery of Linyphia,* placed among the morning glories, from which a gang of Pixies had kept up a continuous and annoying volley of spears and arrows. But not being supported by the infantry, he fell back to the outer line of intrenchments. Here he was joined by Captain Bruce with his troops.

In the meantime, Commodore Rodney and his fleet had retired before the Stygians, and lay under the protection of the great guns mounted at the mouth of the inlet. The Pixie squadron took position before the inlet, thus shutting the Natties in, and Admiral Quench immediately sent three ships to relieve Big Cave Camp.

Thus matters stood on the eventful evening that brought such happy issue to the Brownies on Ellen's Isle. Exciting incidents also had happened at Camp Lawe, as the Brownie encampment before Big Cave had been called, in honor of the Ensign's gallant exploit. Shortly after nine o'clock, the hour for changing the sentincls, Bruce was informed by Vigilant, the Sergeant of the guard, that one of the men was missing from his post.

---

* Appendix, Note A.

"What," cried Bruce in angry tones, "I didn't think we had a traitor or a coward in our camp. Bring the wretch here, as soon as he is found. He must suffer the penalty." The Captain thus spoke, because it is an almost unheard of thing that a Brownie soldier should desert his post, and the punishment for such offence is instant death.

FIG. 110.—"The Bowl-Shaped Battery of Linyphia."

"But, Captain," answered Vigilant," we have searched for the guard, and can't find him. No one has seen him off his rounds. Indeed, he was seen at his post by the nearest sentinel but a few moments before the relief came up. Here is his spear, which was picked up on the ground.   Otherwise there is not a trace of him anywhere."

"Remarkable indeed!   Who was the sentinel?"

"Private Standwhile."

"Ah, a good man and true!   I know him well.   Lead the way to his picket post."

The two were soon upon the ground.   The spot where the missing soldier's lance was found was carefully examined, but there was no trace of conflict or other unusual occurrence.   The approaches to the picket line from the enemy's direction were closely scanned.   Nothing suspicious was seen.   The ground for some distance between the Pixie and Brownie camps was at this point flat and smooth.   Unable to solve the mystery, the Captain ordered another sentinel to be placed.

"See that he is a good man, one of the brightest and most careful in the ranks," said Bruce.   Accordingly Sergeant Vigilant assigned Private Sharpsight to the vacant post.

"And, be sure, Sergeant," said the Captain, as he turned away, "that you keep a bright lookout upon your sentinels during the watch, especially on this one."

Scarcely an hour had passed ere Captain Bruce heard the sharp challenge of the sentinel before his tent door: "Who goes there?"

"Sergeant Vigilant of the picket guard."

Bruce rose from his couch without waiting to be called, and left the tent.   "Well, what is it?   Speak!"

"The second sentinel is gone!"

"Sharpsight gone?"

"Aye; not a sign or sound of him anywhere.   I visited the picket once within an hour after he was stationed.   All was then well.   But I felt restless and nervous about the disappearance of Standwhile, and a few moments ago returned. Sharpsight had vanished as mysteriously as the other!"

"Call out the guard!" cried Bruce, snatching his broadsword and striding off toward the picket line. "Keep this matter as quiet as possible. It won't do to alarm the camp."

Every bush, and clump of grass, weed, stone, stock, or other place that could possibly give shelter to friend

FIG. 111.—"The Horizontal Snare of a Young Uloborus Among the Laurels."

or foe, Brownie or Pixie, within a wide circuit of the fatal picket post, was thoroughly explored. Nothing more dangerous was found than the horizontal snare of a young Uloborus among the laurels and a few young Furrow spiders. The latter lay within their silken tubes which were snugly embosomed within a dainty tuft of dry moss, or tucked within the folds of rolled leaves or curled birch bark, with a trap line strung from the openings to nearby round webs. The Brownies were no wiser than before. The mystery was unsolved.

"Shall we place another picket?" asked Sergeant Vigilant.

"It must be done," answered the Captain. "But call for volunteers."

"You see how it is, my good fellows," said the Sergeant turning to the guard. "Two of our men are gone. Where, how, nobody knows. There is foul play somewhere, and the sort that leaves no trail. The next picket may uncover the villainy, or he may go the way of the others. I shall not draft any one to this post unless necessary. Who will volunteer? Step out!"

There was a moment's pause. The sentinels cast glances from one to another, as though each waited for his comrade to volunteer. Then, as if by one impulse, every one stepped to the front.

Fig. 112.—"Snugly Embosomed Within a Dainty Tuft of Dry Moss."

"Bravo!" cried the Captain. "It is just what I expected of you. But I only meant to test your courage. I shall take this post myself, and do duty for the rest of this watch as one of the picket guards. Sergeant, dismiss the men and resume your rounds. Call here in half an hour. I will solve this mystery, if it can be done. Away!"

Vigilant and his guard began to remonstrate with their leader against this exposure of his life. But when he bade them away in such peremptory tones, they knew that his mind was made up, and there was nothing for them but to obey. Slowly and unwillingly they withdrew; not to sleep however, but to talk in subdued voices over the strange events of the night, and await the issue of their Captain's watch.

The half hour had well nigh passed. A cry of alarm startled the guard. It ran through the camp. Officers and men sprang from their bivouac fires and rude couches, and seized their arms.

"Fall in! Fall in!" shouted the officers. The bugle sounded the call.

"Is it a night attack?"

"Yes!"

"No!"

"Where have the Pixies assaulted the line?"

"There! Don't you see the guard rallying in yonder open space by the ridge. The enemy is coming straight over the plain."

"Pshaw! There's not a Pixie in sight. It's a false alarm raised by some stupid picket."

Thus backward and forward ran question and answer, as the Brownie soldiers swiftly fell into line of battle.

"Where is the Captain?" asked Lieutenant Mac-Whirlie, saluting Acting-Adjutant Bright.

"At the picket line I believe, Sir," answered Bright, "looking after the cause of the alarm. Ah! here comes the Sergeant of the guard. Why—in Heaven's name, Vigilant, what's the matter?"

"Captain—Bruce—is—gone!" said the Sergeant, jerking out the words between sobs.

"Gone—what do you mean?" cried both officers at once. The story was soon told. The Captain had disappeared as mysteriously as the two privates. Lieutenant MacWhirlie after a brief consultation with the officers issued the following order: "Let the soldiers be informed of everything. Appeal to their honor, loyalty, courage and good sense. Dismiss them to their quarters, and bid them sleep upon their arms. Come, Sergeant, lead the way to the picket line."

Accompanied by Vigilant, the Lieutenant strode away, having sent back his pony to the corral. The men of the guard were still scattered throughout the neighborhood looking for traces of their lost commander and comrades. They were recalled by a bugle. There was nothing to report.

Meanwhile MacWhirlie carefully examined the premises. The open space in front of the mysterious picket post ended in a low ridge which ran for some distance in either direction, and was covered with grass intermixed with tufts of moss and ferns. Beyond that and toward Camp Lawe the ridge was covered with a growth of young bushes. It was close up to this ridge that the lost pickets had been stationed.

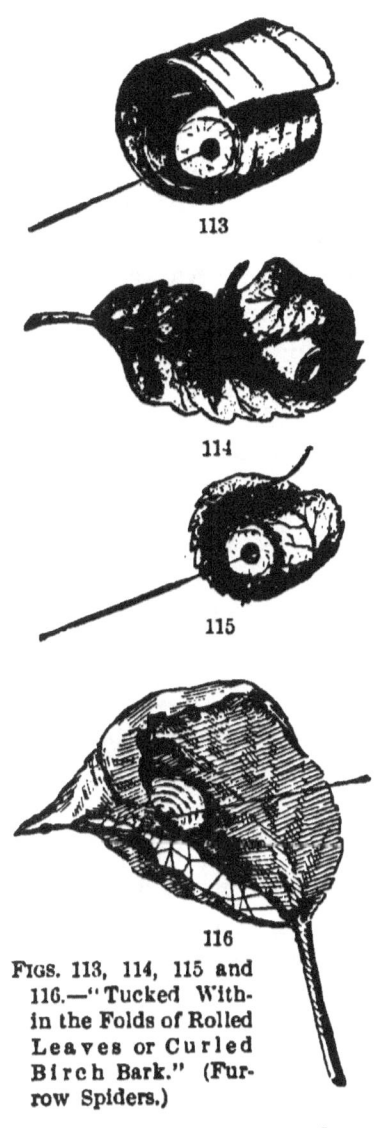

Figs. 113, 114, 115 and 116.—"Tucked Within the Folds of Rolled Leaves or Curled Birch Bark." (Furrow Spiders.)

"Did you observe the position of the men?" asked MacWhirlie.

"Not of the first one," answered the Sergeant. "But the second was stationed here. So also was the Captain. They both stood with their faces toward the plain—outward. I watched them both from a distance, after I had left them. The Captain paced up and down, just there along the ridge, keeping his eyes toward the enemy's camp. He made a half face outward, so to speak, as he walked."

"Outward? You are quite sure of that?"

"Quite."

"Very well. I shall take this post now. You will form the entire guard in a circle enclosing this spot."

"How far away, Sir?"

"Just far enough to have me well in sight. Let the men pace their beats as ordinary sentinels, keeping each other in view, face to face and right about. At the slightest call or alarm of any kind let them close in instantly, all of them at a sharp run."

"Is that all, Sir?"

"Yes; except that I want you to report to me as soon as the men are placed. You may go, now."

"Fall in. Attention. Right face. Forward—March!"

The Sergeant marched away at the head of his squad, and was soon stationing the sentries according to orders. As the guard moved off MacWhirlie overheard muttered words of protest dropping from the soldiers' lips. "Can't afford to lose both our leaders!" "It's a useless sacrifice!—Haunted ground!"

"Humph!" exclaimed the Lieutenant to himself. "Haunted ground, indeed! The cause of this deviltry is somewhere in this neighborhood, I'll be bound. And there's nothing more ghostly than Pixies at the bottom of it. There's no keeping track of their tricks. We are forever coming across some new tribe, with new habits. Their cunning and skill are beyond belief." He turned his back toward the plain and his face toward the ridge, and in that position kept guard until Sergeant Vigilant returned.

"Now," said MacWhirlie, "I want you to take your stand a few rods beyond me in the direction of the Big Cave. Keep your eye on me closely. If anything unusual occurs give the alarm, no matter what it may be. Don't fear to raise a false alarm."

The long watch began. Keeping his face steadily inward, the Lieutenant stood, or walked slowly back and forth, covering his eyes and scanning closely every object before him. Not a motion of leaf, twig, blade of grass, sprig or frond escaped his keen vision. But there was no sign of anything threatening or unusual. Midnight passed. One—two—three o'clock! The first glint of the coming dawn began to show in the horizon. The Brownie camp was as silent as a graveyard, for the men had grown tired of their long suspense, and dropped asleep. MacWhirlie and his guard were also well nigh wearied out. The day was like to break leaving the mystery unsolved.

# CHAPTER XXVII.

Lieutenant MacWhirlie had now almost come to doubt so much of his theory as located the unknown enemy within the picket line. But he was a persistent person, and disliked to give up his theory until he had something better to lay hold of. Moreover, as he still believed the Pixies to be the cause of the late misfortunes, and as he knew they were wont to be quite active about the peep of day, he resolved to bide by his voluntary watch a little longer. He beckoned Sergeant Vigilant to his side and the two sat down to rest among the delicate ferns that covered the ridge. They went over again the events of the night, putting this and that together, in order to frame some intelligent theory for their guidance. MacWhirlie, however, could find nothing to shake his first conclusion.

"The danger must have come upon them unawares," said he; "it was clearly in every case a complete surprise. If an enemy had approached from the front, he would have been spied in time for an alarm. A surprise so thorough could only have come from the direction of our own camp, as that was the only quarter not carefully watched."

The Sergeant's reply was arrested by a curious phenomenon. The ground beneath them seemed to be trembling; it raised slowly, swayed back and forth, and then sank down. The Brownies jumped to their feet and MacWhirlie exclaimed:

(268)

"What is that? Did you notice the shaking of the earth? or was it only the grass rocking in the wind?"

"It was—it seemed to be an earthquake," answered Vigilant. "There! I feel the ground again trembling beneath us."

The earth had, indeed, begun to lift up like a wave; higher and higher it rose, until the officers, finding that they were losing their perpendicular, flung themselves backward, in true

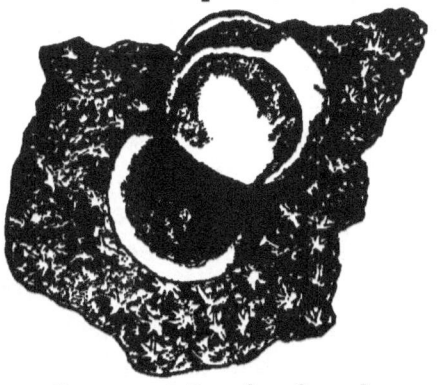

Fig. 117.—A Trap-door Opened.

Brownie fashion, into a bush on the summit of the ridge.

"See!" cried MacWhirlie, clasping the Sergeant by the arm, "there is the enchantress of your haunted ground!"

A trap-door had opened in the ground, and out of the crevice a huge chocolate-brown Pixie was stealthily peeping! The door was semi-circular in form, its edge beautifully beveled and covered with fine white silk, and fitted into the ground as smoothly

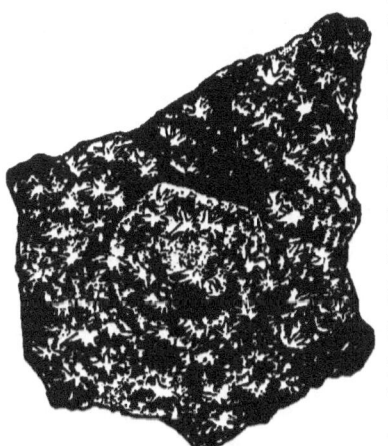

Fig. 118.—A Trap-door Closed.

as a cork into a flask. The top was covered with grass and ferns of the same kind as those on the ridge, so that the keenest eye could not detect the difference. A hinge of strong silk cloth held the trap-door to the upper

20

side of the ridge. All this the Brownies took in at a glance.*

They crouched motionless in the bush, concealed by the leaves, but having a full view of the monster who was slowly emerging from the tubular burrow under the trap. The creature was the largest of the Pixie race that either of the officers had seen. She was several times the size of Spite or Hide, and compared to the Brownies was as an elephant to a child. She was covered with a fur robe of a uniform brownish-red color, fringed with black. Her fangs were huge tusks, her feet immense brushes armed with sharp claws. Woe to the enemy that fell within her power! The Brownie

FIG. 119.—Peep-oh! Pixie!

officers had as brave hearts as ever beat under uniform, but the wonder upon their faces was somewhat touched with terror as they looked from this monster into each other's eyes. There could be no mistake about it. This was the great giantess Cteniza, the Queen of the Pixies!

The giantess turned, clambered up the ridge and made straight for the bushlet wherein the Brownies were hid. They grasped their swords and silently waited. Cteniza reached the bush. She stretched up an arm to—seize the Brownies? No! she fastened a strong cord to a twig and pulled it taut. The trap-door of her cave slowly raised until it stood ajar. Then another line was made fast to the bush and carried over to the top of the door. The trap swung in this wise and thus allowed the Pixie queen to enter her den when she wished to return. This done, she went down the ridge, gazed around her,

* Appendix, Note A.

and began spreading a thick snare over the ground round about the trap-door.* She had not seen the Brownie officers at all.

"We are safe this time," whispered MacWhirlie to Vigilant, "but what shall we do? It would be folly for two of us, or even the whole guard, to attack that creature without some great advantage on our part."

"We must wait and watch," was the answer. "Our action must depend upon the Pixie queen's."

"Aye, Aye," responded the Lieutenant, "but there is one thing I have settled. These cords shall be cut and the monster shut out from her den. If there is any hope at all for the recovery of our Captain and comrades it lies in that. Come what may the giantess shall never get back into her cave; at least until we have had a a chance to explore it."

Queen Cteniza had by this time finished her snare of strong cords, and a smooth silken sheet stretched irregularly upon the grass. She gazed contentedly upon her work, cast a glance upon her trap-door swinging snugly by its lines, and set off in the direction of the Pixie camp. She stopped suddenly. She had caught sight of one of the sentinels in the outer circle of guards, and at the same moment the sentinel saw her. He lifted his bugle and sounded the alarm.

"Ter-ah! Tra-la, la-lah!"

The answer came like an echo from a score of bugles, and the air was full of the notes. Cteniza turned and ran toward her cave. MacWhirlie heaved up his axe and struck a double-handed blow. One of the lines which held up the trap was severed. Again he struck. The second line parted and down fell the trap with a heavy thud, just as the giantess reached it. She was

* Appendix, Note B.

shut out from her cave! A glance showed her the cause
of her misfortune, and then her huge form shook with
rage. She leaped upon the ridge. But by this time the
Brownie officers were well away in hot flight, and the
circle of guards was rapidly closing around them. A
stir throughout the Brownie camp beyond showed that
a general alarm had been sounded, and the whole army
was falling into line. But could the devoted officers
and their little band escape destruction?

"Stand!" cried MacWhirlie. He himself stopped
short in his flight and faced toward Cteniza, who was
pressing forward with uplifted claws and clattering
tusks. Vigilant stopped and stood beside his Lieutenant. The sentinels gathered around them. Scarce a
dozen of them! It seemed as if the Pixie might crush
them all at a blow.

"Attention!" called the Lieutenant. "There is but
one chance left us. We must skirmish with this monster as best we can until the troops come up. Mark
those bushes to the right and left. Ready! Vault!"

MacWhirlie gave these commands in sharp, rapid
tones that seemed to impart his own spirit to the sentinels. Cteniza had approached within half a bow shot
of the Lieutenant as the final order was given. At the
word "vault," every Brownie disappeared into the
foliage of the bushes to right and left, and there perched
on the outer leaves with bows and spears in hand.

The giantess paused and stood with raised arms, rampant and threatening. She panted with anger and exertion. She looked to this side and that, before her, behind her, but saw no sign of her enemies. From the top
of a tall clump of grass above her MacWhirlie's voice
called: "Fire!" Cteniza started; a lance had struck
her face; an arrow had cut through her shaggy robe

and broke flesh upon the abdomen ; a dozen other weapons bounded back harmlessly from the chest, or frayed the skin upon arms and legs. She leaped upon the clump of grass whence MacWhirlie had issued the order. The

Fig. 120.—A Rampant Tarantula.

stalks bent down so quickly under the great weight, that the bulky creature sprawled upon the ground. The Lieutenant was shaken from his perch, and rolled in the dust beside the Pixie, but at once regained his feet.

"Rally!" he cried, and the soldiers ran to his side.

Cteniza now stood looking at her tiny foes. It seemed like a battle between a lion and a litter of mice, so vast was the difference in size between the combatants. In this moment of peril to the devoted band there was a new arrival upon the scene. Ensign Lawe having left camp for Hillside, the command of the cavalry fell to Sergeant Goodnews when MacWhirlie came into chief command after Bruce's disappearance. Goodnews was one of the most famous among the Brownie officers. There was not a fairy in the whole nation so comely in appearance, so valiant in fight, so efficient in all military action, so wise in council, so cheerful, amiable and kind in disposition. Never were beauty and sweetness so well combined with valor and might.

His charger was a goodly sized wasp, whose name was Formosa, commonly shortened into the nickname of "Moz." The creature was thoroughly trained, apt in every duty of war, and devoted to her master. In motion she was the swiftest of all the troop. She had a complete armor, and carried a spear charged with a deadly sting, which she well knew how to use against her master's foes. This was the new arrival. Hurrying up behind Goodnews came a squad of mounted Brownies, and beyond these again the remainder of the army. But they would be too late! What could one soldier do, however brave and well mounted, to save the Brownie sentinels from the monster who was in the act of throwing herself upon them? We shall see.

As the giantess sprang upon the little group of guards, a volley of arrows and spears flew into her face. But these wrought small harm, and ere the sentinels could leap aside three of them had been torn to pieces. Vigilant was wounded and borne to the earth; MacWhirlie was disarmed and dashed to one side, bruised and sorely bedraggled. It was at this moment, when the giantess was turning fiercely upon her prostrate foes, that Goodnews flew to the rescue upon his gallant Formosa. His sabre cut clean and strong across Cteniza's eyes, as he passed at full speed. He wheeled and rode back again. What is he doing? He is hovering above the Pixie queen, skillfully avoiding all her mad efforts to grapple with him. Is he only seeking to turn her attention from his friends? At least, he is making no attempt to use his sabre.

Ah! his tactics are plain enough now. Formosa circles around the dazed giantess a moment, and then darts upon her back. The wasp's bright lance flashes in the light, then horseman and steed are away again like the wind. And what is this? Cteniza reels upon her feet. She has fallen over upon her face. She is motionless. The fatal armor of Sergeant Goodnews' good nag has done the work. The poison within the sting ran instantly throughout the bulky frame of the Pixie queen, and there she lay prone and powerless.*

"Hurrah!" shouted MacWhirlie leaping up in spite of his bruises, and gaily swinging his broadsword. "We are saved! The Queen is dead! We can save the Captain now! if——"

Ah! that if!

---

* Appendix, Note C.

# CHAPTER XXVIII.

The dayspring had begun to streak the east when MacWhirlie, with a chosen band of Brownies, stood again before the closed trap-door of Cteniza's cave. The silken cords which had held the door open were still clinging to it. The ends which the Lieutenant had cut away were now gathered up, and the Brownies vainly sought to pull the door open by main strength.

"Away!" bade MacWhirlie: "call another company to our aid. And send a windlass."

Soon a second company arrived, bringing ropes and a windlass. The latter was a rough machine, a straight twig resting within two upright forked twigs, and having spokes thrust into and around its projecting ends. The windlass was planted on the ridge, a cord wound around the twig, and fastened at the free end to moss growing upon the trap-door. A bevy of Brownies seized the spokes and began pushing and pulling with might and main. Some took the ends of the spokes and threw themselves downward, carrying the windlass around by their momentum; others braced their backs against one another, and with feet upon the spokes pushed right merrily. Brownies are apt to make a frolic of their work, and even on an occasion so serious, their capers could not be quite suppressed. The two ropes were also fastened to the trap-door and manned by a troop of soldiers. A cheery call went up from the Lieutenant!

"Hi—ee—oh! Pull away!"

(276)

The Brownies at the ropes responded in a sort of chant: "He—oh! a long pull; he—oh! a strong pull; he—oh! a pull all together, oh!" At each cadence the busy workers put forth all their strength. The trap began to move. Higher—higher! It was soon fairly above the ground. Workers were stationed below to thrust props into the opening as the door rose. A goodly distance was cleared at last. New props were added. The trap stood ajar, and the mouth of the burrow was exposed to view.

"Now, men," said Mac-Whirlie, "this is my adventure. I shall lead the way into the pit. Sergeant Rise and Corporals Hope and Shine shall go with me. Let the rest be ready for any order or emergency. Bring ladders and lanterns."

Both were

FIG. 121.—The Mouth of Cteniza's Den Opened.

ready; the rope ladders were hung upon the edge of the burrow one on each side. MacWhirlie stepped upon one, battle-axe in hand, and was followed by Corporal Shine. Sergeant Rise led the way upon the other, followed by Corporal Hope.

"Ready?" asked the Lieutenant.

"Ready!"

"Come on, then, and mind the signals."

Hope and Shine had ropes fastened to their bodies, by which signals could be sent aloft. They also had their bugles hung loosely, with which to sound the alarm, and give necessary orders. Down, down into the cave the Brownies went. The light of day was left behind them; all was dark, except where the lanterns shed a narrow circle of light.

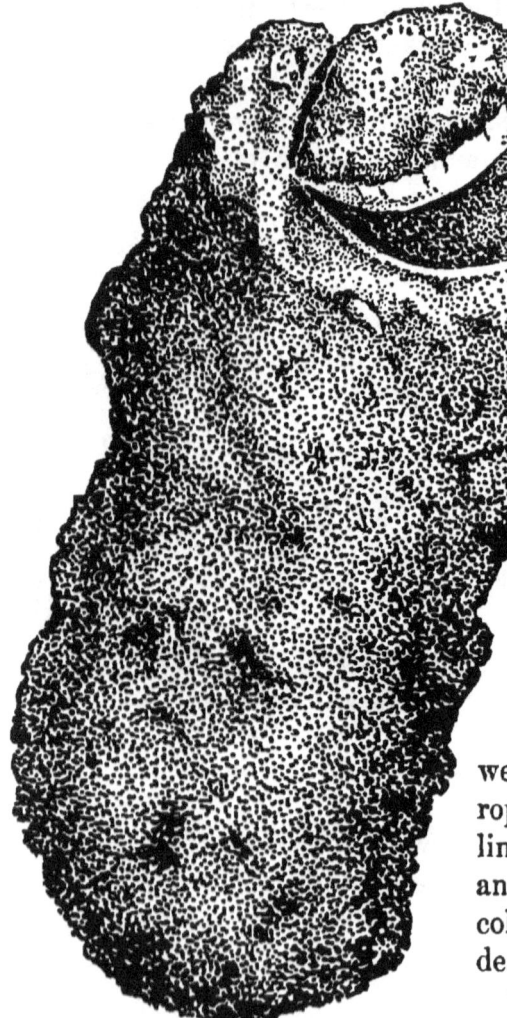

A cry of horror broke from MacWhirlie. On the sides of the cave hung the forms of two Brownies. They were fastened by silk ropes to the silken lining of the tunnel, and swung stark and cold. They were dead.

"Who are they?" cried Hope, as he

FIG. 122.—A Clod Containing the Silken Nest of the California Trap-door Spider.

peered through the glimmering light to recognize, if possible, the dead sentinels. "Is the Captain there?"

The explorers' hearts were very heavy. It was sad enough, however it might turn out. But oh! if their beloved leader should come to this end?

"Is it the Captain?" echoed Rise and Shine.

MacWhirlie, who was nearest the swinging corpses, had been scanning them closely. He made out the one nearest him. "This is Sharpsight—beyond a doubt. The other is—"

"Well, the other?—"

In the dim light it was difficult to determine. Bruce and Standwhile were very like in form and stature, and there were few marks in the Brownie uniform by which men could be distinguished from officers.

"It—is—Standwhile!" The decision was given slowly, but confidently. Yes, the sentinels were gone, but the Captain was yet to be found.

"We must send our poor comrades aloft," said Mac-Whirlie, "before we go further. Pull the signal rope, Hope. And have the ladder shifted a little nearer the bodies."

Hope was soon aloft, and down again; the ladder was shifted, the dead sentinels fastened to the ropes, and hoisted slowly out of their charnel house. Down in the cave the groans and cry with which the corpses of their comrades were greeted, were heard by the little band of devoted explorers. Once more the ropes were lowered, were fastened as before, and the Brownies pushed on in the darkness. They reached the bottom of the cave at last. Not a sound was heard save the echoes of their own voices in the hollow depth. There were carcasses of huge insects, and legs, wings, and heads thereof scattered over the floor. The Brownies stumbled over these at every step. Not a sign of the Captain!

Around and around they went, sounding the walls

with their axes, cutting away the silken tapestry here and there. There was clearly but one chamber; no secret doors or inner rooms at that point at least.

"Then we must look higher up," said the Lieutenant. "There must somewhere be a branch tunnel, in which the Captain, living or dead, has been stored away. Look sharp, my men."

Up they clambered, scrutinizing at every round the circular wall of the cave. They reached the point where the dead sentinels had hung. Some unevenness in the surface here caught MacWhirlie's quick eyes. He struck the end of his battle-axe upon the wall. Hark! there was a faint echo within. The place was hollow! He smote again; a third time the axe fell; but ere it reached the wall a door opened so violently that it struck and put out the lantern in the Lieutenant's hand. Fortunately, as it proved, the axe blade fell upon the bevel of the door, and was thereby wedged into the opening, leaving the door slightly ajar.

"What is it?" cried Rise.

"One of the brood of the Pixie queen," answered the Lieutenant. "I caught a glimpse of the creature's claw and fangs as the trap-door opened. It is a young giant. Our Captain is inside this branch, and this Pixie prince is guarding him. Here, lay hold of the trap!" Rise and Hope joined their comrades upon the ladder. Slits were cut in the tapestry, and seizing the fragments the Brownies tugged with utmost strength to pull open the door. It was hung so loosely that it ought to have opened almost of its own weight; yet the Brownies could not move it.

"The Prince is holding it against us,"* said Mac-Whirlie. "We must have help from above. Quick!

* Appendix, Note A.

fasten these ropes into the slits upon the door. There, that will do finely. Now, aloft, Hope! Let the men above pull upon these ropes. Brace them back when you find them giving away enough, and fasten them firmly. Then descend, and bring my two-edged sword with you, old 'Charity.'"

These orders were obeyed with amazing rapidity. Hope inspired his fellows with the news that the Captain might yet be found. But, withal, there was a cloud upon many faces. It seemed hard to be up there pulling at ropes, while a blow was to be struck for their Captain's liberty. And then, was their noble Lieutenant, their leader now, to risk his life in that cave with so few to support him? The Pixie prince was a youth, it was true;

FIG. 123.—The California Trap-door Spider (Cteniza Californica).

but a giant nevertheless, and a match for a whole company of the best Brownies.

The messenger who had gone down with MacWhirlie's sword returned with an order that pacified this discontent. Two more ladders were to be let down into the cave. Over these soldiers were to be stationed as closely as convenient. Thus there were two lines of Brownies reaching from the surface of the earth to the mouth of the branch, all ready for any service, and in communication with the troops above. These arrangements were soon made.

Then came the signal, "Hoist away!" The ropes

tightened; the door began slowly to yield. MacWhirlie stood upon the ladder close by the edge of the trap, holding the side ropes with one hand and grasping his two-edged sword in the other. The Pixie's black claws came into view; they were fastened upon the inside cover of the trap, and the whole weight and strength of the young giant were opposing the opening.

"Hah! Take that then," cried the Lieutenant, striking upon the exposed claw, which was thus nearly severed from the arm. The giant released his hold and backed slowly up the branch. By this time the trap-door had been well nigh lifted up from the wall, and was held steady by the ropes above, which were securely fastened. MacWhirlie entered the open door of the branch followed closely by Shine, Rise and Hope.

"Fasten your lanterns to the sides," said MacWhirlie. There were hooks on the handles for such uses, which, by a single motion of the hand, were caught into the silken lining, and thence the fox-fire lights threw their glow into the darkness. Sword in hand the four Brownies advanced, the Lieutenant in front. The bulky form of the Pixie prince opposed them. They stood a moment, silent and prayerful, ere closing to the conflict. They knew that their lives hung in the balance, and girded themselves for the issue. Back from the inner darkness, in that momentary waiting, a voice called faintly:

"Hal—loo!"

"Hark, my men; it is the Captain!" cried Mac-Whirlie, waving his sword, while the cave fairly rang with his answering shout, "Hello!"

Again the voice came, stronger than before, saying, "who is there?" It was indeed the voice of Bruce.

"Brownies!" answered the four men in chorus; "Brownies to the rescue!"

They threw themselves upon the Pixie, smiting face and breast, arms and legs with swift, strong blows. Prince Proud (for that was his name) made but a feeble resistance. Once or twice he stretched out his arms as though to grapple with his assailants, but the Brownies easily avoided him, and springing forward again, showered their sharp blows upon the huge foe. The cause of

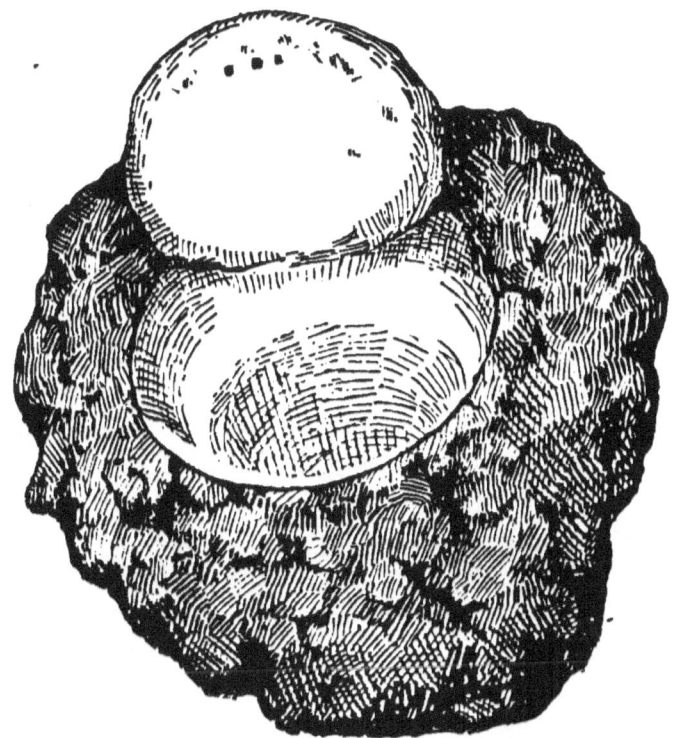

Fig. 124.—"Claw Marks Upon the Inside Cover of the Trap-door."

this apathy was soon explained; he was just over a season of moulting, or changing his skin! Several times before they are grown, Pixies go through this strange process. The whole outer skin peels off. During the change the creatures are almost helpless, and lie still, taking little or no food. After the skin is off, it takes several days for them to regain their strength. During the whole time of this change nothing but the sorest need can stir them up to even as great exertion as Proud had already made.* MacWhirlie saw his advantage at once. He understood how they had escaped thus far so easily. His hopes rose into confidence. He spoke with new cheer.

"Forward, merrily! Sergeant Rise, order in the men who are on the ladders; I shall cut my way past the Pixie to the Captain!" He struck upon the Prince's face, as he ran forward, gave a back-handed stroke as he passed, and then fairly dodged under Proud's legs and passed on into the darkness.

"Captain," he called, "Captain!"

"Here!" was the answer from the far end of the cavern, in the well-known voice of dear old Bruce. "This way, whoever you are. I am bound hand and foot."

On, into the darkness the Lieutenant ran, thinking nothing and caring nothing for obstacles. The little light at the mouth of the cave was shut out from the interior by Proud's huge body; but guided by the voice MacWhirlie strode on through the gloom, and fairly stumbled at last upon his Captain's prostrate form. In a moment the keen edge of Charity had cut the silken cords with which Bruce was swathed, and the strong arms of MacWhirlie lifted him to his feet.

"Who is it?" cried the Captain with trembling voice.

"It is I—MacWhirlie!" And throwing his arms about the captive's neck the brave dragoon sobbed for joy.

Suddenly the darkness of the cave was broken by a

---

*Appendix, Note B.

flood of light that relieved even the shadows of that end of the cavern where Bruce had lain. MacWhirlie turned. Proud was gone! The Brownies at the mouth of the cave were in great confusion, some sprawling upon the floor, some scrambling to their feet, some swinging by the roof, some hanging to the raised trapdoor and some to the mouth of the cave. In the excitement of the moment MacWhirlie let go his hold upon the Captain. The limbs of the unfortunate chief were so benumbed by his severe handling and the tightness of the ropes with which he was bound, that he fell upon the floor.

"Ah, my poor Captain," exclaimed MacWhirlie, "pardon my thoughtlessness!" Without more ado he lifted the fallen officer in his arms, and started toward the cave's mouth. Rise, Hope and several others were already hurrying inward to find their officers. They met MacWhirlie midway of the cavern staggering under his burden. A shout of joy burst from their lips at the sight. It was subdued at once, as the noble fellows caught sight of their leader's pale face. But the note had gone on from lip to lip, out of the branch tunnel, up the walls of the main cavern, along the line of soldiers who hung upon the ropes, to the group who gathered around the open door. The sentinels caught up the cry; it flew from man to man until it reached the camp, and then, led by the sound of trumpets and the blast of bugles, the whole wood and valley rang with such a cheer as never before went up even from Brownie throats:

"Hurrah! Rejoice! Our lost is found!"

The squirrels stopped upon the branches of the trees, threw their bushy tails above their backs, pricked up their tiny ears, listened a moment, then joined in the

21

cry of their friends, with merry barking. The birds stopped in their flight, or alit upon the boughs, perked their pretty heads to this side and that, as though they were asking, "what is the matter?" Then they, too, joined in the shout of their good friends the Brownies, whistling, trilling, carolling until the air was alive with songs. The trees clapped their leaf hands together; the flowers raised their plumed hats; the bees, butterflies and wasps hummed in chorus with the joyful cry. It seemed as though all nature had joined in with their happy friends to celebrate the rescue of Bruce, chief of the Brownies; and happiest heart of all was that of Agatha the good.

# CHAPTER XXIX.

The rescued Bruce was carried by his rejoicing friends and followers to the upper air. The fresh breeze and bright sunshine wrought like a charm to renew his strength. The time of his captivity had been short; but he had been so roughly handled by his giant captors, and the cords with which he had been bound had so galled him that he was quite unable to walk. He was therefore laid upon a leaf stretcher and carried to his tent. A few words explained the manner of his capture. He had been surprised by the giantess who rushed upon him from behind, knocked him senseless by a blow of her claw, bound him, and then carried him into her den. The monster had already slain the two sentinels, sucked their blood, and hung the bodies upon the wall where they had been found. But Bruce was reserved to feed the maw of Prince Proud, and was therefore thrust into the branch cave. As, however, the worthy youth was "moulting," and in the listless estate which has been described, the Captain lay in bonds awaiting the revival of Proud's appetite. To this fact both Bruce and his gallant rescuers owed their lives.

"But what became of Proud?" The Lieutenant naturally raised this question after all the party had got out of the cave.

"Well," said Sergeant Rise, laughing, "he's down there among the bones at the bottom of the cave, alive or dead, I don't know which. After you had dodged by the Prince, we attacked him vigorously, but he did little more than move back slowly, occasionally striking out in a blind way. All at once, however, he dashed forward, and plunged out of the branch into the bottom of the main cave. We were taken by surprise, and were sent flying in all directions in an awkward and ludicrous manner. A score or so of Brownies had just entered

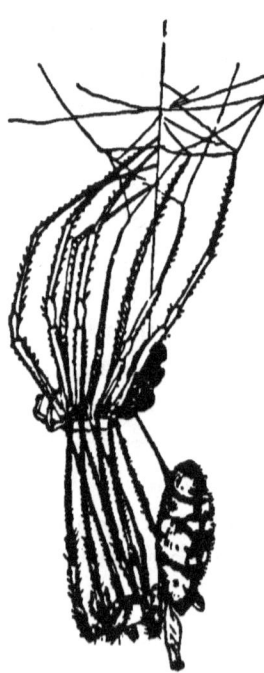

the branch from the ladders, and they were scattered like leaves in a whirl-a-wind. Two of them were thrown upon the Pixie's shoulders, and went down with him pick-a-back into the cavern. Fortunately, they flung themselves off upon the rope ladders, and so escaped. Indeed, we all got off pretty well; a few scratches, bruises and torn clothes, but nothing serious. It was about the funniest scrape we have been in for a long time. We were taken aback and upset by the brute's sudden dash."

FIG. 125. — "Moulting." A Spider Pulling Off Its Old Skin.

MacWhirlie joined in the hearty laughter which the recital of the adventure awakened. "However, my lads," said he, "it might have been anything but a comic affair. See that the trap-door is securely lashed and fastened down, and guarded. We will look after the young giant hereafter."

This order given, the Lieutenant was about following his Captain to the camp when his attention was drawn to a crowd of curious Brownies gathered around the carcass of the Pixie queen.

" Ah, yes," said he, " I must see about getting this thing out of the way."

He climbed into a bush from which he could overlook at once the crowd and the bulky form of the giantess. The greater part of the Brownies were gazing upon the carcass, meanwhile chatting, in their lively way, over late events. A small group of more restless spirits were bent upon getting the fangs or tusks of the immense creature as trophies. They had just finished their arrangements as MacWhirlie arrived, and armed with ropes, swords and axes were scrambling over Cteniza's legs towards her face. The legs and arms were drawn up around the body as they had been when death overtook her. Suddenly the arms stretched forward from the face! The legs shot out backward!

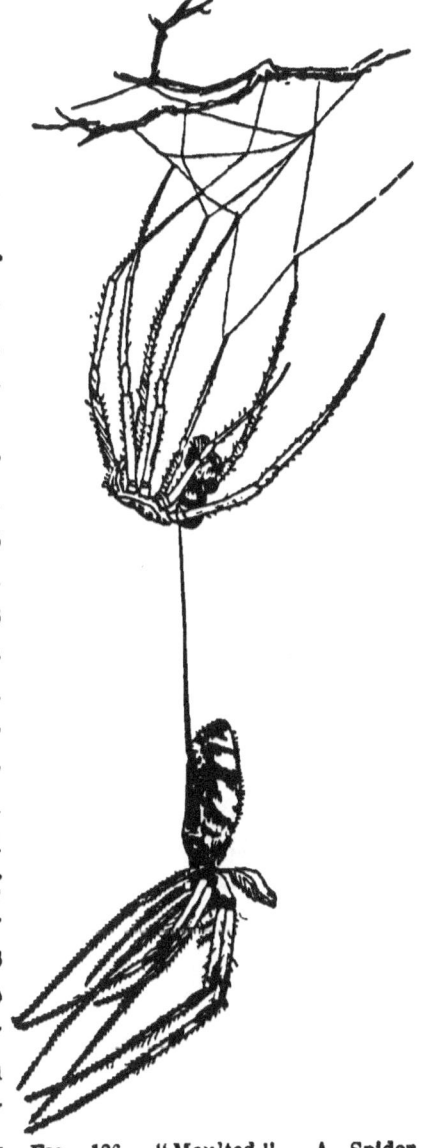

FIG. 126. — " Moulted." A Spider Hanging Beneath Its Cast-off Skin.

" Whew! the Pixie queen has come to life!" some one shouted.

Such a scampering as there was! The adventurous trophy seekers threw themselves by a series of somersaults from the moving limbs, and Brownies, axes, swords and ropes went flying in all directions through the air. The crowd around fell back, pushing, tumbling, clambering over one another, a panic-stricken mass.

MacWhirlie from his lookout observed this strange behavior of a dead Pixie with amazement and alarm. "What, isn't the giantess dead?" he exclaimed. He expected to see her rise and charge upon the confused and struggling crowd of Brownies. But ere he could give a second thought, Cteniza's limbs slowly fell back into their first position. She made no other motion.

The soldiers rapidly recovered from their panic when they found they were not pursued; then, in right Brownie fashion, began to make merry over their own ridiculous flight. But what were they to think of this last movement of the Pixie? Wasn't the creature dead? MacWhirlie left his perch and took charge of affairs. He was about organizing a fresh attack upon the giantess, when Sergeant Goodnews rode up astride his nag Formosa. He had already heard of the strange behavior of the "corpse," and was ready to explain:

"The fact is, Lieutenant, the Pixinee is not dead, but you would quite waste your energies in any new attack upon her. She will surely die. The sting of my Moz is mortal; but for several days, perhaps weeks, Cteniza will be just as you see her. She cannot move from that spot. If you disturb her she will probably stretch out her limbs; but they will fall back again, without doing any harm, and in due time the creature will die."*

The Brownies were satisfied although the explanation seemed very strange. But they had well learned that

* Appendix, Note A.

nature's facts are often stranger than fiction, and so believed the good Sergeant. The giantess was left undisturbed, and MacWhirlie hastened to camp. Captain Bruce rapidly recovered his spirits. But his nerves had received too severe a shock to allow him to resume active command at once. Yet he could consult with his officers as to what should now be done, and a council of war was held in his tent. The reluctant conclusion was that it would be better to raise the siege of Orchard Cave, and join the fleet at the inlet. They feared that the enemy might attack the Brownie forces while divided, and destroy them. The order was therefore given to break camp at once.

Amid the stir of preparation for departure, MacWhirlie had forgotten about the dead giantess. But as the Brownie troops marched by the late scene of conflict on their way to the inlet, he was reminded of the incident by a cry from the vanguard:

" The body of the Pixie queen is gone ! "

" Is it possible ? Call Sergeant Goodnews." The Sergeant reported immediately.

" How is this, Sergeant ? It seems that you were wrong about our giant foe. She has disappeared. The Brownies haven't carried her off; the Pixies haven't been near ; she must have made off herself. You surely did not mean to deceive us ; but explain if you can."

The Sergeant gave reins to Moz, and followed by MacWhirlie on his Bee-pony Buzz, flew straight to the spot where Cteniza had lain. The bulky carcass was nowhere to be seen.

" Now my good Moz," said the Sergeant, " show us what you know of this mystery." The obedient wasp, circled around the spot, and then darted into the bushes.

She soon lit upon an overhanging twig, and folded her wings as though quite contented with herself.

" What is the matter now?" cried MacWhirlie.

" Look for yourself," said Goodnews, pointing to the ground beneath. A mound of fresh earth was thrown up on the margin of a wide hole out of which came the sound of rattling clods and fluttering wings.

" What is this? It explains nothing!"

" Wait a wee. There! do you see that?"

A large Pompilus wasp flew out of the hole, which she at once began to fill with the loose clay heaped around the edge.

" That is your sexton," said Goodnews; " this is her newly made grave, and inside you will find the missing body. The sexton is a full cousin of my Formosa. She has dragged your giantess here by her own unaided strength; has dug that grave which you see, and is just ready to fill it up. Are you satisfied? If not, look for yourself."

Down flew MacWhirlie to the edge of the grave. Away went the sexton in alarm. The Lieutenant peeped into the hole and saw the brown body and limbs of the Pixie queen already partly covered with pellets of clay.

" I am satisfied," he said, and the two rode away. " But tell me, what strange fancy could have turned yon insect into an amateur grave digger?"

" It is not a matter of fancy," replied Goodnews, " but of those strong, wise natural promptings of motherhood which men call maternal instinct. If you had lifted one of the Pixie's limbs you might have found an egg of the wasp snugly stowed away against the body. In due time that egg will become a grub with a most ferocious appetite, and that appetite will find food in the plump body of the Pixie queen. That is why nature has given some wasps the power to paralyze by their sting the prey which they stow away as food for the future grub; it remains fresh and palatable instead of decaying as it would do in actual death." *

When the Lieutenant again reached the head of the column it was about passing the trap-door cave. The Brownie guards were relieved from duty, and Prince Proud was left to his fate. As the trap had been pretty tightly fastened down, however, the Brownies had good hopes that his fate would be such as to deliver them from any further fear on his account.

FIG. 127.—" The Trap-door Tightly Fastened."

It was a pretty sight to see the Brownie troops as they marched to the inlet. First came the cavalry, their bright trappings and many colored butterfly steeds making a brilliant spectacle. Next to these rode Sergeant Goodnews with the color guard, as MacWhirlie was once more at the head of his troopers, and Ensign Lawe was still absent. The great flag of Brownieland was borne by a sturdy dragoon mounted on a Goliath moth. Behind these came the litter on which Captain

* Appendix, Note B.

Bruce was carried. A small downy leaf of silver maple
had been laid upon a mattress woven out of ropes of
grass and fibres of bark. The mattress was slung upon
poles on each side, and these were laid upon the
shoulders of stout Brownies, who thus carried their beloved Captain quite comfortably. Above the litter a
sunshade, made from the blossoms of a wood violet, was
borne by mounted Brownies. Behind this ambulance,
and indeed directing it, rode the Nurses, Agatha and
Grace, with the assistants and accoutrements of the sani-

FIG. 128.—Brownie Troops on the March.

tary corps. The maidens were pale and worn by the
grief and excitement of the last days, and rode along
sadly, almost silently. A number of litters followed the
sanitary corps, bearing sick and wounded Brownies.
Then came the infantry; and last of all, a squad of
cavalry brought up the rear, the buglers piping merry
notes as they rode along.

The Brownie army did not get away without annoyance from the enemy. The Wolf Brigade and the
Vaulters hung upon the rear and flanks, annoying the

troops as much as possible. Gossamer and his balloon corps hovered above, keenly spying the column to note where an assault might be made. The Wheel Legion spun cobwebs across the route to entangle the wings of the cavalry. The Lineweavers and Tubeweavers spread thick sheets upon the grass to retard the footmen's progress. The Stygian ships followed the line of march as nearly as might be, keeping close in shore and watching for opportunity to work harm. The Watermen, Smugglers and Pirates pushed out from their grassy hiding places and joined in the pursuit. The Brownies, how-

FIG. 129.—" Cobwebs Across the Route."

ever, were quite used to all these methods of assault, and knew well how to meet and avoid them. Moreover, a section of their flying artillery, with guns mounted upon bee ponies, accompanied the march. They hovered over the van and rear and above either flank of the column, and pelted their adversaries with shot from their portable davids, thus keeping them at a safe distance.

Before sunset the inlet was reached, and the army encamped safely under protection of the big davids mounted upon the forts built at either cape. One of these was known as Fort School, the other Fort Home; and the guns which guarded these were called "Precept" and "Example," for Brownies are fond of calling all

FIG. 130.—Brownie Flying Artillery and Portable David.

manner of objects after some favorite fact, person or virtue among their human friends.

It was pleasant for the soldiers and sailors once more to be together, and there were warm greetings and happy reunions. But as they pitched their tents and kindled their camp-fires on the beautiful and familiar bank of their beloved stream, their hearts were sad that their foes already had possession of Lake Katrine; were swarming along its shores; and, ere morning sunrise, would have covered the lawn once more with their white tents, and spread their snares beneath the very windows of the Wille mansion. Withal, as the Brownies had learned to take such destiny as befell them with contented or at least submissive minds, they composed themselves for the night's rest, and soon were sound asleep. The sentinels paced the parapets of the forts, peeped through the fog from the lookouts on shipboard, and stood watchful and silent on the lonely picket line beyond camp.

# CHAPTER XXX.

## THE GRAND ALLIANCE WITH SCALY, TWIST AND SLY-MOUSIE.

Next morning the Brownies' forebodings were found to be well grounded; their enemies held possession of the lawn. Lake and lawn both in Pixie hands! It was a sorry day in Brownieland. What could be done? Not a word as yet had been heard from Ensign Lawe, and all were uneasy thereat, for they knew that he would not forget his mission, nor fail of it if success were possible, nor be likely to fall into the foe's hands. Yet his absence showed that early aid was not to be looked for from Governor Wille, and thus hope was cut off from that quarter.

There were plans enough formed and discussed among the uneasy spirits of the camp, but only one had practical issue. Corporal Policy, of the Engineer Corps, proposed a grand alliance against the Pixies. The Corporal was not in high favor among the Brownies, although he was a shrewd fellow, and a useful one too, when kept well in control by Sergeant True and the other officers. But in the present gloomy outlook of affairs many were ready to listen to any counsel that looked toward delivering the nation from its peril and restoring the Mansion to Brownie control. It is not strange, therefore, that the Corporal's proposed alliance was seconded by many in the camp. A delegation, with Policy at its head, waited on Lieutenant MacWhirlie, laid the plan before him and urged its adoption. The plan was as

(298)

follows : Policy had once done a great favor to two land elves, Twist the Serpent, and Slymousie the Quadruped, and also to Scaly, a water sprite. They had promised to serve him at any time in any affair. They were not on good terms with the Pixies at the best and, the Corporal urged, would be prompt and eager to fulfill their promise against the common foe.

"Now," continued Policy, "I propose that we organize an expedition against the Stygians in this wise: let Scaly fall upon their ships, sink as many as she can with the stroke of her tail, and drag the rest by their cables or push them with her head upon the shore. Our troops and ships can attack them, at this disadvantage, with certainty of victory. At the same time let Twist and Slymousie break in upon the Pixie camp, and bite, crush and destroy. Slymousie is a cunning and active adversary, and Twist is so much bigger than the Pixies that they cannot stand before him. Then, there is nothing like fighting these poison breeding creatures with their own weapons. Poison to kill poison, say I!" quoth Corporal Policy; "shrewdness to overcome cunning! That is true wisdom!"

Thus, and with many other arguments, Policy and his friends pressed their alliance. MacWhirlie had little favor for the scheme, as it was contrary to Brownie nature and custom ; but, in sheer desperation, he at last consented that Policy should take charge of a company of volunteers and try his plan ; especially as he thought it could work no harm, and would keep some restless spirits occupied.

The volunteers were readily enlisted and pushed off hopefully to find the haunts of Dragon Twist, Slymousie the Quadruped and Sprite Scaly. Twist was soon found sunning himself upon a limb of a sapling that grew above the big stone under which he had his nest. When the party spied him the Corporal mounted upon the rock and sounded a note or two upon his bugle. Twist slowly lifted his head above the leaves, flung a coil of his tail around a twig, looked down and at once recognized his friend. He hissed forth as pleasant a greeting as he knew how to give, listened patiently to Policy's request, looked wise, nodded his head in approval, and at once promised to do his utmost.

"I will keep faith with you, good fairy," he said, lisping out the words between tongue and teeth. "You may depenth upon me to crush out your old enemieth, body, bag and baggage." Whereupon he wriggled among the leaves, and took an extra coil or two of his tail around the twig.

"Thanks!" cried Policy, "and now, when will you begin operations, and how many of us will you want to help you?"

"Now, I will begin now!" answered Twist; "and ath to aid, I athk for none. If a few of you would like to go with me to thee my triumph over the Pikthieth, come along! I thall make thort work of it, and you can come back and thing my praitheth."

The Corporal detailed a squad of his men to go with Twist, and hurried away to engage the service of Scaly. The water sprite was not so easily found. Somewhere in the lake close by the rocks of the cape she had her favorite haunt. The Brownies swung upon the overhanging weeds and bushes and peered into the water, but could see nothing of her. Policy sounded his bugle in vain. At length a water beetle, of the family known as Whirligigs, thrust itself out of the lake, and began capering upon the surface.

"Hello!" cried the Corporal.

" Her-rr-reep ! " said the Whirligig, skipping nearer
to the shore.

" Have you seen Scaly the Sprite down below ? " asked
Policy, "and would you kindly tell us where she may
be found ? "

" Aye, that I can, Mr. Brownie. But what could you
do even if I were to tell you ? Would you go down to the
bottom of the lake to speak to her ? Ha, ha ! " The
little water beetle, who had been joined now by a group
of companions, cut sundry gyrations upon the lake, and
circled round and round in a merry dance with his
friends. Clearly he was much pleased that he was able
to do something which a fairy could not do.

" Come now, Master Whirligig," said the Corporal,
"you must oblige us in this matter. You know that
Brownies are your good friends; and you know that we
can't do what you can. Go and tell Scaly that we want
to see her."

" So I will ! " answered the water beetle, good naturedly.

" So we will ! " chirped all his companions. Turning
suddenly the whole party plunged into the water, every
one carrying down with him on the tip of the abdomen
a bubble of air to supply him with breath while under
water. They made their way straight to a stone of
quartz whose crystallized sides glittered in the light that
penetrated the stream.

" Sprite Scaly, Sprite Scaly ! " called the beetles in
chorus, while they held fast to the rock with their
claws.

A form slowly lifted itself from the shadows under the
edge of the rock and rose higher and higher until it was
quite on a level with the top whereon Whirligig and his
friends sat. It was a fish, with silver-white scales and

22

red eyes. She floated in the water, which she lazily beat with her fins and tail, opening and shutting her gills, looking all the while very sedate indeed.

"Sprite Scal*ee*! Ah! here you are!" cried the beetles as they caught sight of the fish poised above them. "Brownie Policy sent us down to tell you that he claims your service. He waits on the shore above. Good bye!" Up they went without more ado, and in a moment were again circling around upon the surface of the lake.

Scaly was not far behind them. Lazy as she looked, she could dart through the water like an arrow, and sooner than we tell it, had reached the bank and thrust her face close to the feet of the Corporal. Policy repeated his plan and got as hearty assent from Scaly as from Twist.

"What shall we do to support you?" asked Policy.

"Well, there's nothing very 'special," said Scaly, spitting out half a dozen mouthfuls of water. "The Natties had better follow up my attack in their own way. They'll not have much to do but gather up drowned Pixies, I reckon; or maybe capture some of their boats as the Stygies make off from their damaged ships."

The Sprite and the Corporal agreed upon the time for the attack, and thereupon Scaly turned, gave her tail a few self-satisfied flops, and dived out of sight. .

The third party to the proposed alliance was Slymousie the Quadruped. "We shall find her in the field," said Corporal Policy, and sent off several men to hunt for her. The Brownies climbed the hill back of the Mansion and by and by found the cave, just on the edge of the orchard, where Mrs. Slymousie had her nest. It was quite hidden away beneath the overtopping meadow grass. A round bunch of chopped and twisted hay was balled up within it, which made it snug and warm. The Brownies swung themselves down by the grass blades and roots until they were well within the cave, when the Corporal called a halt and blew his bugle. There was much shrill squeaking down at the bottom of the nest, and a sudden rustling amid the dry upholstery, as the youngsters scampered away into hiding.

Once more Corporal Policy blew his bugle, and then called loudly: "Slymousie—hello! It's no one but I— the Brownie. Hello—come out and see the Brownie!"

At last a low, timid voice squeaked forth the question, "Who's there?"

"Corporal Policy the Brownie! Don't you know me?"

"Oh, yes! to be sure I know you now. But, dear me! you nearly frightened me into a fit. I thought it was Grimalkin the Housecat; or that miserable old Owl that nests in the hilltop wood. Are you sure—it's— only you?"

"Yes, yes, Slymousie; don't be absurd! Who else could it be? I came to claim your help against our old enemies the Pixies."

"Dear, dear! Don't mention it, I pray. What could I do against those dreadful creatures? It quite flusters me to think of it, indeed. Besides, I have a large family now at home; some of them very young; too young to leave alone. Really, you must excuse me this time. Dear, dear! My heart is going pit-apat, pit-apat at the very thought."

Policy was not to be put off so easily, and remained some time trying to persuade his friend. But he quite failed, and was about to leave, when who should come

into the cave but Master Biggy, Mrs. Slymousie's oldest son by the next-to-last brood. He had been out
on a visit to his sweetheart, and dropped in to see if
mother hadn't a nice bit of cheese, or bumblebee bread,
or some such delicacy for him. He heard enough of
the conversation to excite his love of adventure, and
at once volunteered to take his mother's place.

"Do you think you are old enough to measure
strength with the Pixies?" asked Policy.

"Old enough?" exclaimed Biggy indignantly. "Old
enough, indeed! Look at me, now! I'm nearly as
large as mother, and not half so timid as she. Just
you wait, Sir! You shall see that Biggy Slymousie
is no small affair when it comes to fighting Pixies.
I'm a match for any score of 'em in strength; and as
for slyness—well, you shall see!"

Biggy was certainly a stout enough specimen of a
half-grown Slymousie, and as he seemed not to be
lacking in spirit, and had a keen mind for the work,
his service was gladly accepted. It was arranged that
he should attack the Pixie force in the rear, while
Twist assaulted in front; and having instructed him
as to the time of assault, and arranged some details,
the Corporal retired with his squad, highly elated at
his success. Thus the grand alliance was formed. We
shall now see what became of it.

When the sun had gone down, the full moon rose.
It poured a flood of rays upon the mansion, lit up the
lawn, and lay like a golden crown on the top of Hillside. The Pixies were in high glee over their prospects. Their ships had drawn up around the inlet as
near as they dared to come; their troops had been
ferried across the lake, and were already closing up
the lines of investment around that part of the Brownie

camp which lay on the side toward the mansion. From this point the Pixie tents and snares stretched across the lawn to the flower border by the walk. In this direction Twist turned his course. He crossed the brook, holding his head aloft as he wriggled his body through the water. The Brownies followed on their moth ponies.

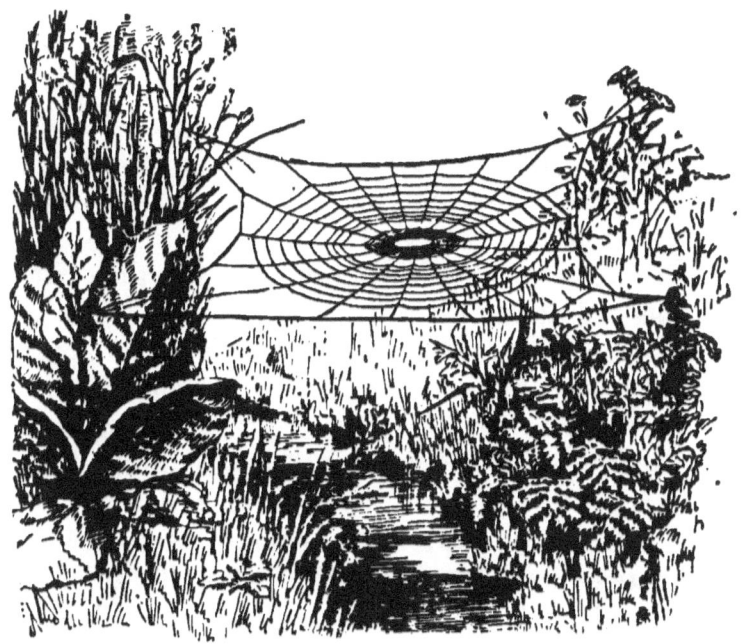

Fig. 131.—The "Bridge That Tetragnatha Had Builded."

The Serpent stopped a moment upon the shore, then dashed at the Pixie breastworks, which broke into fragments before his assault. Many of the guards were knocked over by the swoop of his tail, others were crushed under the coils of his body, others were pierced through by his sharp fangs. The camp was in consternation. A broad swath of fallen tents, broken fortifications and dead Pixies marked the progress of the mighty Twist, and throngs of fugitives fled across the brook by a bridge that Tetragnatha had builded, and which quite reached from shore to shore.

What a small affair serves to turn the tide of events, at times! A little hop-toad, disturbed by the commotion, leaped from beneath a cool leaf to ask "What's the matter?"

"Aha, my beauty," cried Twist, "you're my game!" and he snapped up toadie in a twinkling. One would have thought it a painful thing for Twist to eat his meals, for he writhed, and jerked his body as though he were in torment. However, he appeared to grow more comfortable after a while, and stretched himself out on the grass as though to enjoy a nap.

The Brownies were not pleased to see their friend the hop-toad dealt with so unceremoniously. The poor fellow and his brothers had stood by the fairies in many a stout bout with the Pixies. To be sure the toads would eat their enemies; but as they never insisted upon sharing such rations with their friends, the Brownies made no objections. To have their new ally serve their old friend in this style was sad work, and their indignation waxed warm. But when Twist stopped short in his path, and deliberately composed himself to rest, the Brownies could not restrain themselves.

"How is this," they cried, "do you mean to leave off a work so well begun? Come, this is not keeping faith. Up, and renew the attack! You will rout the whole Pixie army before sunrise if you keep on."

"Thank—ee—kind—le," drawled Twist, winking first with one eye and then with the other. "I nev' e'n work af'r thupper. Muth take time t' digest. Sh'nt do 'nything till '—r—morer. 'M go'n thleep right here. Goo' night, Thir Brownithz, 'll finish job'n mornin'." His head dropped down upon the grass; he was sound asleep.

" Humph," said Corporal Spur, who had charge of the squad, "that ends this campaign. If the Pixies don't serve that gourmand with a rather peppery sauce for his supper, I'm out in my reckoning. Attention, squad! wheel—fly!" He wheeled his own pony, and led his little command back to their quarters. As they flew above the Pixie lines they saw the camp alive with excited troops swarming from every quarter toward the spot where Twist lay.

A squad of reckless youngsters who had jointly mounted the back of a huge Polyphemus moth, could not resist the temptation to let fly a few arrows at the crowd of excited Pixies beneath them. One of the squad, our old friend Highjinks, nearly lost his life, however, for in his eagerness he tumbled off the pony's back. Fortunately, Hosson seized one hand and drew him back safely. But it was a narrow escape, and even Highjinks was for a time quite sedate as he thought what his fate would have been had he dropped into the midst of that angry host of foes. In the excitement, Polyphemus came quite near the ground, and barely escaped being lassoed by one of the Vaulting Legion.

Meanwhile, a circle of Pixies had hemmed in the sleeping serpent; but no one dared to interfere with him until Spite came. Then they began to clamor for orders:

" What shall we do, Captain?"

" Do?" said Spite, fairly hissing the answer through his teeth. "Do? Why, we'll hang the villain!"

" Aha! Captain Spite talks very large, indeed," whispered the soldiers one to another. " Who ever heard of Pixies hanging a serpent?"

At any rate Spite intended to try it now. Already he had climbed upon a bush that overhung the sleeping monster, had fastened a cord to a twig and dropped down upon his head. Twist moved. Spite retreated upon his cord, and in a trice was half way up toward the twig.

"Come back, Captain, you'll lose your life," shouted the crowd.

"Tut! trust me for that! Why, don't you see? The brute is dead stupid from his meal, and perfectly harmless."

Down he ran again. This time Twist did not move. Spite fastened a line upon his head, dropped down by the side of his face, and burrowing into the grass, cleared a path directly under the jaws. Through this he carried his line, then up again along the opposite side of the face, and knotted it. He had thus passed a cord entirely around the serpent's face.

"Now, my braves," said he, "I have shown what I want you to do, and how to do it. Here, a score of you wind up these jaws until they are completely gagged. Another squad may take a knot in his tail, tie it, lash it to a strong rope, and swing it up to that branch. I'll show you what more to do. Work sharp, now, and touch the brute as gently as possible. We shall surprise him, when he wakes up, with a new suit of clothes. He, he!"

The Pixinees and Pixies went to work with a hearty good will, and soon had finished their task.

"Now mount that branch and pull on the rope." The tail was raised a little, and then the work paused. Nothing more could be done in that way. "We must rig up a pulley, then," said Spite. Bring me a dead fly, quick!"

The carcass of a green fly was readily found. It was swung down from the branch, and wrapped round and round until it became a hard silken ball. The rope which had been tied to the tail was now carried over this pulley, or windlass as it might be more properly called. The ball was slowly revolved by the united strength of a number of Pixies; the rope gradually wound around it as it grew taut, and the body of Twist began to move. Thereat the crowd broke into hearty applause, clapping their fangs and claws together until the camp rang. The noise appeared to disturb Twist, or perhaps the effects of his meal were beginning to pass away. He raised his head feebly, shook it from side to side, discovered that his jaws were bound tightly together, and began to wriggle his body violently, whereat the circle of Pixies fell back.

"Pull lively, lads!" cried Spite, who was prudently perched upon the top of the branch. "Lively! a few more turns and we shall have him all right. There, that will do bravely. Now he may squirm as much as he pleases."

FIG. 132.—Twist, the Serpent, Hung in the Pixie Snare.

Twist was indeed bound and hung up beyond hope of recovery, although he was making desperate efforts to escape.*

"Straighten out that cord, my lads, as much as possible," called Spite. "Run up supporting lines to the limb

* Appendix, Note A.

here. Fasten down the coils on the ball so that the rope won't give. Then, hurrah! We'll have a taste of dragon blood before we go to bed." Spite ran down upon Twist's body as he spoke, and fastening himself upon the neck, struck with his fangs again and again. He then comfortably settled himself for a meal. In the meantime a number of the working squad had followed their Captain's example. Poor Twist! he was being literally devoured alive. Like many other wise persons, he had fallen a victim to ill-governed appetite. Thus ended his proud boasts and the campaign most prosperously begun. A Brownie scout, attracted by the great commotion in the Pixie camp, stole through the lines and discovering the cause, returned with the news which was soon known by all the Brownies at the inlet. But Spite was not long permitted to enjoy his well-earned supper. A runner bustled through the crowd and shouted for the Captain.

" Here I am," answered Spite, quitting his hold upon Twist's neck and dropping to the ground. " What's the matter now?"

" Matter enough, Sir! The rear of our camp has been attacked by young Slymousie, and everything there is in panic and confusion."

" The prowling sneak! The Brownies have put him up to it, I warrant. Rally the men! We must try to drive him back."

Thereupon Spite started at full speed to the rear. He found affairs quite as bad as they had been reported. Biggy had cautiously approached the camp and, crawling low in the grass, slipped by the picket line undiscovered. Then with a rush and bound he leaped upon a group of Pixie sentinels who stood at the guard tent talking over the late incident with Dragon Twist. Unfortunately his caution, which is a good trait, was pushed to an undue degree, which is bad practice in a soldier. The fact is, that in spite of his boastings, Biggy's heart failed him a little when he came to face the danger, and thus his approach was so timid and slow that instead of striking the Pixie camp, as had been agreed, at the moment of Twist's assault, he did not attack it until Twist was fairly over his onset. This proved to be a fatal blunder.

However, when he once began work, he pushed it vigorously enough. He dispersed the sentinels hither and thither, broke down their tent and burst into the midst of the encampment. He struck, pushed and bit to the right and left, and soon had laid a broad swath of destruction along his path. In the midst of this high success he came upon the scattered contents of a bumble-bee's nest, which the Pixies had been pillaging. It was a most unlucky circumstance, for all the Slymousie tribe are fond of bee-bread and honey, and Biggy was hungry. He stopped, smelled the bee combs, turned over a few cells with his nose and then began to nibble.

"Just one little taste," he said, "and then I'll go on with my duty." Ah, Biggy Slymousie, take care! Your enemies are all around you. This is the time for duty, not for delicacies. Touch not, taste not, handle not! The temptation may prove too strong for you!

But Biggy silenced the voice of his better judgment, and nibbled away. Now, Slymousies are always dainty and deliberate in their way of eating, which, as a rule, is quite proper and nice. But when one is in the midst of a hard and perilous battle, daintiness cannot safely be indulged. Spite the Spy arrived on the scene just as Biggy had fairly settled down to enjoy a hearty meal. With a curse of thorough contempt hurled at the silly glutton, the Pixie chief began his preparations for revenge. He sent for engineers Tegenaria and Agalena of the Tubeweaver legion, and ordered out Theridion and his pioneers. The Pixies set to work with a will, and ere Biggy had finished his meal had completely surrounded him with a thick, strong and high wall of web work. While Biggy nibbled, nibbled, the Pixies spun and wove around him their fatal snares. Poor Biggy!

At last all was ready. The Theridion pioneers were sent aloft among the overhanging grasses, the Tube-

FIG. 133.—"One of Tegenaria's Thick Snares."

weavers went to their holes, and those in front of Sly-mousie provided themselves with silken blankets. Then Spite ordered a company of vaulters, runners and side-goers to the bushes behind Biggy. They moved to their places noiselessly, and awaited the order to assault. It came at last.

"Charge!" shouted Spite. Stridulans at the same

moment struck the long roll on his drum, and the Pixies rushed in upon Biggy. The poor fellow was so frightened that he made a great leap forward. The Pixies who had fallen upon him were scattered in all directions, but, alas for Slymousie, he alighted within one of Tegenaria's thick snares.* Immediately the Tubeweavers closed upon him with their blankets, as Spanish bull

Fig. 134.—" Wrapped up as Tightly as a Captive Grasshopper Swathed by a Big Garden Spider."

fighters assail a wild bull. They blindfolded his eyes, covered his nostrils, and veiled his face, until they were wrapped up as tightly as a captive grasshopper swathed by a big garden spider. Theridion and his Lineweavers followed this attack, and flung their swathing bands around Biggy's limbs. The poor fellow, in spite of his struggles, was soon wrapped up like a mummy, and at

* Appendix, Note B.

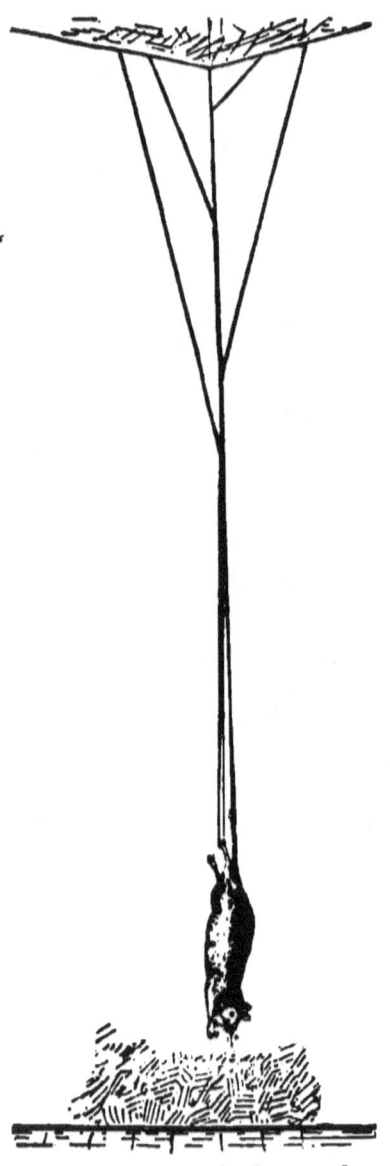

last lay still and subm... d to his doom. Spite rigged block and tackle and wind-lass, such as had been used to hoist Twist; then he fastened ropes to Biggy's tail, and bade the Pixies pull away. Soon the unfortunate young Slymousie was raised aloft and hung by his tail with his nose upon the ground.* His foes surrounded him, pinched him, laughed, jeered, shot at him, until death came to relieve him of his tormentors. Thus the second of Corporal Policy's grand allies came to grief.

But the Pixies were not left to enjoy their triumph long. A runner ran into the circle and hurried to the chief's side. "What's in the wind now?" asked Spite.

"Well, Sir," said the runner, who was quite blowed and caught at his breath between the words, "there's the—mischief—to pay—down at—the lake. The

Fig. 135.—Slymousie Hung up by the Tail.

navy is all in—commotion. The Natties have got the

* Appendix, Note C.

help of Scaly the Fish, and have broken loose upon our Stygies with a vengeance. Scaly has already stove in two of our ships and a half dozen boats. She is like to sink the whole navy if we can't stop her somehow. The Admiral has sent for you."

Spite was as near being overcome by this news as was possible for him, but he soon recovered. "Here, Pixies!" he shouted, "down to the beach, every one of you. This game will keep till you come back,—if you ever do get back!" he added in an undertone; a remark that showed pretty clearly that he thought there was serious work before them.

Matters did indeed have an ugly look when Spite reached the shore. The wrecks of two ships and several boats were floating in the water, with Stygians clinging to them. Boats were pushing out from the remaining ships bent on leaving them and seeking safety on land. Two other vessels were standing out to sea with all sails set, and the flagship Styx, followed closely by the Goodtime, was slowly making for the shore. Spite took in the situation at a glance.

"But what do the Natties mean?" he asked. "They seem quite as much taken by surprise as our fellows. Saving a brace of boats yonder, there is not a Brownie ship under sail. Ah! there they go, now! See those lights on the Emma? That's the signal to make sail. And there goes the signal 'to quarters.' Oho! we'll have our hands full now. But I don't see through it. Surely, Scaly the Fish isn't operating on her own hook!"

The reader will understand Spite's perplexity. Most of the Brownies were indeed taken by surprise. Mac-Whirlie had not even told Bruce and Rodney of Corporal Policy's plot. He had looked upon it simply as

one of the madcap undertakings which his troopers were
always ready for, and in which he liked to please them
when he could do so.   But that it would have any
serious results never entered his mind.   With the exception, therefore, of the volunteers engaged in the expedition, few were ready for action.   But when the vigorous
and successful raid of Scaly was        seen by the clear
light of the moon, the Brownies       were all astir on
lake and shore.  The big davids       were  double

FIG. 136.—Wolf Strangle Leaps Upon Scaly's Back.

manned.   The ships made sail and prepared for action.

At this point Scaly turned her attention on the Pixie
ships Styx and Goodtime.   Mindful of the wishes of her
friend Policy, she resolved to carry these vessels into the
inlet as a present to the Brownies and as trophies of her
prowess.   She therefore darted between the shore and
the ships, stopped the vessels' motion by running
athwart their bows, then placing her head first against
one, and next the other, pushed them by alternate shoves
toward the mouth of the inlet, out of which the Natties
were slowly sailing.

Scaly was in high good humor, and made the lake behind her boil under the frisky strokes of her tail as she urged the Stygian barks forward. The Pixies were in despair. The Brownies from the shore of the lake and the decks of their ships sent up ringing cheers.

Then came a sudden turn in affairs. The master of the Goodtime, Wolf Strangle, was not a person to give up his ship without a struggle. He was a strong, active Pixie, a vigorous swimmer, fierce and brave. He made a desperate resolution: He would grapple with Scaly the Fish single-handed! He laid aside his sword, threw off his uniform coat and hat, and mounted the railing at the stern of the ship. The sailors gathered around him and waited silently to see what was his purpose. They would never have guessed the truth; but they knew their captain and were looking for something gallant and startling in which they expected to take part. This is what they saw:

Scaly had just given the Styx a vigorous shove, and turned to do the same service to the Goodtime. She scarcely noticed the dark form of Strangle poised upon the railing, but thrust her nose under the stern of the ship, played her fins and tail, and sent the vessel merrily ahead. At this moment Strangle leaped fairly upon her back, seized her with his claws on the forward side of the dorsal fin, and sunk his fangs again and again into the fish's flesh.

Scaly wheeled to one side, leaped out of the water, and dived deep into the lake. Her whole frame was quivering with the pain and shock of the sudden assault. The Stygians on the two ships crowded the rails and ladders, and gazed eagerly toward the spot where they had seen the two sink out of sight. They had great confidence in Commander Strangle, but they feared that, famous waterman as he was, he would be worsted in this combat.

"He will be drowned!" cried one.

"He dives like a duck," said another, "and will come up all right."

"No; it was madness to grapple with a fish many times his size, and in her own element," said a third.

Now the voice of Admiral Quench was heard ordering first all hands to quarters, and then to tack ship. The Stygies ran to their posts, the topmen flew aloft, and in a few moments both ships were turned about, and under full sail from

Fig. 137.—How a Spider Captured a Fish.

the inlet. Quench had taken advantage of the diversion to put all the distance possible between himself and the Natties.

Before this movement was finished Scaly had emerged from the water. The black form of Strangle still clung to her back! The poor fish made the most frantic efforts to shake off her enemy, who held on as with a death grip. Scaly plunged under the Styx and tried to scrape

off the Pixie against the keel. Strangle swung his body
over upon the fish's side but never relaxed his merciless
grasp. Frantic with pain and terror, Scaly swam round
and round in circles, plunged into the water again and
again, and finally, nearly worn out, dragged herself toward the shore, and ran her head under the grass.
Strangle held on to her body with his fangs, laid hold
with his claws upon the grass stalks above him, and
drawing himself up with his utmost power, had well
nigh succeeded in landing his huge prey ere Spite and
his friends reached the spot.* In a few moments more
the unfortunate Scaly was drawn up upon the green
bank, where she was at once assailed by a brood of vo-
racious Pixies in the same manner as her unhappy ally
Twist the Serpent. Strangle quietly shook the water
from his hair, and perched upon a cliff, together with
Spite and other officers, to watch the turn of events.
The fate of Scaly had made a great change in the condition of the two fleets.

The Stygians had been much scattered, but were beginning to rally. Their boats put back to the abandoned
ships, carrying with them many of the sailors who had
been picked up from the wrecks. The loss of the Stygians was two ships, several boats and a few drowned
sailors. But the victory over Scaly, and the moral
effect upon the navy, was counted a fair offset to this
loss, and on the whole the Pixies were mightily satisfied
with the night's work.

On the other hand, the Natties had at once taken in
sail, and cast anchor. Some damage had been wrought
upon their enemies by the expedition of Twist, Slymousie
and Scaly ; but the defeat and capture of these mam-
moth adversaries, under circumstances that showed to

* Appendix, Note D.

such advantage the Pixies' skill and power, well nigh demoralized the Brownies. Thrice that night had their enemies wrested victory from the jaws of defeat, and had triumphantly annihilated the Grand Alliance of Corporal Policy. While the Pixies were highly elated, the Brownies were dispirited, cowed, well nigh in despair. But, courage, good fairies! The Hebrews had a proverb—"When the tale of bricks is doubled, then comes Moses!"

"The darkest hour is just before the dawn."

# CHAPTER XXXI.

## HOME AGAIN.

Sightwell, the lookout on the Emma, had observed, during the late stirring events, a suspicious-looking craft hovering on the outer line of the Stygian fleet. It was a yacht, apparently one of the privateers or smugglers that infested the lake. When first sighted it was hugging the shore, the side opposite the Pixie camp, as though planning a raid upon the Brownies encamped on that side of the inlet. When the Stygies had been scattered by Scaly's first onset, this yacht pushed boldly out from shore, and headed directly for the inlet, as though she would come to the rescue of her friends. In the excitement of the closing incidents in Scaly's career, Sightwell had quite forgotten the stranger; but as the Emma came to anchor, he sighted her once more. She was bearing down upon the inlet under full sail.

"Sail ho!" cried the lookout.

"Where away?" called Ask the mate.

"Dead ahead, and bearing straight down upon us."

"What do you make her out?"

"A yacht,—a smuggler, I judge. And—yes, there are two boats pulling along close under her sides!"

"That looks suspicious," said Ask. "Call the Commodore."

Just as Rodney arrived on deck Sightwell called from the fore topmast cross-trees: "Our boats are about to make an attack,—I mean the boats that first went out with Scaly and afterward turned back shoreward. They

(321)

pull up cautiously to the strangers.  The two boats
from the yacht dash away to meet them.  They are
about to grapple.  Hah!  No!  what can that mean?
The men in the boats rise and swing their hats.  The
yachtsmen are hanging in the rigging swinging kerchiefs,
scarfs, bonnets and swords; I can see the flutter of one
and the flash of the other in the moonlight.  Hark!
they are cheering each other!"

It was so, indeed.  Over the shimmering surface of
the lake rolled a volume of sound such as never before
went up from so small a company in all the history of
Brownieland.

By this time every soul on shipboard who could get
aloft, or find place at the railings, was gazing across the
water and wondering at this strange occurrence.  No
one could solve the mystery.  Meanwhile the lookout
continued his report: " The whole scene is now fully in
view.  One of the Brownie boats is pulling for the shore
with might and main; the other has left the yacht
and is making straight for the Emma.  The oars flash
in the moonlight, and are played so rapidly that the wake
of the boat is an almost unbroken line of gleaming gold.
The Kind, Commander Takeheed, lies directly in the
boat's course, and as the crew pass under the ship's bows
they pause a moment,—only a moment,—and then on
again as though making a final spurt at a rowing race.

" But what is this?  The whole ship's crew has surely
gone mad!  Cheer on cheer, wild, loud, uttering the
very madness of joy, goes up from the Kind's crew, till
the welkin rings.  See! the flag is being dipped.  The
sailors are running over the rigging carrying with them
lanterns which they hang upon every available spot.  The
vessel is a blaze of light!  They are manning the yards!
And still the cheers rise up and roll over the lake with

unabated energy. Ah! they have caught the contagion on the shore, which the first boat has already reached. A line of lights follows from the landing to the headquarters tent, springing up at once behind the running boatmen, until every tent, bush and tree-top is gleaming with lanterns and torches. The fort is all ablaze. And such cheers! The camp is wild with joy over some great event."

"What can it be?" .

"Governor Wille has come!" cried an enthusiastic Natty.

Maybe! But we shall know in a moment. Rodney and his brave tars are well nigh beside themselves with excitement and wonder as the boat on which every eye is now centred, dashes alongside. A brawny sailor is at the bow, necktie thrown off, shirt wide open, hatless, and nearly breathless with excitement. Hist! the deck is silent as death, and every ear stoops for the message.

"The lost Nurses are found! Faith—Sophia—they're on yonder yacht! Pipe, True, Blythe—they're all there —all safe!"

Hurrah, hurrah, hurrah!

Never were such echoes wakened from the green bosom of Hillside and the blue face of Lake Katrine, as those which answered back the ringing shout. The tidings flew from ship to ship; land and lake were soon gleaming with countless lights, and the very leaves above them shook with the sound of cheers and singing till the gathering dew dropped down from their quivering sides.

And Rodney? We draw a veil upon his emotion as the tidings came to him. Equally, we drop the curtain upon the scene which followed, when the Fringe—for it was Raft's yacht, the same that bore the Nurses away into captivity,—drew up to the side of the Emma, and

Rodney sprung upon her deck and clasped his darling Faith in his arms. Presently the yacht landed its precious cargo at the foot of Cape Home, where all the return party were publicly welcomed. Then the Nurses were led away to their own tent and the embrace of their dear companions Agatha and Grace.

Faith and Sophia safe in the midst of the Brownie camp once more! Surely the dayspring has come at last!

All this time Spite the Spy stood upon the cliff surrounded by his staff, all of them champing, fretting, cursing, wondering, guessing, well nigh distracted in their perplexity over these strange doings. The whole thing was so mysterious, the burst of joy on the part of the Brownies so sudden and extreme, that awe fell upon the Pixie host. Vague presentiments of coming evil hung upon many hearts. The troops lay down solitary and silent to sleep.*

Spite sat upon the cliff alone, looking at the moonlight upon the water, gazing across the mouth of the inlet into the illuminated camp of the Brownies, venting his hatred and disappointment in oaths, and weaving in his busy brain some plot by which to find out ere he retired the cause of his enemies' joy. He had already sent out scouts to prowl along the outer entrenchments of Fort Home, which divided the Brownie tents on the south side of the stream from his own. As he sat there, awaiting their return, he queried again and again, "What can it be?" Ah, Spite, you shall find out ere long, and it will be the last tidings that your ears shall ever hear!

We go back now to take up the story of the party upon Ellen's Isle, and trace it to this happy ending. We left the little camp settled into happy sleep after

---

* Appendix, Note A.

the rescue of Faith and Sophia from Arachne Hall.
The morning broke calm and bright, early driving away
the mists that hung over the island. The first thought
of all turned upon escape. It seemed beyond endurance
to be shut up on that little spot, so near their friends,
with such glorious news in their keeping. Faith in particular found it hard to restrain her feelings. She was
indeed free, and her lover was by her side ; but how
could she wait for the hour when the load of grief should
be rolled from her father's heart?

But stubborn facts shut the party in. One boat,
which had nearly swamped under the load that it had
carried to the island, was all that they could command.
And now there were three others, Pipe and the two
Nurses, to be cared for. The sailors asked to be left to
shift for themselves, while the officers, and as many as
could be stowed away safely, should make the best of
their way to land. No! that would be selfish and
couldn't be thought of. Besides, there was the risk!
The Stygies were closely guarding the inlet; and the
Pixie camp at Big Cave lay between them and the army.
All over the lake and along shore the pirate crafts,
smugglers and yachts were plying. These facts made
departure in an open boat too great a risk, especially
with such precious passengers to look after. By themselves, no adventure would have been too daring for the
humor of the wrecked Brownies, but with Faith and
Sophia in their company they felt doubly engaged to
caution. Then there was that mysterious boat's crew
from the Doubt. The least imprudence might reveal
to them the presence of the Brownie party, and call
down upon the little band the whole Stygian fleet. It
was a perplexing position, and they must be wise and
patient and make the best of it.

"First of all," said Pipe, who now took command, "we must try to rig up another boat. Now, my hearties, out with your hatchets and ropes and get to work!"

The sailors could turn their hands to every sort of handicraft, and some of them were quite skillful mechanics. Fortunately, Square, the ship's carpenter of one of the sunken vessels, was among the number picked up by Coxswain Help, and to him the boat building was entrusted. First the frame was made ready. A hickory twig was laid upon the ground, and bent at both ends. This formed the keel. Both ends of two similar twigs were fastened to each end of the keel piece, and bent outward to form the gunwale. These pieces were held in position by braces until the ribs were set, which were shorter twigs bent around the frame and fastened to the keel piece beneath, and to the gunwale on either side.

"Very good," said Square, when this work was done, "now for the covering. We must find a birch tree for that, and strip the bark from some of the branches."

The Natties soon came back from the woods bringing enough white birch bark to cover a man-of-war. The framework was entirely covered with this, the pieces being lapped far over one another, so as to make the joints as water-tight as possible.

"Now," said Chips, as the sailors call the carpenter, "if we had a little oakum to caulk these seams we should be all right."

"We can fix that for you," answered one of the sailors. "Here is a grass whose fibres, if well scraped, will give us quite a good substitute for tow. As for tar, we can get on very well with the gum on yonder pine tree."

"A good thought," said Square, "and I will leave you to carry it out, while I get ready the thwarts and bottom boards."

The thwarts were simply undressed twigs laid close together after the fashion of a rustic seat, and fastened against the ribs, and the bottom board was built in the same way. The whole affair had a rustic appearance, when it was finished, but it promised to be serviceable, and that was the main matter. When the woodwork was done the boat was turned keel up, and the caulking began. The fibres of grass were torn and drawn into fine threads, and these made passable oakum, which was thrust into the seams between the layers of bark until they were thoroughly stopped. Now rollers were put under the keel, ropes were fastened to the stern, and by pushing and pulling the boat was safely launched upon the lake. It floated well, and was water-tight. The building of the boat took the whole of that day and part of the following, and all hands were vastly pleased at the results. They now had the means to escape from the island whenever the way opened.

After dinner, whilst Square wrought upon the boat, and Pipe and Blythe guarded the camp, True and Clearview, at the head of a small party, sallied forth to explore. They set out for the head of the island, that is, the end toward the inlet, marching as stealthily as an Indian war party. They were chiefly concerned to find out what the boat's crew from the Stygian ship Doubt had to do upon Ellen's Isle, and whether there seemed any prospect that they would pass over to the opposite end, and thus imperil the Brownies. They had well nigh skirted the entire south shore before they observed any signs of the Pixies.

" What is that?" cried Sailor Filip, pointing to a small conical mound just beyond the path, built of dry grass stalks and small twigs. Thereupon he ran up to it and exclaimed : " It is a tom-tit's nest, built flat upon the ground ! "

"Who ever heard the like?" shouted a companion; and thereat the Brownies began to guy the discoverer, and ran into the thicket to get a closer view.

"Well, well!" they exclaimed as they got quite near, "it truly is a bird's nest of some sort. But what a weenie one! And what bird could have built it?"

"Come, let us explore it!" said a little Brownie who by a well-known rule of contrariness was called Jumbo. So saying, he began clambering up the sides.

"Good for Jumbo!" his comrades cried, and followed close at his heels. It was easy climbing, and the Brownies having quickly reached the top were amazed to find no bottom to the nest! They looked down into a deep crater that pierced the ground below the surface, and led into depths hidden in darkness.

"I'm bound to solve this mystery!" said Jumbo. "Who'll go with me into the hole?" He swung over the edge, and his comrades were about following, when they were stopped by a sharp cry from Jumbo: "Look out there!"

"Look in, you mean," said Filip. And they all looked into the burrow. They saw a row of gleaming eyes that sparkled like jewels as they slowly moved upward into the light. Then came into view a claw; then another, and another, and next the brown head of a great Pixie!

"Whew!" cried Jumbo. "Somersault all, and out of this, instanter!" He swung himself back over the outer edge of the nest and rattled down the rugged side in such haste that he tumbled in a little heap upon the grass, and was presently buried under the sprawling limbs of his comrades. When the Brownies got to their feet they saw a huge ground Pixie of the clan Lycosa, glaring at them over the edge of the nest, and plainly getting ready to spring down upon them.

"Cut and run, lads!" shouted Jumbo, and away the squad scurried out of the thicket, leaving Lycosa perched upon the crest of her nest-like tower. When they told their story to Captain Clearview, he bade two of the Natties remain in the path, and keep watch upon the nest-building Pixie lest she might sally forth and attack the party on flank or rear. Then he bade the squad move on. They had gone but a short march when the Captain called a halt.

Fig. 138.—The Tower or Surface Nest of a Lycosid Spider.*

"See," he said, pointing toward the lake, "yonder is the boat! It is tied to the shore, without any attempt at concealment. Plainly, the crew has no suspicion of our presence here. Their camp can't be far away." The scouting party was halted, and Clearview and True stole through the young willows that fringed the shore.

"Hist! there they are!" whispered True, who had caught the sound of voices. "Do you see them?"

"No, but they are just beyond this fallen sapling. Here, we can climb upon the trunk and overlook the bivouac safely."

---

* Appendix. Note B.

In a small open space, near the point where the boat lay, the camp had been pitched. A large tent with a tubular entrance had been built over the hole made by the uplifted root of an overthrown oak. Another tent was pitched above this on a platform made of earth which had adhered to the projecting roots; and a third was woven over the top of a clump of weeds, its tubular entrance or hall running straight down to the ground. A bridge of silken ropes stretched from the camp to the tops of the willows that skirted the shore, and from the tents to the edge of the water. It was a snug and pretty retreat.*

True and Clearview climbed into the branches of the fallen tree, crept along the trunk, and found themselves near enough to overlook the entire camp and overhear the conversation which had first attracted their attention. They were themselves hidden among the leaves. A sentinel stood in the circular doorway of the tent which occupied the hole below the roots. Just beyond, two Pixie officers walked to and fro, talking loudly and earnestly.

"Do you know them?" whispered True.

"Yes; that fellow in black is Halfway the son of Hide; he is one of the principal Stygian chiefs. The one in the brown uniform with broad whitish band is Agalena Ringster; he is one of the Tubeweaving Pixies, a tricky fellow and captain of the marines."

"Softly," said True, as the Pixies, having reached the limit of their promenade, turned and walked toward the tent. "We shall find out now what they talk about."

"You are sure you understand your father aright?" asked Ringster.

"Quite; he said that the cave was at the head of

---

* Appendix, Note C.

Aranea Isle—head, I think it was; it's the only point about which I feel uncertain. I am positive of all the rest."

"But," said Ringster, "there is no such cave, for we have explored every inch of ground thoroughly. Pity the old man was cut off so suddenly! But we must act on your uncertainty, and try the foot of the island. There's nothing else for it; you can't go to Spite about this matter; that would spoil all."

"There's the trouble. We have wasted too much time already. Our absence will be noticed. We can't do much to-day, and—but will to-morrow be clear?"

"Aye. Look at my marines yonder. Do you see them putting up a new tent?" Ringster pointed to the tall grass near the willows, over which a fresh silken canvas was being rapidly spread. "They never do that in threatening weather. You can rely upon it more certainly than our fine Governor does upon his Old Probabilities." *

"But if we fail to discover anything on the foot of the island?" asked Halfway. "Can we take the time to go over the—"

Here the voices of the officers grew indistinct, as they had turned upon their course and gone to the far end of the enclosure. They were soon within ear-shot again, but the thread of conversation had been lost.

"But where is he?" asked Ringster. "If our search fails we must fall back upon him. He was your father's friend, and will serve you faithfully. Where does he keep his yacht?"

"I don't know. But—I declare! I had quite forgotten it! He was to meet father here to-day!"

"Good!" exclaimed Ringster; "that is the best news

---

* Appendix, Note D.

yet. It was stupid enough in you not to remember it
before. That makes matters plain. We may wait here
until he comes, and save ourselves all trouble. But
where will he land ? "

" I don't know that," responded Halfway. " If I am
right as to the location of the cave, he would touch here,
of course. If not— " Here the Pixies entered one of
their tents and the conversation was wholly lost.

" We have heard enough," whispered True. " Let
us away!" Noiselessly as they had approached, the
Brownie spies stole back again to their friends, and
reported their discoveries.

" What do you make of it all ? " asked Help.

True answered : " That scamp Halfway is after the
cave in which Faith and Sophia were concealed. Don't
you remember that they told us of Hide's plans? The
old rogue had been laying some scheme to circumvent
Spite, and was cut off before he had finished it, or fully
revealed it to his hopeful son."

" And the last part of the conversation—? "

" Refers to Raft, beyond a doubt," answered Clearview. " Now the question is, what shall we do ? These
Pixies will be down upon our camp to-morrow at the
furthest. We must get out of the island, at least out
of our present quarters, very soon, unless, indeed, we
agree to stand and fight it out."

" Well," said Help, " I have thought of a plan that
will save us from our greatest danger. I was sorely
tempted to put it into execution, while you were away.
Look there," pointing to the Pixie boat. " If that were
out of the problem we could solve it a good deal more
readily. What I fear most is that these Doubtmen, at
the first alarm, may pull off to the fleet, and bring such
a force against us as will overwhelm us. If they were

here alone with us we might have a fair standup fight, or a struggle of plot and counterplot, and come off well enough. Can't we get that boat adrift? It is not guarded; we can steal along the shore, loosen the cable and let her drift off on the current. I will volunteer for the service."

The party greeted this plan with approbation, and it was immediately carried out. Help and two of the sailors crept along the shore, under the drooping boughs of the willows, and reached the boat safely. Silently and quickly they slipped the cable by which she was moored to the bank, and placing their spears against the bow, gave a vigorous push. The current was strong at this point, sweeping from the inlet along the head of the island toward the foot, and so out into the lake. In a few moments the boat had drifted out of sight beyond the willows, and was on its way to the outlet.

It had immediately floated away beyond recovery, before Halfway, who had mounted the bridge to look out for Raft, saw that the boat was gone, and raised the alarm. He stormed, swore, questioned, threatened. In the meantime Ringster had quietly ascended one of the tallest bushes, and was carefully surveying the lake.

"I see her!" he cried, pointing toward the outlet. "Yonder she drifts, far beyond the foot of the island, and out of reach. The current is so strong here that she has pulled up the stake or slipped her painter, and the current has carried her away. It's bad business for us, but storming won't mend matters. We must make the best of it and quietly wait for Raft. If he fails us, we must set signals for some of our own ships." So saying he got down from his perch and entered his tent, an example which the rest were not slow to follow.

The Brownies set their faces homeward well satisfied

24

with the results of the scout, and anxious to reach camp
before sunset. But their adventures were not ended.
As the party stealthily threaded the shore in Indian file,
Clearview, who was in the lead, suddenly halted and
threw up a hand in token of silence.

"Hist—softly! See there!"

He pointed to a gaily uniformed water Pixie stretched
upon the ground a little beyond them, sound asleep.
The Brownie sailors lifted their spears, and were about
to hurl them at the prostrate form.

"Hold!" said True in an undertone, "we must capture this fellow. He may be Raft himself. It is his
uniform, at least; and if it be he, no Brownie hand
must harm him save in lawful battle. Let us move
softly, and at the signal surround and capture him." It
was done as ordered, and the sleeping waterman awoke
to find himself in the hands of his enemies.

"Are you Raft Dolomede?" asked True.

"Well, what then, Sir?" answered the Pixie defiantly.

"Then your life shall be spared for a kindness done
in an hour of great need to those whom we love."

The captive cast a keen, inquiring glance into True's
face; then answered coolly, "Humph! that's a temptation to sail under false colors that most of my kin would
thank'ee for. But I don't take kindly to lying, and
don't ask for life at Brownie hands. Do your worst—
and as soon as you please. My name's not Raft."

Again the Brownie spears were poised, and again True
interfered to save the captive. "Beat those bushes
along the shore," he cried; "we shall carry our prisoner
to camp." Presently the sailors returned and reported
that they had found a yacht at anchor under the willows
just beyond.

"Any name on her?"

"Aye; 'The Fringe' is worked in white silk upon one of the sails."

True turned to his captive and asked, "Are you the captain of that yacht?"

"No, Sir," was the stout answer, "the Captain's looking for some messmates down yonder at the foot of the island."

True started. "Haste! Mark the spot where the yacht lies. Bring on the prisoner—away, away!"

The Brownie camp was soon reached. Square and his squad left their boat-building to stare at the new arrival, and overwhelmed their friends with wondering questions. Faith and Sophia left their tent to learn the cause of the commotion. The crowd of sailors around the scouts and their prisoner fell back, bringing the Pixie into full view. Sophia uttered a cry and ran forward.

"Do not harm him, True," she exclaimed, "this is Raft! Save him; he is the only one who showed us kindness in our captivity."

Raft, for it was indeed he, cast down his eyes and said nothing. True looked in amazement upon him, and asked half angrily: "What reason, even according to Pixie policy, could you have had for telling us such lies?"

Raft was silent. In sooth, he could hardly have answered the question. Perhaps he had felt, more keenly than he cared to show, Sophia's refusal to marry him; perhaps he was moved by ideas of fidelity to his own party; perhaps he was simply stubborn and defiant; perhaps he was really ashamed, after the manner of some human beings, to confess and talk about anything so far out of his common life as a good deed. At all events, he refused to speak to any one, even to the

Nurses. He was securely bound and carefully guarded throughout the night.

Next morning Pipe called a council, and announced a plan of escape. " We have, or shall have soon," said he, " two boats and Raft's yacht. We could get off quite well in the boats; but the risks of meeting some of the Pixie craft would be considerable. We can avoid that by taking out the Fringe with us, and pulling our boats close alongside of her. The Stygies will not suspect anything wrong with a craft they know so well. We can get quite near the fleet without challenge, and trust to luck to run the gauntlet of the ships afterwards."

The plan was accepted at once and it was agreed to attempt the escape that evening, when the moon would give enough light to sail by, but not too much to allow close observation. There were two difficulties in the way, Raft and the Doubtmen. The first was happily disposed of. Pipe approached the prisoner in his hearty sailor fashion. He saw at a glance that the smuggler was in a better humor than on the evening before.

" Mornin', shipmate," said Pipe. " We're going to leave these quarters this evening, and take a little cruise toward the inlet. We have need of your craft for a convoy and want to make matters as easy for you as possible. We give you your choice; stay here tied to that tree until your friends at the head of the island can find and release you, or go with us on the Fringe. If you choose the first, you must lose your yacht; if the second, we promise you that when we are safe alongside a Nattie ship, or in the Brownie camp, you shall sail off unmolested. What say you ? "

Raft twisted himself into a more comfortable position, pulled upon the cords that bound him, and answered,

" Well, Bow'sn, I might as well say thank'ee at once. I choose number two. It's not a pretty thing for a free rover like me to be lashed up here like a sailor on a man-o'-war seized up for a flogging. An' d'ye think I'd trust those fellows on the Point to cut these cables and set me free? If it suited their own interests they might; otherwise Raft might go to Pluto for all them. As to giving up the Fringe"—here a tear started into the smuggler's eye, "not if I can help it, Bow'sn! Why, I love that pretty thing more'n my life. She's as dear to me as your daughter is to you. Aye, aye, Sir! I'll save the Fringe, bless her pretty timbers! So heave ahead, as soon as you're a mind to. One cruise with a Brownie skipper won't hurt, I reckon. 'Specially as a fellow can't help it."

That matter being arranged, the boat-building was hurried up, and as the skiff was nearly finished, it was launched as already described. Camp was then broken, and the whole party embarked in the boats and pulled around the island, keeping close under the shadow of the overhanging willows, to the point where the Fringe lay. Faith and Sophia were placed aboard the yacht, and Raft, still bound, was kept under guard in one of the boats.

" Now, my hearties," said Pipe, as the Brownies landed, " we may as well get ready for some rough work. This is my plan. We are to go into ambush, just beyond there. I am satisfied that the Pixies will take this path to the foot of the island. The other side is well nigh a jungle, while here is an open way. You are to wait under cover until Halfway and his party appear. Then at the signal you are to open on them with spears, and rush upon them with swords, making all the noise you can. I count, pretty confidently, that

they will be thrown into confusion, and will make
straight back to their camp and fortify themselves.  If
they do so, we are all right and can sail away at our
leisure.  If they show fight, we must stand up to them
like men and do our best."

The ambush was soon arranged.  A scout who had
been sent forward to the Point, was seen swinging along
under the bushes, stooping as he ran, and moving noiselessly.  He reported that the Pixies were about leaving
camp, and, as had been conjectured, by the path on that
side.  The word was passed along, and all sank into
silence as Halfway and his command strode on carelessly talking and laughing.  When they reached the
fatal spot, the Boatswain's whistle rose shrill and loud
from the bushes above the path.  It was the signal of
attack.

"Faith, Sophia and Rescue !"

The Brownies shouted this battle cry, which Pipe had
given them, as though the voice and strength of ten
were in every throat.  At the same instant a volley of
spears rained down upon the astounded Stygians, and,
ere they could recover from their surprise, the Natties
were upon them with swift sabre strokes.

Pipe had reckoned truly.  The surprise was so complete, the attack so vigorous, the names of the Nurses,
whom the Pixies were seeking, had such a startling
effect as they were shouted and echoed on every side,
and the Pixies were so utterly unprepared for defence,
that they turned at once, and fled in disorder to their
camp, where they began throwing up entrenchments.
Three of their number were left dead upon the ground,
one of whom was their leader, Halfway, who fell pierced
through and through by spears which True and Clearview had hurled at him with sure aim.

"Now, my lads," said Pipe, putting up his sword, "we may as well take matters comfortably until sundown. Then, up anchor, and away home!"

A ringing cheer was the response. Sentinels were stationed, a scout sent out to watch the Pixie camp, and the party quietly rested until evening. When the moon arose above the lake, the anchor of the Fringe was raised, the boats were manned, and the little fleet swung loose from the island. Both wind and current were against them at first, and little progress was made. But Raft, who had been released on parole and was aboard his beloved Fringe, aided heartily in navigating the yacht, while the boats kept close under her sides. Gradually the party approached the inlet, and arrived unchallenged within the lines of the Stygian fleet just as Scaly began her attack. That event somewhat unsettled the plans of our little squadron, but Pipe soon found that it might work to their advantage. He crowded on all sail, and made straight for the Emma, with what results the reader already knows.

The Brownies dealt with Raft as they had promised, and when the island party had safely landed on the Emma, the smuggler was allowed to sail away with the Fringe, untouched. He made directly for Ellen's Isle, took aboard the Pixies there, secured the body of Halfway, and after delivering the living and dead aboard the Doubt, ran his yacht under the cliff whereon we last saw Spite the Spy seated, waiting, in solitude, tidings from his scouts.

# CHAPTER XXXII.

Shortly after the renowned adventure with the Stygian Ram, Ensign Lawe had been sent upon a mission to Governor Wille. He had been told to spare no effort to arouse the Governor from his indifference to Brownie perils and sufferings, and bring him to their help. "Take all the time you need," added Bruce, "and don't let us see your face until you can bring from Wille a fixed decision, Yea or Nay."

These were hard instructions; but the Ensign was used to facing difficulties, and overcoming them, too. He therefore rode away, with a few trusty troopers, determined to succeed if success were possible. Arrived at the Mansion he found preparations afoot for a grand company in honor of the distinguished Major-General Fleisch. Many people had been invited, and when evening came the house and grounds were thronged. There were Parson Prettyman and his wife, Senator Wirepull, the Honorable Mr. Splurge, M. C., Mr. Shearall the rich banker, Mr. Shortweight the wealthy merchant, Lawyers Grip and Gab, Drs. Sugarcoat and Skindeep, Squire Muddle, Mayor Sponge, and Messrs. Taxem and Robb of the City Council. There were, to be sure, some most worthy people besides, but the above seemed to be favorites with Governor Wille, and to them and the great General Fleisch he showed particular attentions. There was no end of merrymaking. A band played beautiful music from a rustic stand in front of the hall door. Chinese lanterns hung upon trees and shrubbery, and these, with the light of the full moon, made the grounds look like a scene in fairyland.

Amidst all this splendor and gaiety the Pixies kept on spreading their tents upon the lawn. Every now and then, indeed, some of the company would overturn a tent and send its occupants fleeing into their holes among the roots. But that is a matter which Pixies count upon, and therefore they only grumbled and got to work again. Indeed they were quite proud of the whole affair.

"Ho! Brother Cito," said Captain Saltus of the Skirmishers. "Isn't this a grand celebration of our victory?"

"That is it!" answered Cito; "a regular jubilee. Good luck to Governor Wille, and confusion to all Brownies!"

"Humph!" growled Heady, "they're a pack of human fools! And you're little better for thinking that they care for our victories."

"Let those laugh who win," thought Ensign Lawe, who was hidden in the rose bush just above the group, and overheard these remarks. "However, there will be little chance to forward my mission to-night. The Governor has given himself up wholly to pleasuring that big general, and will have a heavy ear for Brownie complaints and petitions."

He sat on the bush and swung himself to and fro, and listened to the strains of music, the hum of conversation, the clatter of plates and goblets, until the small hours of the night had come. Then he saw Wille and Dido go off wearily to their bed-chamber, and wondered, "Shall I disturb them? No! I will wait until they are refreshed by sleep, and will appeal to them in the brightness of the new morning."

As the day began to break Ensign Lawe awoke. He

peeped from beneath the leafy canopy under which he had slept sound and dry. Over the lawn the white tents of the Pixies were spread far and wide. Squads and companies of busy workers were rapidly pushing on the encampment to the border of the South Walk, and to the Promenade under the west window.

"I can't stand this!" cried the Ensign. "Ho! Brownies, awake! Hi! ponies, up! Shake the dew

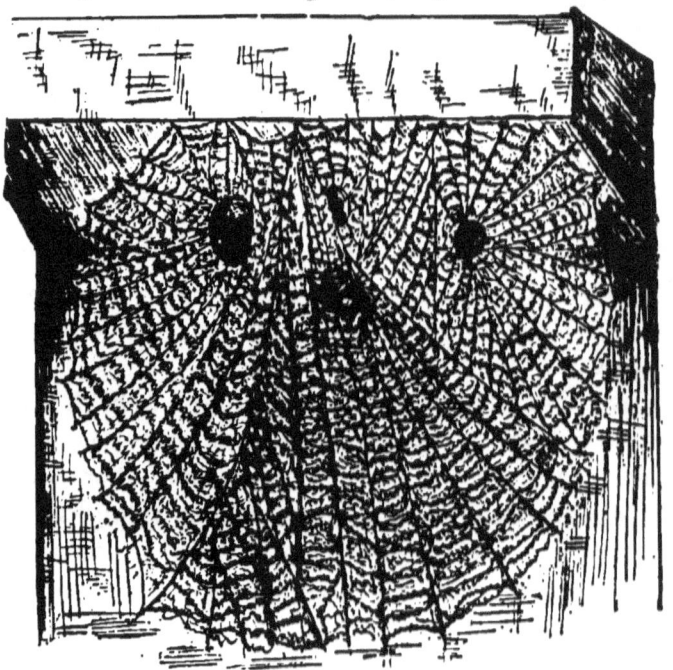

Fig. 139.—The Web of Dictyna the Lacemaker.

off your wings!" He leaped upon his own nag, and followed by his dragoons, flew across to the Virginia creeper that ran over the west wall and twined above the windows of the chamber where Wille and Dido slept.

It was the Ensign's hap to alight upon a leaf whereon a small and rather dainty but vigorous Pixinee, named Madam Dictyna the Lacemaker, had built a snug

FIG. 140.—Madam Lacemaker Tries to Capture Ensign Lawe.

pavilion. Spite had set her as an especial sentinel upon my lady Dido ; and when Lawe and his dragoons made such a rude entrance upon her domain she was sorely vexed. Shaking her lace frills and skirts, she ran out from her tent and threatened the Brownies with high bluster and rage.

But Lawe would not permit her to be attacked just then ; he had other work to do, to which the Lace-maker's presence only spurred him forward. The party left their ponies outside, and crept through the slats of the closed blind into the room. They mounted the bed-post, climbed atop of the carved headboard, and began drumming with their feet and spears upon the solid walnut.

" Rat-a-tat ! Rat-a-tat ! Tat, tat, tat ! "

Neither of the sleepers stirred.

" Louder, lads, louder ! " shouted the Ensign.

" Rat-a-tat ! Rat-a-tat ! Tat, tat ! "

Still the weary couple slept.

" Stop ! " called Lawe. " No use ! Late hours—late supper—champagne ! We must wait and try something better. Away ! "

As they descended the bed and scampered back to the window they were greeted by a loud, prolonged nasal serenade from the unconscious pair.

" Puff ! pu-ff-ff !—oo,—haw ! " breathed Dido quite gently, indeed, after a fashion which goes with some folk by the name of " boiling mush."

" Oo—oogh—ha—aw—*hogh !* " was the answering snore from the Governor's nose, with a tremendous force upon the " hogh ! " In fact, it came out with such a sharp explosion, that Wille's head flew forward, and he awoke.

" **Wife**," said he sleepily—" I say, wife ! " and here he

gave Dido a little tap under the chin. "Don't snore so loud, please! Why, I—I—really you made a terrible racket. I thought at first that some one was pounding the bedstead!"

Dido was quite awake now, and answered indignantly, "Snore indeed! You'd better talk! Pounding the bedstead! It's too bad!" And thereupon the little lady turned over sharply toward the wall, and composed herself to sleep.

However, the Governor had lost the benefit of Dido's speech; for ere she had finished he was sound asleep, and snoring almost as vigorously as before. Meanwhile the Brownies had returned to their rose-bush retreat ignorant of the amusing scene for which their little feet were responsible.

"To-morrow," said Lawe, "we must succeed. If we can once get the Governor to see, in the early morning, while the dew lies upon their tent-tops and reveals them what a vast camp of our enemies holds our old and rightful quarters, I am sure that he will clear out the usurpers at once!"

"Aye; but how shall we bring that about?" said Corporal Trust.

"We must have help. Come, lads, mount and away!" answered Lawe.

He led his troopers straight toward the orchard. Over the tree-tops they flew; on, up, until at last he halted the party on one of the spreading limbs of Lone Aspen. There the Ensign dismounted and approaching the Lone Aspen the first object upon which his eyes fell was a round, horizontal snare of Uloborus, spread within the hollow of the trunk, where the great gateway opened at the foot. His anger was highly inflamed at the sight, and he forgot his mission in the eager purpose to rout this foe lurking at the doorway of his friend, Madam Breeze. He ran hastily forward and smote the web with his sword until it fell to the ground. Uloborus, who was stretched beneath it on a ribbon-like hammock, tumbled down with the ruins of his orb; and thereat Ensign Lawe fell upon him with his sword. But the Pixie, thinking discretion the better part of valor, dodged the strokes, and shaking himself loose from the fragments of his late beautiful net, ran away at top of his speed, and plunged into the thick grass around the roots of the tree. Lawe did not think well to follow; and his wrath being somewhat vented, turned again to the errand on which he had come. He climbed the grass-rope ladder stretched along the trunk, and having reached the upper window at the great knot-hole, blew a shrill blast upon his bugle. The echoes rolled up and down the hollow trunk.

"Oo—oo—oo!"

The round mellow voice of Madam Breeze answered the call, and a moment thereafter the merry Elf bobbed her rubicund face out of the window.

"Hah! who is there? Brownies again, I warrant— Wheeze! More forts to smash? Ho, ho, ho! Why, my sides are aching yet with that last bout. Ho, ho!— Hoogh!" It seemed more likely that the good lady's sides were aching with her hearty laughter.

"Didn't we batter them, though?" she ran on. "Down went tents! Down went barricades! Down went fort—Hoogh!" Here Madam gave one of her little coughs. "Well, no, not exactly that, neither. That was too much for us. But no matter! The vile old den got its deserts anyhow. Ho, ho! Phaugh! And how's Spite the Spy? Has his breath improved any? Wheeze—Dear me! I doubt if he ever scrubs

FIG. 141.—"A Round, Horizontal Snare of Uloborus, Spread Within the Hollow of the Trunk."

(347)

his teeth. Think of a pure, sweet Breeze-body like myself having to wrestle with such as he! Don't ask me to! No, no! It's too funny, ho, ho!—Wheeze—hoogh! You see my asthma's no better—Wheeze!"

All this time the Elf had been seated on a broad leaf swinging like a pendulum, and gazing into the clouds. She suddenly stopped and looked into the Ensign's face.

"Dear me!" she cried, "I—I—and so it's not Bruce this time? The rogue—the scamp—the—ah!—Wheeze! How could he dare to deceive me so?—Hoogh!"

For one minute Madam Breeze sat still, actually for a whole minute! The fact is, she was just a trifle afraid of Ensign Lawe, the only one of all the Brownies, by the way, who ever dashed her high spirits a particle. During that moment the good Elf looked as sober as she could; then threw her heels up and her head down, and swung away furiously for a few seconds.

"Oho! It's you, is it? Well, things must be serious when Lawe comes a-gossiping to Madam Breeze. Well, well! Cheer up, cheer up, Mr. Sobersides!

"Shall we, inclined to sadness,
Strike melancholy's string?
Oh, no! we'll tune to gladness
And merrily, merrily sing
Tra, la!"

The Elf trilled these words to a sprightly strain, and wound up with a laugh, a wheeze and a cough. By this time her touch of seriousness had vanished, and she was swinging as lustily as ever.

"There now, Mr. Lawe. You see I'm composed and ready for business. Go on with your story. Bad news? —of course! Yes, yes—hoogh! I know something about it—bad! There,—stand still a minute, can't you?—and go on!"

Lawe had stood silent and motionless, all this while,

waiting for Madam Breeze to settle herself. But as he saw that this was not likely to happen, he began the story of Brownie disasters, and after many interruptions reached the matter he had in hand.

"Yes, yes! I see it all," said the Elf. "Not another word—it is all right. Here, Whirlit, Keener! Put my ponies Vesper and Vacuum into the chariot—quick!"

The word had scarcely been spoken ere the two pages returned leading a House Martin and a Meadow Lark, who were harnessed to a maple leaf mounted upon wheels of thistledown. The stem of the leaf served as the tongue of the chariot, and the palm of the leaf was bent over at the apex and bent up at the base, so as to make a very pretty fairy coach indeed.

The lark's name was Vesper, the martin's Vacuum, and Madam Breeze had taken the liberty of nicknaming them "Vesp" and "Vac."

"Come; in with you!" cried the good Elf, and suddenly contracting herself into the very smallest compass, as she was wont at times to do, she bounced into the chariot. The Ensign followed. Whirlit and Keener mounted the bird ponies, and waited for the word of command.

"To the cove. Go!" shouted Madam Breeze; and away the party went over orchard and meadow, over town, bridge and river. They stopped at the summit of a hill that stands at the mouth of the cove, whose brow has been worn by frosts, heats and storms of centuries, until it stands up a bald cliff. The naked rock below has a rough likeness to a human face, and the fringe of bushes underneath gives the idea of a vast beard. The top of the cliff is covered with trees that look in the far distance like tufts of frizzly hair upon the Giantstone's poll. From the midst of these rose (when these records were made) two pine trees. Their

25

tall trunks were quite bare, their bushy branches interlocked closely, and thus was left a goodly sized opening,
through which at that time of the year the sun was first
seen of mornings coming down into the valley. The
fairies called this the Gate of the Sun, and it was to
visit four sister Elves who kept this gate that Madam
Breeze had now come. The gate stood wide open, for
the sunshine was already gone through to the town and
hills beyond. In a snug little cave in the limestone
front of the hill, a sort of "mouth" to the Giantstone's
face, the four Elves lived.

Lawe followed as briskly as possible, swung himself
from bough to bough of the overhanging shrubbery,
landed upon a narrow ledge, and found his way to the
mouth of the Cave of the Clouds. Madam Breeze,
now expanded in bodily form to goodly size, had already
entered and was bustling around the place calling for
the sisters.

"Hi! Cirrus! Ho, Stratus! Here, here—where are
you?—Wheeze!"

The dead dry leaves whirled around and around as
the merry Elf called, and the echoes answered her voice.

"Ho—e—oh! Cumulus! Nimbus! Can't you hear?"

The bustling Elf had no cause to be impatient, for
she had scarcely spoken ere four forms slowly rose in
the shadows of the inner cave, and began to move deliberately toward the light. The first advanced with airy
footstep, shaking about her face a cloud of long curling
locks, almost white. She was dressed in a white robe,
covered with trellis-work patterns, inwrought with thin
silvery streaks. This was Elf Cirrus.

The second sister was a plump, sober-looking Elf,
whose hair was gathered in woolly puffs upon her round
head, and was a curious mixture of white and black.

Her robe was covered with figures of cones, hemispheres and white-topped mountains, which figures were touched here and there with many bright colors. This was Cumulus.

Elf Stratus wore a grayish robe flounced with bands of divers colors, many of them edged with bright silver and golden fringe like the rays of the setting sun. Her dark hair was worn smooth, and was crossed by a band of purple ribbons that girdled the crown.

Nimbus, the last of the four sisters, was a gloomy-looking dame, with a kind look in her eyes nevertheless, and a great purse in her hand, through the meshes of which yellow pieces of gold were seen. She was dressed in black, had a gray cloak with fringed edges thrown over her shoulders, and a dainty lace cap upon her head.

"Oho! here you are, then!" cried Madam Breeze as the Elves came forward. They all bowed as she spoke, and stood quite still when she ceased. Indeed, the sisters seemed to be curiously affected by Madam Breeze's voice; for all the while that she was speaking they gently swayed their bodies, and moved back and forth through the cave.

"Come now," said Madam Breeze, "you must be quite good-natured, you know. I have a very, very important duty for you. I want to serve my good friends the Brownies—wheeze! Here, Ensign, let me present you. These are the Cloud Elves." Lawe bowed gravely, and the sisters each made that graceful and dignified courtesy which our grandmothers were taught to be the proper thing on such occasions.

"This is what I want," continued Madam Breeze; "to-morrow morning—wheeze!—do you hear me? To-morrow morning I want to have quite clear. Keep the Gate

of the Sun wide open—hoogh! Wide, I say; for we
have some good work for my Lord Sol to do over there
at Hillside. Stratus, do you hear, lass?—wheeze! I'm
most afraid of you. You're such a regular night owl,
and affect the manners of—hoogh!—of those silly hu-
mans who wake all night and go to bed at sunrise. But,
mark what I say—wheeze!—you must stay at home this
night. Not a flounce, not a frill, not a—hoogh!—not
a—wheeze!—nothing—(confusion seize this cough!)
—of all your fine· toggery must be spread between
the sun and the gate to-morrow morn. Do you all understand?"

Madam Breeze puffed, and bounded about in a nervous way, mightily stirred up by the necessity for making
such a long speech. The sisters bowed several times,
and at last Nimbus, who seemed to speak for the others,
answered in a deep voice that rolled through the cave
and sounded like low distant thunder: "We will keep
the gate open, good Mistress Breeze. You know we
are always ready to oblige you. Your pleasure shall be
our law."

"Good—good! Many thanks. Don't forget. If
you do—bless your hearts!—I'll blow up Brother
Tempest and have him tear your fine robes into tatters.
Good-bye. Come, Ensign, let us away—wheeze!"
Once more squeezing herself into scant space, she got
into the chariot.

"Where next?" asked Lawe, when the top of the
cliff had been regained.

"Where, where? Jump in—quick! Whirlit, Keener,
you rogues, where are you? Oh, you're at your post, are
you?—wheeze! All right. Go!—hoogh!"

"Go? Whither?" cried Whirlit, leaping upon Vesper's back and gathering up the reins.

"To be sure! I had forgotten; all owing to that vile asthma! To the falls in the cove. Away!"

A beautiful stream runs through the cove. As it approaches the river, it hugs the base of the southern hill, enters a short ravine, midway of which it tumbles over a rock ten or twelve feet high, making a pretty waterfall. The sides of the ravine around the cascade and pool are covered with ferns. Thrifty young hemlocks stretch their tops upward and interlock their green branches above.

"What a charming spot! what a cool retreat!" cried Lawe, as the chariot dashed through an opening in the foliage, through which the sunlight stole and rested in a golden plate upon the bosom of the pool.

The face of the pool was rippled and dimpled as Madam's chariot stopped upon a flat stone at the edge of the cascade. The waterfall, too, raised a louder splash and broke its broad sheet into many ribbons and tongues of water in welcome of the good Elf. Vesper and Vacuum dipped their beaks thereinto and having kissed the pool's face, threw up their heads and drank to the health of Cove Fall and its people.

"Wait a moment," said Madam Breeze. She leaped from the chariot and ran under the fall. Presently she returned bringing with her the Fairy Dew, whom she had come to see. Lawe had never seen a more beautiful and dainty sprite. Her face and head were covered with a long white veil which, as well as her gauze robe, glistened with mimic pearls and diamonds. When she shook her head or moved her body these jewels were thrown off in little showers that shone a moment in the sunbeams, and then melted away into the earth or water. But there seemed to be none the less of them for all that. A curious instrument that somewhat resembled Scottish

bagpipes, hung from her shoulders, and rested under the
left arm. Every moment or two Fairy Dew pressed this
instrument between her arm and side, whereupon, from
a number of little tubes there would issue a cloud of
spray, that settled upon the grass and leaves in minute
round jewels like those which covered the Fairy's
dress.

Madam Breeze presented the Ensign to the Fairy,

FIG. 142.—Fairy Dew at the Mouth of the Cave.

and then in her own jerky way told the story of the
Brownies' troubles. Whereat Dew was sorry and ex-
cited, and shook so many pearl drops around her that
Lawe had to step beyond the circle of the shower to

save himself from being drenched. That was the Fairy's way of shedding tears, it would seem.

"What I want you to do," continued the Elf, "is to be up bright and early to-morrow, and cover the lawn at Hillside with these pretty gems of yours. The Pixies—faugh!—have their tents spread out like the camp of Joshua in the plains of Moab. Sprinkle 'em well—wheeze! Make every single thread a string of dew-drops. We'll attend to the rest. What say you, my dear?—hoogh!"

"Will the Cloud Elves be at home?" asked the Fairy.

"Aye,—I've seen to that. The way'll be clear. What say you?—wheeze!"

"Oh, I must consult my husband first, you know. I can do nothing without Dewpoint. I'll run and ask him."

"Aha! you're as sweet as ever on that—wheeze!—hubby of yours. Quite—hoogh!—right! Go and consult with Dewpoint."

"May I go in with the Fairy?" asked Lawe, who was curious to see her home.

"Oh, to be sure," said Dew, "and welcome. Come in, both of you!"

"Not I, thank you," said the Madam. "Shouldn't wonder if I had taken my death of cold already— hoogh! In with you, Ensign, and hasten back."

The water in leaping over the edge of the precipice left a space of a foot or more between the falling sheet and the face of the rock. By this path Lawe passed under the fall. He noted that the light shone through the tumbling stream as through a frosted window, and made every object within visible. Above him was a roof and beside him a wall of rushing water, whose

loud, steady roar, as it fell into the pool, quite drowned
the sound of his voice. In a moment he was drenched
with spray. The stones over which he stepped were wet
and slippery, and compelled careful walking. Presently
Dew stopped before an opening in the rock, and beckoned Lawe to follow her.

He entered an irregular cave which stretched backward into the cliff as far as the eye could reach. It was
dark at first, but as soon as his eyes became uséd to the
change, Lawe could see the objects around the opening,
and faintly those further in. Upon the roof were hanging stalactites white as sea foam, some tapering to points
and dropping like icicles, some just touching or blending
with like formations called stalagmites, which rose from
various spots upon the floor like marble pillars. These
beautiful white formations were also spread over the
walls of the cave wherever the water had trickled down,
and some of them looked like serpents, or roots of trees
carved in marble.

Far back toward the end of the cave Lawe saw in the
dim light an old-looking Elf, who seemed to be in an
uncomfortable state of mind and body. He was clad as
scantily as propriety would allow, indeed was naked
from the waist up. A long white beard fell upon his
bare breast. He sat upon a rude Gothic chair, not unlike
the big pulpit seat which the minister sits in on Sundays,
which had been formed, by some freak of the cave
Sprites, from the interweaving and massing of stalactites
and stalagmites. He held in his hand a huge fan made
from the feathers of a snow bird, with which he fanned
himself so vigorously that his long beard was blown
about over his chest, and his white hair was kept streaming behind him. Considering how chilly was the cave,
Lawe thought this strange behavior.

"Who is that?" he asked. "He looks like Saint Nicholas in his summer retreat. Is that your husband?"

"Oh, bless you, no,—no indeed!" laughed Fairy Dew. "That is my half brother Frost. He gets little comfort in this country until winter begins to come on. He hardly ever goes out of the cave the whole summer, and keeps back there, as you see, in the coolest spot. No wonder that he plays some sorry pranks when he is released in the autumn from his long confinement."

"But he has been out in the summer, hasn't he?"

"Yes, yes," said the Elf quickly, "he did escape the guards once or twice and—dear me! I don't like to think of it! It was too bad the way he carried on. The face of the earth looked as if it had been boiled in a caldron during the night. Farmers and gardeners were well nigh ruined. They called brother the 'Black Frost,' after that trick. Though, dear me! I don't see why, for he's white enough I'm sure. But mortals are odd and contrary folk sometimes!"

Just then Dewpoint came out of a pavilion or chamber which was contrived by using stalagmites as pillars and stalactites as supports. As he stepped forth he threw back the curtain door, and exposed the interior of a snug room, lit up with fox-fire lanterns which were fixed in gnarled stalactite brackets. Lawe was about to take a closer view of this pretty room and its master, when he heard the voice of Madam Breeze calling at the mouth of the cave:

"Ho! Hello, there! Are you frozen up? Have you taken summer lodgings? Here I've been waiting for— for—hoogh !—"

"For three minutes!" answered Lawe a little impatiently, for he was curious and disappointed. Then he bethought him of his duties, and spoke up cheerfully,

"I am coming! You are quite right, it is no time to
loiter. Thanks for your kind prompting, friend Breeze.
Farewell, good Fairy Dew, and you, Sir Dewpoint, too."
He hastened out of the cave and followed the Elf to the
chariot, which bowled rapidly away from the ravine.

# CHAPTER XXXIII.

"Whither now?" asked Lawe.

"Home," said Madam Breeze. "We've nothing more to do but wait for the morning. If all go well, and all shall go well, never fear! we will see old Spite—faugh! —and all his Pixie crew—wheeze!—scattered to the four winds before morning. Be up bright and early. You shall find me on hand at daybreak, and by sunrise Brownieland may proclaim a Jubilee—hoogh!"

When the chariot reached Lone Aspen, Lawe called his troopers, and with many warm thanks bade the Elf good-bye, and hurried back to his former bivouac at the tip-top of the large Rose Bush. The ponies were tethered under the leaves out of Pixie sight, and the troopers stretched themselves upon the branches to sleep, or sat in the forks of the limbs and talked over old campaigns until nightfall. Always, however, sentinels kept watch against surprise. The day passed without alarm, and when night came on the Brownies composed themselves to sleep. Lawe, full of anxiety, was sleepless. He had firm faith that Madam Breeze would bring deliverance, but as she had not told her plans, he could only guess what they were from such hints as had been dropped while arranging matters with her friends. Still, there was so much doubt in his mind that he could scarcely compose himself to wait until the morrow. He descended the bush, dodging on the way the round beautiful snares

(359)

of the Wheel Legion swung among the daisies, and
the criss-cross and knotted nets of the Lineweavers.

On the ground beneath him a party of Pixie officers

FIG. 143.—"The Round Beautiful Snares of the Wheel Legion Swung
Among the Daisies."

were gossiping over current events.  There was Saltus
of the Vaulting Legion, a large-eyed, intelligent fellow,
dressed in a black uniform, with gold and scarlet facings,

and a bright metallic green helmet and sword sheath. He was famous for his long leaps, being able to make at a single jump the distance of several hundred millimeters. There also were Lieutenant Heady, and Cito of the Wolf battalion, and Dysdera of the Tubeweavers, who lived in a sac-like tent from which the Brownies had nicknamed him "Pixie Silk-poke." They were all in high feather, and were making merry yarns and jokes over the late disasters which had befallen their enemies. Lieutenant Heady was in the midst of a boastful prediction of the utter ruin of all Brownieland when a runner arrived with news of the strange excitement among the Brownies, and the illumination of the camp and ships, as related in a former chapter.

"What can it mean?" asked Saltus.

"No one knows," replied the runner.

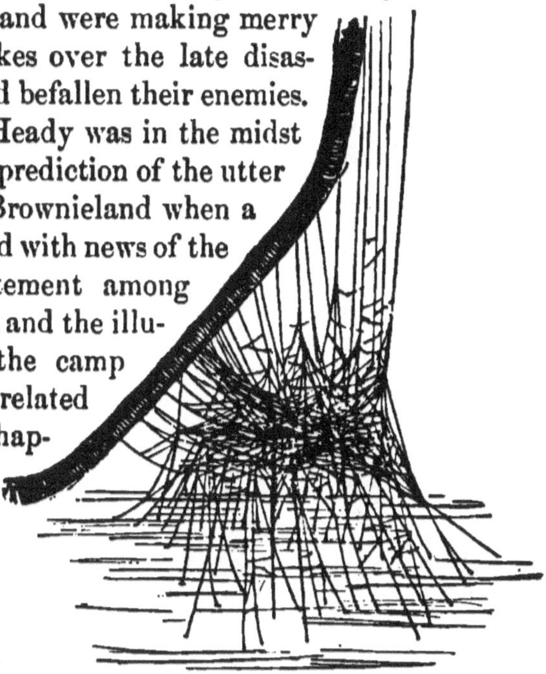

FIG. 144.—"The Criss-Cross and Knotted Net of the Lineweavers."

"P'raps they've got up a big feed and pow-wow for some pompous general," growled Heady.

"Aha!" said Ensign Lawe; and having doubled the guard, he sped away through the moonlight. When he came back with the glorious news of the rescue of the Nurses, his squad of troopers could not restrain their joy, and broke out with a round of cheers.

"Whew!" cried Cito, "Brownies here, as I live!
After them, lads!" and he ran up the Rose Bush full
speed.

"Heigh-ho!" cried Saltus, leaping upon the leaves,
"mount for them, Vaulters! Jump, jump quickly!"

"Confusion seize 'em," growled Heady between his
teeth, "I'll put a stopper on your throats, my pretty

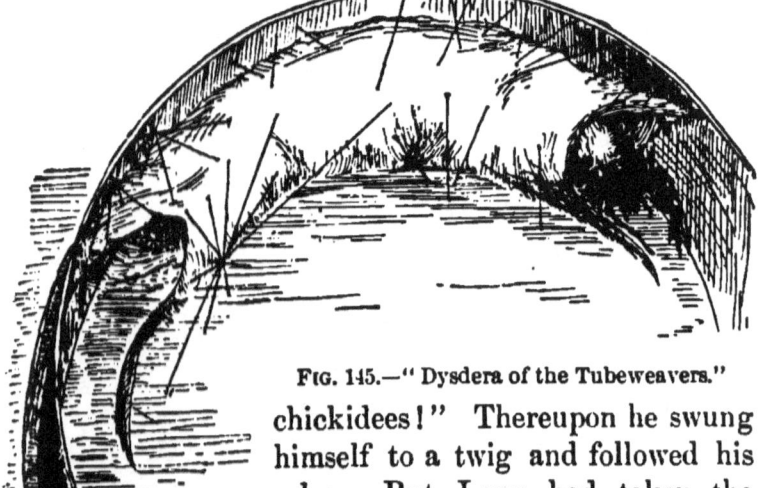

FIG. 145.—"Dysdera of the Tubeweavers."

chickidees!" Thereupon he swung
himself to a twig and followed his
comrades. But Lawe had taken the
alarm, and betook himself and troopers
to the Virginia creeper above the parlor
window, where they were out of harm's
way.

Now the night passed merrily along.
From the depth of despair the Ensign and his men were
suddenly lifted to the height of joy. The news seemed
too good to be true; moreover, it was like a prophetic
assurance of further good fortune on the morrow. Lawe's
spirits rose to the highest pitch; and when at last he
fell asleep it was to dream of victory, love and Grace.

"Oho, oho! Did I surprise you, Mr. Ensign?" was
the greeting which came to him as he awoke. It was

daybreak. There sat Madam Breeze on the Virginia creeper above him, smiling good-humoredly, and shaking the vine gently. He hurried to her side, bade her good morning, and told her the news of Faith and Sophia's rescue. Madam shook with joyful excitement until the vine clattered against the wall.

"Hist!" she cried, "that will never do! Silence— do you hear? Softly—hu–sh! We must keep cool a while longer—wheeze!" She choked off her cough as she spoke, and sat still, at least as still as she could sit.

Lawe looked out upon the lawn. There was Fairy Dew giving the finishing touch to her night's work. As she flew with quick wings above the grass, her arms played rapidly upon the sacs beneath them, and from the many tubes attached thereto the spray flew in all directions.

"Humph!" said the Ensign as he watched with curious interest this fairy spraying machine. "What a busy little body Fairy Dew must be! See what an immense work she has wrought during the night!"

"Aye, aye! That is what we want. Look how the dew brings out to view yonder Pixie tents on the lawn and in the bushes. Ha, ha! Good, indeed!—wheeze!" The Elf clapped her hands merrily at the sight. But Lawe could hardly enter into the pleasure of the view, for as he saw almost every square foot of his beloved homestead grounds covered with the tents of his foes, showing white and clear under their load of dew-drops, his heart beat tumultuously with grief, shame and anger. He therefore shrugged his shoulders and said nothing.

"Never mind," cried Madam Breeze, "we shall see presently. Aha! lookee yonder! There comes the sun! All is well! Hoogh!—hurrah!"

The first rays of the rising sun were beginning to

peep between the Two Pines, touch the tip of the Giant-stone's poll and shoot out across the river.

"Bless the kind Cloud Elves," exclaimed Madam, "they have served us truly, and left the Gate of the Sun open wide. Welcome, welcome, good Sol! Here, this way now, Fairy Sun-beam, follow me."

The Elf tossed herself off the vine and bustled away

FIG. 146.—Dew-Sprinkled Tents Upon the Lawn.

to the front window that looks toward the northeast, facing the great bend in the Ohio River. She shook the window shutter until the slats rattled and fell open.

"In with you now!" she cried to the Sunbeam. "Right in! Off the floor now, please. Up the white bed-spread.

There—that is it; that's it! Just the spot, full and fair in the Governor's face! Now—wheeze!—rest there a moment, will you? I'll finish up these shutters—hoogh, wheeze—*puff!*"

She laid hold of the green slats and shook them again and again. Harder, Madam, harder, if you would get them open! Once more the Elf threw herself against the barrier, until the window shook.

"Here, Whisk, Keener!" she called. "Come to my help. And you, Lawe, creep in here and pry up that catch with your spear. All together, now!—Whoo-ooo-*whooff!*"

One of the shutters flew back with a loud bang, and as good hap would have it, the hasp or catch on the end thereof struck the leaf on which Lacemaker the Pixinee was nested and broke it loose from the vine. It floated off upon the wind and Madam Lacemaker was sorely tossed about upon her aerial voyage. Seeing this, a Fairy Sunbeam seized the stem of the leaf and darted off westward with it. Thereat Elf Keener plunged away after careering leaf and flying Sunbeam, and with stout puffs of his breath drove the leaf before him, Madam Lacemaker all the while tumbling back and forth, holding on to the lines of her dainty web, and ever and anon from her kneeling or half-prone posture shaking her fists, and sputtering forth her helpless wrath.

Now through the open space the sun sent in a broad sheet of golden light that fell full upon Wille's face. The Governor awoke, rubbed his eyes, grumbled at the wind, grumbled at somebody's carelessness, got out of bed and crossed the room to close the shutter. Madam Breeze threw around him the freshest and sweetest breath of the morning as he approached. He leaned

26

out of the window to draw the truant shutter to its place. He was wide awake now. The soft sunbeams fell upon him. He drew a full breath, and sent it forth again with an "ah—aa-ah!" of hearty relish.

"Well, this is a glorious morning," he muttered. "Ah, Nature gives us our sweetest tastes of life, after all. How still it is here! A real relief from the excitement and clamor of my life." He stood and gazed quietly upon the lovely scene before him. His eyes were fixed upon the rising sun, the glowing hill top and golden zoned river. A feeling of sadness fell upon him. It deepened into regret, as he silently looked and mused. He was thinking,—and who has not so thought? —of the earlier, the purer, the happier morning of life, ere the ambitions and struggles of manhood had awakened within him to warm the heart to fever heat, and taint the freshness and purity of nobler and holier desires and aims.

"Heigho!" he sighed, as he slowly drew the shutter to its place.

He felt a light touch upon his hand. A small, thin voice, but very sweet and familiar, fell upon his ear. It was the well-known greeting of his Brownie friends.

"God speed, Brother Wille; hail and good speed!"

He looked down, and saw standing upon the window-sill Ensign Lawe and his troopers.

"Welcome, brothers; hail and good speed!" he answered. There was a heartiness in his tone and genuine pleasure in his face, which made the hearts of the fairies jump for joy. It was so like the tone and look of old time!

"What do you bring me, brothers?" continued Wille. "What can I do for you, or what will you do for me?"

"Look yonder, please," said Lawe, pointing toward the lawn.

The Governor leaned over the window-sill and followed

FIG. 147.—Fairy Sunbeam and Elf Keener Banishing Madam Lacemaker Beyond the River.

the direction of the Ensign's pointed spear. He started! The Pixie encampment covered the place! The dew drops on the tent-tops were glistening in the sunbeams like jewels.

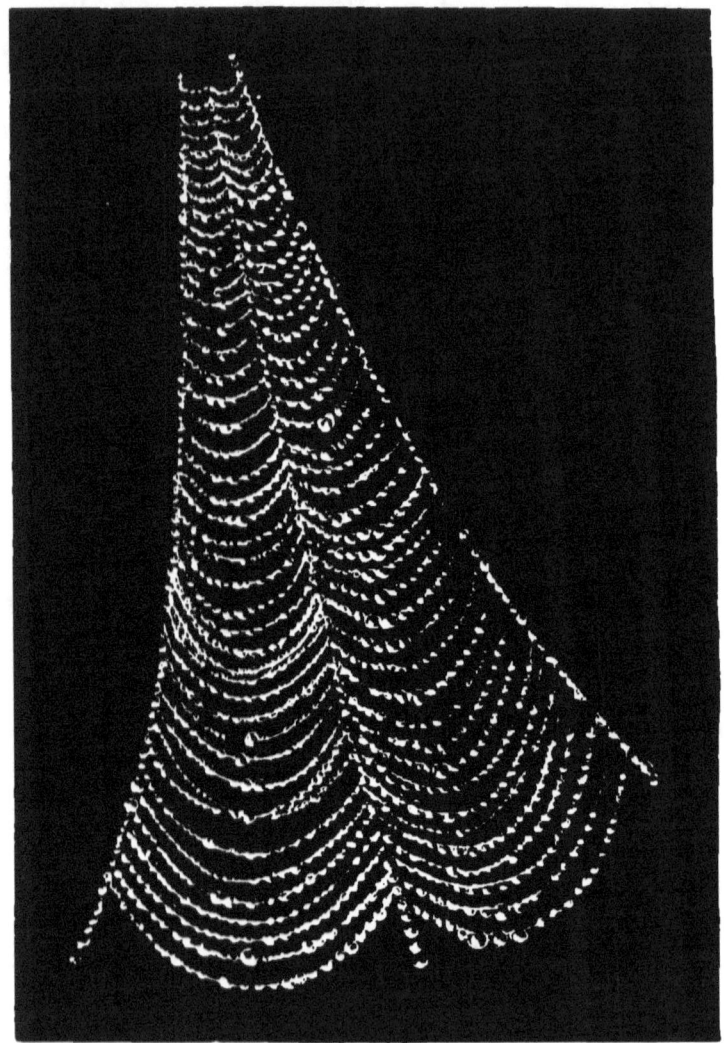

FIG. 148.—A Dew-Laden Web.

"Look out of the west window, now," said Lawe. The Governor threw back the shutter and saw the same dew-laden webs and silken tents stretching in close array up toward the orchard to the very bauk of the lake and inlet.

"And has it come to this, my good friends?" cried Wille. His voice trembled, and a tear started upon his cheek. "Have your old foes driven you from your homestead, and shut you out from the mansion and from me? I see, I see! Not another word! I know that it is my fault. Forgive me! I will right the wrong without delay. I will, indeed! And Dido will do her best to help me. Depend on us. When the sun has dried the dew from the grass, meet us at our old trysting place by the Rose Bush, and you shall see us scatter the Pixies, and give back the Home Lawn to my Brownie brothers. Good-bye!"

He lay down again, but could not sleep. His thoughts were too busy with the past, and too sad, in sooth, to allow rest. He aroused Dido and told her all. Like a good wife she heartily sympathized with him in his new resolves, and agreed to join him in the crusade against the Pixies.

Breakfast over, the two went out to the lawn. "Let the gardener bring up the lawn mower," said Dido.

"Not I," answered Wille. "I shall do the work myself. It is quite as little atonement as I can make for neglecting my old, true Brownie friends."

He threw off his coat, donned his wide-brimmed hat, and brought the scythe from the tool house. The hone rung merrily upon the steel as the Governor sharpened the blade. He had not forgotten his skill of earlier days, and while he was bringing the scythe to a good edge his mind followed along the path of his life to the quiet village among the green hills on the banks of Little Beaver Creek, where his boyhood had been spent.

One spot very dear to memory came into view—
Aunt Fanny's farm! The good, strong face of dear old
Aunt Fanny arose before him. What happy days he
had spent in her quiet country home! He felt again
the thrill of holiday freedom that stirred his young
heart on those summer days when he set out upon the
four miles' walk to the farm. In imagination once
more he passed the old Factory Dam; he saw the water
tumbling over its breast; he stood on the Sandy and
Beaver Canal locks, and watched Sam Underwood and
Ike Clunk pull up their dipnets from the bays. With
what eagerness of interest did he gaze when the net was
swung ashore with a silvery sucker or a pink chub
swaying down the centre!

On, on, along the Elkrun Valley. There is Orr's;
and there is Meldrum's; and there is Charters' farm;
and there is Kimball's mill; and there is Squire Clem
Crow's cooper shop; and yonder is Elkton. One mile
more! The road turns here to the left, winds down the
deep cleft of Pine Hollow, shady the whole summer
long between its sharp ridges crowned with hemlocks,
and musical with the ripple of its clear mountain run.

There is the old District School house!—and many a
lusty conflict he recalls with the country lads who waged
with him the traditional feud between "country haw-
bucks" and "town boys." Now he climbs up the hill
road; there to the right is the Crow place, and the
Governor smiles as he recalls the easy boyish wit that
dubbed it the "Crow's nest." At last through the trees
comes the longed-for glimpse of the white house on the
knoll, and Aunt Fanny sitting on the porch!

"Hurrah! she rises; she has seen me!"

Up the lane on a run now, and soon at rest before a
bowl of snowy bread and fresh milk.

What days those were! full of pleasure from early rising with the sun to twilight bed-going with the birds. The wanderings in wood and orchard ; the expeditions after gay field lilies, aromatic calamus and sweet myrrh ; the long hunts after hens' nests in the fence corners; the walks, musings and amusings among the sheep and their frisky lambs, the cows and calves, the colts and piggies, the hens and their yellow puffy broods of muffies ; the big roosters, the speckled guinea fowl,—how keen was the zest of these engagements and pursuits !

Then came the warm bright days of harvest, and the mowers came with their scythes. What fun to toss the fragrant hay ! What glorious fun to see the mowers run from the stirred up bumble-bees' nest ! What fun, most glorious of all, to fight the insects with wisps of new mown hay ! Ah ! the odor of the fresh mown meadow on dear Aunt Fanny's farm ! The Governor seemed to smell it again, as fresh as on those long past harvest days, while he stood there whetting his scythe and living over in memory the scenes of his bright, pure boyhood.

He drew a deep sigh ; he dropped the whetstone into his hip-pocket ; he threw back the scythe, then bent down to the grass which had so long marred the lawn by its overgrowth, and swept a broad clean swath up the hillside.

" You shall not do the work alone," cried Dido, and seizing her reaping hook began to trim away the struggling tufts along the border walk.

When Ensign Lawe had received Wille's promise to break up the Pixie camp and disperse and destroy the Pixies, he straightway sent messengers to Bruce and Rodney to follow up the proposed attack. Swiftly but silently the orders went forth. Fort Home, which commanded a point of the inlet nearest the Mansion, was strongly reinforced, and the big david, " Example," manned and made ready for use. The ships were cleared for action, the crews sent to quarters, and all things made ready for weighing anchor. Never did Soldiers and Natties await the command with a more cheerful, willing and confident courage. The rescue of the Nurses had given them new life ; the good news of Governor Wille's conduct lifted them all into the height of hope. The battle cry was passed : " Wille, Dido and Victory ! " All was ready. All were waiting.

Now came a trooper dashing post haste into headquarters. " The Governor has prepared his scythe and is just advancing to work."

Then came a second courier : " The Governor has begun the attack ; Dido joins him in it ! "

A third came : " Wille is cutting a broad swath up the lawn ; the Pixie tents are swept away before him, and our foes are fleeing in all directions."

Close upon this messenger came Lawe himself, spurring at topmost speed into the Brownie camp, swinging his sword around his head in high ecstasy, and crying, " Forward all ! Forward at once ! Fall upon the foe, and we are saved and safe forever ! "

" Forward ! " cried Bruce.

" Forward ! " at the same moment shouted Rodney, and the signal flag flew to its place.

The ships moved out under a favoring breeze, and opened full broadsides upon the Stygian vessels. Ensign Lawe, once more at the head of his gallant troopers, led across the inlet and dashed at once upon the retreating Pixies. The footmen poured out of the gates of Fort Home and marched away to join the attack.

The Governor had now reached the bank of the inlet,

and as he swung his scythe merrily, and bowed to the good work, he was greeted with three times three from forts and ships :

"Wille, Dido and Victory! Hurrah, hurrah, hurrah!"

Wille paused a moment and swung his hat above his head, while Dido waved her handkerchief in recognition of the Brownie cheers. Then the Governor turned, and mowed down the lawn, throwing off at each swing of the scythe a bunch of grass mingled with the ruins of Pixie tents and huts, whose inmates lay struggling beneath the wreck of their homes, or fled to the standing grass, or burrowed and hid around the roots. The Brownies followed them up, searched them out, dispersed or slew them. It was a complete destruction and rout. In a few hours the fragrant grass lay curling in the sun, and not a Pixie tent was left upon the lawn. Spite and Heady made a strong effort to rally their soldiers, and succeeded in forming a line of battle. But the Pixies were so demoralized that the troops broke and fled before the Brownie charges. Many found hiding places in holes and dens of the earth; some escaped in the small boats of the smugglers and pirates; numbers were taken aboard the Stygian ships, and were borne down the lake, closely pursued by the Natties.

Lieutenant Heady lay dead upon the field. What had become of Spite? When we last saw him he was sitting alone upon the cliff, filled with rage and wonder at the Brownie rejoicings over the rescue of Faith and Sophia, and waiting in the moonlight for the return of the scouts whom he had sent out to get the news. Not a whisper of tidings could he hear. Bruce had ordered the Brownie pickets to keep the matter from their foes, and no breath of the good news could be gathered from them. For good and sufficient reasons Raft the smuggler had held his knowledge secret, and had kept away from Spite's presence. His yacht, the Fringe, was now anchored just under the cliff, hidden from view by the overhanging grass. Raft had heard for some time the commotion on the lawn, but gave little heed to it. It drew nearer. The singing swish of the scythe against the grass, the cheers of the Brownies and Governor Wille excited his interest. He climbed up the cliff and reconnoitered. He took in the situation at a glance, then turned his eyes toward the inlet. Thereaway the Nattie fleet was under way, and bearing down straight toward the cliff.

"It's all up with Pixiedom!" he cried, "for one good long while at least. Good-bye to the lawn! I'm off with the Fringe to safe quarters; I wouldn't lose her to save the whole nation. Every fellow for himself, and deil take the hindmost! That's good Pixie doctrine, so here's cut and away!"

He spun out a drag-line, Pixie fashion, and fastening it to a rock, thereby swung himself down the cliff to the grass at the water's edge. Thence he boarded the Fringe, set his sail, pulled up anchor, and was just about leaving the harbor, when a shower of sand and small pebbles rolled upon him. He looked up, and saw a Pixie officer lowering himself down the side of the cliff by blades of grass and ferns. The form seemed familiar; he looked more closely. Yes, it was Spite the Spy.

"Hold on,—hold!" cried Spite.

"Aye, aye!" answered Raft. "This way now—down that tall rush—so! Now swing upon the mast. There, —you're safe. All right!" He unmoored the yacht, and pushing against the cliff sent her out with one vigorous shove into clear water. The wind caught the sails, and the Fringe flew merrily over the surface of Lake

Katrine. Raft now had leisure to give some attention to his chief. Spite had thrown himself upon the deck, and was fairly panting with fatigue, and livid and trembling with passion. Wrath, terror, disappointment, shame were in turn and in quick succession reflected from his face. The smuggler had little love for the chief, but he pitied him now, and in his rough way tried to comfort him.

"Better luck next time, Cap'n," he said. "We've had many a backset before, and have come out all right again. Cheer up!"

"Backset, indeed!" growled Spite. "It's annihilation! There's not enough left of Pixiedom to make a decent funeral. But—" and he rolled out a string of oaths—"I shall have such revenge as they little dream of! I'll tear the accursed Nurses limb from limb and fling the pieces into the Brownie camp! Say! what are you putting her head down the lake for?" he shouted, suddenly starting to his feet.

"That's the way of safety, Sir," answered Raft. "We must make for the outlet or Orchard Cave at once. Look there at the Natties hard upon the wake of our fleet. We must get out of their way, Sir!"

"Curse the Natties!" answered Spite fiercely; "and confound you for a coward! Put her toward Ellen's Isle, I say! I will land there if the whole Nattie fleet were following us. But they'll not bother us now; they have better game at present than the Fringe."

Raft's cheeks burned at the word "coward," and he could hardly refrain from tossing Spite overboard. But even the worst of Pixies have some reverence for a chief, and Raft was one of the best. Besides, he really pitied Spite, and was willing to allow for his bitter disappointment. He saw that he had not yet heard of the escape of the Nurses, and resolved that he would tell him now, so that he might be persuaded to give up the trip to Ellen's Isle. It was pretty hard to get started, however, with the story. Raft hemmed, stammered, and at last began :

"Cap'n, there's no use going to the island now. All's up, there, as well—"

Spite interrupted him. "No use? What is that to you? Do as you are bidden, and do not dare to question or comment upon my orders. Change her course at once, or—or—" he fairly screamed these words, and stopped suddenly in the midst of his threat, choked by passion.

Raft trembled with anger. He dropped the helm, laid hold upon a marline-spike and advanced toward the chief. Then he suddenly changed his mind, and retraced his steps.

"Very good," he answered quietly. "You shall have your own sweet way, my dear! Ellen's Isle it is!" He pressed his tiller and shifted the sail; the Fringe swung around, and in a few moments was quietly riding in one of the secluded harbors with which the smuggler was familiar, at the head of the island, and not far from the cave of Tigrina and Aranea Hall.

"Wait here until I return," said Spite leaping ashore. "I shall be back soon."

There was a strange look in Raft's eye, that caught the chief's attention, for in a moment he turned back, and shaking his clenched hand at the smuggler, said :

"If you fail me, I'll follow you to the ends of the earth and drink your heart's blood! If you prove true you shall be Admiral of the fleet. Beware!" He turned again and was soon out of sight.

"Admiral!" sneered Raft, when Spite had disappeared. "Admiral, indeed! That sounds grand, verily. But I wouldn't stand the fury of his wrath and disap-

pointment to be the chief himself. That is, even if—"
Raft shook his head, and glanced toward the cave.
"However, he would have his own way, and he may find
out for himself how much better it is than the one Raft
advised." He pushed the Fringe out of the harbor, and
spreading full sail ran rapidly toward the outlet.

Let us follow Spite. He came to the door of the cave
without noting any signs of the Brownies' recent camp
in the neighborhood. He found the door fastened on
the outside. What could that mean?

"Curses on the old hag Tigrina," he cried, "she is out
on some expedition, and has left the Nurses locked
within. Well, they're safe enough under these fastenings," he muttered, as he cut away the thongs, "and I'll
have the Brownie beauties all to myself. But I'll flay
the vile hag alive for this disobedience. It's time that
I were rid of her, at any rate."

The strong fastenings which the Brownies had put
upon the door were at length removed, and Spite entered
the cave. All was as still as the grave. Not a sound
from the bright and busy world without fell inside those
silent halls. He pushed on. The fox-fire lights had
burned out. He was well used to groping in the dark,
but he could scarcely make out the objects before him.

"Hello!" he called.

The echoes of his voice rolled back upon him again
and again from either end of the cave. A strange sensa-
tion came over him. His heart began to quicken; a
cold chill seized him. He threw off the feeling. He
cursed his timidity and superstition. "On, on!" he
cried. "Revenge is near." He reached the silken curtain that formed the door of the fairies' room. He drew
it aside, gloating over the thought of the terror which
his sudden appearance would excite. A single lantern

burned upon the wall, and by its light he saw that the
room was empty! Signs of confusion were everywhere.
The stand lay just where it had fallen, and under it the
" Wisdom of the Pixies " was outspread upon the floor.

" Faith! Sophia! " he shouted. The voice died away
among the arches. There was a faint noise at his side.
He turned quickly. There stood Tigrina. Her face
was gaunt, her cheeks hollow, her eyes burned like balls
of fire.

" Hag! fiend! wretch! " yelled Spite. " What have
you done with the Nurses? " He drew his sword and
took a step toward the old Pixinee.

" Oho! " said Tigrina, uttering a harsh cackling
laugh. " You have come at last, have you? The
pretty Nurses! Where are they? Ha, ha, ha! That
is good—good! You didn't know that the Brownies
had been here, hey? Didn't know that Faith and
Sophia are safe in the Brownie camp, hey? Oh, no!
that is very good—very! You didn't know that I had
been left here sealed up in the cave—oh, no, not you! "

Spite stopped, then staggered backward as though he
had been struck a violent blow. The whole truth flashed
upon him. He understood now the mysterious outburst
of joy in Brownie camp and fleet. Faith and Sophia
were gone,—safe from his power and revenge; among
their own friends! Fortune had again failed him.
His breast was torn by a tempest of passions. This
last defeat was even worse than the loss of his camp
and the rout of his army. He broke forth into wild,
blasphemous reproaches of Tigrina for failing to keep
the fairies in her charge. Again he lifted his sword
and again he started toward the Pixinee.

There was something in the attitude of Tigrina which
caused him suddenly to pause. Her eyes shone in the

dim light of the cave; her sharp, long fangs swayed back and forth, touching each other with a grating sound; her back curved; she sank into a stooping posture. Spite felt her hot breath strike his face as it hissed through her clattering teeth. He knew too well what all this meant. The "blind fury" had seized the Pixinee!

Fly, Spite, fly! It is for your life!

He turns, flees! Too late! The rush of Tigrina's form is heard as she springs upon the doomed chief. Her fangs are fastened in his throat. He is borne down to the floor, and without a struggle and without a cry he yields up his life. The enraged and hungry Pixinee drank up his blood, and left the dry carcass hung against the wall by broken strands of web-work, to moulder into dust with the silken ornaments of Aranea Hall.

Summer passed. Autumn came and hung her gaily colored banners upon the trees and shrubbery of Hillside. The Brownies dwelt in peace upon the lawn, and Governor Wille and Dido held the Mansion with happier hearts than ever. The winds blew more and more keenly around the hills. The Fall had well nigh merged into Winter. Thanksgiving day came. Great preparations had been making at the Mansion, and now the family meeting was being held. Gray-haired sires, strong men and matrons, and fair-haired children, down to crowing baby Paul, all were there. How the halls rang with merry-making! What a happy, hearty company sat down to the Thanksgiving dinner!

It was a bright crisp day, and when dinner was over, all went out upon the lawn and gathered around the great Rose Bush. There was a quadruple wedding in Brownieland: Lieutenant MacWhirlie and Agatha, Adjutant Blythe and Faith, Sergeant True and Sophia,

Fig. 149.—A Dead Orbweaver Hanging by Broken Strands of Web-work.

Ensign Lawe and Grace, all stood up together, and were joined in holy wedlock according to the simple rites of the Brownies. Then, amid shouts of the children, cheers of the older folk, and the wildest hurrahs of Brownie soldiers, sailors and people all, the eight happy fairies rode away, escorted by a gaily uniformed troop, to the Lone Aspen, where Madam Breeze had prepared for them a grand reception. Fairy Dew and Dewpoint were there, and the four sister Cloud Elves, and Whisk, Keener and Whirlit, and before the merry-making ended, even Elf Frost looked in, quite happy to be once more free to roam abroad.

As the evening was fine, and the moon full, Commodore Rodney and Pipe the Boatswain arranged to give the party a reception on the Emma and a moonlight sail upon the lake. The sailors had beautifully decorated the ship; fox-fire lanterns gleamed from every part of the forts, and shone all along the shore. Our old friends Captain Ask, Help, Clearview, Mate Angel, Howard, Hope, Rise, Shine, the Twadeils and many others were aboard. The wind was fresh and the lake was a little rough, but that only made matters all the merrier. How the ship did scud along!

It was passing the Point of Ellen's Isle, when suddenly a small vessel pushed out from the brown grasses at the water's edge, crossed the wake of the Emma within a stone's throw, and stood away toward the shore.

"Sophie, Sophie!" cried Faith, "look yonder! Do you know that yacht?"

Sophia glanced a moment at the beautiful vessel as it rose and fell on the waves and sped swiftly through the moonlight.

"It is the Fringe!" she cried. "And there—see! There is Raft the Smuggler. He has raised his hat!

27

He is waving it.  Hurrah! hurrah!"  Perhaps had she
stopped a moment to ask whether or not such conduct
were orthodox in a Brownie bride, she would not have
done it, but she simply gave way to the impulse of her
heart; she plucked her bridal veil from her head and,
quite unconscious of what she did, waved it again and
again at the fast flying yacht.

The Natties had sprung to their guns at the Fringe's
appearance, prepared to pour a broadside into her; but
when they saw Sophia's greeting and heard her shout,
they took their cue from her, and
instead of shot sent cheers after
the smuggler and his pretty craft.

"Poor fellow!" sighed Faith,
as she leaned over the rail, and
watched Raft's vessel disappear
under the shadow of the shore;
"poor fellow; what a pity that he
should be a Pixie!"

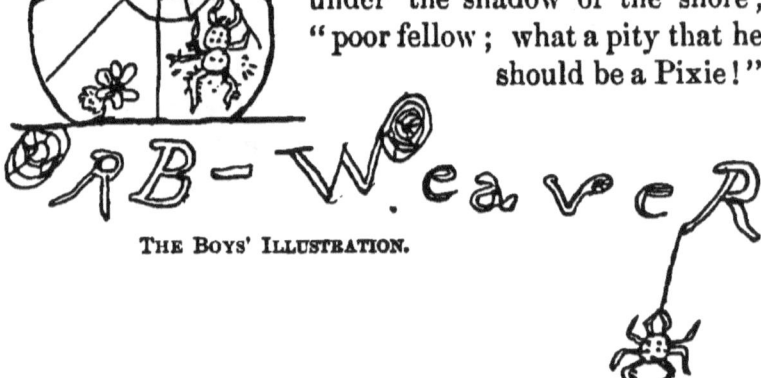

THE BOYS' ILLUSTRATION.

THE END.

# APPENDIX.

# APPENDIX.

## CHAPTER II.

**Note A, p. 14.**—Atypus piceus is a European species of Tunnelweaver (Territelariæ), which inhabits Great Britain. It resembles in habit our Atypus Abbotii, the Purse-web spider, found in the Gulf States, especially Florida; but supports its external tube upon the trunks of trees, instead of on the grass or surface.

**Note B, p. 16.**—Spiders are extremely cleanly in their habits, and brush and comb the various parts of the body with their hairy and spinous legs and palps. When brushing the head and chest (cephalothorax) the resemblance to the cat's toilet habits warrants the reference in the text.

**Note C, p. 18.**—Some of our American spider species have been imported from Europe, and I have seen them on vessels stowed away in divers crannies and under sundry parts of the ship, and overspun in the method attributed to Spite and his companions, and shown Fig. 15.

## CHAPTER III.

**Note A, p. 22.**—Epeïra globosa is a species of Orbweaver, which spins above its round snare a bell-shaped silken tent, represented at Fig. 17, p. 21.

**Note B, p. 22.**—One of the most common webs spun upon grass, on box-wood borders of flower beds, on arbor vitæ hedges, and such like positions, is that of the Speckled Tube-weaver, Agalena nævia, here described. It is a broad sheet, usually concave or funnel-shaped, with a circular opening near the middle or at one side, which leads into a long silken tube extending downward among the branches, or to the ground. At the opening the spider is usually seen waiting for prey.

Lines are attached to the sheet at various parts and reach upwards to bits of foliage, forming a network of lines which support the sheet. Insects in flight strike against these cross lines, and fall down upon the sheet, and become the prey of the Speckled Agalena who rushes upon them from the opening of her tube.

**Note C, p. 24.**—The cables here referred to are the upright lines described in Note B. (See Fig. 28, p. 54.)

**Note D, p. 26.**—The turret of Lycosa arenicola is here described. It is popularly known as the Turret Spider. This animal is widely distributed throughout the United States, and may be found along the Atlantic shore where it burrows in the sand, and sometimes selects small pebbles for the foundation of its tower. The shape of the tower is not always a regular pentagon, but inclines to take that form. Beneath the surface is a tubular burrow extending straight down as far sometimes as twelve inches. The spider is frequently found on guard at the top of the tower.

**Note E, p. 26.**—See Note A above. The web of the Speckled Agalena when spun upon grass often takes this form and shows a striking likeness to a miniature circus tent.

**Note F, p. 27.**—The Turret Spider is sometimes seen at the summit of its tower with head and fore limbs thrust over the edge, apparently on the lookout for passing insects.

**Note G, p. 35.**—The above description and Fig. 22 are of the cocoon of the large and beautiful Orbweaver Argiope cophinania (or riparia). It is a pear-shaped object about an inch or an inch-and-a-quarter long, and is suspended in the manner shown, among the branches of bushes, etc. The outside is a closely woven silken cloth of a dull yellow color. Next to this is a coating of bright yellow flossy silk, and in the centre is a closely woven ball of purplish or brownish silk, within which may be found the eggs of the mother spider. These sometimes number more than a thousand. When the little ones are hatched out, they live within this silken house until they are strong and old enough to cut their way out and form webs for themselves.

## CHAPTER VI.

**Note A, p. 52.**—The lodge here referred to as used for a guard house by the Pixies, is supposed to be a snare of the Speckled Agalena, which often spins its tent-like web upon the low grass of a lawn. Fig. 27 shows a web spun upon a honeysuckle vine, whose over-arching tendrils form a little cavern or booth which might well suggest a lodge.

## CHAPTER VII.

**Note A, p. 62.**—Spider webs are often destroyed or injured by wind storms.

**Note B, p. 62.**—A common habit of ground spiders and those that weave snares upon the ground is to thus hide themselves when molested or alarmed.

**Note C, p. 67.**—"Hand over hand." This roughly describes the method of some spiders in raising their prey when swathed, and in moving building material and debris.

**Note D, p. 69.**—See Note C. The figure is from life.

**Note E, p. 73.**—The achievement attributed to Spite is based upon a recorded account ; but the author is bound to say that he has seen no examples of webs that had been counterpoised with intent, as above described. Webs are sometimes found thus balanced as at Fig. 34; but it is doubtful if this is not the result of accident.

## CHAPTER VIII.

**Note A, p. 75.**—The mandibles or external jaws of spiders are shown in Fig. 39, and described in the text; the poison gland is shown at Fig. 40. The outlet for the poison may be seen at the tip of the fangs in Fig. 39.

## CHAPTER IX.

**Note A, p. 84.**—Certain species, especially Orbweavers (Fig. 86) and Lineweavers, swathe their prey when captured and before eaten. (See Fig. 33, p. 69; Fig. 134, p. 318.)

**Note B, p. 88.**—The bridge-lines here described are common objects in Nature. Spiders move freely from point to point, thereby often crossing considerable intervals. Fig. 44 shows the way in which these bridges and webs may block a path.

## CHAPTER X.

**Note A, p. 97.**—The egg-bag within which the mother spider places her eggs is popularly, though not quite correctly, called a cocoon. It is sometimes simply a wad or ball of loose silk, but more frequently is a bag of stiff and closely woven silk as at Fig. 22. Fig. 47 is the cocoon of an Orbweaver, Nephila plumipes; Fig. 48, of a Saltigrade or Jumping Spider, Phidippus opifex McCook.

## CHAPTER XIII.

**Note A, p. 115.**—Dolomedes fimbriatus, a rather common English spider, makes or utilizes a rude raft of leaves, and drifts over the fens thereon. The American Dolomedes frequents the water but has not been observed to act as above.

**Note B, p. 117.**—As a rule spiders prey upon one another, without regard to species or sex. Fig. 55 represents two males fighting.

## CHAPTER XIV.

**Note A, p. 123.**—Lycosa tigrina McCook abounds in the Eastern and Middle United States, and makes the burrow here described.

## CHAPTER XV.

**Note A, p. 128.**—Herpyllus ecclesiasticus Hentz is a common American Tubeweaver. It is black, with a dorsal pattern in white like that shown in the figure of the "Pixie parson."

**Note B, p. 135.**—The aeronautic or ballooning habit of spiders is the basis of these engineering feats of the Pixies Lycosa and Gossamer. A pleasant October day is the best on which to observe it; but young spiders may be seen in aeronautic flight during all warm months. An elevated spot is usually sought from which to make the ascent. Ground spiders, as

Lycosids, ascend in the manner shown Fig. 57; Orbweavers drift off as at Fig. 59. This interesting habit is described more at length in my "Tenants of an Old Farm."

**Note C, p. 137.**—Mother spiders of certain species carry their egg cocoons until the young are hatched; some take them in their jaws as our long-legged cellar spider, Pholcus, others beneath their bodies or lashed to the end of the abdomen.

## CHAPTER XVI.

**Note A, p. 144.**—Tetragnatha is a genus which has several common species in the United States and Europe, T. extensa being most familiar. Its colors, especially when young, are green and yellow, and when its long body and legs are stretched upon a leaf or twig (Fig. 64) it is difficult to detect it. The species here personified is one that keeps close to streams and ponds, Tetragnatha grallator HENTZ, the Stilt spider. The method of sailing, Fig. 66, is not imaginative but drawn from nature. The Pixie "Sixpoint" is a Citigrade spider, Dolomedes sexpunctatus HENTZ. I have known it to stay under water for forty minutes.

## CHAPTER XVII.

**Note A, p. 153.**—Many Orbweavers spin together several leaves, or roll up the end of a single leaf and form the nests described and shown, Fig. 69. That at p. 158, Fig. 72, was made by Epeira trifolium HENTZ. (See p. 194.)

**Note B, p. 154.**—"The Cardinal Company." Phidippus cardinalis HENTZ has its abdomen and venter covered with brilliant red hairs. Phidippus rufus HENTZ resembles it but is less brilliant. These are jumping or Saltigrade spiders, belonging to the Attidæ.

## CHAPTER XIX.

**Note A, p. 188.**—The Sedentary spiders, those which capture their prey by means of snares, commonly fling bands and threads of silk around the captive before feeding upon it. (See p. 69.)

## CHAPTER XXII.

**Note A, p. 216.**—The habits and spinning work of a common Orbweaver *Epeira labyrinthea* are personified in the Pixie jailer Labyrinthea.

**Note B, p. 218.**—The male spiders of Orbweavers when they "would a-wooing go," hang around the edge of the orbweb, and are not always received kindly. Sometimes, indeed, they are eaten.

**Note C, p. 220.**—"Hyptiotes." The Triangle Spider, Hyptiotes cavatus HENTZ. Its snare and mode of capturing prey are most interesting and ingenious.

**Note D, p. 223.**—This rigidity of limbs is not exaggerated, and is common to both old and young of this species.

**Note E, p. 226.**—The Labyrinth spider makes several cocoons, strung together as the several figures show. Each one is made of two circular caps united at the edges, so that Brownie Dodge could thus open an edge and peep out.

## CHAPTER XXIII.

**Note A, p. 238.**—"The water Pixie's den." The water spider of Europe, Argyroneta aquatica, makes a cocoon upon the water, somewhat in the manner described. No species with like habits has yet been discovered in America, and the author in locating the same at "Hillside," has sacrificed the facts of geographical distribution to imagination. But no doubt he will be pardoned for the sake of the incident which brings the lost Boatswain Pipe to life again.

## CHAPTER XXIV.

**Note A, p. 240.**—There is some, though little, variety in the color of silk with which spiders spin their snares; but their cocoons are often woven with bright colored silk.

## CHAPTER XXV.

**Note A, p. 250.**—The tradition that spiders are sensitive to music is old and widely spread, but appears to have little or no basis in natural habit. However, the reader may find, if he will, some pleasant stories based thereon.

**Note B, p. 250.**—"Feigning death." This habit is strongly developed in many spider species.

## CHAPTER XXVI.

**Note A, p. 259.**—"Bowl shaped battery." Fig. 110 was drawn from a snare of Linyphia communis HENTZ, woven among morning glories. Compare with that of Linyphia marginata HENTZ, Fig. 68, p. 151, in which the bowl is reversed.

## CHAPTER XXVII.

**Note A, p. 270.**—The Trap-doors drawn at Figs. 117, 118 and 121 are from Moggridge, and are not of American species, though they differ only in size.

**Note B, p. 271.**—This habit has been attributed to the Trap-door makers, but needs to be confirmed.

**Note C, p. 275.**—The mother wasp, which lances and paralyzes the big southwestern Tarantula, Eurypelma Hentzii, is Pepsis formosa, called popularly the "Tarantula hawk." The author has seen it pursuing the above species, but does not know positively that it attacks the true Trap-door maker, Cteniza Californica.

## CHAPTER XXVIII.

**Note A, p. 280.**—This is no doubt a true representation; see the three claw marks on the inside of the lid shown at Fig. 124.

**Note B, p. 284.**—The moulting period (see next Chapter), is attended with great weakness.

## CHAPTER XXIX.

**Note A, p. 290.**—The sting of the spider collecting wasps destroys the power of motion, but does not at once kill; it is certainly fatal in the end, if the young wasp larva does not in the meantime eat the victim stored away for her by maternal foresight.

## CHAPTER XXX.

**Note A, p. 309.**—Spiders have been known to thus suspend a snake, which is not so remarkable as it seems if we consider that a small garter snake ten inches long may weigh from one-eighth to one-fourth of an ounce.

**Note B, p. 313.**—The Medicinal spider, Tegenaria medici-nalis HENTZ, builds in cellars and shady spots a strong sheeted web with a tower at one angle thereof.

**Note C, p. 314.**—The capture of a mouse in a spider web has been proved, at least to the author's satisfaction. Fig. 135 is a sketch of such a captive made by Governor Proctor Knott, of Kentucky.

**Note D, p. 319.**—This "fish story" is quite true. The incident occurred in a draining ditch near Eagleswood, New Jersey. The fish was three and one-fourth inches long and weighed sixty-six grains; the spider was three-fourths of an inch long and weighed fourteen grains. It was one of our large Lycosids, probably a Dolomedes The facts on which the incidents of this chapter are based, are given in Vol. I, "American Spiders and their Spinningwork."

## CHAPTER XXXI.

**Note A, p. 324.**—Most species of Spiders are solitary in their habits; not like the social hymenoptera, as bees and ants. In this respect, the social characteristics of the Pixies are not true to nature, except in the case of spiderlings, or quite young spiders. However, some recent discoveries, especially those of the eminent French araneologist, M. Eugene Simon, seem to point to a decided social habit in several South American species.

**Note B, p. 329.**—This nest, so muc hlike a bird's in form, is that of Lycosa Carolinensis. It is made from the needle-like leaves of the white pine, or other available material by bending and pasting the same, as in the cut, Fig. 138.

**Note C, p. 330.**—The snares of Agalenanævia are often seen in such situations, and are sometimes of immense size.

**Note D, p. 331.**—The belief that spiders can prognosticate the weather is widely spread, but seems to have little or no basis in fact. The author has shown the groundlessness of the opinion at least in the case of Orbweaving Spiders.

# "Tenants of an Old Farm."

Leaves from the Note Book
of a Naturalist.

...BY...

## HENRY C. McCOOK, D. D.,

with 140 illustrations from nature by Dan Beard
and others.

---

### 460 PAGES WITH INDEX.

---

## EIGHTH EDITION.

12mo, Cloth  -  -  -  -  -  $1.50.

Sent postpaid on
receipt of the price
by the Publishers,

# George W. Jacobs & Co.,

## 103 South Fifteenth Street,

PHILADELPHIA.

# TENANTS OF AN OLD FARM.

# PRESS NOTICES.

"Belongs to a class which might with great profit take the place of much of the literature, sentimental and otherwise, which finds its way into the hands of our children through Sunday School and other libraries. It is pleasantly written and beautifully illustrated with original drawings from nature."—*N. Y. Examiner.*

"We will venture to say that the Colorado beetle, the apple-worm, moths, bumble-bees, caterpillars, ants and spiders, were never before made so picturesque, never so idealized. The author likes them, humanizes them, lives among them, finds an inner meaning in their little lives, makes in every way the most of them. . . . Housekeepers will surely be amused and probably surprised by learning just how moths go to work, and the chapters on crickets and katy-dids are very fresh and animated; the same is true of the bumble-bees and spiders; and what is not really new is put in new shape."—*Boston Literary World.*

"The illustrations, 140 in number, were prepared expressly for the work, are finely engraved, and are a great aid to a clearer understanding of the text."—*Philadelphia Evening Call.*

"We wish that our farmers, who are giving their sons a Christmas present, would choose this book. It would help them to see many things to which they may now be blind."—*Presbyterian, Philadelphia.*

"Heartily recommended to the attention of all who are themselves interested in natural history or are seeking some means of interesting young friends in this subject."—*Portland Press, Me.*

"We have not seen any book this season more worthy to be put into the hands of an intelligent youth, or indeed of any one who is interested in the direct and face-to-face study of nature."—*Illustrated Christian Weekly.*

"Of the highest order of interest. The author has made studies and drawings of the insects which can be found on any old farm, and has made discoveries which give him a high place among entomologists."—*Chicago Advance.*

"May be said to be a perpetual passport to the minor kingdoms of nature. It is the work of an accomplished and practical naturalist who is hand and glove (so to speak) with the populace of the leaves and fields, the woods and waters."—*N. Y. Mail and Express.*

"Dr. McCook has already achieved an enviable reputation by his valuable contributions to science, and in this charming book, so full of amusement and instruction, he has given us another proof of his being one of the most clear, concise and attractive writers of the day."—*Christian at Work, N. Y.*

"It is well known that Dr. McCook is one of the few ministers among us who have made a specialty of studies in the natural sciences, and that he has in this line built up an enviable reputation beyond our church and beyond our land."—*Presbyterian Journal, Phila.*

"The illustrations are a noteworthy feature of the book. Many of them are admirable illustrations of their subjects, while to these have been added a number of comical adaptations from the pencil of Mr. DAN BEARD."—*Illustrated Christian Weekly, N. Y.*

"The scientific accuracy, the good illustrations and simple descriptions make it a valuable book for amateurs and a good book of reference for advanced students in that department of natural history."—*Springfield Republican.*

"The author is not a mere compiler of other men's labors; he is a close and patient observer, and his book has an original value."—*N. Y. Home Journal.*

"He is rarely qualified for the task."—*Troy Daily Times.*

"Scientifically, Dr. McCook is authority on all these matters."—*Presbyterian, Philadelphia.*